#  THE SNARE

*Books by Elizabeth Spencer*

Fire in the Morning
This Crooked Way
The Voice at the Back Door
The Light in the Piazza
Knights and Dragons
No Place for an Angel
Ship Island and Other Stories
The Snare
The Stories of Elizabeth Spencer
Marilee
The Salt Line
Jack of Diamonds and Other Stories
On the Gulf
The Night Travellers

# THE SNARE

A NOVEL BY

Elizabeth Spencer

BANNER BOOKS

University Press of Mississippi / Jackson

First published in 1972 by McGraw-Hill Book Company
Copyright © Elizabeth Spencer
Introduction Copyright © 1993 by
the University Press of Mississippi
All rights reserved
Manufactured in the United States of America

96  95  94  93    4  3  2  1

The paper in this book meets the guidelines for permanence and
durability of the Committee on Production Guidelines for Book
Longevity of the Council on Library Resources.

Library of Congress Cataloging-in-Publication Data

British Library Cataloging-in-Publication data available

For David, Nellie and Lewis

# CONTENTS

*le Diable*
*Fait toujours bien tout ce qu'il fait!*
—BAUDELAIRE

# INTRODUCTION

Elizabeth Spencer's Julia Garrett, the protagonist of *The Snare*, is a haunting presence among American literary characters. A woman who feels to the marrow of the bone a sensuous responsiveness to life, she finds no ways to give expression to her passionate intensity but in experiences that her society marks as destructive or evil. Julia's time is the post-World War II South; she is a child from Tennessee who, motherless, grows up in the New Orleans household of her aunt and uncle in the 1940s and 1950s. She comes of age during the same years that Walker Percy's Binx Bolling, in *The Moviegoer*, is tooling between the Gulf Coast and New Orleans, trying to escape everydayness, or to live with its toll of existential dread and despair. Like Binx, Julia confronts a world in which society's absolutes have largely come to be forms of behavior, postures, costumes, menus, decors. But what is memorable and haunting about Julia is her appetite for and ease with living in an utterly uncertain world.

Believing that literary reincarnations are at least as possible as corporeal ones, one might imagine that, in Julia, Hawthorne's Hester Prynne has found her way to New Orleans, a temperate setting hospitable to her passionate nature, a murky, swampy place of wildness and sensuality, but a place that is real and believable, as the allegorical woods of Salem, Massachusetts, never quite were. Whatever New Orleans signifies in the collective psyche of this country—perhaps a distilled essence of whatever "South" symbolizes—is what Spencer suggests and invokes in the story of Julia Garrett. Julia is something of an inverse fictive sister of Willie Morris; she goes South—downward, inward, where meanings and judgments are blurred—to find home. Complexity, indirection, opacity are the qualities of life she trusts.

In *The Snare*, published in 1972, Spencer creates a remarkable novel, one that rewards a rereading and rethinking for
those who first encountered it nearly a quarter century ago.
For those who are reading *The Snare* for the first time, Spencer
offers a wide, transparent window opening upon the middle
years of the twentieth century. I find that, among all her
works, it is in this novel that she most fully explores the consequences for the individual consciousness of the vast shift in
personal values and public behavior that, looking back, one
sees so sharply focused in the 1950s and 1960s. Contrary to
much of what one reads—or remembers—of the fifties as a
time of dullness and conformity, it was a decade when unset-
tling social adjustments were being made. In the space of a
few years the country moved from the depths of the Great
Depression to an exuberant war victory that elevated the
United States to world dominance. But prosperity, prestige,
power, and ascendant democracy came to be heavy freight
for the nation and the individual American, and there
occurred in the fifties, as in the nineties, a determined turning
inward, an effort to understand the new condition, and a
questioning of what might lie beneath the placid con-
sumerism that had come so quickly to seem natural and
desirable.

The postwar affluence is represented in *The Snare* by one of
Julia Garrett's suitors, the rich Martin Parham of Mississippi
oil, gas, and timber money. Julia's comfortable world is also
furnished with the upper-middle-class New Orleans presence
of Aunt Isabel, sister of Julia's dead mother, and her husband,
Maurice Devigny. For a time Julia holds a respectable job in
an ophthalmologist's office, accepts invitations to respectable
parties and dates respectable men, but ultimately she finds
the milieu of gentility does not offer the life she seeks. When
Julia meets the handsome musician-vagabond Jake Springland, who first appears in the ophthalmologist's office in the
company of the weird and frightening Ted Marnie and
Wilma Wharton, she leaves the safe, everyday world and
commences a tour in the counterculture, a world of drugs,

crime, music, sensuality and radical individual freedom. Like a mermaid escaping a constraining, inhospitable land, she swims out into deep water and finds—not the suicide that awaited Kate Chopin's Edna Pontellier—but a medium that sustains her. For Julia, human experience constitutes "the great life snare," but she neither wants nor seeks any alternate vision to the "great, muddy stream flowing toward the sea."

In a 1964 short story, "Ship Island," Spencer first depicted a mermaid-like girl who anticipates Julia Garrett in her attraction to New Orleans, to unpremeditated sex and the risky excitement of fast cars and underworld figures, and in her aversion to respectable boys and acts of obedience of any kind. Nancy Lewis, a woman younger than Julia, flees the "nice" world because it is threatening and deadening. She senses, though she cannot articulate, the stultifying feminine mystique represented by the sorority girls in the story. If the only alternative to what they offer is flight and loss of reputation, then that is the price she will pay.

When Elizabeth Spencer came to write *The Snare* a few years later, she undertook a more complex critique of the alternatives for an independent life available to Julia Garrett. In doing so, she composed a profoundly female-centered novel, in many ways a feminist novel, though an unnerving one. The final circumstance that is imagined for Julia—that of single mother with child, of a slightly-better-than-amateur artist whose art consists in arranging found objects of glass into "frozen jazz" compositions, of a woman largely isolated from other people—is little changed from one's parting image of Hester Prynne. Even in a cosmopolitan twentieth-century city with a reputation for moral laxness, a city known far and wide as the Big Easy, Julia Garrett seems a misfit, a woman enlivened by sexual experience and nearly destroyed by it, a woman bored by status-seeking and acquisitiveness, whose indifference brings her to the edge of hunger and homelessness. And yet in shunning a sheltered life, Julia, like Hester, embodies a life force. Her aunt acknowledges to her husband Maurice near the end of the novel: "I collect antique figurines,

I join societies to preserve the old houses, the cemeteries, I belong to the best clubs, I go to church. But all of this is not life any more" (394). Rather, as Isabel comes to understand, life is with Julia.

In *The Snare* Spencer depicts the malevolence and violence associated with drugs and underworld terrorists. She once remarked, in fact, that a friend suggested she had imaginatively anticipated the Patty Hearst story. The more compelling threat of destruction that pervades the novel, however, lies nearer to original sin than to societal breakdown, a kind of menacing evil at least as theological as psychological. At a young age Julia is introduced to the "human swamp" by Henri Devigny, "Dev," the brooding sensual father of Maurice. An orphaned, "throwaway child from the hill country," she is initiated by Dev in some unspeakable way—the adult Julia never quite decides, or admits, whether the experience with Dev was sexual abuse. Nonetheless, it is through Dev, with his connections to a world of violence, sexuality, and even voodoo forces that Julia comes to understand the intensity of human seductions and revulsions.

Central to the suspense of the novel—and the focus of many characters' speculations about Julia's psyche—is the absence of certainty about her relationship with Dev. Martin Parham is obsessed with the need to know whether Julia hides a story of victimization. In fact, the possibility of shameful corruption in Julia's past intensifies her attractiveness for him, as she well understands. Maurice Devigny is likewise stimulated by an imagined scenario in which he finds his father with the girl child. And Julia's own effort to recall a pivotal day with Dev, one in which there is a memory of blood and death and sexual urgency—narrated dramatically through the device of a diary entry—leads only to deeper uncertainty and ambivalence. The indisputable fact seems to be that Julia does not regard the relationship with Dev as injurious. If corrupting, it was a necessary and inevitable introduction to the "crooked world," as she explains to her reporter friend, Tommy Arnold. "People draw life from the crooked world. There's a conversation going on with the straight world, all the time. It's what makes this city and it's what makes the world" (110).

In a 1980 interview with Elizabeth Broadwell and Ronald Hoag, collected in *Conversations with Elizabeth Spencer* (1991), Spencer spoke of *The Snare* as a "study of evil," and she said that, of all her works, it was the "most intensely thought-out." Asked about the novel's relation to the work just preceding it, the 1967 *No Place for an Angel*, she emphasized the different conceptions of evil that distinguished the two novels: "In *No Place for an Angel*, evil is simply an absence of good, the result of a vacuum of despair. I'm not a student of philosophy; but a friend of mine, who is scholar enough to give me the right context, says that this is evil in Augustinian terms. But I happen to believe that evil is also an active force with an existence of its own, and it occurs to me now that it's this active force of evil that's loose in *The Snare*. That book rests, so the philosophers might say, on a Manichean understanding of evil as an independent power to be dealt with" (72-73).

An even more direct influence informing Spencer's conception of "active evil" comes from the French poet Baudelaire. The book's epigraph is taken from Baudelaire's "L'Irremediable" in *Spleen et ideal* ("le Diable / Fait toujours bien tout ce qu'il fait!"), and it points directly to the ineluctable attractiveness of the devil's seductive world. Julia Garrett, protege of old Henri Devigny, the shaggy, massive, minotaur-like lover of Baudelaire's poetry, has been well instructed by Dev in the nuances of the poetry and its expressions of the Baudelairean world of sensual appetites. Quotations and images from the poetry pervade the novel, giving a rich intertextual resonance to Spencer's portrayal of Julia, who is "alive with creature feeling" and who finds vitality in both pain and sexual pleasure. The parallels between the poems and the pattern of the novel, which I discuss in detail in *Elizabeth Spencer* (Twayne, 1985), all have the effect of intensifying a vision of the human condition as a vast snare, in which human beings vainly struggle to reconcile a desire for transcendence with a knowledge that no such transcendence is possible. Baudelaire's view of human nature as inescapably dualistic reflects in many ways the Manichean conception of a divided cosmos actively and eternally in conflict.

As a final note on the fertile intertextual play in *The Snare,* one should call attention to the breadth of literary experience invoked in the novel. Spencer's protagonist, Julia Garrett, brings to mind not only Hawthorne's Hester, but a long line of Jamesian heroines who confront nameless, mysterious evils let loose in the world. Perhaps she is most vividly a legatee of Faulkner's Temple Drake, though Julia would seem to be a far more familiar and humanized woman to the author who creates her than Temple ever was to William Faulkner. It is particularly interesting to follow the unfolding strength and resilience of Julia, whom Spencer depicts as a woman who sees, accepts and enters a "life snare," but who ironically succeeds in evading entrapment and defeat. In many respects she suggests an Eve before the Fall, or, perhaps, an Eve who passes all the way through history and who reenters an Eden where mother and child replace Adam and woman. In her passage from childhood to motherhood, Julia does present a counterpart to the American Adam, the young male hero who passes from innocence to moral maturity, who has been a central figure in the nation's literature since European settlement. She is not an innocent, however, but a sensualist. She descends into a Dantean hell and survives, making her way to a quiet, safe place, because she finally assimilates evil.

The critical reception of the novel when it was published in 1972 was mixed. The novelist Madison Jones in the *New York Times Book Review* (17 December 1972) praised especially Spencer's evocation of New Orleans (the "sense of the living city, rendered in its uniqueness, with its customs and its lights and shades, is probably the novel's solidest single achievement"), but he voiced some reservation about the structure of the novel. Other reviewers, such as Patrick Cruttwell and Faith Westburg in the *Hudson Review* (Summer

1973), responded favorably to the characterization of Julia but less so to the novel's thematic ambiguities. Ultimately, *The Snare* was a puzzle to many critics who reviewed it.

When one considers how familiar in modernist fiction is the interplay of past and present, of memory and current experience, it is difficult to understand critics' resistance to the chronological juxtapositions in the novel, a resistance Spencer herself notes in an interview with Terry Roberts in 1990. She goes on in that conversation, collected in *Conversations with Elizabeth Spencer*, to discuss other elements of connectedness and interplay in the novel, such as those between character and setting, which give rise to a complex symphonic structure.

> New Orleans is a very sexy place, and I needed a very sexy heroine to make that connection plain. Most of the men who are attracted to her are attracted sexually. Her early experience with her guardian mentor, Dev, a French Cajun man who may or may not have seduced her, had a profound effect on her.
>
> This shady part of her life was happiest and yet at the same time was not subject to approval by the proper side of New Orleans, of which her family was a part. She kept trying to make these two parts of her life come together. In search of a synthesis, she went deeper and deeper into seedy, cruel, even criminal life. Finally she hit rock bottom, and it's a wonder she even survived.
>
> What I hoped would happen is that the reader would catch the connection between Julia and the city and so read it as an exploration, in depth, of both simultaneously. She's a human compendium of the city. New Orleans reveals the woman and the woman reveals New Orleans (228).

For Spencer, as for so many others of the lower middle South, New Orleans is the quintessence of city. In contrast to small and middle-size towns, to county seats or state capitals, to countryside and farms, it is exotic, sensual, opulent, splendid. Spencer remarked to Hunter McKelva Cole in 1973 that, for small-town southerners, it is a "cosmopolitan, European city." For her, she said, "it's been a city of life-long fascination." In *The Snare* she employs a great variety of stylistic devices to articulate the mysterious power of New Orleans. Frequently, she reverses a familiar technique in modern fiction, that of suggesting interior states of mind through images of setting, and suggests rather the mood of the city through descriptions of characters' responses to it. The newspaperman Tommy Arnold attempts to free-lance stories that bespeak the power of New Orleans to express "the nation's true pulse beat," which he identifies as "voodoo, jazz, sex, and food—who could go further than that," he thinks, "toward what was really important to people in the U.S. and A. . . . All they knew out in the great money-making complex that was the Yewnighted States was that strange things went on down there, and then they hummed a tune or ate a meal that they didn't connect with 'down there' at all. Yet both the tune and the meal would have started from down there and only from there. And the down there of their own hearts, the dark tangle, the lurking mysteries, did they know how much of that was a dim carbon of the original which lay spread out before his wandering feet, every day that rolled?" (82).

It is New Orleans that is seductive and unfathomable to Julia, more a mystery than the Devignys, more the fated attraction than is Jake Springland. In fact, Jake appeals to her because he "had caught the city's rough corruption with its core of feeling, its peculiar tolerant knowledge. She had circled it for years, but now an outsider had come to discover it, claim it, experience it and give it to her whole. Orphan girl in a voodoo city. . . . And so she clung to the stranger who had come and soaked the essence up. She gave to him to get in return what he had found there" (117-118). In this novel New Orleans embodies a heart of darkness, and the central characters, particularly Julia, are impelled to seek its depths to put their imagination and courage to an ultimate test. It is not surprising that Spencer has spoken of Joseph Conrad as a significant literary model in the years when she first began to write, for the Conradian motifs, though perhaps not so pervasive as the Baudelairean allusions, are significantly implicated in *The Snare.*

I think it is true, finally, that the power of the novel to compel the attention of a reader rests with the characterization of Julia and with Spencer's articulation of the city's gripping mystery. The author of *The Snare* is clearly not interested in simply invoking stereotypes, either of New Orleans or of a sensitive, intense young woman betrayed by a callous society. She is trying rather to press some essences from essential oils: what is it about mid-twentieth century respectable society that young adults then found so revolting, so unsatisfying? What were they (we?) searching for in the 1960s? Why, with so much material advantage, did they so adamantly flee their comfortable homes and so often find drugs and violence and self-destruction? What is there about human nature that finds a snare, especially a snare fully exposed, to be so enticing?

---

ELIZABETH SPENCER, a native of Carrollton, Mississippi, has registered in her fiction much of the societal conflict and spiritual confusion of her era. She began her literary career writing three novels set in Mississippi, *Fire in the Morning* (1948), *This Crooked Way* (1952), and the remarkable *The Voice at the Back Door* (1956), one of the most astute and compelling fictional portraits of local politics in the American literary canon—especially the politics of the rural South during the first half of the twentieth century. In the 1960s, after a sojourn of several years in Italy, marriage to an Englishman and a move to Montreal, she began to produce a shelf of stories and novels that mirror a broader social and geographical landscape.

The new directions are immediately apparent in *The Light in the Piazza* (1960) and *Knights and Dragons* (1965), novellas that portray American women in Europe. In *The Light in the Piazza*, for the first time Spencer writes in a novel-length work of a central protagonist who is female, creating in Margaret Johnson a woman whose self-possession is partly a posturing, partly a centered sense of identity and purpose. This book, which was originally published in *The New Yorker* and then

made into a successful Hollywood film, is the most widely
known of Spencer's work. She has often been asked about its
celebrity, and she invariably responds with a rueful comment
about the vagaries of publishing luck, noting that the time she
spent on composition was "all told . . . about a month."

In a number of ways both novellas prepared Spencer for
the writing of *The Snare*. She would return to the theme of
female self-possession in the later novel, and in developing
the character of Julia she would explore further the conflict of
female goals in conflict with patriarchal power. Particularly
in *Knights and Dragons*, in the character of Martha Ingram and
her former husband Gordon, Spencer imagines a young
woman-older man relationship similar to the bond between
Julia and Dev. In fact, Gordon Ingram bears a physical resemblance to Henri Devigny; he is described as "shaggy," "huge"
and menacing, like a dragon, or, more precisely, like a mino-
taur. The aura of mystery and the penchant for self-destruc-
tiveness that characterize Martha directly anticipate Julia Garrett.

*No Place for an Angel* (1967), which followed shortly, is a
long, complex novel about a group of Americans whose shut-
tlings around the world reflect the fluidity—instability is perhaps the more accurate word—of their familial and moral
lives. We see especially Catherine Sasser's dislocations, as she
moves from a girlhood in Texas through a marriage that
allows her no sense of self or spirit, to a single, though not
lonely, life in a Walden-like home in Massachusetts. Despite
the female stereotypes that confront her, Catherine persists in
following a path of her own choosing, maintaining throughout the novel a mysterious reserve of feeling and strength
that belie her appearance of vulnerability and fragility.

A gifted writer of short fiction, Spencer published her first
collection of short stories, *Ship Island and Other Stories*, the following year, in 1968. In the title story, one finds in the characterization of Nancy Lewis the continuing grip upon Spencer's
imagination of a certain kind of woman—sexual, reserved
though not repressed, curious, wounded in spirit, and threatened by a larger world that is both spiritually hollow and

oblivious to sensitive, intelligent women. Nancy is an adolescent, however, so her story, while richly suggestive in both imagery and interior discourse, is after all short. It is, rather, in *The Snare* that Spencer develops her most complex and satisfying exploration of such a female protagonist.

The mixed critical reception of *The Snare* was undoubtedly a disappointment to Spencer, and she did not publish another novel until 1984. The intervening years saw the publication of a number of short stories, as well as the critically acclaimed collection, *The Stories of Elizabeth Spencer*, in 1981.

Despite her achievement in short fiction, the novel has always been the serious form for Spencer, and she returned to it in *The Salt Line* (1984) to explore again the effect of the traumatic 1960s upon contemporary Americans. Set on the Gulf Coast of Mississippi, the novel focuses upon the adjustments of Arnie Carrington, formerly a professor at a nearby state university, to the consequences of a storm that is both actual event and the central trope of the story. *Jack of Diamonds and Other Stories* (1988) and the 1991 novel, *The Night Travellers*, give still further indication of Spencer's imaginative engagement with the decade of the 1960s and of her efforts to understand the continuing effects that the civil rights movement and the Vietnam era had upon individuals and the collective psyche of the country.

Artistically and thematically, the fiction of Elizabeth Spencer warrants attentive reading. It is a rich and varied body of work that gives not only a moving portrait of the twentieth-century South, but, uniquely, a portrait of a South viewed as inextricably connected with the larger world. And among the nine novels and over forty short stories to date, no other work more surely or profoundly communicates the tangled web of relations that distinguishes the recent South than does *The Snare*. What it reveals is a place and time representative of twentieth-century confusions, a human milieu one can recognize as one's own.

Peggy Whitman Prenshaw
Louisiana State University

# ❧ THE SNARE

# Part I

# 1. THE SQUIREMEISTER PARTY

 It had been the most wonderful party, all the better because nobody had expected it to happen—no party at all had been planned or intended.

It was just that Bucky and Marie Squiremeister suddenly found themselves with more and more people dropping by, and it was New Orleans, and it was spring. More: it was a noticeable, a particular spring, which kept coming on (they talked of it in New Orleans at the time and later) forever. It kept coming on, and on and on, from January when the camellias bloomed in the small green yards along the broad flat residential streets out toward Highway 90 and the Mississippi coast, about the time of the New Year's game in the Sugar Bowl, when they beat the big drum boom-boom and the little majorettes strutted on their thin little legs in white tasseled boots and white satin skirts up to high-water level.

Distinctly feverish, the whole show, the reporter thought. He was sitting on a couch at the Squiremeister party.

But the spring was not feverish. His vision basked in a diffuse glow of softest sunlight, westering without glare, fading without elegy.

The city was mellow and knew itself, and the spring had crept in, after the scarlet of poinsettias, in yellow and pink, rose and white, a bloom here, a scent there, here a raised window, a warm terrace, a splash of sun. Then, teasing, there would come a raw wind, a gray afternoon, a sudden explosion of hail bounding in the

3

streets. Once in a while a hell-sky threatened, roiling in over the river or the lake or up from the swamps, livid with lightning, with the suspicious look of being able to toss automobiles, roofs, and shrimp boats around as easily as children's toys. But that would fall, fade, fail, drop away like a gruesome Mardi Gras mask, and then, smiling, the spring had returned before you knew it, saying like a gracious young mother soothing a dream-troubled child, "I'm here. I was here all the time." So one's own forgotten Easter feeling waked up again. (What was it like? the reporter wondered, looking closer inward. An Easter child with the scent of a rose pinned in safety-pin firmness to the lapel of a navy-blue double-breasted little-girl coat, arriving on the punctual stroke of the church bell to slip a white-gloved hand into a waiting palm in a moment not-quite-awkward and sure with joy. . . .)

"What are you sitting there thinking?" a girl, distinctly not a little girl, asked him.

"Not thinking, just drinking," returned the reporter, who had been uncritically letting his own purple phrases rejoice him because nobody could black-pencil him.

She sat down. "Isn't it a marvelous party?"

He nodded. "It's the best ones you never plan for. Can't. They just happen."

"What do you do?"

"Hey, be careful. Questions like that, even one or two, and this misty creation will crumble to dust. You know that. Save it for the next Junior League open house."

"I don't belong to it, and anyway I really wanted to know. I wanted to know what you do."

"I'm a guesser. What I've guessed is: you already know what I do. You've guessed it."

"Newspaper?"

He nodded and braced for the next dull question to put up its little comic strip balloon above her pale rather narrow forehead, when she suddenly left him. Then he wished she would come back.

Then he felt old, for she had looked about twenty-four at the most; then he went and threw his weight around a little, kissing the hostess, Bucky Squiremeister's wife Marie, and getting another drink. But nothing would quite do it; the peak was past; from now on it was only coasting, drifting down. He wandered into the garden and back again through French doors thrown wide, sampling shrimp, cold chicken, olives, and almonds, watching the fish in the garden basin, joining one cluster of people, exchanging it for another. But always wafting down.

It took a long time because the point had been a high one, really remarkably high. The damp weightless iridescent bubble had not come out of any bottle, but was after all what people were only trying their best to purchase whenever they bought a bottle. So the coasting, the wafting down, went on until long after dark. By the time they spilled out the front door and into the open, it was past three, a dark quiet hour dim with a mild sheen of stars, moon melted away completely, street surface gray with dew, street as full of wide-eyed country air as though a deer had wandered into town.

And the reporter knew about such things. He had seen that very story, checked on it, and rewritten it for the *Picayune*. A deer had wandered into Jackson, Mississippi once, in the early dawn hours when all were sleeping. Where had it gone, what had it thought, before they had got up and about and started seeing it, frightened it, run it down, attacked and killed it . . . no need to remember all that horror. Only remember the animal wandering, unknown, unknown about, not knowing even itself, but creating wonder. It had seen itself in a department store window and jumped straight through the glass, damaging—what? "The finest in ladies' dresses, bags, hats and shoes"?

He looked up from trying to open his car door with the wrong key. The deer he saw was two-legged (have I really got this corny? he asked himself) and it was still

in pale green linen with a coral scarf, with the narrow
forehead, the cropped dark slightly French look.

"I am a newspaper reporter. Yes, I am," he told her.
"You have guessed it exactly, Miss—?"

"Garrett," she said. "Julia Garrett."

"Gah-Ray, no doubt. Old Creole family. Julia, how are
you? I believe we had a brief exchange, dedans, là-bas
bas, back yonder." He put out his hand for a very good
reason and she took it just in time, to hold him upright.

"You can't drive home like this," she said, like a
sensible girl. Her dark hair lay in thick half-curling locks
about her brow. He didn't know whether to like or dislike these level-headed girls who knew how to drink, how
not to overdo it. In his day the girls had tossed it down,
you had to race to keep up, they had to have it before
you could touch them. "Where are the keys?" she asked
him.

"Listen, kiddo, I've flown airplanes a damn sight
drunker than you've ever seen anybody get."

"That so? Well, you're obviously quite a guy, then,
so go right ahead." She suddenly dropped his hand and
he stumbled, listed, groped, and gained the car door. He
put his hand to his head. "Sometimes it hits you," he
complained. "It's funny—I feel sober, vision good, it's
just that my coe-ornashun is not too A-1."

"I'm going to drive you out to the lake. I didn't have
any plans for going to this party. Nobody knows where
I am. Do you follow me?"

He squinted. "Not well."

"I mean it's after three. I mean, nobody knows.
I've got two addresses, you understand."

The wheels in his brain turned, a bit slowly, but at
last he got something. "So if you don't show at either
one——"

"They'll each think I'm at the other one."

"Oh-*ho!* Oh-ho-ho-*ho!* They each know about the
other. That's a new one. Now the kind I've heard
about——" What was the kind he'd heard about? He

couldn't get there. His own train of thought had departed without him. He was left in an empty station. He pressed his forehead against the cool metal of the car. "There's nothing like a newspaper office for sleeping it off. Empty as a canyon, gray as a vault, head on folded coat. Sideways on copy desk. All the old smells."

"There's nothing like the cool front seat of a car with the top down, out on the lake with the morning breeze."

He thought a minute and looked at his watch but found he could not see if he had one on, let alone make out the time.

That was when he soundlessly passed over the keys.

Out on Lake Pontchartrain, where a girl can walk barelegged on a lot of evenings while the spring comes on, from January to May, feeling the warm wind beneath her skirts and generally thinking things over if alone, or talking things over if not, Julia Garrett woke up with a straight-up-and-down jump. She was at the wheel of a strange convertible and she was alone. She might have been asleep for five seconds or two hours, not longer because it was just dawn; the long low-lying clouds to the east, along the water-pale horizon of the lake, were pink, turning intense red now, staining to a ravishing deep dye, through watermelon and crêpe myrtle, right on back to lipstick and roses.

In the small waterside park ahead gulls, hovering at tall-man height, clustered about the refuse of somebody's last night's picnic—beer cans and crusts of hamburgers, doubtless; paper cartons with shreds of cole slaw and French fries stuck to the paper. They screamed now and again, pure in color, white and faint brown. They lowered tremulously with greedy outstretched claws.

The lake, cross-furling and easy against the breakwaters, rustled; and she stirred, shifting back against the doorframe, tilting back her neck, which had a crick in it. She would certainly have fallen asleep with the scent of salt and spring-stirring growth in the deep nobly-named mysterious old lake, while the blood color drained from clouds to the health of gray, pearl-gray to firm white, except that back to her left and behind her she heard the noise of a man throwing up what sounded like every-thing except his shoe leather. Then she really woke up.

He came back to the car. His eyes, fish-damp, dis-enchanted, but sober, sought her out from over the door-frame where he leaned with folded arms.

"I hate you," he said. "You look fresh as a daisy."

He mussed his hand through his eyebrows, then smoothed them back, laying flat and straight the few longish damp strands which were all he had left of what must have once been a rich, thick crop of hair, back when he came out of some country town to be a big-time reporter.

"What time did I pass out?" he asked her.

"Right after we got here."

"I don't remember."

The street-cleaner truck trundled by, spraying water in palmetto-shaped jets, colorless, close-hauled to the charcoal-colored asphalt. Fallen azalea blooms carpeted the grass of the park; a few camellias still bloomed in partial deterioration among their dark green leaves; gardenias starred a single low bush near the drinking fountain. The water flapped against the rocks. The gulls sought out their special altitudes.

"Well, what do we do, now we've got this little history behind us? A stroll in the park? Would you care for a swim?"

"How can you discuss it?" she said. "As long as there is a single cup of coffee left in this entire city, how can you even ask?"

"Right. Right, right. And there's an all-night stand, or used to be, back before they tore down the V.A. hospi-tal—just down there and around." He circled the car quickly, and opened the door.

Julia Garrett slid over in the peeling leatherette seat,

which was torn jaggedly, revealing the cotton stuffing beneath. The sun, in circumference as long as the convertible, now cleared the lake's pale gray horizon line with clouds still laced about it, visibly gained an inch of the horizon. The reporter put the car in motion. The muffler snorted. The gear worked loose as a hound's shoulder.

"I picked this car up second-hand three years ago," he remarked, suddenly needing a shave. "You can say one thing for it. I bet you've never been out in anything like it."

"What do you take me for?" she asked him. "Some sort of ex-debutante?"

It was the second occasion she'd had to ask him that and she was by now finishing her coffee, having cleaned up scrambled eggs, toast, bacon, and marmalade, and was lighting a cigarette.

"I don't know what to take you for," he said, risking a little cream in his second cup of coffee. "After all, this is the first time I've really been able to see you."

"It was a good party," she said.

He paused, spoon dripping. "Wasn't it good? Wasn't it good? I'll always remember it. What were you doing there? And alone too? No, don't tell me. Let's not postmortem it. Let's never do that. Will you promise me?"

"Okay," she said, too quickly, he thought, as though pulling back from him, from the entire last twelve hours. He felt let down a peg; the magic carpet turned into an elevator, going down. But she suddenly saved the moment by smiling warmly, and saying, "I do promise, yes. And you're right, too—what you feel is right."

He looked off at the wall. What was all this about? he'd begun to wonder.

"To continue a conversation," she said, looking carefully down at her cigarette, "I asked you what you did. Way, way back I asked you. You said you worked on a paper. That's the *Picayune*, I guess."

"Yes," he said, "and a long time ago I asked you what you did and you didn't answer."

"I guess I didn't hear you. I don't remember. You can always ask me again."

"Okay, so I have. What do you do, Julia—Julia—?" He snapped his fingers for the last name.

"Garrett," she supplied.

"Julia Garrett, what's your occupation?"

"I'm a model."

He broke out laughing. She had come out with it too flatly, self-consciously, her sophistication after all was only a thin little manner, it now seemed. She traced his thought accurately and blushed. "I just got the job," she explained. "In a week I'll know how to say it. It'll be a snap."

"And your family doesn't know what you do. And— wait now, don't tell me—you keep two addresses."

"I got the apartment first, then the job. I've always had the family."

"Where does the family live?"

"St. Charles area, generally speaking."

"Garden District, generally speaking?"

"University section, to be exact."

"But out St. Charles?"

"Yes, out that way."

"Do you model downtown? Parade around at lunch with price tags dangling off you? Murmur one hundred twenty-five to ladies on their second slab of chocolate cake?"

"Not like that, not at all. It's for artists. You know, life class. Sitting."

He whistled. "No wonder you didn't know how to say it."

"It's not like you think."

"How do you know what I think?"

She put out her cigarette and folded her hands together firmly. "It's just that from the outside things have this imaginary quality. I say sitting for a life class, you think nude with a lot of lascivious young men in smocks. I'm not nude; they're mainly queer, in jeans and dirty shirts; and it's so academic it's boring. Then I say University section and you come out with some ex-debutante talk. Well, when you say reporter don't some people go all bug-eyed? You flash your press card, you sling a camera over the broad shoulder——?"

"I don't think you're really so worldly wise," he interrupted, "so cut it out. You're still self-impressed—it's nice to be, you know."

Then she said: "How's the murder trial?"

"The one I'm on. How did you know that? Wait a minute . . . you heard them talking at that party. And that's why you——"

"I wasn't sure I overheard it," she nodded. "I just thought I did."

They were both silent for a moment. Because he was a good reporter, he had the sense to know when he heard the central point of what was going on; he knew a heartbeat from every other racket. This, all the time, had been what was going on.

"What's my name?" he asked her.

"Arnold. Thomas B. Arnold," she answered correctly —and why not? He was good for a by-line, several times a week.

"A lot of people are curious about this thing," he mused. "Women, especially. Yes, indeed." He squinted at her, then, fumbling in his coat pocket, drew out a packet of aspirin.

"For just one little pristine while, you can see. You can see better than you ever saw before. It's the reason for all vice, what I just gave you. Vice clears the mind for seeing. Then the old head tunes up. The little red man with the forked tail is up in there clanging away, and why doesn't he go find him another old murky foundry to work in—why pick on the one on the inside of this poor old skull, vintage 1920? It's the kind of golden philosophy I hand out to my wife. Now you're getting it and you don't like it either."

He went to the counter, past the big quiet electric fan on its stem as tall as a camellia tree, and leaning at the counter with the dark arborite top between two of a row of empty stools, empty except for one lone truck driver in a cheerful white uniform with some sort of nauseating advice about bread stamped on his back, he got a glass of water, tossed down the tablets, and returned to her.

Hamming it up, she sat thinking; all reporters are like that.

"So should I interest myself?" he said, sitting down. "Here I think it was my intelligence, charm, my je ne sais quoi, my definite appeal, my—— I thought it was me you liked."

"I don't dislike you. In fact, I like you fine."

He frowned at her, for a moment totally self-absorbed, for the good reason that his stomach was spinning like a stunting airplane over a cow pasture; then the aspirin stayed down and took hold; he bent to his coffee, with caution and a certain piety. "A great party," he repeated. Clear-eyed he focused straight on her face. She was real and getting realer. There might be something better than magic carpets. "You've got something to tell me about the Springland affair. I haven't even asked you what. You know he didn't do it?"

"I do know that. I do know it."

"So do a lot of people, but still nobody can prove it. Least of all him. He was with the goofy victim when last seen. Or I suppose you're going to say you saw him that night, at the very hour of the crime?"

"Well, yes, I did. I wasn't checking watches, but it was close enough." She was cool and final with her shocker, the message she'd wanted to get through to him for the last twelve hours, and he saw she meant it, much more than he would have seen it if she'd just looked him up at the paper or sent the words burbling through the alcoholic seas at the party. Now he had it, like a note on a silver dish. He watched her tapering long aristocratic fingers extract another cigarette from the pack with the off-beat brand name.

His reaction was protective. Why should she get into it? It's sleazy with dirt, it's cruddy and it smells, at times literally.

"There are too few good times in this world," he said aloud. "I have to be at the office at eight. Leaving time for a shave and a stop by the laundry, I'm just about on schedule, ready for phone calls from my ten addresses. So now I'm writing down Julia Garrett with the double R and double T, correct, and now I'm passing on my name and number to you." He wrote it down and tore it off. "Got a telephone?"

"No."

"Thought not."

"How did you know?"

"Didn't know."

His gaze on her now was speculative, enfolding, detached. He ticked the yellow copy pencil against the table top, then he was picking up the check, paying, clearing her through the door, out into the full fresh spring morning, letting her into his car, swinging out into the boulevard with the grassy pretzels between the crossovers, plots for stunted palms. He dropped her by a cab stand, as she asked him to.

"Good-bye, Mr. Arnold," she said.

"Tommy to you," he said. "Considering we spent the night together."

"Okay, Tommy."

"Marvelous time," he said. "It's just that I have to live on it for quite a while, you understand." But she wouldn't know what it was like—aspiring to so many things, coming down to so few. To her everything must always be a little of an adventure; she took for granted a forever-coming spring.

"One thing: are you on his side?" She squinted through sunlight, demanding, shielding her eyes with one hand.

"Anybody would be, wouldn't they?"

"I'll make it do for an answer."

They all try to talk like Hemingway, thought Julia Garrett of reporters generally. Looking for a cab, she thought it sounded better than usual when Tommy Arnold did it, maybe because he gave her the feeling that his disillusionment was real.

# 2. THE TOUCHSTONE

Of the two addresses that Tommy Arnold had teased her about, Julia Garrett gave the cabdriver the more distinguished one, in the University section. It was called Audubon Place, a cul-de-sac of residences off St. Charles Avenue across from Audubon Park. She chose to dismiss the driver just short of where the iron gates stood open, high and graceful in the warm spring morning. The hibiscus thrust its fluted trumpet through the palings; bougainvillea crept into bloom along the wall of a neighbor's plain house, enhanced by that one proud vine. Julia went past deep lawns richly plotted in flowers, shuttered living-room windows, recessed and morning-dumb in the shadow of the verandas.

The house she was going toward, the one she had been brought up in by her aunt and uncle and her uncle's father, stood well forward in the cul-de-sac, three houses from the entrance. It was pleasant white-painted Victorian, not overly ornate, considering the period when it was built and the kind of money that had been back of it in that day and age, and it was still kept fleecy white by her uncle Maurice Devigny—up-keep was an expression of his nature.

This gentleman, a man of such pronounced sensuality and good humor that he could even bring off a sort of sartorial elegance of foulards, ascot ties, jade cufflinks, and brocade smoking jackets without seeming to give himself airs or risking labels of effeminacy, was now in one of his favorite attitudes in the kitchen doorway, an enormous ironstone cup of café au lait on a shelf at his elbow, lounging, arms folded, against the door frame. The green lattice work of the breezeway behind him, he was talking to his wife. He was commenting, rather, while his wife talked; she could feel herself the while, moving in his vision, the creation of his vision curling about her, setting her with the firmness of a jewel in her own world. And nonjewellike she responded, living and breathing within her body's life, almost as conscious as he of her roundly set hips, low-slung beneath the flowered cotton wrap-around, the plump knees and elbows, the broad handheels and rather wide feet, neither of the last pleasing to her—she would have liked to be daintier. But having made the turn into her forties, she was inclined to take relaxed views even of things which did not altogether suit her. Her sense of style continued; her fashion sense lapsed and returned by fits and starts. Someday it would go altogether.

"I suppose that what she wants is to make a distinct life for herself," Isabel was saying. "I think she has her motives; we just don't have her confidence completely. She's not dumb."

"Brilliant school marks," said Maurice. "I wonder what they mean, in living terms, I mean. No correlation, maybe."

"I wasn't thinking of school. Intelligence—well, it makes responses greater, I guess. Julia responds, every which-way. We know that."

"What are you making? Potato salad?"

"That's right." She looked up over her chopping board, almost spilling off the glasses outlined in fine gold wire that had slid down as usual to the flare of her nostrils. They were comic and she knew it—a little clown's façade to her riches. An enormous green pepper was giving up its strong crisp odor as she chopped it fine with a knife a bushwhacker might have used in a pinch. "So juicy, these peppers."

"What's with that for dinner?" Maurice's perpetual

interest in food had something sanctified about it, like a devotion.

"Oh, this is for lunch."

"Isabel, you're not going to waste that succulent mess on yourself and the maid and whoever might drop in, like our straying niece. I bet she's got a whiff of it clear across town, wherever that mysterious apartment is located. I wonder what she eats? Can you imagine? I bet she gets those instant things that all taste like woodpulp and soap, dissolved cardboard with food coloring. Isabel, *don't* eat up all that salad."

She pushed the glasses up with the tip of her little finger, cocking her head slightly, experiencing fake innocence. "I'll try and make some more, to leave some for supper." She nibbled for a moment at the dish, then dumped in a small pyramid of riced hard-boiled egg. She turned to three uncut stalks of celery, their yellow-green leaves still cool from the refrigerator. Her mouth could almost feel the ribbed pressure of the stalk before teeth sank in, and she nibbled again, a sprig part leaf, so that the pale innocence of the leaf leaped into positive odor; its virginal strength rushed through the senses. She stood munching a larger bite. No frozen woodpulp for her.

"We're up so early," Maurice complained.

"The sun," Isabel recalled and riced another hard-boiled egg. He would think of that salad all day. "It's just the spring, too nice to waste."

"Bed . . . waste? Since when? Are you going to feed me, now I'm up?"

"Breakfast." She once more touched her glasses in place with ritualistic delicacy, rinsed her hands at the sink and dried them on a cup towel. She rattled about in a cupboard for a skillet, and bending over a drawer near her husband, felt his touch and stroke across the hips that rose up before him as she bent. The sheer cotton wrapper pleased her.

"God is merciful," said Maurice, with a sigh.

She came up laughing. "What?"

"Why is it women always want a compliment repeated?"

"She's got a man, I bet you," Isabel said, beating eggs at the stove, back to Julia again in her mind.

Maurice put himself down at a white enameled table, before a bright mat of varicolored straw, plate, and cutlery, a glass of orange juice. "More coffee?" "Please." He watched the glossy stream pour out.

"If she's got somebody," he reflected, "it's amazing she never talks about him. We always used to meet them, before the Parham deal broke up. Since then she never talks about them any more."

"We got our hopes too wrapped up in the Parham affair," Isabel said. "So much *money*. I wonder if she ever loved him."

"Love," said Maurice, speculatively. "He was bored up in that godawful bailiwick. Baptists and swamps."

"Filthy rich," said Isabel. They had had this conversation so many times and what it always meant was the same. In spite of the fine address, the good old house, the excellent silver and china, the admirable circle of friends who knew about painting, opera, history, politics, and local lore back to the days of the French and the Spanish, the Devignys needed more money, and it was entirely within their rightful way of looking at things to believe their niece might be the one to bring it in. More often than they cared to think about they had had to dip into capital.

Isabel's large cup, stamped in blue, exactly like her husband's, full of black chicory coffee with hot milk stirred in, now sat a neighbor to his near her elbow on the white table.

"Maurice, do you know that the Parhams objected to us?"

"Objected to *us*? Ridiculous! Who could object to us?"

"They could. And did. Indeed, they did. Do you know why? Because we're Catholic."

They both burst out laughing.

Maurice sampled his eggs which were scrambled dry, just faintly browned in one or two quarters. In other words, perfect.

"If they only knew what kind of Catholic you are," he said, amused at the entire world. He was handsome when ironically pleased. His light-colored eyes, between gray and blue, shone agreeably; his skin, supple and moist like fine leather that had been expertly treated, lay in a justly apportioned line from cheek to chin, marked by a wrinkle line or two, shading into brown temples.

"No good getting started on my sort of Catholic," said Isabel. "Look at yourself. Anyway, it didn't matter what *kind* of Catholic we were. The worse the better. Just that we were it. That awful thing."

"I'm Catholic enough to know there's something awful about Protestants like the Parhams. Money-mad, narrow, grasping, critical, mean, self-righteous . . ."

"Maybe we're better off without them, after all."

"Oh, I didn't mind the boy. Martin Parham was put off by them, too. That's why he wanted Julia."

"And she didn't want him."

"It may not be over yet—he's never married anybody."

"Umm," said Isabel, thinking that things once dropped hardly ever resurrected themselves.

"Where did you get this thing about Catholics? How do you even know it's true?"

"I felt it. No, I'm serious. I distinctly felt it on more occasions than one. Then there were two little things—little but important, I mean——"

He waved a smooth brown hand. "Spare me." These deductions of Isabel's—she knew very well how he thought of them. They wound around, it was true, through labyrinthine paths, but they did emerge at a point where, she was convinced, the full truth was to be seen. Strange, then, how reluctant Maurice was to follow her step by step until her cry of triumph: "You see!" But then he often did not see. He was sometimes amused enough to listen, but that was different from agreeing.

Not wanting to ruffle a sunny morning, Maurice said soothingly: "I shouldn't think it would matter what the Parhams thought of us; it was what Martin and Julia thought of each other that mattered. If religion had been a sore point between them, they would have told us, back in those days. No, love, I can't accept it. All I know is what I know. She found herself a great catch, nice boy with money to burn, and she let him go."

"Do you actually think we'd have got any? What do you think?"

"Any money? Not just handed over in the form of a check. I think it creates an atmosphere, and you and I— oh, Lord, what's the use?" Dryly, he folded his napkin.

She glimpsed his vision, and knew why he turned away. In having so much—and Each Other stood foremost on every list anyone could draw up of the much that they had—what they'd been denied was galling, like two personal insults from the Almighty. No children. No money. A slap on either cheek. In place of children, happenstance had brought them Julia. And she, in turn, might have got the other also. It had come within a breath of working. On some great grim one-armed bandit way down deep in some sleazy back room in the French Quarter, the giant of all jackpots had trembled before spilling out its total insides upon the willing waiting head of Maurice Devigny. Child Julia, almost daughter, bringing plenty: a rich marriage and her children, too, good as his own line.

It hadn't worked.

He pushed back his chair. Time to go to the office.

"Who's she got now?" Getting out his coat, he salved his soul on the thought of green turtle soup at Kolb's. Fridays always brought that benison.

"We don't know for sure she's got anybody at all."

"Come on, she's always got somebody. Don't let's start

kidding ourselves. And furthermore, since moving down into some crummy area it could be anybody at all."

Isabel sighed. "You mean an organizer or a painter who doesn't sell or just an intellectual——"

"I mean some horse of a different color from us. It's what those good grades meant all the time, Isabel. Not that she's more fit for living, but less!"

"Color!" Isabel had seized the one word from his flow of talk.

"Oh come on. I hadn't really thought of *that*. The religious question is one thing, the race question is another." But he had, rather, stumped his toe on a possibility. How to explain her silences? A line knifed between his brows. He knew it and smoothed it away. "Enough for one day—agreed?"

"More than enough. Oh, yes, I do think so!"

From far up past the pantry, the china cupboard, the stairwell, the parlor, and the entrance hall, they heard the front door open and close, and a familiar step in the hall. The looks they exchanged were complex, containing their own quality of life—but happy.

So she did come back to see them, after all.

The quick clear stride broke from the carpeted area of the living room on to bare dark floors. Trailing morning air, Julia burst into the kitchen. Lime-colored linen. Fresh lipstick. A crown of dark curls.

"Any coffee left?"

"Hello, Julia!"

"What a nice surprise!"

"Grand morning out, don't be lazy."

"It woke us up early. Oh . . . the paper. Since I was too lazy," Isabel continued, "to go out and pick it up."

"Sorry. This is mine. I didn't see yours. But it's out there, I guess. Here, take it anyway. A present."

"Give it to Maurice," said Isabel, busy with coffee.

Maurice peered at it critically. It had been hers or

somebody's long enough to be opened and read past the front page and refolded. Questions about her life woke up. He wondered if she'd been to bed at all in any ordinary sense of the word, but said nothing. He was averse to opening a mussed newspaper. Nothing but the fresh-printed word would satisfy his morning mind, his morning eye the first to rest upon it.

"Never mind. Whether you saw it or not, mine's on the porch where it always is. Give that to your aunt. Keeping up with the murder, Julie?" The thought had come to him while getting into his coat. He kissed his wife and then his niece, who had not answered him. "Thought once you'd grow as tall as me," he remarked, regarding her from no great height. He gave her an affectionate slap on the behind. "You'll never make it now. Glad to see you, chère." Going toward the door, he turned back to say, "If it's the sack of books you're after, I put them in the entrance closet."

"How'd you guess?"

"I don't know . . . they're your bedside books. You forgot them." He looked at Julia more directly, started to ask her something, hesitated, then turned and left.

While her aunt glanced through the paper, Julia sat and thought: it is unusual to have made the acquaintance of a murderer, or at least of a man a whole city thinks is a murderer.

"Do you think he did it?" her aunt inquired, coming up with a bird-look bright with the gleam of gold wire that rimmed her glasses.

"Who?" Julia asked, mask-faced: an inward bracing had gone on.

"This boy—this Jake Springland."

"Who knows? Do you?"

"They're all mixed up together, people like that. It's what I always think. He's got a nice face, that's what's made it odd. It's what's got everybody interested. How could anybody that looks like that kill anybody? But all that's deceptive. No matter how he looks, they're all equal and all dirty."

"Dirty, Aunt Isabel?"

"I mean those streets they live on, all those places. You know they aren't even halfway clean, and if you think in the summer time, in hot weather——"

"Some crooks are rich," said Julia. "They stay clean all the time."

"I don't know any," said Isabel, "and glad of it. Aren't you going to be late for work?"

"Running me off?"

"You said you'd eaten. Don't you want a piece of toast?"

"No, nothing."

A pause fell between them, continuing by its nature the hesitance of Maurice, leaving, refusing to ask her anything. Now Isabel was deciding not to ask either, but as they were alone and both of them women, the silent question got louder. She could have got those books anytime.

"It was such a beautiful morning, that's why I wanted to see you," Julia said, in a burst of all-at-once affection that her aunt knew had something of truth in it. Good at receiving warmth, Isabel smiled. But she said nothing and the silence grew again. "You see, I was coming here yesterday but got mixed up with some people going over to the Squiremeisters—you remember them —and we got started partying and it went on and on. . . ." She trailed off.

"And on," her aunt concluded, getting up to go to the window and swat a fly. "Maurice and I used to get mixed up in things like that, back when sleep didn't matter so much as it does now. If you so much as lie down and close your eyes——"

"That's it! I had to keep going. Never make it through the day if I stop."

Isabel returned and sat facing her again. "So noth-

ing's wrong, then?" Her gaze lost itself in one of Julia's
opaque silences. As always when that happened, Isabel
wished for Maurice, whom Julia did not scare. Trying to
open up confidence with Julia, she always wondered if
she really wanted it. Did she . . . didn't she? The
moment, for both of them, ticked past. Her question went
unanswered.

Julia gathered up her bag, gloves, and dark glasses.
In the entrance closet she found the books, as Uncle
Maurice had said, neatly piled in a carry-bag. And he
had chosen a small white bag from one of the smart
Canal Street shops rather than a regular grocery store
one. The touch was like him and seeing it made her
slip her gloves on. Peering inside, she saw the copy of
Baudelaire's poems that the old man, Dev, Maurice's
father, had given her before he died; and her missal,
little used, bound in white leatherette, but always present,
because, she had thought from time to time, what do
you ever do with it except keep it? And the two or three
other books she kept by her bed: a Brontë book, *Villette*,
which she had not re-read since freshman days but
which had given her a firm idea of how life could center
around a woman's impressions of it. The modern poems
also came from her freshman year, and the book (rather
battered; she had picked it up in an old bookshop) of
folklore about a community down in the bayou country,
and that brought her back to Dev again. It had been Aunt
Isabel and Uncle Maurice who, childless, had thought
they wanted her for their very own, but who had been,
she at least believed, themselves like children who want
a pet until they get it—then someone else has to take
care of it. That someone had been the old man, Maurice's
father. Dev. A heavy face leaning down; a wide-lipped
mouth, dark within as a wine-drinker's, with a gleam of
gold from out the cavern. All dead now and laid to rest,
but present to her still, a constant heavy sun along the
horizon of her spirit's self. Would he ever either rise or

set or show any change? The companion of her childhood: no blood kin (Isabel's sister had been Julia's
mother). She imagined Dev would always remain exactly
where he was with her, dominant and unmoving. Sometimes, true, he spoke. Right now he was saying what he
had often said: "There's creatures and varmints, Julia.
Cree-chures and var-mints. Be sure to be a cree-chure.
Nothing wrong with females, good ones." He snapped off:
gone.

By then Julia was well out of the dark heavy front
door, down the steps, past the iron gates of Audubon
Place and on to St. Charles Avenue, where she would
stand waiting for the old streetcar to lumber along. But
because Dev had come and spoken, the old dead man,
still the same, and in good voice, she had been caught
up in a well-toned personal rhythm, had come to feel
herself and more. She knew why she had come to Audubon Place, not to confide in her aunt and uncle, not really
for books either, but to touch home, to find her touch-
stone, now when she needed to. In other words, to touch
Dev. Now that she had, her glory was with her.

It was partly the self-glory of twenty-four, alive with
creature feeling. Her heels crackled on the pavement and
all living odors of fresh bloom and morning swirled
around her. She crossed the tracks just before the streetcar trundled to a halt, iron wheels shrill on iron rails.
She pulled herself up and in with one smart string-gloved
hand, bag and parcel held in the other. Her coins tinkled
clear in the clicking box; the bell clanged. She sat down
on polished wood, reposed behind dark glasses.

> *Voici venir les temps où vibrant sur sa tige*
> *Chaque fleur s'évapore ainsi qu'un encensoir. . . .*

The book that said that was now all innocent-seeming
down in the shopping bag. The voice that had often read
those lines was reading them still, at least in her head—
old and tremulous, perhaps, but rich with savor.

Late to work was what Julia let her aunt think she
was. The truth was, she had no regular work at all any
more, only the part-time modeling she had told Tommy
Arnold about.

Up until two weeks ago she had gone each morning
to a brown-paneled, polished, and carpeted ophthalmologist's reception room where she had sat decoratively at
a desk with pads, pens, pencils, typewriter, and telephone.
Sometimes she had been busy. Her presence was necessary to the doctor within. Anyone's presence, however,
she knew very well, would have been equally as good as
hers. And knowing this was what brought her, one day,
to just up and do it: serve notice and quit.

Dr. Pollard had stared at her when she told him; he
had pushed up his ophthalmoscope, which was sitting
crooked on his brow. He who six months before on a
warm fall afternoon, eyes wild, breath whistling through
his nostrils, had chased her round his desk, his charts,
his lamps, and his elaborate examining chair, a real race
into the reception room, around her own desk and on
through the outer door, where she guessed he would
have kept right on down stairs and through streets and
all over the French Quarter, had not the cleaning woman
herself, upholstered top to toe in sweaty overstuffed black
flesh, the greasy gray-black hair strained back into a wad
behind, but still a woman, looked up and right at him—
and he never went another step. Julia, vanished by this
time around the corner of the stairwell, hanging on to
keep from slipping on the freshly mopped marble,
spiraled down three flights to the lobby. By the next day
she had put aside the incident and so, she judged, had
he. When he brought in some letters for her to type and
compose properly (he had earlier confessed to being
weak in grammar), he colored slightly as he finished his
explanation and hurried back to work. Since then they
had scarcely had a conversation, but life was more peaceful than not with him, now he'd made his pass: Dr.
S. M. Pollard, gruff and bossy and accurate with patients,

angular brown bristly hands, unpressed trousers, sloppy jacket, long ago desentimentalized. He had his own office air-conditioned for the summer, but left the reception room as it was, high-ceilinged and airy, with tall windows and flawed marble floor beneath the carpet. "It's cool enough in here, isn't it, Miss Garrett? . . . It always seems cool to me when I come back from lunch." "Oh, yes, Dr. Pollard, perfectly satisfactory." "However, if it gets too much just tell me. I can call them in the morning and they can have a machine in before you know it, the same day." "Yes, I will, Dr. Pollard."

The day she gave notice he was sitting in the inner office between patients, crowned with his ophthalmo-scope, scribbling notes. The pencil continued to move while she told him, then it stopped. He did not look up. "Is there any specific complaint?" he inquired, eyes studious on the pad. "No, Dr. Pollard, I honestly can't think of a single one." "You're getting married, perhaps?" "No, Dr. Pollard." "Another job?" "I will get another job. I'll have to. It's only that secretarial work . . ." "Is dull?" He looked up. Now she was smiling at him and there he was, a human, for the first time to her knowledge, Samuel M. Pollard. He had been there all along. "You've been okay," she told him. "You've been just fine." He grinned, angled off from her by swaying aside slightly in his chair; she noticed the expressive quality of a swivel. He turned once, not fast, not slow, then a half-turn, finishing with his back to her, tilting, hands clasped behind his head. He might have been watching clouds. "You've been fine too, Miss Garrett." They agreed she would stay till he got somebody.

He found a replacement, laggardly, a month later, a blond girl in white high-heeled pumps worn too early in the year, a baby-blue wool suit too bulky for her height, and a squeaky voice. Julia told her everything to do and left her with it. She went in to say good-bye to Dr. Pollard, who was on the phone. He put his hand over the mouth-piece. "Take it easy, Miss Garrett," he advised. Closing

the door, she felt a real pang of love for Dr. S. M. Pollard,
whom she had seen only once, really, surprising his
creature-self there in his office the day he admitted it:
the job was dull. She had the impulse to go back and say
something further, but this was not her style. She went
down the steps in memory of him, and at every turning
of the old-fashioned cracked marble flight on which her
heels, in every weather, struck out a crisp reverberation,
she thought she would certainly try to keep in touch with
Dr. Pollard, in some way or other. Then she was through
the lobby and out on the street: Jackson Square. Through
the trees General Jackson, outsider, cocky conqueror,
canted back on his rearing horse in perpetual salute; but
the city had snared him nicely, balancing him off between
the docks and the cathedral in the middle of a little
square; he was framed, and served up motionless. That
fate would not be hers. The fresh windy March air,
harshly brilliant as broken glass, charged with odors
from the wharves of fish, oiled machinery, sea and river
water, a dark sluggishness of passage by river, snatched
at her breath. Birds chattered, darting, near one favored
tree. A colored nurse with a gray sweater over her uniform held children eager at a corner back from certain
death. Julia's first step forward was into a city old and
new all the time, but newer in this moment than she
had known it for a long time now. She had brimmed
up with its mystery without noticing. With her first step
out the door, the quick of life moved in lock step with her:
she knew she would never be back.

Now it seemed years ago she had left Dr. Pollard,
but it was only a week or so, so why didn't she tell her
aunt and uncle? Well, she hadn't and she didn't—that
was all.

She got off well before the streetcar reached Lafayette
Square, entered a drugstore and bought a paper to replace
the one she had left in Audubon Place. She sat down
alone at a booth and opened it. The picture on the front

page confronted her silently. She lowered her eyes to it slowly, then fixing her gaze more deeply, for one minute chained to the next, let it come entirely in to her. It seemed that the two of them—she and the man in the picture—were alone at last.

# 3. THE UNHOLY VISIT

 As she stared at it, the photographed face would seem to rise vibrant toward her vision with unknowing force. Then she laid her hand over it quietly and firmly.

The picture took up a very large part of the page, almost as much as her hand covered. Now the keen level intelligent eyes probed into her palm, the long square chin jutted up against her handheel, the definite declivity from cheekbone to jaw ran equal length with her palm's outer rise toward the small finger. Her whole hand became alive with the face. She lifted it. The pulses in the tips of her fingers were awake and throbbing. The face still looked evenly out into the world. It did not defend itself, was not alarmed.

The underworld, thought Julia, the crime world—what was it? Like a revolving beacon it was always flashing, come and gone on elsewhere before its nature could be known. Julia knew as little about it as though she really were the ex-debutante the reporter, Tommy Arnold, had accused her of being. What she did know was that one day it had turned up in Dr. Pollard's office.

Her first impulse when she thought of that winter morning was still what it had been then: to burst out laughing. But that was before the fear had struck her, and now, before the memory of it, sharp, metallic, corrosive as acid, returned. Because she had been scared, all right. She'd been scared to death.

The buzz had sounded ("RING AND ENTER," said Dr. Pollard's notice), and the door had opened, and there they were, the three of them, disreputable, unlikely, and wild, realer than real.

They would be famous afterwards. For weeks on end every detail that could be raked up about them would turn into grist for the New Orleans papers, but Julia Garrett, being to all appearances someone out of the straight world with some idea of what she was actually seeing, and whose imagination could guess at further actualities still, saw them first, before the city did. The man Ted Marnie was fragile, with thin mouse-gray hair limp and untrimmed about his neck and brow, and a spare apocalyptic look, shabby and sanctified. God had bit him like a rattlesnake, was Julia's instant impression, and on the very stroke of her thinking that he approached, leaned carefully across her desk, and spoke.

"God's grace is yours. Only believe."

Eyes without their accustomed glasses, she had noted by now, show it by the whitish over-tender area around them and a naked look. His, in addition, were glittering and gimlet-sharp. They took her breath for the moment, ripped it straight out of her. Innocent was the word that came strangely but accurately to her later on. Because he was that, as in the old comparison of the savage and the precious watch, smashed between rocks to get the tick out. Innocence can do anything, devoid equally of doubt or guilt or fear. To the totally innocent, flowers and garbage are exactly the same, allowing for slight differences in color and smell. Her gaze fell away, fleeing from his, and landed on the two hands placed before her. One wrist was crooked and the hand from it set off at an angle like a flag on a stick, obviously broken. My God, doesn't it hurt? was what she all but gasped. Evidently it didn't.

The woman had followed him and stood at his elbow. She nodded in agreement to what he'd said, staring down deeply into Julia's face. Whatever the man said, the woman would support it. She had got converted, Julia decided, by methods none too original. Sex and religion had strongly combined. Now with a prophet in charge, she was even letting the red dye grow out of her hair. Stoop-shouldered, overweight, and sullen, some idea of her own sexiness had got into this woman's head from girlhood on; it had become all that mattered, up to the recent past when religion had entered her life and down she'd gone before a new master, much like the old but with some additions. A smell like rusted metal reached to Julia and she drew back, not wanting to have to think about it. She looked past the pair, not answering, her eyes seeking for the third, seeking for an answer: whoever could possibly have fallen in step with that pair, been amused by them enough to want to spend any time with them? Much less get attached to them? Well, there he was, the third member of the party, off and to the side, letting the scarecrow who'd taken the foreground obscure his good nearly six feet of height, in the same way he permitted the cheapness of the two of them to be part of him, going without shaving in a stained windbreaker and checked wool shirt. Julia guessed that he must *be* cheap, else he would have resisted them. In the lenses of her vision, they stood until set in permanent form, microfilmed and filed and catalogued; then they moved. Something was bound to happen, ran Julia's young feelings, about every place she got involved with; about this one, something told her that this was it.

"Do you have an appointment?" she inquired.

"No."

Her eyes were on her note pad. Her head had run out of things to think, and still she couldn't stop her heart from its panicky racing. In that town you could always find yourself on the bus next to somebody with glazed eyes and fumbling motions; strange combinations of humanity showed up in bars and movie houses. Tales were spread about—houses with nothing but quadroons, nightclubs for nothing but queers, snake ceremonies, voodoo rings and fortune tellers, conjure packets for sale, mail orders all over the world. Dr. Pollard had not told her what to do if a bunch of weird characters wandered in.

"Just have a seat," she said. "I'll have to ask if the doctor can see you."

"I've got money. I can pay cash."

It was the young man, speaking out suddenly, over the heads of the other two. Up to now he had given her the impression that he was thinking of something on the outside. He lifted his hand from his pocket, holding a wallet of smooth-worn leather.

She nodded, showing nothing, and went through to the inner office, closing the door quickly, and appealing to Dr. Pollard. Her heart was still hammering like crazy.

"What is it, Miss Garrett?"

"Some people—" She swallowed. "These people—"

"Well?"

She stepped away from the door toward him. She wanted to tell him in a low voice, and so leaned over the desk, but at the same time she became aware of the door having opened behind her, of a stepladder-structured frame shadowing her back. Its head was too small. Her spine tingled. She did not turn, but saw Dr. Pollard's face change as he looked past her.

"Miss Garrett," he said, "would you just fetch me that last month's record book out of the study." He jerked his head toward the opposite door. There wasn't any study, but she caught on and obeyed, thanking God for Dr. Pollard (since God had been so recently mentioned). She entered a back passage where his and her coats hung and closed the door. She held on to the edge of the wash basin, ready to bolt for the door which opened on the fire escape, noting the tiny flakes of powder which had scattered from her compact that morning, listening. She heard nothing but a long exchange of low voices and presently Dr. Pollard called out, "If you can't find the book, Miss Garrett, would you be kind enough to go back to your desk?"

So it's all right, she thought; it's okay.

The pair, the thin one and the woman, were with Dr. Pollard. She had an instinct of shying, like a mare at a snake, when she went by; an aura clung round them; they were, at least she could already find herself reassuring herself, the "real thing."

She went through the door and resumed her place at her desk, straightening her skirts, rubbing her palms together slowly to calm down the sweat that was breaking out on them. Further to steady herself she stared at the back of the young man, the third one, who was looking in turn at an old framed Victorian engraving of two hunting dogs, a pair of setters, black and white, pointing a pheasant.

"The gentleman has broken his glasses," Dr. Pollard had said when she passed through, and there had been Samuel M. Pollard sitting there without turning a hair, not even smiling when he said "gentleman."

Now the young man said without turning, "He broke his glasses. Or rather I broke his glasses. I sat on them. Anyway, they're broken." He turned around, looked right at her, and smiled. In the smile, his near-whiskers went shooting out to all compass points, like a trick mask. "You may be surprised, ma'am, to learn that people like him have glasses. Or if they break them they don't go to the ten-cent store, or steal another pair off somebody else. But his are special, he's got some kind of rare defect in vision. Either that or he's lying. How can you tell? I still have to fork up."

She looked at the tip of her pencil and said, "Is he a friend of yours?"

"He'd say so, I suppose." He had an out-of-town way she rather liked of not toying with what he knew, but simply dishing it up straight. "He's more than a friend," he continued, after a pause. "He's supposed to be converting me to the Lord. A lot of characters down here," he added, seeming pleased with himself for meeting some choice ones.

"Where do you come from?" she asked.

"Ohio. Nearly Kentucky."

Up there somewhere, she thought. Looking slant-eyed at him for a half-second, she placed two letters unfolded in a wire file.

"I'm real gone on this place," he told her. "But like I said about Korea, I just hope I get out alive."

The door from Dr. Pollard's office opened; her heart flinched. She lowered her eyes and counted paper clips, making herself rigid in the chair. When she looked up again, the room was empty, the young man was gone, and there was again a fading whiff of something which was not a physical odor, but more like the odor one imagined from corroded metal, mixed in with cheap perfume. Steps faded down the stairwell. She began cautiously to breathe again.

Presently Dr. Pollard stuck his head out the door. "It takes all kinds," he said.

"Weren't you frightened?"

"Well, no. . . . You see, Miss Garrett, practically everyone needs glasses at some time or other."

That was morning.

In late afternoon, the young man returned. He came unannounced as before; the door simply opened and he appeared in it. Now she saw him on his own—the wasted fanatic, who, preacher-fashion, had shamelessly drawn attention to himself alone, was removed. He had shaved and put on (it looked brand new) a soft-collared beige shirt with a tie that had seen better days, knotted inexpertly, but, at least, done. He was a big blond young man with long fine features.

"I was just passing by," he said.

It was such an obvious lie that they both laughed.

"You must have about got to quitting time, haven't you?" he asked. "Aren't you ready to leave? Oh, excuse me." He saw that there were two patients still sitting in the office. Julia saw them smile indulgently. All they thought was that a young man had stopped by to see a girl. Rising, she went through the door with him into

the corridor and stood talking with him outside for a
moment. She had meant just to say she had a date or an
appointment, but that was before his face, bending
toward hers, showed, in addition to curiosity, an appealing liveliness. The morning's event had jarred something
loose in her, something jammed up maybe for too long
a time. She felt curious, now, as well as he. For she did
not know what this something was.

Strolling with him that day after work, late on the
winter afternoon, black coat buttoned close against the
wind, she was living in her own impulses, wondering at
them, at the same time listening, taking in; for, open,
voluble, he could not quit talking.

"You're a different side of New Orleans from what
I've been able to see," he confessed right off. "I knew it
as soon as I saw you. I've not got enough money hardly
to live on, and no connections here. So it's been strictly
the low life for me. I like it, understand—in a way, I eat
it up. I was out there in the war—Korea, Yalu River—
frozen dead bodies, K rations, booby traps. Hell, just
being warm is as good as the Hilton, a long time after.
I said when I got out I'd just bum around the States a
while, some warm climate. Not so warm here yet, but not
so bad either. No ties or anything. What I really wish
was that I was a writer, a painter, something like that.
I meet guys that claim to have it made along those lines,
but I don't know—it's hard to know. Can you tell?"

"I guess not."

"All I've got's these songs. I can do guitar, steel guitar,
zimbalon, some bass, oh, and (don't laugh) banjo. Yeah.
The old Dixieland combos got me interested. Always
some guy in it with a banjo. I thought I'd try it. I teach
myself mainly—get some music. It's just a natural gift,
good for helping me get around. Then—this is important—it puts me on the right side of things. You know
that guy this morning? He knows one or two of the Negro
bands; he's got some sort of in. I stick around because I

can't tell what it is. Religion? Dope? Voodoo? What's the angle? One day I think it's one thing, one another. Could be anything. Not that the bands would let me play with them, just for the asking, not on the main circuits. But practice sessions, and all that—maybe. I'm investigating stains. There's some sort of rub you can buy and turn colored. Crossing the color line in reverse. I guess then you wouldn't speak to me."

"Can't you join a white one—or a mixed one? It just seems like a lot of trouble, staining yourself."

"Mixed ones are scarce now. So far I can't find any."

"Then you'll have to dye your hair too, or get a wig."

He thought about it. "What schools? What colleges?" he inquired of her.

"Newcomb. Then Tulane."

"I've heard of Tulane. Football. Sure, that's it. That other one—I don't know. I bet it's the best. You think all that good-college stuff's a lot of crap?"

She kept smiling, kept walking, keeping quiet enough to let him go right ahead making her up to suit himself. He was inventing her; she saw that. Julia had observed that men would do that if you let them, and if they were good men what they made up would be pleasant. Seldom true, but pleasant. Maybe in the course of things, you could believe in it a little too, and then maybe it changed you a little. Her mind idled on such thoughts which did not, she knew, matter very much. Idling, she listened to his voice, tuning in to the frank, amused quality, the sharp, tidy sound of the out-of-town R's; a voice too head-long to be tricky.

"The crime that goes on in this town! I've learned a lot."

Something Julia had noticed about outsiders: when they came to where you lived they wanted to tell you what it was like, as though you couldn't find out for yourself. The worst of them would tell you what you yourself were like, as though you'd never noticed.

"Most of these guys," he continued, proving her right, "are just hopped up and trying to make enough to buy what keeps them alive. Some of them are hoping to make the big time, get with some operator, somebody who knows somebody big. I don't know if they even know enough to mean any harm. It's crummy. A real crummy life. Thank God down here at least it isn't cold—not all that cold. You probably think it is. See that?" He leaned his head to her: part of his ear had been snipped away. "Frostbite. Korea. I know about cold."

"Then there's all the Negroes. I love their kind of talk, all that music. Just eat it up. You have to be careful, stay in place with them. The other night, I was over in —well, you don't want to hear about all that. What do you want to hear about? Don't tell me you have to go! Now I've found you! Where do you live? I'll take you there.

"Where I'm living, it's hardly what you'd call halfway decent. I'm trying to work out this fool idea on too little money. In summer I plan to go to work on the shrimp boats, down south of here. I'm worse scared of one thing than running out of money. You know what it is? Running out of feeling—the feeling of this time in life. You know how things are like that? That they can run out? Do you?"

The talk poured over her. He looked down at her face more than he had to. From time to time she felt small, as though he were carrying her along tucked beneath his arm like a black kitten he had found. From time to time she felt happy. The wind had sprung up, rustling some fallen leaves in the park. She drew her coat more tightly up under her chin. He tugged her against his shoulder, stroking her hair. Once he placed a sidelong kiss against her head.

"You've hardly said a word. Hell, if life isn't about things like this, what is it about? Do you know?"

"Yes," she said. "No," she said. "I don't know," she said. She was shaking with laughter, and halfway long-

ing to break over into sheer joy except she knew she'd
needed something to happen for quite a while, ever since
she'd broken things off with Martin Parham, the rich
boy from up in Mississippi. "Wait till Mardi Gras," she
advised. "You can dance in the streets if you feel like it.
Nobody will notice."

"Are people noticing?"

"Well, there just went my boss, for instance."

"Is he in love with you, too? Is that why he hired
you?" He caught her arm up close and walked her on.
"I think we've got something here, Julia. Julia—what
is it?"

"Garrett."

"Julia Garrett, I think we might have something.
Let's at least go have a drink before you have to go. It'll
cost me my dinner, but it'll be worth it."

He let her go to hasten ahead of her into the French
Quarter, down Royal Street, as if he knew where he was
going, a good dog on a scent. But he didn't know. He just
turned corners wherever they appeared to interest him.
He glanced into streets he meant to visit someday. He
caught overhead supports and swung round them happily,
suddenly aware of architecture. Julia's mood was chang-
ing; she didn't like his shirt any more. Her college-girl
criticizing was about to start: was he good enough?
Obviously not. She had met a lot of other men who
weren't good enough either, for one reason or another.

"Here, what about this place?" she suggested.

"I don't know it; is it okay?"

She said it was okay and they went in, sat in the
corner and scarcely said a word. After two drinks she
heard herself agreeing to meet him the following Saturday. She said a hurried good-bye and went off smoothing
herself together, taking a taxi which she really couldn't
afford, wondering what she thought she was doing. He
had thrilled her once or twice and made her laugh. Then
she remembered the glasses and whose they had been—
those nightmare people. That wasn't so funny. They gave

her pause, and a long shiver, keen and fine as a razor. Would she go on Saturday or not? She had promised, but she didn't know.

She went principally, she said to herself, to tell him that she couldn't stay but a few minutes. She scarcely dressed for the occasion—skirt and high-collared shirt under her black coat and then he was before her, outside the hotel lobby with impatient watching in his face and a notebook under his arm. Sitting on a sofa in the hotel lobby, the Monteleone, he showed her the song lyrics. "All I've got to say for myself," he explained. "The theory is—" He was turning pages, murmuring, leaning close into her vision while she read. To her surprise she saw and felt the words he'd written down. Not bad, some of them. And so it meant . . . He was off again. He couldn't wait that day to see her, he said. He caught her shoulders, one in either hand, and squared her around facing him. Holding her firmly, he unbuttoned her black coat a little way, looked with approval on the white shirt-blouse, then let her go. She leaned back, withdrawing slightly, but at his touch her flesh had reassembled itself, face to ankles. Desire was an old acquaintance of Julia's; its candle-flame intensity was known to her in every grade and flicker. The lobby was garrulous with out-of-towners. Suffocated with too many voices, she half-sank into a permissive languor. If the street could snap her out of what he made her feel, then she would have no problem.

"Look here." She caught his hand solidly in her own. "This city just goes crazy on Saturdays. People show up from everywhere. I don't like it."

She was pulling him out. Through revolving doors his blue eyes trailed her; she sensed his vision catching against her head, shoulders, legs, behind, as she moved before him. Wind in the street, cold and damp, off the river, took her strongly in, pummeled at her, beating out her feelings, like a rug swatted free of dust on a line. She let them all go, gasping a little, noting her own weakness for sexual occasions.

"I just came to tell you I couldn't stay. I don't know anything about those song lyrics," she continued, apologetic, but crisp and firm, "except that they sound good even without the musical background part. I'm nobody that can help you here. So——"

"Can't stay!" It was all he had heard. "You can't go, Julia. Of course, you can't do that!"

"But we've nothing——"

"In common? You're going to say 'nothing in common'? Christ, of course we haven't!"

"Yes, but I've got a life here and—— Oh!" She had cried out for he had taken her arm and crooked it back upon itself, the forearm unnaturally bent behind her back and at the same time deprived of any possibility of moving itself, as thoroughly as if it had died. "What are you trying to do?"

"I didn't mean to hurt. No, honestly, I—— There. I was just disappointed. Overcome for a minute. Can't we walk a little way, like the other day? You couldn't be in such a big hurry."

"I think you broke it. It feels dead."

"Not really." His arm circled her gently. They had got half off the curb and a foam of people swirled about them. He pulled her across a pedestrian-jammed street, edgy with cabs in demand, over to the opposite side. They stood at the entrance to Royal Street.

"Must be a convention," she remarked. "That or football." She was ready to turn away, go back out St. Charles, do a little weekend shopping, lunch at a barbecue counter, not much but clean, warm, and cheap. She was ready to see him turn and plunge off into the Quarter, another outsider to test the labyrinth there, a custom in that town centuries old now. He wouldn't be the last. "Good-bye, I——" She was about to put her hand out when a group of college boys, arms linked, drunk, lunged out of the Quarter shouting and singing and bumped into her, an attractive girl before them, in an accidentally-on-purpose way they obviously all thought cute, except that instead of just one brushing her in this way, all of them had had the same idea so that she caught the weight of what felt like the whole Georgia Tech team and went down on one knee against the wall.

"Can't you watch what you're doing? Christ a'mighty!" The young man with the songs in the notebook whammed its black cover in the face of the nearest boy.

"Sorry, Mac. Sorry, we didn't mean—" They were running.

He was bending over Julia who was sitting against the wall with her stocking torn at the knee. He pulled her up and, seeing nowhere to go, drew her off the street into an antique shop, not a very fancy one, the objects for sale being not much better than second-hand furniture, and nobody about but a woman with blonde untidy hair, talking on the phone, her back to them. Julia leaned down over her scuffed knee, then let herself be led to a second room and sat on a couch, dusty, with scrolled mahogany arms, covered with worn blue velvet. There was a Tiffany lamp done in panes of red and ivory-colored glass on a table inlaid with a cracked wooden mosaic of a St. Bernard. The smell of dust and shabbiness came out of the blue velvet. She felt drowsy, out of the wind and the shouting crowd. "On Saturdays, I hate it down here. Everybody in the world keeps coming. I forgot your name."

"Jake. Jake Springland."

She was looking at him now, he who had struck a noisy boy in the face for her and before that had made her arm go curiously dead so that she had been momentarily frightened. It was private here and unlikely— an unlikely place to be. Her throbbing knee said that hurt could occur anyplace, anytime, a weed always busy under the soil. Julia would not have wanted anyone to know how much a place with things like these, that sort of street incident, filled in her particular sense of life. She settled herself on the dusty old sofa as if in a house of her own. She knew then what she wanted to do, and she saw him know it too, in the same instant. He had left off touching her.

"It's those people you were with, in the doctor's office. When I think of them——"

"They frighten you?"

She did not answer. A fissure, something like that, had jarred loose within her nature. She could get dizzy, she knew, peering into that cool-flavored dark. Were those people, trailing their fearful world, a repellent or attracting force? Were *they* really why she had come and why she was here on the blue sofa?

"Forget them," Jake Springland advised.

In the room beyond, the street door opened. The woman at the telephone had hung up and was approaching new customers who had entered.

"I'll try," Julia said. "But I doubt—"

"Doubt what?"

"Succeeding."

Seated beside her, he laid his notebook down in his lap. His wrists coming out of the tan raincoat looked raw and strong. His long regular-featured face, slightly hollowed between the cheekbones and the strong chin, forced its straight regard upon her. He took her hand up. She saw avidity gather around his mouth, but his eyes remained blue, steady, clear.

She rose presently. I'm crazy, she thought. Really nuts. She had run through her share of misbehavior, all right, but never with anybody who appeared in the sort of company she had seen this man with. Why did she keep returning to them—the skeletal, broken-wristed man and the woman with fading red hair, those two horrors? When her arm had hurt in the young man's grasp and gone dead, she had thought of them. Why? Was her fear, maybe, the real treasure in it all?

She turned her eyes from him, but her mouth was dry. He was waiting and she knew it.

"Let's go out of here anyway," she murmured. "Walk
—eat something. I'm starved."

From that moment, eat where they chose, wander
where they would, it was settled. Sooner or later they
would find the room.

It was after dark before they found it, after a good
deal of talking, some eating, some drinking, and many
silences. The room was dreary and anonymous and
neither of them noticed it in much detail, for by the time
they got through the door they were cased and strait-
jacketed in such an iron seizure of desire that even waiting until he turned the key in the lock and switched off
the center light was anguish—it was agony. When they
fell at last toward one another, she heard his breath like
sobs pounding through the intricate tunnels of her ears.
Her letting go took half a century. Release . . . oblitera-
tion, it was gaining them that made her one with all the
shadows in her mind about him. She knew that all the
way through, before, exhausted, she blanked out in the
cool dark.

When she woke it was nearly two. She squinted at
her watch by the light of the dimmest possible lamp. The
hour could still seem to be explainable on Audubon
Place. Her uncle and aunt never exactly asked her anything. That was when she got herself together and Jake
Springland too. Her black coat finally resumed made
valid her return to the world, though she liked herself
none the better for having got out of it, not to mention
blouse and skirt and all the rest, so easily. But it was done
now, she thought, moving quiet beside him on the cheap
stairway; it was done instead of fighting about it for a
week or so, which was never her style. Her feelings were
drained. Wanting to please her in minor, preliminary
ways was not in this man's bones; and she remembered
Martin Parham, so eager a pleaser it would make her
smile anytime to think of him. Had she been missing
Martin, and didn't know it? If so, she didn't know it

yet. She was tired, blurred out, and in the taxi, snuggled beside the strange young man in the damp, exhaust-smelling cold, she looked down at the flesh of his hand and wrist pressed fast to her shoulder. She promised to meet him again without much conviction.

This time she didn't go.

Only several weeks later did the tumult in her ear, not to say the cries and harsh demands, come back to life for her. Disembodied and repetitive as the sea in a shell, they murmured time and again, restlessly. The song lyrics, too, returned—in scraps and phrases—they weren't so bad, not at all. But at Dr. Pollard's office, if waiting for Jake to show up was what she was partially doing, she waited in vain.

And here she was, several months later, looking in the newspaper at the eyes again—steady, clear, direct—the same that she had first seen lightly probing into hers when he had confessed to sitting on the glasses. Here was the face—but with a certain depth that had not been there before. Did she imagine that?

Jake Springland was supposed to have murdered the man, Ted Marnie, one dark night last winter, after helping him hold up a filling station. The body had been buried south of New Orleans, down below Gretna, in a swamp. The henna-haired woman, whose teeth had been yellow below a satchel mouth, was missing and searched for. And Julia herself, though the story did not mention her, was not where she had been when that curious threesome walked through the door of Dr. Pollard's office. Neither by day nor by night was she in the same place. She had left Audubon Place and now lived without a telephone in an old section down on Amelia Street. She posed for a life class to earn enough to eat on. She thought a good deal about the cheap life, that sluggish drifting river, the languor of untidy afternoons, where the common goals have all got shifted, shuffled like an old deck of bicycle cards.

In the booth in the hole-in-the-wall she leaned closer to the picture. The shadows under the high cheekbones, those long declivities, had blurred; the eye sockets looked shadowy. "Oh," she said and yawned, thinking, I'm so sleepy.

She remembered then that she hadn't slept all night, except for that indeterminate time in the convertible, out on the lake with the reporter. When she folded the paper, sleep came on so strongly, she half-staggered in the door of the café. She remembered what the reporter, Tommy Arnold, had said about falling asleep on the copy desk at the newspaper office, coat rolled up for a pillow, the comfortable, patchwork-quilt smell of familiar things.

God, she thought, seeing double with fatigue as she searched her purse for coins. She still had walking to do. Feet heavy as lead took her at last through a side gate, her entrance to a walkway past an old house. She entered the back garden, climbed the back stairs, her entrance. The unkempt old garden lay silent under spring sunlight. The broad flight of steps falling down toward it from the veranda above still kept, in outline at least, the idea of former splendor. In the wide upper hallway, doors stood half ajar. Shuttered, her own room looked dim and cool with all the flooding force of strong New Orleans light blanked out.

> Voici venir les temps où vibrant sur sa tige
> Chaque fleur s'évapore ainsi qu'un encensoir. . . .

The sonorous old voice trembled, accompanying her steps.

She plunged face down across her bed, barely conscious of the thud of her shoes slipping off onto the floor before she fell asleep, the paper falling from the bed. And Jake's face in the paper, it had dropped as well, she knew, but could not summon the motion of her hand to retrieve it. He lay on the floor below her. She longed to draw him, in the flesh, up beside her.

In trouble, was he? Those people . . . those people . . .

Jake Springland.

# 4. MAURICE DEVIGNY

 As he went to work that morning, catching a taxi because he had gossiped too long with his wife, Maurice Devigny thought things over as regards his niece and could come up with nothing except increased feelings of curiosity, vague anxieties. Several years back he had been anxious about her for different reasons; then one day it had dawned on him that she had certainly by now lost her virginity to any one of the number of young men who had called to ask her for dates from high school age on, and had done so moreover without making any production of it or embarrassing anybody or letting it in any way affect her poise and good humor. From then on he had had almost too much confidence in her life sense and had gone so far as to be a little jealous of the air of freedom and lightness which surrounded her comings and goings. In other words, he'd proved it: he wasn't prurient, he wasn't a prude. It was not his style to be so. If he had ever really resented Julia, it had been when she was a child. She had entered a household already complex with his father's presence and added to it another layer of complexity. She wasn't even his own—she was Isabel's sister's child, not a Devigny at all.

In love with his own marriage, he had dreamed away whole sections of his life on children that never came about, now never would. Early in their eager young passion, Isabel had miscarried once, then conceived again ridiculously soon after. His father had let him know what the trouble was: "There's such a thing as too

much, son. All your carryings-on upset the little things."
"Stop, Father . . . hush saying it to me. It's too late to
talk about." And so it was, the second time. He'd got one
of those medical pronouncements that made his heart
freeze up, his blood run backwards as though drawn off
into a vacuum. He had even been shown the second child,
a tiny boy, well-formed. The doctor had brought it to
him. It was an ultimate cruelty, perpetrated by a cold
young medical man who did not even know what he was
doing, doubtless thinking of it as a friendly gesture—a
man should be able to see his son, even though the son
is stone dead after premature birth and three hours of
breath and daylight. The young doctor could forget in
the next few minutes and probably had done so, but the
precious outline was cameo-carved for good and all on
the memory of Maurice Devigny, a father for three hours
only. No use to dwell on it. Their fault, was it? His father
had been pointing it out, but he had thought so too, long
before, after the first one. It was one of the irrational
sexual convictions that people carry, more real than
truth. And back of it in time, but continuing forward
into time, always behind, around and before them
simultaneously, remained the great joy of their marriage.

It lived with him always, from the ceremony onward.
A winter marriage, church fresh with green smilax,
masses of white chrysanthemums, and Isabel, nineteen
and a virgin still, a gardenia circlet on her brow; he could
smell the flowers yet as she knelt by him and turned,
leaning toward him for the ring, sense the chill-warm
in the petal flesh, too much sweetness to draw in.

A New York honeymoon: his father had given it to
them. Neon-lit nights very black and tall, the buildings
straight and so lofty their heads could not be found, their
sides sleek and rich, all polished granite was the impression he had then. A gloss of snow slanted past,
through dark and light and into dark again, dampbrush-
ing their fresh cheeks, catching in their enchanted lashes.
The hotel room smelt of its own rich carpet. Going back

to New Orleans on the Pullman, little towns glowed past in early evening or slept by starlight, and at stations, porters trundled baggage past in the dead of night, groups clustered in the cold on wooden platforms, seen through a crack in the green curtains; the human mystery seemed near and precious as their own breath, infinitely receiving and giving love. Back in New Orleans, outside their bedroom window, a giant poinsettia in full spike-petal scarlet bloom stood on the upper gallery. Even with that plant he felt a kinship, a link of being, individual by either the plant or himself.

Then the first pregnancy, and the first small blow. He had felt puzzled, but only vaguely, worried, but not alarmed. Then it happened. Maurice had been an only child. To say "I want" had always been very nearly equal to having. Now he had been refused by something in tractable and perverse in the blind nature of things. The mystery which had seemed so accessible and precious was more precious than ever for having, for some unknown reason—worse still, for no reason at all—been refused him. His love for Isabel intensified—if he felt thus and so, how must she feel? He used to find her, rabbit-soft, curled up in unlikely corners of that huge house, face streaked with tears no paw could wash away. Then he would embrace, caress, and murmur, but at last, as she said nothing, he would shake her gently, like a doll she herself might have had as a child, to win some outcry from her.

It did not come. In those days, her dress, her taste, her ornaments took seeking and testing and encouraged in her a privacy of choice, an intricate movement in areas she did not share with him. He was thus so unprepared when the first news of Julia entered the house that he had no means to resist. Isabel's sister, victim of a bad marriage (not only bad but unattractively, dismally bad) had died, leaving a child, a young girl child, scarcely six. "But that's too old," Maurice remarked. He wanted a baby fresh from the vine and so went back to his idea of adoption. At his objection, his wife flew at him like a small hurricane. Importunate, he thought later, dwelling on the old-fashioned word, his sensuous, hoarse, almost theatrical voice entering into the accent of his thoughts. To stop her he would have had to strangle her. Her own flesh and blood left in the hands of that worthless husband, a man named Frank Garrett! What God had taken from her, God was now returning to her. This was what she said. Maurice thought it was going too far into things for Isabel to mention God personally. Her weekly attendance at Holy Name of Jesus was more like a social observance and often finished with sherry at somebody's house. Who would have guessed her to be involved in personal events with le bon Dieu?

Brought low with misgivings, Maurice repaired to his father's apartments high up above Audubon Place, and sat down in that atmosphere—male, not as robust as once, but full-toned still—a sprawl of flesh behind a desk piled with books of every nature. "Take the house, son," his father had said, after Maurice's marriage. "Isabel will enjoy it." "But what about you, Father?" "Me? Oh, I'll take over the third floor if you don't need it. Ask me down to dinner, temps en temps." It was Sunday dinner that they asked him to—and they ate it at night. Other times, one of the Negro family who worked for him, who lived out in the old carriage house, and with whom he kept up some sort of constant spiritual communication, would enter the kitchen and, having consulted with Isabel's cook, would load up a tray. They would carry it up the outer stairway in warm weather, the inner dark narrow carpeted one on cold or bad days. Afterwards the tray, well-pillaged, would sit out before one of the apartment doors—inner or outer, whichever it had come in by.

Maurice had sunk in an armchair, one of the smaller ones with carved walnut arms, covered in wool worked in pictures of men and women in costumes of three centuries before. "It's Isabel," he said. "You remember

this Garrett man, the one her sister married?" "Never
had the pleasure." His father cast him a dry gleam of a
glance across the desk. Not a fatherly glance, not friendly
either—just different, since Maurice had married; but
how to define that difference? Diffuse perhaps? Determined not to come too close, determined to possess itself.
Yet (Maurice was an optimist) maybe his true feelings
for his son were still there deeper than ever, like Isabel's
for God, or maybe what he felt released from was simply
responsibility, not that he'd buried it for good and all,
the way he'd buried wives, two of them, one loved, the
other not. How could Maurice tell? His father's next statement seemed at least to express concern.

"Don't tell me Garrett's descending on you, now his
wife's died?"

"No, not that. At least, not that. It's the child. Isabel
wants it—all her own idea. Garrett's no good—an accountant or bookkeeper—ought to do something for the
WPA if anybody would have him even for that. Thinking
of that child and Garrett together, Isabel just goes crazy."

"And when they go crazy—" Henri Devigny remarked.
Women in general was what he meant. Nobody could
question that he knew more than enough on that subject.

"I wanted to adopt. Still do. A boy, preferably."

"You still can."

"She's got something against adoption, any adoption."

"Blood," said the father, at once.

"That's it. Whereas, I—I can't see that it matters
much."

"Later you might not think so."

"What do you mean? I'll love it more for Isabel's
family blood?"

"Was Garrett wild? Or only foolish?"

"Nonentity . . . a nothing man. Maybe he thought
he was wild. I doubt if he could even be that. We're talking about him as if he were dead. That's enough to say.
As for Isabel's side, they're docile as chickens."

His father's sun- and liver-splotched hands searched

for a cigar, stripped and trimmed it. A lighter glowed. "Have you got a picture? A photograph?"

Maurice glanced up sharply. Henri Devigny looking over a little girl's photograph was different from the same man looking over a little boy's photograph. Maurice's own nature, love-seeking, had its innocent side: he was deep-drawn in faith to what he felt was good. What was his father like? He had been shocked as a boy, many times. Yet for Maurice personally things had never been rough. With the same order with which when he was sixteen his stepmother had had him measured for his first suit, his father when he was eighteen had introduced him to the young woman who was so light-colored as to have almost no skin color at all except a certain wanness, like ashes. Her room had had white clean ruffled curtains and pull shades, and she wasn't much older than he except in experience. After he married, his father settled with her at Maurice's own wish, playing the New Orleans gentleman of fifty or a hundred or more years ago, the old-fashioned grandee. Hadn't Henri Devigny dreamed it all that way, back where he was raised, poring over history books down in the moss-hung bayous, practicing a French that he would never find more than one or two to appreciate? Long after New Orleans had forgotten its former ways, Devigny kept them still: his way of doing things right. Maurice, though not present, could see him plainly, shifting his cigar to the side of his mouth, thumbing out bills to set in the slight ash-colored hand.

Thus ended Maurice's only venture into the other, illicit side of love. Why was this, when he had had his chances all along the way, had them still? No false pride or shame or fear restrained him, though he was aware, for all his true claim to love, that uxoriousness itself has its shameful side and like any other sexual trait brings out the knowing glance, the half-heard word, the snicker and the sneer. So he kept it to himself, generally, like some awful secret practice which brought untold joy. He did not speak of it to his father, who took a dim view of tender

natures. Opening confidences with his father anyway
occasioned him his only dread. How to start? He experi-
enced a kind of tension also, something akin to fear, when
his father asked for the little Garrett girl's picture. Now
for yet another reason he debated the wisdom of taking
her in. But that reason was too ridiculous to declare—it
lay in the land of instinct and hunches. Isabel, who had
so far managed a relationship with her father-in-law
which was as clear and delightful as herself, would have
attributed lewdness to her husband for even stating what
he now felt. So maybe he was being crazy. When did you
know where the craziness in thoughts met the craziness
in life? Thus Maurice was lost in deep meditation before
he gave in about taking Julia. But he did give in, at last.
By him, Isabel could not be refused.

Importunate, that she was. He sighed to think the
word, and thought: Oh, my love. As if with fruit or lilacs,
he longed to fill her arms with what she most desired. Was
there a picture? he asked her, returned to the lower
floors from above. Yes, Isabel had said, and got it to show
him. It was a year old, but she couldn't have changed so
much, this thin little girl in shorts, barefoot, up in a
sunlit country-town yard, squinting under a tousle of dark
hair. "She looks like both of us—Alice and me," said
Isabel, though Maurice could see no resemblance whatever. "But it's no place for her," she went on, "way up
there, dressing like that."

"They all look like that up there," Maurice said
vaguely. "They fish all the time," he added, just as
vaguely, forgetting that Cajuns and Gulf Coast people
fished incessantly.

"I can't help that," said Isabel.

So they got her, ordered off for her, like something
pictured in an advertisement, Maurice put it to himself.

The first night after she arrived, train met in the
morning, home, bath, and room, new clothes to try, and
then the thundershower—how vivid even the acrid smell
of it came back out of that lost summer!—they had dined

by candlelight, and the father had come down. It was the most natural thing in the world, wasn't it? Except that Henri Devigny had taken his rightful place at the head of the table. From then on, Maurice, a young man, his emotions that evening confused, his heart anxious, started calling his father "the old man," if only to himself. Not "the dirty old man"—not that, no, not ever that. He saw the child's head bending forward, lost innocence above a full plate she didn't want, her tears barely held back. The whole evening filled with tenderness for her, slowly, like a filling basin; even the servants felt it, and waited on her silently, taking care.

She'd had all their hearts then—he could swear it— his own, and Isabel's certainly, and the servants'. But what had the old man felt more than they? Interest? It was a girl-child, after all; that was what Maurice Devigny sat trying not to know, above the candlelight, that first evening. How to be angry at his father? How not to be angry when the old man had obviously wanted this child's first impression in the house to be of himself, hulked large at table's head, assuming authority. When she looked up, she saw him. Tears would not erase him. When he spoke to her—"Was this your first train ride, young lady?"— "Yes, sir," was what she managed to say. Her little voice was comical. Maurice ate mechanically that evening, discontented with the shape of things to come.

But Isabel had never looked more beautiful. The candlelight glowed in her crystal beads; her heart was drinking joy. Together, he and she took the little girl upstairs to her room after dinner. Outside the windows, the trees still smelled of rain. How sweet life could be! How sweet, in that journey up the stairs, it had been.

Arriving at work in his taxi, not late to amount to anything, Maurice rounded out his reverie by recalling with a start that he had still been in his twenties that long-ago evening. Now he was in his forties, an amiable, alert, attractive man, arriving at a brokerage house which once having retained him as a lawyer had gradually found him indispensable. He was brisk and confident on the broad steps of the building, for he had thought of something that had changed his mood. After all, the way Julia was now making him feel was exactly the way his father had made him feel, all his life. What was it but unease before the suggestion of moral laxness in every direction he could think of and a good number he doubtless could not imagine? Yet Maurice would vow he was no Puritan. That was laughable. He was just a man who dealt evenly with life and loved a woman, and that woman was, always had been, and always would be his wife. What gave him the unease was that he loved them too—had loved his dead father, now loved this living girl. But the dark glossy eyes below the heavy brows had fallen on that child, from that first evening after rain onward. What could Maurice have done? Look at it their way, he thought. The wounding force of living with a privacy of happiness such as he and Isabel knew, of being outside that magic circle. Wouldn't they have teamed with anything, a servant, an animal, a chum, if they hadn't found each other, an aging widower and an orphan child?

He gained his office. The firm was anxious to be protected against a possible lawsuit involving a local oil firm it had refused to list after too-long consideration . . . the smell of a commitment retracted. Cases involving oil companies and brokerage houses . . . issues of common stock. . . . His secretary knocked, bearing a sheaf of papers.

Her purse had been snatched the evening before. Still in broad daylight, near the grocery, shopping. Some young man who shot off down an alley, clutching it like a football. Crime everywhere, she lamented. All around us, we just don't realize it.

As she left, he thought of the worrying element, lifelong, the surrounding character of things one had to live and breathe without ever shaking free. His father, then Julia, then the two of them, now Julia turning into his father again. The loose weave of their characters, their puzzling pride in this very thing. And, in this day and time, the danger that looseness ran. She was too young yet. . . .

The secretary reappeared, bringing files. "Did you read about the murder? That nice-looking young man. It's hard to believe, but it just goes to show—"

Oh yes, the murder. "I forgot to look at it. Thank you, Miss Saunders." Purse was about all she had worth snatching, poor Miss Saunders. Geraldine.

I do not like the name Geraldine, thought Maurice Devigny.

# 5. THE SECOND ADDRESS

 When Julia Garrett woke up, it was afternoon, and the girl who lived across the hall, Edith Williams, was standing in the door.

"Oh, excuse me, I didn't know you were asleep."

"Okay, it's okay. I must have dozed off." She sat up, shaking her tousled head. "The air is heavy." (*Voici venir les temps où vibrant sur sa tige . . .*) "I would have called you last night to say I wouldn't be home, but . . ." Salty waves of memory came spewing back into her head; she reached for her comb off the dresser, coming up out of the sea, reducing life to words of explanation. "But I went by the Squiremeisters'—you remember them, Bucky and Marie. No? Well, they were married when they were in school and nobody knew it, they just assumed they were sharing, but it was marriage all the time. They had a little place over a garage where we all used to drop in. Now they've a house out near the Lake. Marie called me about a week ago for a shrimp recipe I had. I went to drop it by and there were some other people there, from out of town, and then one or two others, and somebody called somebody, so in the end . . ."

She trailed off.

"It's okay," said Edith Williams—"Edie" was what they all called her. "I just thought I'd hear you at the door if you came. I locked up about twelve or so. Miss Louise is sick, you know."

Julia found her hair so badly matted she could have been a skunk fresh from the swamp, she remarked. She hunted her brush. The small, plain girl talking with her in the doorway had something anonymous and pleasant about her. She always looked like clean cotton blouses, scrubbed brown hair dried in the sun—a stubby, intelligent female creature, with neither vanity nor pride. "Oh, Edie," said Julia, "I'm too sleepy to think. Are you going out or coming in? In? Then do put a record on and leave the door open so I can hear. I'll come to in a minute."

"Is the Prokofiev okay?"

Edie collected records, one of her mild, pleasant habits. With the help of her boyfriend, a student physicist, she had rigged up a small hi-fi for these singular quarters. She had also put cheap but colorful rugs on the floor, had enameled white an old wrought-iron bedstead scrolled in two dividing fan shapes. She had even got curtains up and refinished a second-hand rocking chair. This was all beyond Julia, who had looked on these rooms from the time she had seen them as being all the more what she had in mind because they were not pretty but rough, old, and bare. She herself had nothing but a mattress with springs beneath set on peg legs, shoved in the corner and surrounded by cushions pushed back against the wall. She had one chair, bought second-hand from the Salvation Army, with a bright Mexican-printed throw draped over it, and one straight chair at a card table for eating, though generally she ate her breakfast standing up at the refrigerator in the hall, and shared her dinners with Edie at a lawn table the old ladies they rented from had caused to be put on the back gallery. Edie lived at the end of the hallway in a small room, but Julia's room overlooked a fine old garden now returned to seed and semi-jungle because the ladies downstairs could not afford to keep it up. As they could not actually see it unless they went out on a back porch they never used any more, they had probably not thought of its existing for many years. (At least, this is what Julia would have said. It was the opinion she held them in. Edie had the ladies much more firmly in mind than that. She knew that they knew more about that garden, overgrown though it was, than she and Julia together would ever know, and she knew that she herself was better informed about both garden and ladies than Julia would ever care to be. Can people be everything? Edie would have asked, making it clear she did not want to criticize. Her name in full was Mary Edith Williams, and she came from somewhere in Georgia, some dusty little dried-up town called Beatrice, pronounced Bee-*atris*. Julia Garrett, at least, thought it was a dried-up little town when she thought of it at all, which wasn't often.)

What Julia had been looking for when she found this place, what she had really wanted, was some place for cutting ties painlessly. Last year she had had marriage plans with Martin Parham, and if they hadn't worked out, still a broken engagement made a breaking point in life, to be noted in some significant way. The receptionist's job wasn't really significant enough: she could have been anybody else as far as that job was concerned. So what then? So she found it, the what-then—on one of her afternoons off from Dr. Pollard's. She had found it first in the library, in a book. A picture of that particular old house with the balustrade, open-air, a wide staircase dropping down off the second-floor back gallery to the walled garden. The old Mulligan house. Mulligan? She'd never heard of them. What on earth was anybody named Mulligan doing in New Orleans? Well, the Irish had got there, just as the Germans had, and the Italians. What, for that matter, was anyone named Garrett doing in New Orleans? We can't all be named Devigny, Henri and Maurice.

It was no longer fashionable, nor was it bohemian, to live in the particular part of town where the Mulligan house stood. It could hardly be dangerous either, she thought, when she went past, strolling along, casing the streets all around, noting (with the proprietary affection of a person whose neighborhood this already is) how the tree roots had forced the old brick sidewalks to heave up around their growth and then how the bricks, adjusting themselves individually and collectively to each new change in the contour of what they had to live with, had settled in, grown moss where it was shady and damp, or taken in dirt to smooth the areas between.

The Misses Mulligan—she had learned about them from the logical place, the corner grocer. She had found the wooden, pie-shaped little market right around the block. The old man and his wife, bent from leaning down to pack things evenly in paper sacks. Oh, yes, they said, that house. Nobody there but the two old ladies, they said. Miss Louise and Miss Katherine, they said. Never married, getting old. Telephone? Well, yes, but they're so deaf. When they call up an order, if we don't have an item, one of us has to walk over there and tell them we don't have it. Otherwise, they'd never understand. And oh yes, said the grocer's wife, we often just walk over two blocks to the supermarket if it's not too hot and get it for them, whatever they want—they can't get out and it saves time, explaining and all, you know.

Ten minutes later Julia was ringing the old Misses Mulligan's jangly doorbell. It turned like the winder of a child's toy. But my God what a racket, she thought. . . .

So now she could be sure they didn't hear the Prokofiev or the Stravinsky on Edie's hi-fi, or, if they did, it was only as a distant murmur, something familiar, no doubt, and something they thought might have been going on all the time, all their blessed lives, as Uncle Maurice would say. All their blessed lives. But Edie Williams claimed to know better than that. Sure, they're deaf, she would have said. But a lot of times it's more convenient than not to be deaf. They're onto everything, she said.

Julia came out of the shower. And that felt better, a lot better. She felt she might live now. No food since God knew when. Early morning out near the lake, that was when. Edie had gone out to telephone Paul, her boyfriend. They had a steady arrangement, right down to hours and minutes. It always worked. Nothing about Edie ever failed. Why, to Julia Garrett, did that quality seem ob-

jectionable? She didn't know. She herself, far more haphazard, at once darker and lighter, saw them as background, essential and small. Yet now that Edie was not
there she felt impatience as she snacked out of the refrigerator. Edie should come back and catch her up on
things.

"Miss Louise sick?" she inquired as Edie's unhurrying
steps cleared the staircase, the veranda, and entered the
hall once more. "I thought I remembered your saying so."

"Oh, yes, something . . . Nothing serious, Miss
Katherine said. But they're failing, you know. I think one
day they'll turn frail enough and dry enough to blow
right out the window and sail off. It makes me feel sad
and gentle, but not unhappy. They aren't bitter old ladies.
Do you know the difference?"

"I never knew many old ladies," said Julia, whose life,
except for Aunt Isabel and at present Edie, had been
lived almost totally around men.

"Bitter old ladies are the worst," said Edie, who had
apparently some claim to authority. Maybe she'd had a
bitter grandmother. "Do you like my shrimp salad?"

"Oh, is this yours?"

"It's okay. I hoped you'd eat some."

"But I've got masses of stuff. Ham, cream cheese,
chives, and some mocha pastries! I bought them yesterday. Nothing to do till tomorrow but eat and sleep."

"Are they painting oranges and apples instead of you?"

"They just don't have a class on Friday. Otherwise
they'd be painting me. I've still got a month to go. Did
you get the evening paper yet?"

"All about that murder still. Everybody in the lab yesterday was talking about it. Somebody had made sulfa-
nilamide for an experiment and the professor came in.
He said a corpse in a swamp would be a welcome change.
Do you think he did it—that Springland man?"

"Looking at his picture," Julia murmured, "it's hard
to believe."

Edie took on her look of scientific ascertainment

through questionnaires and statistical averages. "You think that fine-looking people never commit crimes?"

"I don't know," said Julia, a liberal arts major. "Do they? Okay, the averages are against me. But I just know that murdering in a quarrel over money—well, looking like he does, it doesn't seem true."

"Unless money was just the excuse," said Edie. Did she have to be so consistently bright? "There was bound to be some sort of involvement or what was he doing even knowing this guy?"

"There's such a thing as slumming," Julia said.

"It might have been sex," Edie said. "The man had a sexy red-headed wife, it says."

"She couldn't have been so much if he was so crummy."

"Or dope," Edie went on.

"You mean the money reason is fishy?"

"Worse than fishy," Edie said, smiling. If ever any face looked like freshly washed gingham, Edie's did. "Did you know that human flesh smells worse in decay than any sort of fish?" she asked.

"No, and don't describe it to me," said Julia. She was getting a kick out of talking about Jake Springland to Edie, who didn't dream she knew him. She was also getting a chill—it ran concurrently with the interest, the words that brought him back to her. And both feelings kept spreading and threatening, not wanting to stay within bounds. He had swept her, after all, that one time, Jake Springland had; his touch had gone deep. It could happen again if the chance occurred. Mightn't he have been able to do this because he had himself been drawn to her, and if she could do that to him couldn't other circumstances find him vulnerable to the point of violence? What was it Dev, the old man, had said? "Passion is what you've either got or haven't got. . . ." Out of such scraps she had stuck her own truth together.

What if she told Edie that she knew him, and knew not only Jake Springland, but the other two as well, the whole

weird trio, one or two of whom had evidently murdered
the third by bashing his head and face in with the jack
from the trunk of the car they owned and buried him in
a shallow grave out in the marshy swamps to the south
of the city? What could poor little Edie say? Edie would
have just thought the odds were against these people having crossed paths with a girl she had known slightly at
Tulane, who had asked her to take a room in the upstairs
of an old house on an old street near the university. Edie
did not believe in the extraordinary until it appeared in the
test tube. When it did, she did not hesitate. Obedient to
her training as a bird dog, she set about in the next instant reducing it to terms.

"When I said that about murdering someone, I meant
he might have just got mad enough, all the more if he
was a nice enough guy who got mixed up with the wrong
kind. There was this man in Beatrice, Georgia, that murdered his wife. He said he could never get anything
through her head, so he put a bullet through it. Everybody that knew her thought the same thing. He got off
with manslaughter."

"Ummm," said Julia. She had mixed a gin and tonic
by this time. Feet wriggled into scuffs, she was sitting
showered and cool, wearing a loose cotton robe. She was
glad her back was to Edie because Edie's transparently
simple reasoning not only had its value but also sounded
like it might even be the truth. Steady, she kept telling
herself, steady. You only slept with him once. You've
thought you were in love before. But could he get that
mad or not? As mad as Edie said? Yes. Get mad enough
to be that foolish? Yes. Yet why couldn't he have walked
right away from them, the specter and that awful woman,
whenever he wanted to? What stuck him with them?
Was it real involvement? She came within an ace of
saying out loud to Edie Williams: I know them, see? I
know them all.

But she didn't. It was the reporter she fell to thinking
of. Tommy Arnold. She had promised to call him. He's

not going to hunt me down, she thought, for the reason that—Well, why? He feels protective, doesn't want a girl like me exposed, involved, name in the papers, and all that. I don't want it either, think of Aunt Isabel and Uncle Maurice. But if it comes to saving Jake Springland, then I'd have to think of some way. The way must be Tommy Arnold, else why did I feel the trust in him that I did feel?

"The grand jury's bound him over," said Edie. "That's in the afternoon paper. I wonder if the police aren't trying right now——"

"Oh hush!" said Julia.

"See how everybody feels?" said Edie. "You too!"

Once again Edie had given her more than she wanted to think about. She had heard the police defended once at a party by a businessman she knew. "If you get a bad dog you have to whip him—what else does he understand?" Her heart constricted. She went inside and dressed quickly.

"I've got to go out . . . something I promised to get," she explained to Edie, who assumed she had a date, but did not ask.

# 6. THE MISSES MULLIGAN

 As Julia passed by the flank of the old house, she heard from within the low wispy murmur of old ladies' voices. Oh, the Misses Mulligan.

As Edie said, they would die some day.

How did it feel if death was all that was left to call happening to you? What did they sit and talk about in a world where not even the milkman was a possibility? Edie had the answer, the first time Julia had mentioned it. "They talk about us," she had said. "I've heard them. You've no idea. They notice everything. Then they talk about it, over and over. It's all written up inside them, everything they've ever known is, and stored like player piano rolls. When they play a subject over it's always the same, word for word, like a tune. They've got almost a whole roll on us, didn't you know?"

Well, let them, Julia Garrett had thought. Let them, let them.

The day of this conversation with Edie, she had been sitting on the back steps on a warm Sunday afternoon in winter, thinking of Martin Parham, the boy from up in Mississippi she had planned for so long to marry, sitting with her long hands resting on either side of her blue silk skirt, a broad silver bracelet on one wrist, her feet in low-heeled pumps placed side by side, her head bent and medi-tative, a characteristic pose. Let them let them let them anything. Right now I could wish them both in the swamp for an afternoon with Martin Parham. Where is he? What did I think I was doing, calling it off for good?

When Edie went down the steps past her, she had

started, nervous as a cat. A bitch (not a cat) was what she would have called herself at that moment, with good reason. How did she call it living, if you didn't have a man? There went Edie through the worn, untidy garden, down the old paved walk, past the dried-up lily pool with rust stains in the basin, out to the overgrown prickly camellia tree near the back wall, the one all shaggy with jasmine and honeysuckle vine. "What are you doing?" she almost said, but was too full of fresh desire, which came welling up in her breast like a spring, to care, really, what Edie was doing. Her senses hammered against the walls of solitude. I have to go somewhere, she thought impatiently, I have to call somebody or drop in on them, Bucky and Marie, for instance. (But they'd moved, way out toward the lake.) Maybe I'll just start screaming. There was bird-screaming instead from way down near the wall, where Edie was bending, pulling limbs aside, lifting. Then Julia realized that for some time a racket had been going on down there, that there was agitation in the bird world and that signals were streaming out all over the place. Once Edie got there to help out, the fool birds had attacked her. Maybe she was even in danger. A mother mockingbird, wild with nothing but instinct and passion, dive-bombed poor Edie, who had all human kindness on her side. She kept ducking and dodging, leaning and picking up, now reaching and tiptoeing and placing, and then she fled, pursued way past the fish pond by that crazy bird, whose babies she had just saved and returned to their nest.

"Good Lord, Edie," said Julia Garrett.

"It was these two little baby birds," said Edie, now on the steps, flushed, trying to put her hair straight. "Somehow they fell out of the nest, wriggling around, I guess, and so I put them back. The camellia tree was too thick for her to reach them, but even if she could have reached them, I doubt if she could have done anything. Do birds pick up their young? I must find out tomorrow."

Edie and her boyfriend, Paul Fowler, had wanted to

spend all one of their weekends cleaning up the Misses Mulligan's back garden. They had wanted to re-lay the old walks, clip the overgrown grass, sod the soil, pull up the old plants gone to seed, prune and straighten the fine old shrubs, trellis the forsythia, the jasmine, the honeysuckle, and train the bougainvillea symmetrically against the old brick walls. They had wanted to clear out and mend the broken fish pool and put water in, lily pads, and real fish. They went to get permission from the Misses Mulligan and were given instead tea in tissue-paper-thin cups with a clove in each. Then they had come and told Julia.

Julia had seen the whole of the affair in a flash and did not like it. She saw how it had happened and how she should have known that something like it would happen from the minute Edie had said she'd like to come and stay there, it being so cheap and all. Like the smoothest of new motor cars, sleek, silent, and perhaps foreign made, Julia had barely avoided a head-on collision with them (Ford and Chevrolet types if ever there were any). Julia did not say a word for a time, or even turn to look at them. She was holding a beat-up silver handmirror with a lady's face framed in flowing silver hair at the center of the mounting, something she had laughed at with Martin Parham once and come away with out of a dusty antique shop down in the Vieux Carrée. He would buy her anything. "Well okay," she finally said, finishing off her lipstick job in the mirror, laying it aside, turning to pick up her gloves and bag. "Well okay. I'll just be on my way and leave it to you kids. Don't let me stop the flow of fresh young ideas."

There was a silence, a definite silence, the kind only strong people can cause. "Oh, well," said Edie. "It was just that we thought it would be fun to work on, something we could do for them. Well, good *night*, Julia! We're doing it for nothing!"

"They just can't afford to do it," said Paul Fowler. "That's all there is to it. They're not going to be able to help but like it." He stopped. Julia had said nothing. Then she turned.

Paul Fowler looked at her straight on, a highly intelligent young man who would never attract her very much, as both of them knew. She brushed a thread from the cuff of her navy coat. Paul Fowler went around in blue jeans and loafers, broken, scuffed, and soiled, wore wool plaid shirts in winter, even to lab instruction. He would have given lectures without a tie. He got things done and had a sort of keenness about life, an almost exalted sense of reason. Activity delighted him. He thought everything worth working at worked if you worked at it. He thought that things not only should be fun but usually were. If they were not fun, why should you do them? Julia's surpassing lack of interest in him was the natural result of the cleanness of his own mentality—an ordered mind without surprising turns or dark corners.

At this point Edie let Paul down perceptibly. She suddenly, belatedly, saw Julia's view of the scheme. "We should have consulted you," she came out and admitted. "You found this place, after all. We just didn't think, we got so enthusiastic. We thought it would just be such a lot of fun and that everybody would thank us for it."

"I'm sure it would be just like something in a magazine," Julia relentlessly said. Within she was full of doubts. She hated to take stands. Quarreling meant that stands must be taken. To Paul Fowler she was causing trouble, messing up his good idea. His mouth had become a straight line.

"We'll just forget it," said Edie. "You do, too," she implored Julia. "That's the best thing."

"Oh, *no!* I didn't say that. Listen, kids, I've got to run."

And out she'd gone, late last summer, passing the flank of the old house, passing along the mossy brick, passing the too-shady, a bit too-damp old front porch, freshly painted every spring, painted gray, the one concession they made to time and keeping up, the Misses Mulligan.

That day Miss Katherine had been out front, or was it Miss Louise? (Julia was never sure, unlike Edie.) A beckoning hand in the afternoon. Within the cool-warm parlor, cups neatly cleaned away already. "Oh, Miss Garrett, I know you're in a hurry, but I— Well it's just too sudden, don't you see? My sister—please excuse my looks—she had to go right upstairs and lie down. Well, we just didn't know what to say. All this machinery nowadays, and who *is* that young man?"

"They've changed their minds," said Julia Garrett. "Please don't worry about it. It would be too much work and now they aren't going to do it."

"Oh, Miss Garrett, we did try to be *nice!*"

"Oh, Miss Mulligan, I'm sure you did!"

"But the garden!"

"Miss Mulligan, I like it just the way it is!"

"Well now!" Miss Louise (or was it her sister?) sat down very quickly in the front porch rocker. "I said that myself. I said it was my impression that as far as you were concerned it could stay as it was. You were the one who found the apartment."

"You were right."

"We agreed on one point, Miss Garrett. Pruning is necessary. The camellias especially, by this time, must need it. But there is one thing. How can other people go about touching what doesn't belong to them?"

Here the great point was made.

"Oh," said Julia, "I think that too."

So she quieted the Misses Mulligan, one at least of whom might have died of anxiety had Paul Fowler and Edie Williams moved a power mower in through the side gate.

The subject of the garden was not brought up again, might as well have been buried in a shallow grave down by the dried-up fish pond. Edie never mentioned it; nor did Julia; nor did Paul; nor did the old ladies. That the air had tensed up so suddenly between Paul Fowler and Julia had been an eye-opener to Edie. If those two got really angry—Edie liked her peaceful ways; she caused no upheavals.

Now as Julia Garrett let herself out by the side gate, the murmur of wispy female voices dropped behind. The episode of the garden must by now have been duly recorded on the piano roll having to do with Edie and Julia. Maybe they were playing it now, over their tea, camomile today, since one of them was ailing? That other day they'd made the tea for getting Paul Fowler inside, to look him over.

And he doesn't like me worth a damn, thought Julia. For that matter, she could imagine him and Edie, looking up bird habits in an authoritative book, bending their heads, their voices a low twittering, not that far in kind from the way the Mulligan ladies sounded each time she passed the house's flank. She'd wound up among a lot of birds, she thought impatiently, banging her bag against her bare leg, walking.

But Tommy Arnold, he'd liked her worth a damn. She was going to have to be careful where she set her feet, doing this little ballet that had an honest-to-God murder in it somewhere. Tommy Arnold, maybe at least partially recovered from his hangover of the night before, was still the best hope she'd found for getting through it all.

# 7. CONVERSATION IN A DRUGSTORE

 "Well, if you keep saying you saw him that night, what can I do but believe you?" said Tommy Arnold. He was once again across a table from her, but this time in a drugstore. She had fished him up out of the newspaper office by telephone. "But it doesn't cut any ice, one way or another. So why break it in the paper? You want to wind up with that sort of image, having half of everybody assume you're laying out with the low life?"

"That wouldn't be true," said Julia.

"I hope not."

Young, she put her head up high. "I guess I'd say so if it was."

"Yeah, sure . . . don't you ever give a thought to that St. Charles Avenue family?"

"Family?" she echoed. Uncle Maurice, Aunt Isabel. "Of course I think of them. But I think about what's true, too," she told him. "About telling the truth."

"You want to know what happens when you tell the truth?" he asked her, sincere now—dogged and sincere.

"What?"

"People start twisting it. Half-truths, lies, subterfuge, roundabout statements—people accept those because they can't do much with them. It's the truth they can't leave alone—it's not good enough, not true enough, it's never quite right enough, or wrong enough. Most people, that is."

"Not me," she said.

"You don't want to tell me, I think. You want me to tell you. What I think happened. Right?"

"It would be desirable," she admitted.

"You're an interested party," he said, "and the boy's in jail."

"He's important to me," she told him quickly.

"That's obvious. I could see it all along. But why? I asked myself that about the time I decided not to follow you up. Why would she go for the low life? There're other good-looking boys around, have been, and will be. Don't tell me this one is different."

"I didn't say that."

"The funny thing is a lot of women have got this feeling about him, that they want him to be all right, they want to get him out of it, it's all a mistake, something like that. What interests me about it is different. There's a classic quality to it . . . seems now that I always knew something like this would happen here. A stranger shows up, strong on making it in jazz, getting in with the local types, seeing the real true city life. Then first thing you know this other guy that can barely pass for human (though he's got a name, an address, a job, and a woman) is murdered. And by whom? The handsome young stranger, with all the ideals about it all, and maybe even some talent, something to give. He's yearning and pure. He would even have turned nigger for a while, if that would have helped. . . ."

"He told you that?"

"I've talked to him."

"When?"

"In jail."

"How often?"

"Time or two?"

"Is he okay . . .? Well? *Is* he?"

"Being in love . . . that's your trouble. Yes, he's well. Troubled, disturbed, but well."

She tucked her trembling hands beneath her thighs, out of sight.

"I can see him and you can't," Tommy Arnold pursued. "I've seen him and magic's rubbed off on me. I

glow in the dark. You smell me across the room at the
Squiremeisters'. You track me down outside. You whirl
me away drunk to Lake Pontchartrain."

"I heard your name called. I had it in mind to look
you up anyway. I thought of lawyers, but they all know
the family. The police—I've never had dealings with the
police."

"Just as well you don't start."

They fell silent. Tommy Arnold had ordered a sandwich. It arrived and he ate it.

"So far as I know, Springland hasn't mentioned you.
I would never have known you existed, not from him.
Either he's not getting you into it, or you've made it up
that you saw him."

"Say what he did tell you," she begged. "Not what he
didn't. I don't know anything. Nothing about it."

"You've read it, same as everybody."

"I mean I've no impression. You must have got one,
and so you can give it to me."

"He said he was just down here on account of being
out of it alive and whole—out of that messy little war
over there in Korea, that is. I could see that. It even made
sense. So he had the music and the song-writing, no vast
talent is claimed by him, but a need of using it as a path
to something right in life: you're with me and I was with
him there. I mean I get it. Anyway, he wants to explore
the city here and give what he has a chance to develop.
Then he meets Marnie and the Wharton woman. No
motive but curiosity for sticking around with them. They
live near him and they're always hollering over the fence,
feeding him supper or something. Marnie got him a
part-time job, driving the Salvation Army pick-up service
truck. It's grimy but he gets to see the city, more and
more of it. He wanted to slum. Couldn't take regular
work because he had his lines out for music possibilities.
He had to be ready for night hours, for sudden openings.
He had to have enough cash to get by on. Then Marnie
came up with the Big Idea. He'd drive the car for Marnie

while Marnie robbed a few filling stations; then they'd split the dough. This happened only three times. He did it because he was flat, then the experience angle again, wanting to know about it, how'd it feel, how'd it work? Then he got a job, a real one. He'd moved on from Marnie to another set of friends. Maybe he'd met you; how am I to know? The last time he pulled a filling station holdup was on account of Marnie. Marnie was flat. Springland had money by then but he wanted to get rid of Marnie, so he said he didn't have money, none to lend. Marnie put it to him, all those meals he'd fed him, all that friendship. Jake promised to go, but for the last time. The 'last time' angle . . . that's strong in it, it comes out too strong. What hold did Marnie have on Jake Springland? I keep asking myself. Why couldn't he just say no? Is Springland so convinced that nothing matters much—that he might wind up anywhere, doing anything? Or is there a hold? Fear? Religion—Marnie was a preacher-type, a Bible quoter. Was that the chord? If Springland did kill Marnie, it was over something besides money. It had to do with hatred, with wanting to get free of him, with revulsion.

"Attraction and revulsion, both together. The pull is as strong both ways. From the outside it looks ridiculous."

"Go on with it," said Julia.

"They brought off the filling station job and then—predictably—once he had the money, Marnie didn't want to pay. Later, he said. But Springland wants his now. He never wants to see Marnie and the Wharton woman again. So they got into this squabble. Went back to Marnie's place, still squabbling. The Wharton woman was there. She'd been hopped up for days—dope, likker; likker, dope—and she wants a share of the cash too. For what reason? Just for being there. 'You don't appreciate me,' she says to Marnie. 'If you do you'll split it three ways.' 'I sure don't appreciate you that much,' says Jake. 'It's me you're taking it from.' Then he turns around to go. 'Keep it,' he says, and feels he's going to be well out

of it. At this point the Wharton woman picks up a broom.
She fetches Marnie such a wham on the head he goes
down, out cold, and the broom's busted. She hits again
with the broom handle, bringing the wire binding at the
bottom into his head and out comes the blood. He comes
to and yells like a goon, but Springland says go on and
die, the hell with it. Marnie passes out again. The
Wharton woman yells out that he's really hurt, Jake
can't leave her with him now, so he throws some cold
water on Marnie and gets a towel to mop up the blood,
then the neighbors start hollering for them to shut up
in there. All the neighbors remember it now, and it's
all pretty incriminating. Because what does the Wharton
woman manage to do but persuade Springland she's got
to drive Marnie over to Gretna where she knows a doctor,
instead of trying one of the hospitals here where they'll
all be picked up by the police. As a last favor—here comes
the 'last' again; that gets me curious—why should there
have been a first one? As a last favor would Jake Springland help her? Just put them in the car and good night?

"Okay, says Springland, as long as you're clear that
with me it's good-bye forever. Out he goes with her and
Marnie, the two of them holding Marnie up between
them, and fold him into the back seat. Springland rode
with them out of the neighborhood and a good way out
St. Charles to get them on the way to Gretna, then he
gave the wheel to the Wharton woman and got out, he
says. Marnie was still alive and he'd never touched him,
only tried to help."

"He got out in my neighborhood," said Julia, "or near
there. Not my family's house."

"That other address," said Tommy Arnold. "He came
to you?"

"Yes, and I wondered how he found me. We hadn't
seen each other since I moved. It turned out he'd followed
me home from town one day and I never knew it. I
think of myself going all that way, bus and streetcar and

grocery and drugstore and him following, never saying—
It's why I—"

"You what?"

"I can't quit wondering. I wonder about him."

"He never mentioned you."

She leaned back, taking in this piece of information
for whatever it was worth, one way or the other, breathing in a certain quiet way.

"I could give him an alibi, but he's protecting me."

"Maybe partly. I hate to get rough. The point to drive
firmly through your pretty head is that whether he saw
you or not that night does not make any too much of a
difference. Marnie could have been dead already. There're
no witnesses, even within earshot, after they drove off
in that car."

"You mean I'm unimportant?"

"In a gang like that, I wouldn't think you'd have much
ambition for importance."

"Ambition! It isn't that. Their lives are what I'm into
now. I can't get out—that would be a fake thing to do.
Not after he followed me home like that. Not after he
came to find me."

"You're not involved unless you want to be."

"It's not wanting to be—it just is."

Tommy Arnold sighed. He followed it all, how she
looked at it—but he just wished he didn't have to. "So
tell me then: what time did he come?"

"About three-thirty, some time around then. Can't
you check it against what time they say he left that rooming house?"

"If it were my business to I could."

"I'm not getting into it with police and lawyers unless
I have to, unless it really will matter."

"Did he stay long?"

She sat still as a model. It was the question she hadn't
wanted, yet awhile, to be asked. He hadn't stayed long,
no; and the next one—had anybody seen him besides

herself?—the answer to that was no, she guessed. Was
he just alibi-searching when he had rushed toward her
house, stepped out of the night as though she was an
oasis of light, cleanness in dirt, water and green leaves
in a desert? Because if she was just alibi and he'd not
mentioned it yet . . .

"Was he hopped up?" Tommy Arnold pursued. "What
was he on? What were you on?"

"Nothing that I know of. Not him, anyway."

"And you . . . you?"

She shook her head.

"Is it a life game you play? Is that it?"

She nodded. "Something, that if I can't get into, I'm
not alive even. The girl that stays over there with me—
she's good, steady, hard-working. I hoped a little would
rub off on me; but it's no use. It never does. It was my
uncle's father's doing. He made me like a dream of
everything he'd ever known. And that was plenty."

"Who was he?"

"Devigny. Henri Devigny."

"The name is familiar."

"It would have to be. I think he invented New
Orleans."

"He's dead?"

"Dead as Ted Marnie."

"And murdered, too?"

"Oh, no. He died in bed, I guess. On an August afternoon . . . quoting Baudelaire. *Je suis comme le roi d'un
pays pluvieux.* . . ."

"I guess you're no ordinary girl."

"It's the human swamp. That's what he got me used
to. If there's no way out you have to live it."

"And love it?"

"Ummm."

Julia sat answering him absent-mindedly. She was
thinking of the soft little sun splotches, skin discolora-
tions, something like freckles, that Tommy Arnold had
on his brown, nearly bare top of head. She knew because

he had slept such a good while, head in her lap, passed out, the night before. The profundity of sleep had got between them; it was how she could answer him so honestly, readily. She couldn't accept him entirely. He was old-fashioned; that meant sentiment, it meant lack of finality. By being involved in goodness, he removed himself from her total trust. She had discovered this through Edie. Now, twice proving it, she found it so again.

She picked up the newspaper from the leatherette seat of the booth and unfolded it. She renewed acquaintance with the photograph. Then Tommy Arnold, with his newsman's hands near a paper unable not to touch it, to right it with his own vision, took it, and looked where she had done, turning it toward himself. Both of them had acted sacramentally, for different reasons. The face made contact with their separate lines of thought.

"Quite a face," said Julia Garrett.

"Out of a filthy tangle," said Tommy Arnold. "That's my source of interest. He looks fine. You are not inclined to value that."

"Why do you think I'm not?"

"You'd separate it out of the filthy tangle, if you did." He dropped the paper and was looking at her. "You've not got a bad face yourself. Ever think of it?"

She smiled, quoting what she'd heard to date. "Not pretty. Interesting."

He stared contentedly on. "I think of all the crazy great-looking girls in the world, staying home wasn't good enough. It's always dishonest, or something. I don't get it. But you do, all of you. You've got to be honest, you say. Oh, yes, ma'am. What's all this modeling business? How'd you get on to that kick?"

"Somebody I knew at Tulane, in the art department. I ran into him downtown and said I needed to earn some money. They were looking for faces with angles, something like mine, and right attitudes toward sitting still."

"Angles within and without."

"What's all this to you?"

"Just curious."

"You think I should have stayed home, learned needlepoint?"

"Something like that."

"Then we wouldn't have known each other."

"You can't tell. You and my wife might have met at a church bazaar."

She stopped liking him, at least for that day.

They went out onto the springtime street. He wound his arm around her, the air so warmly glorious.

"What'll you do with what I told you?" she asked.

"We both know that, don't we? There'll be ways of finding out if what you know is crucial to him or not. That's all I can do."

"And then let me know?"

"And then let you know."

"I wonder—" She had moved off a step or two from him, but now came rushing back, her brows drawn together in the sun, but there were tears too, sunlit and genuine, blurring him to her. "Are the police as tough as they say? I wonder—"

"You mean what are they doing to Jake Springland? You've got a small bare room in your mind——"

"Yes, I have!"

"Isn't it always there? Isn't there always bad news? Pain, ache, trauma, explosion, shock, torture, death?"

Trying to worry her off into some genteel corner. Trying to say, don't let it bother your pretty head. "You make it worse, thinking I don't care about him."

They turned and walked away, in opposite directions.

# 8. THE MARNIE CASE

Day by day around New Orleans, people followed the Marnie case. It was the springtime event, since Mardi Gras had come too early, scarcely much after New Year's. More than anything else it had an impact, this curious affair, on the New Orleans mentality. For one thing, it reminded people what a singular town they pertained to, and the collective face of it, haglike betimes, but often bewitching still, took a cautious peek in the mirror. The weather helped, and the fresh air. This young man—this Jake Springland—had come from afar to seek them out and had got himself involved, not with two derelicts, underground and underworld at once, but with a whole city. It was enough to make it take a wash and comb its hair and put fresh lipstick on. For another thing, it half-illumined, as one brief flash of an X-ray might illumine a hidden bone structure, the ways of the dark world that lay all around them, not confined to one quarter or area, but a second life webbed invisibly in with their own.

Tommy Arnold had been aware of this world for years. Maybe he was a little in love with it. Certainly it was his one abiding interest, since his wife had turned into a nag—their most serious conversations, held regularly every two months, concerned divorce—and since he could not look at his three children except in terms she put to them, one such being that "orphans went around better dressed." So he thought about crime. And he thought too that he ought to be earning more. His train of thought went something like this: New Orleans was the nation's true pulse beat, but the nation did not know it. Voodoo, jazz, sex, and food—who could go further than that toward what was really important to people in the U.S. and A. Not much to do with money maybe. All the better. Once he got one story out, others could follow. All they knew out in the great money-making complex that was the Yewnighted States was that strange things went on down there, and then they hummed a tune or ate a meal that they didn't connect with "down there" at all. Yet both the tune and the meal would have started from down there and only from there. And the down there of their own hearts, the dark tangle, the lurking mysteries, did they know how much of that was a dim carbon of the original which lay spread out before his wandering feet, every day that rolled? But all his reasoning did was frustrate him. He could not get it out, no matter how he wrote it. He could have got it out, out into the big world, if he had put Julia Garrett in it, but he wouldn't do that. He was convinced that this angle would make it, would sell it. But he wouldn't. Protect Julia? Protect that girl! She was already asking for it, courting danger everywhere she turned, determined to do the offbeat, turning herself on with whatever swamp-light shone. A tramp? She didn't think of it that way. A tramp anyway? Here he would throw down his copy pencil (he worked at odd times on the copy desk), whip off his eyeshade and go out for coffee. Coffee ran out of his ears all day. At night, alcohol ran out of his pores.

He knew what he was trying to do. He was trying to lift that story out of New Orleans and make it fly just the way his father, when he was a boy, wanted to stunt in World War I airplanes (a wonder he lived to tell about it). He'd wound up in stockcar racing instead, picking up money on the side at county fairs. The way that same father in later life took to making over junk cars, souping up the motors, showing great tenderness for their old, beat-up inner parts, then putting on a brave paint job, all for racing Sunday afternoons up in Arkansas, Oklahoma, and East Texas as well as nearer home in Louisiana. The father worked for a farm machinery firm all week, but on weekends retired behind high board fences in the back yard where a different world came seeping in to look on. It was a world Tommy never saw except for the intense, brown-faced, sometimes crazy-eyed men who came to talk to his father in their own curious jargon. His father never let him talk much to these men. But they were "getting through"; that was how Tommy thought of it—just as he now wanted to "get through" to the outside world. In the newspaper world you "got through"; his stories about the case had got to New Orleans. The world beyond was the bridge he couldn't build; it was the gap he couldn't close. He could have done it with Julia Garrett in it, for a fresh, classy feminine angle, but he wouldn't.

Still, he wrote and he wrote. He wrote in top form, at night, with wife and kids asleep, trying to slant it so the AP would pick it up. Or *Time*. Or *Newsweek*. He went to see their local stringers. "I've been with this thing from the first," he said. "I know it backward and forward." "It's too complicated," they complained. "There's nothing to get hold of. The Wharton woman is missing. Even if they find her, she's all junked up all the time. That boy hasn't really made a name for himself, musician or not. What's there to say?"

"It's got a certain flavor, this case," he would insist. "There's the comic side. Don't you see it's almost a satire on crime? The criminals don't think of themselves as doing much of anything out of the way. Then there may be a dope angle. . . ."

"Yeah, but that's getting speculative. You can't tamper with that unless you know it's true."

"Don't you see how people are reading it here? That's news in itself. Then, why are they reading it? Don't you ask yourself, don't you wonder?"

"Springland's good-looking. That's why the women are reading it."

"It brings out a whole locale."

"Right. It's way too local."

"Local to the world . . ." But here he'd go off on his theories and they'd stop listening.

# 9. A REAPPEARANCE

 For weeks before the trial Julia had been scared, worried, fretful, given to dreams. Everybody in New Orleans thought, at one time or another, they had seen Ted Marnie before the murder; it took Julia to think she'd seen him afterward. A rickety man with a long neck aslant, an air of concern for all human concerns riding hazy about his shoulders, was coming out of Bourbon Street onto Canal. There was only one thing to do, close the distance enough to see without being seen: she did and it wasn't.

Another day she ran straight into what really was Wilma Wharton. It was downtown, near the lingerie counter of Maison Blanche, and the woman caught her shoulder and swung her around. Julia understood from the papers that Wilma had been located and held as a material witness. She had been found in Texas City, where, having bought a New Orleans paper for sentimental reasons, she had read about the Marnie case, then had got drunk and talked it over with one intimate and trusted friend too many. Somebody had blabbed to somebody who had owed a favor to the police. Once located, she had decided it was better not to run. Besides, she was curious. *She* didn't do it: her conscience was clear as anything. Furthermore, she said to Julia, still with her hand large on the girl's narrow shoulder, she was grief-stricken. Would Julia believe it? It was the first she knew he was dead. She wondered why she hadn't heard from him, that's all. One of her dearest friends, Ted was. Who could have done it? He had had some enemies, that was

for sure. He had a second sight with people, could see
right through to their souls. He knew the soul existed for
a very good reason: he could see it. To some he would
say: "Your soul is black," or "Your soul is blood-colored,
streaked with blood," and if that person had done something or other guilty then what they'd feel for Ted would
not be gratitude. But the Springland boy—could they
really see him getting that mad at Ted? If Jake had a
weakness it was wildheadedness. Poor old Ted, just the
same! Poor old Ted, anyway! Wilma Wharton was crying.
She had a large face, big round cheeks, prominent as
breasts. Now they were wet. It seemed to Julia the cheeks
were crying, not the eyes.

"I thought 'twas you, minute I saw you," said Wilma
Wharton, mopping off the wetness. She began to smile
in a game, middle-class way, as though she and Julia
were hanging up wash on the same line and discussing a
death in the family. She was wearing a suit—too warm
for mid-May. It came over her slowly as a negative being
developed that Julia had so far said not one word. "Don't
tell me I'm wrong? You *are* the one worked for the eye
doctor. Ain't you? Ain't you the one?"

Julia slowly nodded. "Yes, I did work there, but——"

"Well, then, could I be mistaken and you didn't
know about it? It's all been in the papers, honey. All
about what happened to my dear friend and husband
Ted Marnie? The one that broke his glasses? Nobody
coulda missed it."

"Yes, I did. I did see it." What could she say? The
hand was still fixed to her shoulder. She felt white,
blanched out, thin, and tense, but stuck in one spot, no
way to leave. Didn't this woman know that she was
Jake's alibi? Or did she?

"You remember Springland? You must . . . all the
girls liked him. Well, he liked *you.* Classy girl, that's
what he said."

"Good luck," Julia said. Groping, she produced an
explanation: "Back to the grindstone."

How did I get by? she wondered, moving away in disbelief, allowed to go with the cheap words she'd found moving like a passkey in the lock, so that the heavy detaining hand had dropped away from its position of arrest. Was she really coming out of it without a threat? No dark message pressed into her hand?

She moved away to another part of the store, gripping the edges of counters until one clerk looked up sharply, thinking she was trying to shop-lift. The smell of Wilma Wharton's strong, sad perfume had clogged permanently, it seemed, in her nostrils—Jungle Gardenia, some name like that. All of what she said was murky unless it was, by some strange chance, the truth. Hell is murky, thought Julia, steadying herself on a college-girl quotation. She had made it to a phone booth. Her knees were like liquid and she sat down on the small bench within, closing the door, and thus starting the tiny fan above her head. She was about to dial Tommy Arnold.

I saw her, I saw her, she was going to babble when Tommy answered, if he was by chance at that hour in the office. She must have trapped me, tracked me down, it couldn't be coincidence. Don't tell me she doesn't know I'm the one who can back his alibi. That leaves her with the corpse when last seen alive and breathing.

Hell, she doesn't know all that, she could hear Tommy Arnold answering. Don't overestimate these people. She just ran into you, that's all.

"Hello," said Tommy Arnold, not in her head but over the phone.

"I saw her," Julia said calmly. "I ran into the Wharton woman."

"Still with her?"

"I was scared. I got away. I thought she'd——"

"Thought she'd know you were Springland's alibi?"

"Something like that."

"Did she mention it?"

"No."

"Then she doesn't know it. How would she? Listen

kiddo: if she's still around, go ask her who went bail for her."

"I'm not asking her anything. You tell me. Who did?"

"It's either a fake name or somebody no one can find. I think it's a fiction. But the thousand bucks is real. What's she like?"

"Awful. Something wrong with her teeth." She replaced the receiver.

Unable to see Jake Springland in jail, she had got the message to his lawyer by way of Tommy Arnold. She (Julia Garrett) had seen him (Jake Springland) the night of the murder and would attest to this fact if necessary.

That step taken, she had to make her mind up to it: the world was going to seem booby-trapped until the trial had come and gone, settling something, one way or the other.

Things like this encounter with Wilma Wharton, or the fear of them, were going to come out of the woodwork, swarm out of the crowd, every day that dawned.

All the while, her infatuation was growing. A hundred times a day she recalled the pressure of Jake Springland's hand against her black-coated shoulder back in the winter's longest night, darkest hour, tugging her against him in the taxi on the way back to Audubon Place, their cheap hotel experience a common history now . . . and there lay the shape of his wrist outlined against the black fabric. She was looking down at it still, every day, minute to minute, nothing could make her stop. As for the hotel, when she looked back to that, even got in the area of it, passing by, her ears roared like the sea. Who could relieve her? Only Jake could and he was in jail, locked up, while all was noisy ebb and flow within her senses. When she had sent her note in to him, how could she know whether or not it reached him? She was refused, but by him? "You can't see him, miss." That was all she could get out of them. Did it come from him, and why?

Julia was here and yonder, now picking up her pittance at the art class, now passing Paul Fowler without speaking because she had not seen him. He was angry and said to Edie Williams, "What's the matter with that girl? What's she got on her mind?"

"I don't know. She's been worried lately. You know she broke up with this boy she was engaged to. That was last summer. Maybe she regrets it."

"Was that the one with all the money?"

"That's right, Martin Parham. I never met him. He was already past history when she moved over here."

"It's why she came here," said Paul Fowler immediately. Not liking her made him have a feeling for what she would do and why.

Paul was sitting with Edie on the back porch overlooking the garden. Julia was not there.

"Do you think anybody would throw a conniption fit if I went and stuck my head under your shower? I'm getting hotter'n blazes."

Edie agreed to shout if she heard anybody coming. They had the back porch to themselves. "The ladies never come back here," she said. "Julia wouldn't care."

He came back, replacing his damp shirt, rubbing his wet head with a towel.

"That's better." He sat down. "You say Julia wouldn't care, but you don't know. I don't really like that girl. She's good-looking, but she's still one of those smooth sorority types. She's not right for you is what I think. Now say I can mind my business."

"She's not my type, I guess," Edie ruminated. She did not often get mad at Paul Fowler. "But then who wants to get involved? It's just an experiment in living."

Edie was drinking iced tea which she herself had made. From time to time in recent weeks, an ancient colored man came past the steps that led into the garden, trundling an old-fashioned wheelbarrow which he set down carefully in the shade of the wall, lifting from it several worn garden tools, paintless and weathered

almost to fragility. He scraped and stirred a little here
and there around certain plants, pulled certain others
up by the roots, and cleared back the weed clumps from
the fish basin and the garden paths. He had started
coming after the incident of Paul and Edie's wanting to
rework the garden, and he therefore seemed a reproach to
Edie, who cared, and to Paul, who did not, except that he
liked to see a good job done: the old colored man hardly
seemed alive, let alone able to garden. That day they
sat and watched him and thought about Julia.

"I think I got fascinated with Julia just for that
reason, because she wasn't my type. Secretly I always
wanted to be one of those aristocratic girls, just for a
little while, to see what it was like. I never went with
that crowd, you see, but after all, this was New Orleans
where I was in school. People back home used to ask me
about that sort of life here—she's not all that French or
Creole or something, but her relatives are—and I'd say
I'd never seen it. Then when she asked me to come over
here and share expenses—I didn't know her very well—
I think I said okay just out of curiosity. Finally I got fond
of her. She has a lot of feeling about everything under the
sun. She's not all that happy, so disliking her's not really
fair."

"Okay, she's got a heart of gold——"

"I didn't say that," said Edie.

"—but let me ask you this. Has she let you know her
crowd? All those aristocrats you mentioned?"

"Well, I met the family," said Edie.

"No kidding!"

"Sure I did. Didn't I tell you I had Sunday dinner at
Audubon Place? Before I met you, before I moved here?"

"You don't mean they sit down to chicken and gravy
on the stroke of 12:30 same as all the rest of the world?"

"Well, not exactly."

"No, I bet not."

"What I mean is, they have it at night."

"Ah-*ha!*"

"Gossip!" she teased him, giving him a shove with her shoulder. "What's so significant in that?"

"You look cute," said Paul Fowler. "I'd kiss you but it's too hot to get worked up. So go on, Edie. What do they do?"

"Well, you know, out in the garden till dark, in informal clothes, then they disappear, and Julia and I went up to look at her old room (she took me round the house), then out everybody came again, dressed, elegant, a drink on the patio with that sort of white-painted furniture, cushions, just so comfortable, and some sort of protective lamp for getting rid of bugs."

"Not even French bugs allowed?"

"Oh, you're cute! They're really nice, the Devignys. He's sexy. He has this rich caressing voice."

"So drinks but no bugs. Then what?"

"It's not all that grand. Very simple. You eat at dark. Servants off on Sunday, they say, so it's all cold. Cold platters of food. Candlelight, windows open. Big table, mirrors. Wonderful china and silver. I never saw such china in my life."

"Better than the Misses Mulligan?"

"Well, just a lot more of it. And anyway theirs was not matched, didn't you notice?"

"No! I, Paul Fowler, drank tea out of cups and saucers that did . . . *not* . . . MATCH!"

"You'd never have known the Mulligans and I'd never have dined in Audubon Place if it wasn't for Julia."

"Our lives are changed," Paul Fowler mocked. "We are permanently altered."

"She does have dimensions," Edie reflected. "She is still mysterious."

"Balls to that," Paul Fowler said. He said it about the word itself, as much as about Julia. Mysterious anything did not suit him.

## 10. THE TRIAL

---

When the trial date came round, not as many people showed up as one might have expected. The courtroom was not air-conditioned; this was one reason. For another, newspaper coverage of the whole affair had been overdone for a while, it was felt, and so had fallen off. The search for Wilma Wharton, for instance, had been given a lot of space in the *Picayune*, but once she was located, she turned out to be a champion witness of the underworld variety, for she could and did, on every occasion, give the police completely differing sets of testimony. She was evidently convinced that each of these sets was completely true at the time she was giving it. Everything she said, wherever it crossed paths with what could be factually verified, turned out to be true. But the inside stories, which only she and perhaps Jake Springland could know, conflicted wildly. It seemed a kind of talent she had. "Invaluable," murmured Tommy Arnold, "like old half-witted men who can remember the exact dates of everything from the fall of the Bastille to the biggest hailstorm ever to hit Tuscaloosa, day, month, year, hour, minute. Then they suddenly tell you they remember it because they were there too. She should be an international spy. She's being wasted here, like all great talent, mine included. However, since so much depends on the mood she's in, how could anybody count on her?" She was given a lie-detector test and her statements were dutifully analyzed. It turned out scientifically that she was telling the truth even when she contradicted herself. There was not even an inverse proportion of reaction indication to be charted, as she sometimes gave a magnificent lie reaction when she simply hadn't heard the question.

Over in Audubon Place, all this was being read about daily.

"That's what dope will do, in time," said Isabel Devigny, who followed the case. "That's the trouble with her. Isn't it clear to you?"

"Oh, I don't know," said Maurice. "I've heard you tell one story over six different ways."

"Yes," said Isabel, "but what the Wharton woman tells over is not the same story. In one story she married Ted Marnie; in another she was never married to him. In one version she was there the night he disappeared because she wanted to see the Springland man, in another she came because she wanted to see about Marnie's dinner, in a third she wasn't there at all, though she had thought about going, but came in later and found he had got drunk and fallen down and cut himself. In one story she didn't know any doctors in Gretna because she had never been there; in another, she had lived there five years ago in order to be near a doctor who was helping her, but she couldn't think of his name; then again she could think of his name but he had moved to Shreveport. But she and Ted Marnie never got to the doctor that night of the fight because, she says, Marnie woke up in the car and said he was perfectly all right. In a final interview the police report her as saying she gave Spring-land the address of the doctor who wasn't there any more and left both him and Marnie in the car because she didn't know anything about Gretna at all and didn't want to go there. There is no record of her having lived in Gretna and the house address she refers to has burned down. But she succeeded in throwing more suspicion on Springland, though after she's said so much of a contradictory nature he will probably not be harmed by it. . . .

"And . . . oh, here's some more: Wilma Wharton was suspected insane until tests were given her which show a remarkably high I.Q. with especial reference to mathematical reasoning. She is well up-to-date on recent European history, especially as regards the NATO countries and Common Market economics. Rather better read than average."

"Clearly an addict," said Maurice. "Why don't they come out and say so?"

"But once they get them off it, can't they go back to making true statements? Don't they know the difference between true and false?"

"Evidently not . . . she doesn't. She may be in with some big outfit and doesn't even realize it. These things work through connections. The police are always partly involved, more than they'd like anyone to know. The local boys probably get rake-offs."

Certainly Maurice knew more than a little about how things really worked, thought Isabel. "This Springland man——" she began, but Maurice flung aside his book and walked out on the gallery. "I've been tired of it for a week!" he declared, and went into the garden for a turn among the plants.

Isabel realized that she was tired of it as well, as at perhaps that very moment everybody thought they must be tired of it, too, all over New Orleans. The mood of the city shifted. People began to think of how to get away for the summer. The ones who could were going up to New England to summer in Maine coves and out-shore islands. The ones who couldn't were planning to summer at the Mississippi coast. The in-betweens might go to the Carolina or Georgia or Virginia mountains. The rock-bottom ones, who had to stay on, holed up in air-conditioned bedrooms with plenty of books from the library and plugged and unplugged the telephone. Down-town the heat fell on your head like brickbats. Some grimy old murder case—what was the use?

The day of the trial, Julia Garrett, scared to death, nevertheless put on the dark glasses she had bought to

hide behind and, having put a rust-red rinse in her hair
the night before, pulled on a cheap black straw hat at an
unattractive angle and prepared to go downtown, into
the middle of things. Her dress was old, with an uneven
hem. In the upstairs of the Misses Mulligans', peering
in the mirror, she had almost laughed, for it was next to
impossible for her to obliterate a certain set, a smartness,
about her looks. As soon as she had got into it the old hat
took on the very aspect of the lost twenties which was
now being cultivated. Her bare white arms above the line
of the dress obscured its disrepair. She couldn't help it.
Might as well try to de-sex herself, she thought, as stamp
out her natural looks. She thought perhaps she had at
least succeeded in looking like somebody else of her
general type, but Tommy Arnold, who had agreed to let
her sit beside him in court, had recognized her at once.
"What have you done to yourself?" he said. Then he caught
on. "Have you been scared? Has somebody threatened
you?" "Nobody's done anything," she said, "which means
you were right about the Wharton woman." "She doesn't
know you saw him?" "I guess not."

"She's mangled this case," Tommy Arnold complained. "I wanted to keep it straight—crazy and beautiful. All her lies, she doesn't even know she's telling them.
I know what they mean now by that old saw: The truth's
not in you. There's no way for her to tell it, because it
just ain't there. The only trouble is, the jury's apt to con-
vict just from boredom and general suspicion."

"The lawyer never called me," she whispered.

"I doubt they'll need to call on you here," he returned.
Then he looked at her straight. "I hope it's worth it to you,
risking this much for him."

"I had to." She straightened up, sitting stiff and small,
like a small mast against a storm. The judge's gavel
whammed the desk. She had a feeling most of what was
done and said was going straight over her head. But she
was there anyway, present. "I had to come."

# 11. THE TRIAL CONTINUES

 Julia sat and looked at Jake Springland. The whole time, her eyes scarcely left his face. Sitting, in profile, he looked taller than she had remembered him, but that would be because he had lost weight in jail. His face looked quiet and reasonable. Something had got knocked out of him; something had matured, she thought. He might have just gone blank, as far as sensitivity was concerned, and all the edge in his fresh mind, that might be dull. Could it happen? Maybe it would have to happen, if he was going to last through it all.

His head swung round; he looked out, but over and past her. The strain was apparent then, around the eyes, and she startled herself with a wave of desire to protect, feed, nurse him back to where he was that first day when the door of Dr. Pollard's office had swung wide on him alone. Then she began to hurt, inside herself, and the pain was real. Love made it, she guessed. Oh God, oh Dieu, she thought. His profile returned. They were the only two people in the courtroom. Mentally she tore her drab dress open wide and also the tissue, flesh and bone of the rib-caged and flesh-cushioned tenderness beneath; on that portion of her most deeply set and securely private the long profile minted itself like a head on molten gold. He had got into this mess, she thought, through not knowing his own value.

Julia had known wild boys from high school on. But Southern boys, New Orleans boys with their pedigreed French names and their casual pursuit of excellence—

the tops in living, sport, girls—were self-conscious; they were tied to a smaller statement of life than what she wanted made to her. Besides, something had happened which had crystallized them all for her, way too soon. When she was seventeen a sweet wild one she was dating had shot himself playing with an old dueling pistol. It had been during a house party on a fine plantation dating back to the eighteenth century. All week, through beautiful nights, pavilion dances, through layers of wit, rounds of eating, and almost perpetual drinking, it had seemed that they were all too much of something. Too beautiful, too soft-voiced, too brilliant, too casually enhanced with everything that tended toward a racial deserving, an eternity of a paradise of simply knowing they were the only ones in the world with those particular redolent names, the poise and repose of that singularly spared plantation house resting in neoclassical outline upon the banks of that one languid bayou. Beaurivard. "Garrett," the boy had said. "It won't do for a name, Julia. If I had a name like Garrett, I'd shoot myself straight through the head." And he had spun the cylinder, and drawn back the hammer. It had clicked dull and empty, but the gesture remained, printed before her vision. All that afternoon (as well as other afternoons before that day) he had been initiating her sexually down in a boat house on a daybed covered with old chintz. In the breeze from time to time, a torn shade flapped and slapped like a sail in a hot calm. Now he was in the side gallery at Beaurivard, after dinner, alone with her, sitting carelessly, leaning back against a white-painted column, his leg cocked up as though he sat a horse he knew well. Julia felt like a wild orchid just come to bloom. Don't, she wanted to say, when he spun the chamber a second time, but her spirit overruled it. They both were free, that was the good thing. A word like "don't" on that long party and the house might catch fire, or a tornado come plowing in through the woods, or, more magically, all might turn to cobwebs and dust. A light breeze sprang up, fanning the

damp warmth of the flesh at her neck and armpits, moving
along her bare shoulders. The moon had risen. A second
time, the boy pulled the trigger. She did not hear the
sound till later. The face regarding her own transferred
itself from the support of his neck to that of the white
pillar beside it. Julia screamed.

He had been supposed to die as though it didn't
matter and he had done it, they said. They had dragged
her away before he actually expired, but she guessed he
had succeeded, all right, and this more than anything
could bring tears to her yet, to this day, because fiercely
she knew it wasn't worth it; she knew now they had
been so much better than the aristocratic games they'd
been so greedily playing. But René, who hadn't known
that, had signed them off for her forever; she could
never make herself believe in all that self-charmed world
again. For years she had cherished the notion that he—
René—had been her one love, but then Martin Parham
had come along from up in Mississippi, and she'd
changed. But that, too, though entirely another story, had
reached an apex, a climax, which had not been marriage
—a marriage so confidently awaited by her aunt and
uncle. By now she felt that every man—and each world
that every man brought with him—might be expected to
do the same.

The witnesses were passing. Her mind was forming
over words to one of Jake Springland's songs, the one
she couldn't forget; he'd sung it for her that day they'd
wandered so, winding up in the cheap hotel room.

> *Who's got the heart to mind the time*
> *When you know the wine*
> *Is nearly finished and the evening's*
> *Gone to where all evenings go?*

She listened to the witnesses with the words and tune
running in her head.

Yes (the witness, a taxi driver, was relating), Jake

Springland had been seen often with the Marnie man.
Seen where? Well, around the Salvation Army where
they both worked. Salvation Army? It seemed an unlikely place. Well, Marnie was religious, a sort of self-
appointed preacher. Wondrous things had passed before
his eyes. He would lean back in his chair and chant
about them. When he chanted, Springland would get his
box out and knock it, working the phrases over. Would
the witness interpret? Get out his guitar and compose
tunes, or chants, based on the talk of Ted Marnie. They
turned each other on—that way, anyway. Would the
witness please rephrase the answer? Did he mean they
inspired each other? That would do. (Laughter.)

The witness himself used to hang out around the
corner from the Salvation Army, taking coffee and beer
(after hours, of course) at a corner shop there. Sometimes he played gin, a hand or two with Springland. A
good type, Springland: one he liked, but peculiar. Peculiar,
how? Well, just coming here . . . he could have got on
somewhere else, couldn't he? But still people did come
to New Orleans like that, especially musicians, or writers,
people like that . . . so that was it, the witness supposed. Immediate question: So he had taken Jake Springland for a crook? Immediate answer: No, he hadn't.
Didn't say that. No evidence that Springland was a crook,
or involved with crooks. Not unless Marnie was a crook,
and he didn't even know that, one way or the other. Just
curious types: a fanatic maybe, that was Marnie; a
loner, you could say, that was Springland. The fans
flapped on; one had a wobble in it, a loose bearing perhaps, which made an infinitely small clucking sound on
each revolution.

Jake Springland's long blond head, the strict withdrawn profile, looked contained but not mysterious. Plain
facts were there. He did not, Julia realized, thinking now
that she'd known it all along, wrestle with angels. Yet
he might have a demon lurking in him somewhere—was
that what drew her, on and on? That might be why he

had taken up with Marnie, who had been all demon, partly for the personal Springland demon's sake, partly out of the good will of simple time-wasting and the curiosity that went along with it. One thing she knew, for he'd told her more or less apologetically the day they'd wandered so: Marnie and the Wharton woman didn't look as bad as that at first. Marnie's look was getting crazed, he'd thought at the beginning, from dipping around in too much philosophy—Oriental wisdom and all the hang-ups of the mystics. But Wilma, believe it or not, had been trim and blond, a dye job, and she was cheap, God knew, but generous and a good enough cook. This was how they were at first. During the summer they'd gone down to Grand Isle below the city, down on the Gulf, and taken a cottage. Jake had rambled everywhere, talking to people. At night he and Marnie talked about the books. Suddenly, Wilma started getting fat. It was something glandular, he guessed. It was awful. He'd thought Ted would drop her but he didn't. It was her spirit that he loved, Marnie said.

Jake left them, but in New Orleans they had showed up again, again next door. Marnie had got him the pickup job with the Salvation Army. What better way to see the insides of various homes and houses, rich and middle-class and poor, than by moving out furniture, old wardrobes of deceased aunts and grandmothers, worn-out baby carriages, a clutter of old shoes, a rickety fumed-oak sideboard, tarnished sets of plated silver, lamps that would have disgraced a sailor's whorehouse, moth-eaten sweaters, old wicker garden furniture with peeling gilt at the joints, and tables with match scratches and chewing gum stuck underneath, always with one rickety leg, and on top of everything, a cardboard box with old knitting wool somebody had bought and never used. A warped tennis racket in a press. A reading lamp with a metal hood, a student's lamp, wrapped in a worn slicker. He would understand all that stuff, and would be good at picking it up just so, for his tact in how to touch what was there to be handled was not unknown to her. Placing things. And setting things in order in the van. Close packed. All space utilized. Then, mounting, riding beside that skeletal companion, bespectacled and inwardly intent on God knew what. How could he not shudder? On the other hand, why should he? All it was, was life. Everything that was, was life. Whatever isn't dead. And, scientifically—here she remembered Edie and Paul— what's dead is life too, only somewhat altered. Our generation has lived beyond shock, Tommy Arnold would have said. He sat beside her, scratching with a blunt yellow copy pencil, notes undecipherable except to himself, on coarse oyster-white paper.

And the night of the crime?

Here in the questioning there was a statement to be read aloud which Wilma Wharton had signed, but summoned to the stand she broke down, became incoherent, burst into tears, and screamed at the lawyer that someone else had forged her name. The court adjourned amid general chaos, and it was suddenly (to Julia, anyway, dizzy with so many strange experiences) the next day. A lot of crazy dreams had rampaged through her head in the night, but here she was back, sitting beside Tommy Arnold the same as before, in the row beneath the crippled fan.

The night of the crime?

Jake Springland took the stand.

# 12. THE TRIAL RESUMES

 Jake talked in a deliberate way, bent forward and attentive, and leaned his head slightly to catch the questions accurately. His accent sounded somewhat Northern, correct and grammatical in the syrupy atmosphere stirred by the fans. It gave the impression of directness and honesty which his words reinforced. It also accomplished a subtle thing: when an outsider is called on to speak clearly and does so, he gains a better audience than a native would.

There had been, he at once admitted, a series of robberies. The robberies were generally of filling stations in out-of-the-way places, usually at dimly lit state highway intersections, or in semiresidential neighborhoods, rather poor, where few people came out at night for gas. He himself had either held a gun on the attendant while Marnie lifted ready cash out of the register, or Marnie had held the gun while he had lifted cash. Later, they had split it up. Why had he done it? They needed money, for rent and food. (Pause.) Anyway, he added, nobody was really being robbed. (Note of surprise.) Weren't the attendants' wages docked by however much was missing? Jake did not even think that was true—the companies were insured against such eventualities. A certain number of stick-ups were counted on statistically during the year. Anyway, if you thought about money long enough, it did not seem to exist unless you were hungry, or had to pay a bill or the rent. (This spread another surprise wave, and one or two people laughed, then more.)

Q. And well . . . and then?

A. Then there had been the night they had taken all of $20 from a station with a few cents over, and Marnie had refused to split it. He, Jake Springland, had told Marnie this was the last time for him and he wouldn't even go inside with him, but only held the truck ready, back in the shadows with the motor running. It had been a mistake to tell Marnie they were all but finished. They had gone back to the apartment together and the woman, Wilma Wharton, had come in. Jake was determined to have his money and go, he was tired of them, of both of them.

Q. Why was he tired of them? Weren't they his best friends?

A. Friends! He'd got mixed up with them for somebody to talk to, and for the interest in Marnie, a real type, something you wouldn't believe was real. A source for his songs as well. But they quarreled too much, he and the Wharton woman, and it had got tiresome. Besides, the robberies—— He didn't feel right about them. It was not any way to live. He wanted done with it. He had made his big mistake in telling Marnie they were finished, that that was his last time to go out with him. Marnie didn't like to lose anybody. Marnie needed an audience for his crazy ideas. He was a see-er, a man who could see souls, but he needed somebody to appreciate him, somebody to see him seeing. The woman wasn't enough. Jake had been an audience. Now it was over. He wanted to take his money and go. Then the woman. She wanted to make it a test of Marnie, of how he might be Jesus Christ but he couldn't keep promises. She kept screaming that he'd promised her things too, but they'd never materialized. That put her and Jake in the selfsame boat. It made a gang of the two of them, against the anointed one.

Marnie had been sitting in a chair with a beatific smile on his face, listening. There is one thing to know in life and that is how far a belief in God can take you along with all who happen to fall under the spell. All you have to do is switch on the connection you have with

the Almighty and everything clears up. You listen with
a benign smile while others go through their long rig-
marole of error; you just wait until it's over with so you
can get moving once again along the one true pathway,
leading the disciples forward. Not too many months
before, Jake Springland had toyed with the idea that
Ted Marnie's gaunt frame housed a true saint—a man
disinterested in all materialism, giving himself totally
up to the pursuit of truth in all its forms. Now he wanted
nothing but to get out, never to have to see that fatuous
smile, that lofty air. Was there anything worse than a
self-appointed Jesus? He didn't think so.

Q. Would he say then that he had hated Marnie?

A. No—well, yes, in a way. But hated in a sort of
past tense way. Right then all he wanted was to get away
from him, get clean away and gone. Clean away was a
good way to put it. When he'd met Marnie and the
Wharton woman they were not too badly off, it seemed.
They had at least been clean. Now they were dirty—they
didn't care. That rubbed him wrong, more than anything
else. You could draw God up to be anything because
nobody could prove it, one way or the other. But dirt was
something you had to take seriously. Also, he had needed
the money or he wouldn't have agreed to go along.

He had waited while the Wharton woman turned the
light on herself, like an actress, and went into her long
harangue. She had wanted to get married, it now seemed,
to have a regular place for herself, and Ted had turned
out not to mean it when he promised her that all she
wanted would be hers. He had meant it in a spiritual
sense; wasn't that convenient? Once she got rolling it
was hard to stop her. Everything got into her speech,
every memory she ever had, all her folks had done to
her years ago, all bad, all the men she'd known who'd
treated her wrong . . . it was like a three-hour movie
with no intermission, and Jake Springland was held, not
certainly because of the ten dollars, not exactly out of
fear, but as he had been many times held by the two of

them, because he'd never heard anything quite like it. Then he realized he'd got stuck with them, like falling into a barrel of blackstrap molasses.

"Ted," he said, interrupting Wilma Wharton, "just give me that ten."

"You don't understand, Jake," said Marnie, very kind and gentle. "I got a place for this. I expected more, but what I got is not for myself. Do you think I care for myself? You've known me all this time and you think I care for myself. You yourself must have some deep trouble to think that such a thing could be true. I can only sympathize with the pain of your trouble. You can have my week's wages when I'm paid. Did I ever break a promise?"

"If that money's not for you, who's it for?" Jake asked.

Marnie smiled. He was vague and deified. Who could ask him anything? How could you turn on a saint? Well, a lot of people had, in the past, and would again, for it was at that point that Wilma Wharton shouted, "You're poison, ain't you?" and whammed him over the head with a broom. Poor old Ted! This was what Springland thought as the man went crumpling, awkwardly, to the floor. He fell to one side and rolled over, holding his head, and groaning while the woman grabbed at his pockets. Astonishment! Bills came out, over a hundred dollars. Jake saw them fall all over the floor. He picked up his ten and was about to leave, but Marnie turned over and sat up. The Wharton woman was reveling in money, throwing it around her, gathering it up again. Then she saw Marnie sitting up, and "Liar!" she yelled, as soon as she got her breath back. She had broken the broom on the first blow, and now taking up what was left of the handle she hit Marnie again with a downward chopping motion, as though the broom were an ax. There was the wire wrapping close to the straw that hit into Marnie's head. Springland guessed that this must have burst a vein or something because the blood spurted out, jetting. He

really went down then. Springland was at the door about
to go. The Wharton woman changed completely when she
saw blood. She ran to Jake and caught hold of him.
"Poor man!" she said, over and over. "Poor old Ted!"
"You did it yourself," said Springland, "so what d'you
mean, poor man!" "Just let me get him somewhere, Jake.
I owe it to him, Jake. He sees us as we are. He sees the
soul. You know he has that power, more than anyone.
We said that, Jake." "Listen," said Springland, "I'll help
you get him in the car, and that's all. That's all I'll do."
They wrapped a towel around his head and cleared up
the room a little; then they got him out and downstairs.
On the stairs, he started shouting at them to leave him
be, rousing up the neighbors until Jake smothered a
coat over his head. The woman kept pretending she
knew the way perfectly all right, but he knew she couldn't
make it through the center of town. . . .

Q. Was she drunk? On drugs?

A. He didn't know. She'd been drinking, he guessed.
But mainly she was hysterical. Anyway, to help her, as
a parting gesture, Jake drove the car as far out toward
Gretna as the ferry stop, then he got out and left it with
them, as though having towed a strange boat free of
swamps he now abandoned it to open water. He thought
in that neighborhood she would actually be able to get to
a doctor or a hospital or to somebody she knew. Marnie,
the poor old scarecrow, was still mumbling and stirring
now and again. He called for the Lord. And Wilma Wharton was sobbing, Let him live, oh Jesus, so that made both
of them praying. It seemed her love had returned as soon
as she had come near to killing him. (Laughter.)

As for Jake Springland, he had had it. He got out of
the car that night and walked off, a free man.

Q. To where?

A. Well, he couldn't recall. He had walked a lot,
spent part of the ten dollars for food and had a drink
in a late bar in the French Quarter, then come back to

a rooming house he was staying in. He wouldn't go back over there near them.

(. . . He came to me, Julia sat thinking. To Amelia Street and found me outside too, out on the sidewalk having had a drink or two too many and got rid of a man I didn't like, I was walking the evening out of my system and he came strolling, the first I'd seen of him in ages, it was like an appearance, an apparition, but real, with real, strong, sweet arms holding and pure. It wasn't sex he was after, but touching, holding, and the long sweet kiss and the walk in the air that was a lot like spring, a false spring. He came and went and we didn't talk much or ask any questions. But I went upstairs alone and slept, oh, slept like never before, feeling myself a sweet fresh stream he could draw from and he knew it and he had . . . feeling fulfillment and the deep-taken breath of sheer content.)

He had made a resolve that night, Jake Springland said in court, to make a fresh start. He had come to New Orleans and some way or other had succeeded in drifting to rock bottom, now he was ready to come back up, try to swim instead of sink. He'd had to get into the element here, maybe that was what had motivated him; he didn't know. Marnie and the Wharton woman—all those talks, all those books, the few followers Marnie had drawn to him, what did it mean? All it meant was that Marnie was secretly weaving everything into his own web, like a spider. As for who killed him, though, Springland hadn't a clue. The blow with the broom wasn't hard enough, he didn't think, even at the time. . . .

"But you signed a confession."

Julia Garrett sat up straight. There was a long pause, an attentive silence.

The police confession was produced. Jake Springland acknowledged the signature and a clerk read it aloud.

". . . When he wouldn't pay me the money and Wilma Wharton couldn't get any sense out of him, we

both turned on him and knocked him down. If he was
alive after that I don't know because he never said any
more. We got some more of his friends out playing poker
in a house near Gretna and carried him out into the
swamps. I don't know if one of them buried him or not.
They all went off with him together. I stayed in the car,
smoking for a long time, then I went back into town."

There was a long silence and then Springland, leaning
forward, said quietly and distinctly:

"I want it understood, the police beat that out of me.
They didn't tell me his skull was broken. So I figured well
maybe she did kill him when she hit him. And in a way
we were both in on it—who could prove anything? They
said I'd get off with only a year or so for involuntary manslaughter if I gave an explanation of his death that included myself. If not, they said it would be murder. So it
was near enough to the truth, give or take a little, and I
felt bad about the robberies. I said I'd think it over and
that was when they—they roughed in on me."

Then he leaned down and in front of all of them rolled
back his trousers, the bare legs half-healed over, but the
bruises still purple and the flesh tears still crazily pat-
terned from knee to ankle. Sitting there, self-exposed, he
looked young and confused, committed to an action, a
decision to act, that might let him in for more troubles
still, might turn once more into a blind alley he'd run into,
half-expecting the whole city police force to walk in lock-
stepping and drag him off for more tortures yet. Would
he ever be heard from again?

Everyone seemed tired and slightly sickened by the
whole mix-up. At some obscure moment the prosecution
itself seemed to feel he was one for letting go. Now the
courtroom feeling plainly spoke of weariness, of disgust
at sleazy human behavior. They had had—jury and
spectators and judge, too—an overdose of Wilma Wharton, wild as a starved cat, pulling and jerking at her
hair and badly needing what she had more or less lived
on for who knew how long. The young man—now rolling

down his trouser legs with that kind of steadiness which means the world is there to be confronted, often in utter loneliness, out of despair—was clear-eyed and fine-faced. Anybody can go wrong once, especially when young. He was blond.

In the end, the jury passed the hat for him. He left $150 to the good, with a subpoena outstanding in case anyone wanted to bring charges for the filling station robberies. The feeling was that nobody would have the heart.

# 13. AFTERMATH

 Tommy Arnold and Julia walked out together. He took her to lunch and teased
her a little. "You were trying to be noble
and nobody needed you."

Julia wouldn't laugh. "He saw me," she
said. "In spite of all this get-up. As he was going out of the
courtroom. I know he recognized me. It was just a glance."

"I have to admire him," said Tommy Arnold, thought-
fully. "Though if the police ever get hold of him again
any time soon, it's going to be a lot more nursery games
than that. I still admire what he did. It was something
that took nerve because there wasn't any precedent for it."

"I admired it too."

To Julia and Tommy Arnold it now seemed they had
known each other for years instead of weeks. She knew
his typecasting in her life, the not-quite-brother, not-quite-
lover, the kindness and confidence of it all. Her plate
arrived. She took off the floppy, disguising hat and laid it
on the seat beside her. Then she took off the dark glasses.

"My idea is," she said, "that people draw life from the
crooked world. There's a conversation going on with the
straight world, all the time. It's what makes this city and
it's what makes the world. Haven't you noticed?"

Letting that out with one sidelong glance, half-inno-
cent, and she'd nailed him so completely he was speech-
less. For the shady world to him was irresistible. He understood why cops took rake-offs, half the time because in
the first place they had got to be cops from wanting in on
it all. Deep within him he knew, too, why the nice girl

wound up third floor front at an address known to many. Why, for that matter, was good old Tommy Arnold always on the trail of crime? It reminded him: if he couldn't get this story out any other way, he'd write it up for *Detective Story* magazine, the fiction one, inventing a fake ending which would solve it.

"Yes, I've noticed," he at last, dryly, agreed. And then: "What happened to the Parham boy?"

She looked up quickly. "How'd you know him?"

"I didn't. I looked through the society files until I found you. Something nagged at my memory when I met you. The name sounded familiar. I checked to follow up that feeling and there you were: engaged to the Parham boy, out of that wealthy family up there in Mississippi. Do they own half the state or just three-quarters? What happened?"

"I let it go."

"Christ, you were fixed for life."

"That's just it. Would you like to be fixed for life?"

He grinned. "I like you, Julia Garrett," he said. "No," he admitted, "I wouldn't like to be fixed for life, still, for a woman—you've got to be fixed one way or another."

She sighed, acknowledging the counterblow. "You're right there."

"What was the matter with Parham?"

"I told you. I as good as told you. Even Cadillacs get dull. I wasn't ready for the long pull."

"You weren't in love?"

"Martin Parham was a real sweet boy."

"Enough said," said Tommy Arnold. He was eating. Like a good reporter he was not looking at her closely, but she knew that he could have re-told from memory every expression in her voice and face.

"So now you go chasing around after new experiences."

"Is that how it seems to you?"

He did not reply and she felt close enough to him to

add: "I want the depth. I have to have it and, when I get it, then I'm with it, with life, you know, the way you have to move."

"It's a point of view," Tommy Arnold admitted. "Especially if you don't have a wife and children to support."

"What did your father do?" Julia asked him, unexpectedly.

"He was an accountant. On the side he souped up old cars for racing drivers." Mentioning this to her, he could see them once again, the leather-faced men with hard-set eyes, sometimes with a bright blue handkerchief knotted at the neck, passing through the back yard in spring, past the privet rich with scented bloom, heading for the high board fence his father kept. He went on: "Before that, he used to drag-race himself, weekends, all over the place, but after one smash-up too many, he thought his timing was off because he was over forty-five, so he kept his hand in by doing the mechanic's part, buying up the old wrecks and setting them up."

"He got to see all those people," Julia nodded. "It just goes to show you. Why I'm like I am—you, too."

"You can't go *on* like this!" Tommy Arnold scolded her, but remembering his own father like that he'd lost his right to father her. She had a way of neatly taking the starch of his authority right out of him; they were all at once in step again, equals, and she was smiling her cat smile and he his dog one, he guessed.

"Did he really come to see you that night? That very night? Springland?"

"He did, yes, honestly. I looked up and there he was. I'd been out late and I was coming in. It was warm and nice, a false spring. A spring-night feeling. Under the trees. And he—well, it was good, the way he appeared that way. Not the way you think, not the way anybody would think. That's the real reason I didn't want to let it out."

"It was innocent, you mean? And nobody would believe that?"

"That's exactly what I mean." She added: "Can't you tell he's capable of innocence, not only innocence but directness, honesty, standing alone?"

"It's that that's hooked you: I can tell that."

"But so few people are!" she insisted. "Capable of it, I mean."

"I might be capable myself," Tommy Arnold said. "Why, sure. On occasions, I could surprise you." But his tone had a cut-back, a banter in it, which was its own best comment. She looked at him sharply, thinking that sort of voice might indicate something unsatisfactory, something almost as deep as cowardice, but she did not remark on it. She mused on, instead, resting on what she believed about Jake Springland. He had won by himself, without her, and she liked it better that way.

# 14. JAKE

Like any song writer in jail, Jake came out with his pockets full, scraps of this and that for putting into music. He had paid for something, some debt to life was canceled, and now the songs could come and flow out freely. Julia would be his prime listener. She would listen to the ones made up in jail and later to all the rest that came, not once but many times; she soon would know them all. Every street Jake moved on, free air swirled around him, full of songs.

But New Orleans was an instrumental town. How to score with songs in any significant way was Jake's big problem. A girl singer in a night club, maybe one who could strip too, might have a chance, but balladeering, like country songs, while it found some audience, was distinctly not the New Orleans thing. Couldn't he pretend to be a mountain boy? It was suggested to him more than once. He would instantly refuse. He wasn't hillbilly-inclined; he wouldn't whang. The mountain ballads maybe, but even people who sang those had to give out cheap music ninety percent of the time, and if you went on the art circuit, plucking a guitar like a mandolin or a lute and singing tenor, you'd get checked off as a fag so quick you'd never be taken for real. So he tried the impossible, in New Orleans, working with an old tradition to create a new.

He was stubborn, a refuser of things he didn't really want. In the early fifties he'd left college, one reason the draft caught up with him so quick. His father had owned a vacuum cleaner company in Ohio, just across from Kentucky; he had invented in *his* own father's machine shop at an early age a device found better suited to vacuum cleaners than to city sanitation trucks. Lately he and the device and the company had all been bought by Hoover, but he continued to "earn big," as he put it, and would keep on putting it, right up to the last, being stubborn himself—he saw where Jake came by it. When his wife left him he never would get married again; women he loved could milk and trick him all day long, he never would be tricked into marriage. That was one step beyond them, no matter what other tricks they knew. Jake wrung him, refusing college, but he couldn't sweat over it forever. "You'll be all right, Jake," was his conclusion. There was sweetness in it and forgiveness but along with those qualities and deeper than both was the abiding desire not to get worked up and lose sleep.

In college Jake had started out big as an intellectual, then he hadn't liked himself. The intellectual role out of college suited his imagination better; he thought of wandering for a year or two, letting America digest him until it dumped him out somewhere: in other words, he hit on the best and shortest route to Korea. Was it authority he was dodging? Something of his father in him at this point? When the police kicked him crazy he thought of it: life was getting back at him for the many fine opportunities he had turned down by leaving college, but when the pain stepped up he couldn't think of anything but standing it, getting through in one piece. Later, out of there, he thought of the moment when men turn bestial to one another, knew that he had done it too, wantonness mixed up with the logic of destructiveness, out there in the crazy East. Is what we think in extremities, pain or danger, the real truth? No, because some people start thinking about a dog they had when they were seven years old and others about isosceles triangles. Some act without knowing why. The greatest truth Jake had at the moment was that Julia cleansed him. Rotten experience had accumulated in his mind and blood and she had been in on it enough to know. So after the trial was over and done, he had finally come to her and she had taken him—straight on, dead on, never wavering; she had not failed. She had been a refuser, too, it turned out, much to Jake's relief, not to say enlightenment. She had turned back, he learned, from some rich boy who had offered her a long, safe, happy life. . . .

All Julia knew was that the day after the trial Jake had simply appeared, unannounced, like all the other times, except on that one date they had had in the lobby of the Monteleone. It was around one o'clock, and she was sitting on the back steps at the Mulligan house reading Sartre. He had passed the walk and the flank of the old house. Then he was there on the overgrown flagstones. A green lizard left the sun for the shade, and Julia looked up. It was the first she knew of him. She sat quietly, book in her lap, squinting through the sun. Her hand rested on the top of the book, holding the page in place. In order to shade her page, she had sat near a pillar which supported the upper story gallery. The round-necked cotton housecoat she wore was the color of cherries. Glare lay between them, but she had known him from the first glance; his outline had flashed instantaneously against her nerves without any recourse to her brain process at all. The effect was shocking, direct. Between them the sun whitened, and flattened. She raised her hand above her eyes to shade them. He came nearer.

The distance closing between them, their faces did not smile, but, grave, might have been struck for themselves—Jake and Julia—in stone portraits to last for good. He stood above her, one step lower than where she sat, and moved to take the book from her hands. Taking it, he trembled, his fingers fumbling against the cover for an instant before the bright book fell into the shrubbery below. Then he touched her shoulder and groped to find and take her hands. She felt him steady himself, out of touching her. He sank down beside her.

"I saw you at the trial," he said.

"I know you did."

They sat silently facing out toward the empty, half-tended garden, then turned at the same time, slowly, in a half-arc, and kissed, in a soft, tenuous, questioning way.

"You came because I saw you that evening, the one when he got killed. Maybe you tried to see me before, they said that some girl—I don't know."

"Yes, it was me, at the jail."

"I wouldn't come out. Why should you get into the mess because I was?"

"But I had to try, didn't I?"

"You didn't have to, no. For all you knew I did beat his brains to a pulp. He made me mad enough. You remember, Julia, the night I came and found you out on the street, you didn't say anything? Not a word."

"It didn't seem real."

"To me it was more than real."

He could gather her surely in now, she noticed; it was all coming true. He kissed her with what at first seemed tenderness and weariness combined because the trial would have worn out of him what force he kept in reserve for living and loving, but then she felt his presence freshening as he drew out her own strength, now spreading its petals wide and new, to mingle with his own, increasing each. When they drew back they knew much more, and tried again, and everything came new entirely. She took his hand at last, as firmly as she had that day in the hotel lobby, but with different intent, and rose, drawing him up with her, across the gallery, through the door. Within the room already many times, his spirit had walked, breathed, turned, and spoken. Now it became flesh. Now.

Giving totally this second time was better than the first, different, and better because a past had happened. From the doctor's office onward events had moved them forward to common ground. To Julia, Jake had caught the city's rough corruption with its core of feeling, its peculiar tolerant knowledge. She had circled it for years, but now an outsider had come to discover it, claim it, experience it and give it to her whole. Orphan girl in a voodoo city, she had answered when Martin Parham said, "What's wrong with me?" "You're way too good for us down here." Martin Parham would never be accused of burying a corpse in a swamp. And so she clung to the stranger who had come and soaked the essence up. She gave to him to get in return what he had found there; so went their exchange until all mingled in a common element that began demanding of them both, until they spent it all.

Light had drained from the faded walls of Julia's shabby room in the astonished old Mulligan house before the two of them, fallen at angles across each other like two people recently stood up before a firing squad, slept.

Another long portion of late sweet afternoon ebbed past before Edie came home. It was she who found the book, the one Julia had been reading. *Les Mouches* by Sartre, a paperback, its cover presuming to radiance, orange, flame and yellow, a designer's spectrum. It was lying in one of the partially kept-up shrubbery plots near the flight of steps, caught by the edge of a triangular piece of broken brick border. Edie picked it up doubtfully. She had felt the quietness of the house when passing along the narrow walk toward the back. Julia, always a mystery, had been gone a lot recently, suggesting a new man, though surely she wouldn't bring him here; they had decided never on that, keeping their vows to the old sisters. Now holding the book, Edie mounted slowly, with caution, feeling that somebody was with Julia and that she hoped nothing downright quarrelsome or embarrassing would happen. She passed Julia's silent door.

But when Julia at last emerged and came to look for her, no one else was evident. Though she had the air of having made love, Edie had no way of asking about it. Julia confided nothing and went off to eat, saying she would be back in an hour.

# 15. DIVERGENCE

 When Julia returned to the Mulligan house it was dark. Edie and Paul Fowler were waiting for her, and now it was she who stopped, in moonlight, where Jake Springland had stood in the afternoon sun, and she knew that something was about to happen this time, too. The same day. It wasn't over.

A taste of steak lingered in her mouth. Hamburger and coleslaw for lunch, steak, potatoes and tomatoes at night. She and Edie had given up cooking some time ago; the camaraderie over mutually planned menus was a game that could not interest Julia very long.

Edie, who had to stick to her little budget regardless, had gone on cooking; she and Paul went halves, when he was there; neat as a small animal cleaning up its daily portion of newspaper, she ate alone when he was not. The little wood-creature, Julia thought.

Now, the creature, immaculate, you could be sure, in low-heeled white pumps and clean cotton, waited in shadow and beside her rose the dark, intelligent but nondescript head of the boyfriend, whose purpose was to back her up. Only it would be a little more than that in it now, Julia thought. Backing up Edie would not satisfy Paul Fowler for long. They were going to turn into a chorus quoting self-evident truths both of them had held through the centuries. She felt her back straighten. It wasn't only Jake who got judged.

Julia thought for a minute that Edie was going to get up and come down the steps as she had done from time to time to retrieve a fallen book or save a bird, but this did not happen. Instead, as Julia reached somewhere about the fifth step up, Edie called to her.

"Hi," said Julia, pretending to notice for the first time.

"Can you sit down a minute?" said Paul, out of the shadows.

"What for?" Julia asked.

"Just a piece of news," Paul Fowler said, the first she knew that something had actually happened. He told her.

The Misses Mulligan, it seems, had noticed Jake Springland that afternoon. Not only noticed but identified him. He was that young man you saw in all the newspapers, mixed up with criminals. They were not interested in criminals, but they did not wish to be around them. They were made uneasy to think he might be a friend of Julia Garrett's. It was as though, all this time with them, she'd been wearing a false face. Where would it stop? They were scared now, those two old sisters.

"Dieu," said Julia. "What those two can sit there and know. They've got X-ray eyes. They can see through walls."

"They've got eyes like anybody else," Paul Fowler corrected her, coldly. "They keep them open, that's all."

"Well, so what?" said Julia.

"Just doing guesswork, we think Springland's in with a lot of pushers," Edie confided.

"There's something else you ought to know," said Paul Fowler. "The Misses Mulligan have a cousin on the police force. They hated to mention it. It didn't seem polite."

The young couple (as Julia sometimes ironically called them, mainly to herself) had bent their serious heads. Out from the swirling clouds of her own exalted day which should have ended with the quiet grace of consummation and a new beginning, she knew her experience was not of much consequence to either one of them. Who can judge me today? she wondered. Well, they could; they were doing it.

"Nobody ought to get killed," she murmured, "and nobody ought to be frightened. But I—"

Paul Fowler's intelligence snapped like a light in the deepening dusk. "You what?" he asked.

She turned aside, groped in her bag for a cigarette, lit it, and sat down on the steps, looking out. The two of them sat behind her, off to the side. It was more or less where she had sat reading in the afternoon before Jake appeared. So much had happened, time had got bigger to let it all in. Love had happened; time had stretched until it broke. She placed her hand against the post and the strong colliding texture, wood still warm from the sun, recalled the long afternoon, the man at one with the scent of himself, the rise and beat of desire. She stirred without meaning to; her body stirred in the rough rank ocean still present within her.

"I don't care who comes," she said without defiance, almost to herself. "I don't care who upsets the Misses Mulligan. We're all in the same world."

"But they care," said Paul Fowler.

"It was me that saved their garden," said Julia. "From you." She laughed. "Anyway, what else has ever happened to them? Anything this interesting in their whole lives?"

"We can't know that," said Edie, fairly.

"We can come pretty close to knowing it," said Julia. "However——"

"However, what?" Paul Fowler asked. He had the patience of a man who worked a step at a time through month-long laboratory experiments.

"I have to live," said Julia quietly. The night was shaggy with growth. In the night you felt the city wasn't there. It was a natural city. In the night it almost went back to nature. There could be snakes out in the yard, a loon on a tree branch, high up against the moon. "It's life that opens things, opens them up and changes——"

"Changes what?" Paul Fowler pursued.

"What there is."

"But life to you is all mixed up with what's offbeat, dangerous maybe," Edie interposed. "I'm just not like that, Julia."

"What she means is, you and the Mulligan sisters are not her problem," said Paul.

"She didn't say that," said Julia.

But Edie did not contradict him.

"You're taking her away," said Julia to Paul. Her heart, then, really did sink, almost to despair.

Little Edie whom she hardly noticed, whose equipment as to brothers and sisters and what she read and what she thought and where she shopped and ate were hardly worth taking mental notes on, represented something Julia hated to lose. She was going to lose it, she saw that, now that that damned Paul Fowler had taken a hand. He loved Edie, that was his only crime, of course. Loving her, he meant to protect her. There's something awful about him, Julia decided; he's out to defeat me. But not even this was true. To her, his imagination was deficient, but this was not awful; and though he did not like Julia he would not have disturbed her except for Edie. Julia was already missing the quiet early-morning footstep in the hall, going out to work, the long story about some professor's error in class—you didn't have to listen. Edie was the stout little mooring ring that kept the boat from drifting off into the swamp. I'll have to get a cat or something, Julia thought, unable to stay up there in stark loneliness yet pained to give up the place she had worked so hard to find. It had been perfect.

"Edie," she said, "don't go. I'll probably never see Jake Springland again. I promise I'll never see him here. I didn't ask him here anyway. You've got to believe that. He just came."

"It goes deeper than that," said Paul Fowler.

"Oh, to hell with you," said Julia. "You've been welcome here. Did I ever ask your opinion on marijuana before I let you sit down?"

"The trouble is, I've got worried," said Paul. "I'm like the Mulligan ladies. This town is filthy with crime."

"No more than anywhere else," said Julia. "It's more open, that's all." Then she added, quietly, "It's me you don't like," not turning her dark cropped compact head, but speaking once more to Paul. "It's me you think is dangerous. Not crime. Not New Orleans. It's me that scares you."

"That's how you see it, is it?" Paul asked at length. He was brainy, Julia had to recognize. And Edie was no slouch in the head, not at all, a rare little intellectual who had kept hold of her firm little country traditions. They'd be a great couple. They'll go a long way, Julia thought, without me.

"We could move somewhere else," Edie ventured. "Somewhere nice."

"I doubt that would work either," Paul said instantly, and that proved all she had said. He didn't like her, so she and Edie had to part.

Julia felt the sort of qualm only the young and brave can feel. It was a turning point.

"I have to live," she said, and set her face so straight into the moon, which had risen in silent magnificence at the foot of the garden, that she did not know when they left her.

## 16. MAURICE

 "Jake Springland?" said Isabel. She had started repeating it over and over, in different tones of voice. "Jake Springland!"

"Oh, she won't marry him. I don't guess she will." Maurice stepped up the pressure with delicate persistence. He did this, as Isabel knew, because he did not think they had a loophole for creeping out of it, for pretending she wasn't doing what she said she was doing, hadn't done what she said she had done. After three weeks of their not hearing a word, not being able to find her, thinking of going to the police, the letter had come. "You'll probably hear about it anyway, so I'd better tell you . . . I'm down in the Quarter to be near the man they said was mixed up in the murder case, though none of that was true . . . he's from the outside and didn't know how to stay out of things . . . but okay, he's okay . . . wish you could meet him but not now as we have to see how things work out. . . . I was never in love before, I now realize, but making things right for everybody is too much for me to think about . . . wish it wasn't. . . . Love you both, Julia."

All day Isabel strove, at times with real strength, to get it firmly in accord with her image of Julia that a defining thing like this had actually, finally occurred. She wandered in the house and garden and did something Maurice remembered her doing from long before, back in the thirties when she lost her chance at motherhood: she sat in the window-seat corner with her legs tucked up before her, arms encircling them. He recalled this to her, tenderly, having stayed home from work to be with

her. "You look as young now as then." "If age was all
I felt . . ." She could not finish, her voice broke, and his
had trembled. In the bright sunlight streaming through
the window they held together, merging, then parting
with lingering fingers, though even in parting, as Julia
had often observed, they still seemed together.

"To ruin herself!" Maurice kept saying.

"New Orleans can take in anything, I've always said
that."

"It's not New Orleans that's in question. It's the men
in it, singly and individually, a conservative bunch when
it comes to marrying, and you know that after this——"

"Someone from outside again?" Isabel was hopeful.

She was even beginning to identify a little; who
wouldn't have a romantic heart if a handsome young
bandit came along who also played a guitar and sang?
Yet in the same moment Isabel knew this wouldn't do:
Julia was not a romantic, only Isabel was, and thinking of
Julia it seemed that in the dappled thick of a still swamp,
something wild and beautifully marked and half-seen
shot by; the leaves flickered, slapping together, as she
passed, vanishing. From this moment, observing clearly
perhaps for the first time, certainly for the first time in
a final definitive way, the separateness of Julia as creature from herself as woman, Isabel knew that the worst
of the shock was over. Inevitably, something wild and
reasonless would be done by this strange child one day.
Stirring about the big house, morning-fresh, on chores
which healed her, she remembered once when Maurice's
father—she'd called him Dev like everyone else—had
gone into a rage over something in a note which had
been delivered to him by hand from the world outside.
Whatever it had said had driven him up into the attic
and there he had rampaged like a mad old elephant (she
had said to Maurice) hurling old furnishings about,
rummaging in crates, breaking them apart at the seams.
He had gone on for hours like this until she telephoned
Maurice at the office. "Well, it's all his stuff up there,"

said Maurice. His voice had a wry smile in it. "Unless he
sets the house on fire, just let him have it out." That was
before Julia. Dev had fallen asleep up there, or so she
always supposed, after it was over with. She had tiptoed
up the stifling narrow stair that led above, peering
through the keyhole, and seen him sprawled in a chair.
She would have believed him out with a heart attack,
except that he was snoring. In the afternoon before
Maurice's return, leading on far past dark and even into
days afterwards, Isabel had known a peace as profound
as dreams. Life with an animal that could rage and
rampage meant that she and Maurice were humanity
itself, often confused and blundering, but alive in a
human way. Had the fire-breathing presence of that old
man increased their love? She could suppose so. Then,
Julia . . .

She went to find Maurice.

"If she gets pregnant, what then?"

"I think they get an abortion. 'Get fixed up' is what
they call it."

"You can't believe she'd do it!"

"I can't believe," he said relentlessly, hard on them
both equally, "that there's anything she wouldn't do."

"Are you going to see her, talk to her?" Isabel thought
of such a journey with apprehension, as though Maurice
was going off on a safari in the jungle to find a venomous
specimen; she'd much rather Julia would tame herself
or get tamed somehow and return home. "Just write and
wait till she calls, or comes?"

"Christ," said Maurice, to the world in general.
"Every time we swallow it, it comes right back up."

"Maybe we're making things worse than they are,"
said Isabel. "Maybe he's a nice boy, certainly he had a
good face. He wanted to be a jazz musician. He had to
see life. He's found Julia and perhaps he loves her. We
think she's thrown something away. Maybe she's found
something."

Maurice rose from his study chair. Together that day

they had wandered through the house, room by room, talking it over. Separated, they went and found one another.

"Do you think she's thrown away everything?"

"I think she's thrown away us," said Maurice.

Isabel pondered. "I could ask them here some day, if it lasts between them. Maybe we could get to know him."

"Why would she refuse Martin Parham and take up with Jake Springland?"

"Love," said Isabel, in a brief, distant little monosyllable that made Maurice chuckle.

"We've that letter from Martin," said Isabel. "Maybe we ought to read it again."

"What'd it say?"

"He's coming back from France. He wants to see us."

"Still keeping in touch?" Maurice paused. A gleaming thought, slow as a shooting star, passed across their common sky. Devotion like Martin's just might pick her up again, once she'd finished with this foolish passion. There was still all that money. "Jesus," said Maurice, sighing, pleating between his knuckles the fine supple leather of his cheek and chin. "She'd given up her job with that doctor, long before this, apparently. Until last week she had a job with a life class."

"A *what*?" Isabel sat bolt upright.

"A life class. You know, artists. They pay fairly well for girls willing to sit there for an hour or so in their spare time."

"Nude, I suppose," said Isabel.

"It's possible. . . . I'm not sure."

"How did you know all this? Who told you?"

"Remember the Mulligan sisters, or did you ever know them?"

"Not those two . . .? Oh, years ago. My mother knew them. They went to her confessor, I think. The last people I'd imagine that Julia . . ."

"Me too, but just the same a Miss Louise Mulligan

called on me the other day. You remember the night I couldn't eat . . . you thought it was indigestion. I had to think about it all. This old maiden lady. Why, I bet she hasn't been into town in twenty years. She lost her way twice."

"What did she say?"

"Among other things that Julia has been living there. They let her and some girlfriend have the upstairs. Now she's out. They had to put her out. The reason is that Jake Springland came by the Mulligan house to see Julia the day he was acquitted. She next said that in his wake other hoodlums—that was her word, not mine—might well appear. None so far, but the ladies felt they weren't safe any more. Did you ever see the old Mulligan house . . .? I have but didn't make the connection. It's back in a forest of magnolias. I took Miss Louise home in a taxi and looked in. I can understand what Julia saw in it—it's nothing ordinary. A big old square garden gone to rack and ruin behind. Long broad drop of back steps. Something very profound about it. If I was there I'd stay drunk all the time."

"And they knew about the life class, or did somebody else come to see you?"

"Oh no, the Mulligans knew it all, even to her being our niece, though Julia may well have told them that. It seems there's a Mulligan on the city detectives. The old ladies can apparently get the goods on anybody they want to finger."

"I think our crime language is out of date."

"Undoubtedly. I sound like *Dragnet*, don't I? Sergeant Friday all over."

Isabel laughed till she cried, literally, then she kept on crying, gently, like persistent rain. She could stand it now, but sadness would set in. All her hopes. Her mother feeling for Julia. She found her little gold-rimmed glasses and when they streaked and dampened she would take them off and dry them on her handkerchief. The rest of the day she avoided Maurice. When he came into a room where she was, she turned her back and stood beside windows, touching the draperies and looking out. Maurice stayed on. He put records on, Brahms and Chopin, Mozart and Mendelssohn . . . all her favorites softly filled the house on Audubon Place. In this loss she was returning now to her other loss, the lost children, the blank night which had taken them forever. At dusk Maurice closed the shutters up and took Isabel in his arms. They dined late and elegantly, by candlelight in their most formal room. It was a day of great depth, another marking point in their love.

Thus they made their life—Maurice and Isabel—as Julia, wherever she was, well knew. Every event was channeled toward the main stream of themselves, in which they always moved together.

Nonetheless, Maurice Devigny went down to find her. Off past the French Quarter but near it, off Rampart Street, too far over near the Negro section for him to feel at ease, he got a boy to take up his card, the first engraved card to appear in that section, he could imagine, since the Spanish left, unless you counted funeral directors. A door opened three flights up. "Uncle Maurice!" He climbed. At two levels he saw her and at the third, up close. Her face was outlined in the doorway, like a canvas waiting to be framed. She had on slacks and sandals and a loose tunic in a harsh color.

"Julia . . . oh, Julia." He was panting a little from the steep climb. "Child," he said, "child."

Trying not to watch her, he just the same remarked the line of moisture at the corner of her eye. Would he always see that when he thought of her? The unframed portrait suddenly alive with tears, like a saint's miracle? Had he ever seen her cry before?

He came in and sat down, gingerly, where she indicated. She was the only person there. The furniture was cheap: iron rings with leg supports looped into chairs, a bed covered up to look like a couch, a chest of drawers that looked like a dormitory room in a third-rate school. He laid his cane across his legs. Why had he brought it along? Some idea that he might have to defend him- ·self, that was it. Literal, physical defense against some anonymous male who thought he had a better right to define Maurice Devigny than Maurice Devigny did. Or who at the least would be like a beast defending a lair. Instead she was alone, giving him a chair, offering him a Coke.

"Julia . . . It must be fun, living like this for a while. I came to let you know that. I thought you'd build up things about us, about how we feel and so on." For a lawyer, he got it out badly, but maybe this only made it sound more sincere.

"Jake isn't here . . . he's practicing, down over in Gentilly. They wouldn't let him in with the Jolly Bunch any more after the trial—that was the group he'd played with. He'd told them he was part Negro, but then it was something about how he'd come up against the police, right out in the open. They just said they'd found a replacement and not to come any more."

Maurice was silent.

"So anyway," Julia said, bitter and witty and wry, "at least you can know he's all white."

"Julia, why did you say that? Why?"

"Oh, I know, I know. I hurt you. And why have I done this to you? That's next, Uncle Maurice. Isn't it?"

"I haven't reproached you. I came here to say I under- stand. I understand, that is, as far as you'll let me. I came here to say we care, Isabel and I. We'll never stop caring. There won't be any way to."

She groped her hand to his, touched and held. It would seem the world would reorder itself out of that grasp which had begun awkwardly—her left hand toward his right—but spread quickly into firmness. He had called her child, but she was not one, maybe she had never been: she did not throw her arms around his neck One throb of life was what they shared, then it faded

He remembered her mystery and the old man, Dev, shadowlike, not only stirred in his grave but was threatening to rise from the tomb. And she remembered him and Isabel, always at the heart of things, a love continually consuming itself. "I believe you." Their hands dropped apart.

She tucked a foot beneath her and reached in a painted wooden box for a cigarette. The cigarette suddenly loomed as large in Maurice's eyes as if it was printed on a billboard. I won't ask, he vowed. I won't even think about it.

"It's just a Kent," said Julia, with her half-smile. "Have one."

And there before his eyes, she was back, at one with Dev—a threat, a mocker, and an enemy, but what his life knew itself by.

"Will you still come to dinner? Sometime? Anytime? Drop in? Or we'll go out if you like. Jake—why can't we just privately get to know him?"

"Not in that house you won't. Don't kid me, Uncle Maurice. First thing I know you'll have just privately and quietly arranged to get him a good position with an oil company down south of here and pretty soon not a restaurant or a dive in the city will have him playing there! It's why you didn't let me know you were coming down here. Uncle Maurice—you knew I knew . . . how you were."

But she'd trailed off. The quiet sensuous throaty voice now sure of its strength cut across her young wild complaining. "I've done none of that and you know it."

A long silence came between them. "Sorry," she said at last, putting out the cigarette, getting restlessly to her feet. She stood at a window, looking down on he did not care to know what.

"He can't come to that house. You know that."

"You don't want it so he can. And you know that. Anyone who could come there wouldn't interest you."

"As bad as that, am I?"

"Not deliberately," he muttered, considering her feelings if it killed him. "Instinct, it's your instinct."

"But that's bad, too, you mean—all bad."

They fell into what seemed an unbreakable depression, a silence like still New Orleans heat, the kind there was no way to end, as far as Maurice could see, though he twice drew breath and twice said nothing.

"You didn't deserve me," Julia at last volunteered. The room seemed alchemized and Maurice felt the bad spell break. It was perhaps what he had come for, though not all, and for what would follow, he lingered, not asking for it, not knowing really what it was, but counting on her to come up with it. And she did. "I'm not your fault, you know," she said.

His relief was sheer blessing. Now, gallantly, he could rise, draw her face to his, kiss her on either cheek.

"Nothing that's you is all bad. You know I don't go that far, Julia. And never will, dearest child."

She did not come to the door but rose and stood back as he went away. She was once more, to him, the portrait unframed, propped against the wall.

# 17. ISABEL

 And what right did she have . . . I have my memories and know how I felt and that my intentions toward her were nothing but tender and loving and how can she scorn us by choosing to live like that, in a place like that with no taste, if she got anything from me, anything at all? And I know what my motives were, and the example I set, dress and food and taste in things, and my style of doing. Could anything be better? Mistakes at first, but she came after those were made. She came when it was all perfected, ready for her like a palace prepared for a princess. So what was wrong? What could have been wrong? How could any crazy idea get hold of her unless it's love for this boy, that great force, except that she's played with it before, been too off-again on-again, while I—I knew, I knew at once and always, and my nature worked with it, not against. And as for experimenting, tearing what's the most beautiful, the best, to see what's to be fitted up for new pleasure . . . well, boys tear wings off butterflies, and she's the female version as far as I can see, and yet it was her love I wanted, child-love of me, returning motherliness. How little I was permitted, for they got together, she and Dev, like conspirators, from the first moment of entering. . . .

Here Isabel, alone and wondering, wandering her lovely rooms in the morning, cool-warm and green-flowering at the windows, remembered the wild crashing from the attic, her sense that the house itself, solid, three-story, almost vast, was totally endangered. The

memory brought its own sound effects and she clapped
hands to her ears. By him the child had been snatched
from her arms before it grew firmly fixed there. Against
him what had she really done to stop it? Treated him as
a convenience for minding Julia when she wanted
evenings out with Maurice, pretending that even though
something was going on she did not know what it was,
pretending that only with her and Maurice could life
discover passion. . . . And so, cats away, the mice
played, happy and spiteful, inventing revenge.

And so it all went back to that.

And now.

And now.

And now.

# 18. THE SEARCHER

*Who's got the heart to mind the time*
*When the wine's nearly finished and*
*The evening's gone . . .*

 It was good, thought Julia, repeating it to herself, but not good enough. Look deeper, she would think, getting it through to him as he gnawed a pencil, pondering. "Remember the scent of hair, dark hair; that would make another song." She'd got this out of what he'd told her in the dark about herself, and there lingering in the back of her mind was the Baudelaire old Dev had liked to read. "Too poetic," Jake would object, but just the same would fling aside the pencil and pick up anything to make music on, a child's guitar bought in a toy shop, which was nothing to stumble over at least and once tightened and tuned could make an adequate basic sound. Anything she said would get in his thoughts, he had to admit to her; her ideas would show up days later maybe, appearing on his path; then he would move up to them, begin to shape them for himself. Anything she put in his head took life there, she could see it happen, see the way he couldn't shake off what she was able to start his mind running on. Then she saw him begin to get it, to discover new lines of thought, gentle and romantic at the start, like flowers, but with their roots gone deep in flesh and blood. His moving up to her actual self was surer, not reluctant—he could turn and lift, adjust, and form whatever he fancied, arrive on a strong wing wherever desire demanded that he go. He'd pretend she was

French and speak phrases he'd picked up in college or different places, and phrases in the poetry she showed him. "La chevelure," he'd make her repeat, mimicking with his mouth the motion of her own, his even teeth white and moving with the word's rhythm and the tongue just lifting behind them. "Is that right? Is that right? Now une autre fois, once again . . ." But the word would turn to kissing, they would tear it straight apart between them as his fingers plunged deep into her mat of rich hair. Any word would do, in those days, it seemed, but the French ones were the best for taking words away altogether. Her voice would fade and vanish before his increasing desire like a tide shuddering back only to find strength elsewhere; she came back to him voiceless but with a natural beat of rhythm, harsh and swift. Anytime, thought Julia, it being a great part of her pride to be there for him, never to fail. "Just anytime," she'd say, when she could say anything again.

Then he'd try to write it. . . .

> *Hair beneath my fingers brings to me*
> *From seas I never saw,*
> *Lands I never dream to come to. . . .*

"Oh, good, oh, good, you're getting there!"

"I want to talk a show, play the background but talk the words, that's a sort of music. Not any sadness in it, though."

"Nor sentimental either—just straight, just saying it."

"That's what I mean. I'll make French names, then say the songs in English."

"That won't go down here. There's no real French here, just a feeling maybe."

"Won't I get the feeling that way then?"

"I don't know."

What he strove to get hold of was something for this time and this time alone, also by coincidence their time. In their search he saw them joined mysteriously with thousands like them, couples who'd got together, didn't care for the go-ahead world, wanting to find the underlying beat, the true pulse of things. Tall, Jake lounged in the window, looking down on laundry lines, a washtub full of green plants, a hydrant dripping, rust stains spread on the paving. As a searcher must, he looked at every face he passed in the street, for any one might have the secret, feel the connecting force, the tie that bound.

But until his songs came on full and sure as she did, he told her, in a languid hour, as serious as he'd ever be, then he was content to find groups to play background with—the banjo, clownlike though it might be, was good enough. For he knew he wasn't expert enough to get with the best. And not well-known enough to go it on his own. The non-Negro part, that made it harder still. White bands talked cold; he preferred the Negro players, they were keeping something ancient, good, and mainly voiceless still alive.

Thus Jake's struggle, cross-grained with the time, the fifties. But not against the grain of those who like himself were trying to find it, whatever it was, to get hold, take hold, of that good, tender, human
WHAT?
A big question.
Julia had been brought totally to life by him. She thought of it, in her own terms, not as a search but a find. Call it miracle, discovery, or chemical accident, or say some stranger had picked her up by the heels and pitched her into the sea and she never wanted land again. So she did not really care if his search went on forever.

# 19.  CUL-DE-SAC

Around New Orleans, around the Quarter, especially after dark and into the small hours, they got to be well known. Bartenders talked to them, and late night entertainers adjourned with them at dawn into the French Market or some early morning coffee place. They slept through every morning, rousing only in the afternoon. Daily they stirred up the pot of song lyrics. She went to get more poetry books out of the library. Some of those phrases, warm or wild or sensuous, too long mouldering in classrooms, returned now by this strange route to the sort of place that had first inspired them. She went with Jake to the all-night sessions, hearing him play in groups sometimes—banjo or bass—sometimes seeing him alone with his guitar, spotlight on his long serious face, speaking out words he and she had put together. She sat on sawdust floors or tucked herself away in corners, getting high at times on what she might be handed to smoke, not questioning.

(And why do that, flirting with danger, addiction, damage to a good and lively brain, needing neither the shock-chill nor the slow disintegrating music of oblivion? Why do it? It was in the path, that was all. The world was peopled already with those who turned around and went back.)

She stood waiting in doorways for Jake while a pack of bodies squeezed past. He would catch her arm. The dark corner would be out there before them to turn, and they would turn it, like having wheels under them.

They ransacked the city in search of the extraordinary,

whatever might bring true meanings in. One evening found them, for instance, at a snake ceremony where a boa constrictor, having been called upon willingly to swallow a live guinea pig, was accidentally killed in the attempt, for whoever was responsible for drawing the guinea pig's teeth out had forgotten to do it and the snake was destroyed from within. A funeral for the snake was announced, but Julia had become sick by this time and was outside getting some fresh air. Undaunted, Jake got them both admitted to the new church of a Negro sect which sang and danced a ritual cry for the Lord's help. They were not angels, it was explained "for the benefit of white friends," but were dressed with wings to be as birds, someday to be gloriously transformed. Jake said the only soul they needed was in the music. Julia suggested they do it right and find some real voodoo, she was getting tired of all this exploring and decided she would have to live another kind of life, a resolution that must have lasted for an hour or so.

Julia had once gone to a fortune teller regularly, and believed, but that had been decorous and quiet—cards falling softly on a cloth-covered table, colors mottled on paper, iron filings with a magnet waved thrice across them, lines in her palms. (The woman—clean and light-colored and cordial—once said, "You done caught the flu, honey," not as revelation but to sympathize with plain fact.)

Julia when alone often found herself telling herself that Jake was not a great performer and never would be. What she loved about him: he was hard and honest, tough on himself; he knew it too and didn't let it matter. His idea was to get right with things. Not to be found in the wrong combinations. He must have had a religious streak, too, she reasoned, for he'd come out with it that every day was Judgment Day, so you had to be careful. His music was a way of going with the right things. He might wind up in jail, but wouldn't be caught dead at a cocktail party being nice to nice people. He didn't believe in nice people. He wanted to meet her aunt and uncle no more than they wanted to meet him. (He assumed they never wanted to meet him.) Beliefs were what he had, and they were what gave his songs their character when he talked them into the blue light where the smoke went coiling, eddying, rising; they also gave force to his loving and suspended her doubts about him, about his not having what it took to get to some big-time success. Suppose he didn't have it, she would silently argue; so what?

How could she afford to mind, knowing that whenever he got up from a chair, walked away in a street, turned in a window, or drew her urgently toward him in the night, nothing faulted the easy accuracy of his motion, nothing struck off center, or failed to carry her deeply along. Did it matter if he couldn't carry the world with him, too? She could not answer. Her pretty linen dresses were all past tense; she went in slacks and sandals, feeling right and thin. But sometimes too she felt singular to the point of being waiflike, as though she'd moved to a distant city and had no society in the world of other women, and this put her alone with a circle drawn round her, melancholy. Jake remarked the look and said he liked it; he explained it to her well enough—it was the dark side of their moon. But where was the money coming from? It came from somewhere, for they lived. Sometimes from Uncle Maurice; he would put a small check in the mail.

At times the spell Jake and Julia cast over each other fell upon them with such intensity—like a panther leaping from a tree—that they were lost in the hot tussle, buried in the warm, seething tide for days on end. To Julia it would seem that her hands turned to furry paws, her flesh became the leaves and branch of every vine; they both turned contentedly in the noose cast about them, let it tighten to the ultimate without any outcry except of joy. Separate they did not part; the air breathed with them; crowds thickened to tease their meeting again, or opened like an obliging sea to hasten it. Somebody had painted a picture full of banana fronds which they hung above the bed; somebody else had dug up an Indian relic from Bay St. Louis; they placed that on the chest of drawers which Maurice Devigny had found painful to look at. Julia bought a rug. "Looks like home," said Jake, "better stop before it's too late." "Home's where you leave from," said Julia, calming his fears. How not to care that there had been other lives, the ones she'd walked out on? Martin Parham, Edie, the Misses Mulligan, Uncle Maurice and Aunt Isabel? She lay down on the rug, arms flung wide and ankle crossed on one bent knee, staring at the ceiling. She lay on the rug as on a pelt in a cave. If he wasn't going to be great, only mediocre, there could be a kind of purity in that, too, was how he looked at it, she knew; so why was the dose a bitter one for her, and why was it daily, this getting down of the bitter dose? Was it love trying to stay motionless, all the while the world moved? Was this always the anguish of lovers, no matter who or where, that the world won't stop and it won't go away?

Marnie!

"Marnie!"

Jake cried it out one night, out of a nightmare, slamming his hand into the wall. He was so under the nightmare spell that he had to get up, douse his head in cold water, turn on the light, open a beer.

"Marnie's dead," Julia kept repeating.

"Not when I dreamed him," Jake replied, but wouldn't tell his dream. He sat at the table, drinking beer and talking. "We were down at Grand Ile that summer before I met you, and Wilma hadn't started getting fat. Ted was always skinny as a rail but he went around clean, in faded cotton trousers, spouting quotations out of books, and she was a little admirer, hung on his every word. Once I went way out in the Gulf to swim, you had to go out a long way to get any depth, and I came wading back, and they were on the front steps of the beach cabin together sitting side by side, watching me. There'd been a sunset and everything was still and I felt holy, I felt a blessing on us all. I believed then that Marnie was a holy man and that he was succeeding in what he called his one ambition: to make his grace-gift, as he called it, real, to share it. At supper, he said, 'I know what you were thinking when you came up out of the water. It's been your baptism day, going out like that.' I lived three days, maybe more, in such a state— I never was so happy, or so quiet. It couldn't have been a fake, could it?"

"I don't know," said Julia.

"But if it wasn't," he went on, "why did it go away? It was real while it lasted. Then, the week after, she started gaining weight. It was like somebody being blown up with an air pump at the filling station, ten pounds a day, more or less. And she got lazy. Everything was clean there one week, filthy the next. I caught the bus one day, just wrote a note and left. It was fall before they found me again. 'Why bother me?' I asked Ted, but he said, 'Don't you want it back?' and it was the grace-state he meant, only now everything was changed. He had started smoking—speed, hash—anything, just to make it happen, short-cuts to grace, even getting hit with hard stuff for all I know. And he'd worked in with the crowd that can get all that, the same as a lot of people will, finding ways of not having to pay for it. I think it was that crowd that killed him for something he failed them about. I don't think Wilma did it, but how can I know?"

That was before Nashville.

Nashville was where they said Jake ought to go. New Orleans was no good for songs. He had built up a small audience which followed him from the restaurant where he'd got his first spot, to the Vieux Carré hotel bar, to the back room at the all-night bar on Dumaine Street, to the post-girlie-show session at the night club on Canal. Through an old acquaintance of Julia's, left over from her Tulane days and now in the record business, an LP was styled and cut but still to be released. The radio contract, long-promised, halted; the TV stations had administrative headaches and hangovers from some unfortunate gambles of the last season. It was while they were waiting to hear from everybody about everything that Jake decided to take a chance on Nashville. Because everybody said that New Orleans had a cult for Dixieland with some blues, but singers, unless they were names already, didn't get far. He'd only to wail those songs a little more, put rhymes in, and twang a bit; then Nashville might be able to place him. So a friend made the phone call and he got himself ready to go, in a rented beige suit that didn't fit too well and brown shoes he'd had as long ago as when he'd first come back that day in the ophthalmologist's office to find Julia, and the same shirt and tie of that vanished afternoon.

Before he left he talked with her, walking, holding her hand. "If I know I can't be good enough, then I'll just decide to get a job and do it on the side. Some of the best ones down here have sort of halfway made it that way in the bands, for years on end. You don't have to be a name player to get by in terms they like best."

"I know," she nodded. Then she said, "It's funny how often 'making it' has got into things."

He walked on silent. Finally he said, "It's the first time I remember saying it, though."

She did not answer.

Jake had a friend, the one who had made the phone call to Nashville. His name was Abe Purdy. He came on strong as a knowledgeable guy around the entertainment world, a smart talker with a florid face. Jake and Julia knew him for what he was. His wife, a redhead, frequently left him. Then there were the Carters, Bill and Joan, who had two babies and wanted others, they liked having them so. Bill was a professional Southerner who was always being funny about Yankees, how they'd won

the war but lost the country, the country had a Southern
heart or none at all, etc. Jake tuned out on the talk, he
said. But theirs were the only parties he'd go to, and the
Purdys came as well, to a third-story shambles of a
place, halfway up Conti Street.

When Jake got back from Nashville he and Julia
met Abe Purdy alone out on Carrollton Avenue at a
beer place and talked all afternoon. The men talked, at
least; she said nothing. Jake's ego had taken a beating up there; he was doing the kind of talk and the
kind of drinking that followed on the heels of it, smoking with a cigarette like a plucked berry between
his fingers. The people up there were commercializ-
ing too heavily on the country sound they'd inherited by
nature; simple as rain, rich as Croesus, they could treat
you any way. They didn't want innovation, had a personal grudge against New Orleans, were determined to
put it down . . . the bastard had had the nerve to wear
high-heeled boots and a ten-gallon white hat. . . . Jake
had said, Where you think this is, Texas, for God's sake?
. . . What's it to you, son? the man had answered. . . .

Julia went outside, into the quiet spring sunlight.
So it had been a year since the trial last spring. There was
a Negro woman making crosses from green fronds for
Palm Sunday. That was day after tomorrow and you
could buy them off the street for luck as well as get them
in church. (They were stolen off palms in ladies' front
yards, usually.) Julia bought one for want of something
to do, then she said, "Will you be there for a while?"
"How come?" the woman said, not looking up. "Because
I'm inside and I can do some for you and come back
after a while." The woman said nothing, but silently
handed her a handful of fronds. Then she walked to the
corner and got a paper. On the way back she picked up a
clear jewel, the set out of a ring, in the dust, and then
she went in the dark bar and sat at the table while the
two men drank and talked, fashioning crosses from the
fronds, still green and tender, for Palm Sunday, and

glancing at the paper. When they got ready to go they were both loaded, she knew, so she set the jewel down in front of them. "What's that?" said Jake. "I don't know, I found it," she said, and he and Abe both looked at it without surprise. "It's fake," said Abe. "Yeah, just glass," said Jake. They paid and went on, waiting while she gave the plaited fronds to the Negro woman; they never asked her what she was doing with them or why. She put the jewel she had found in her bag. They parted with Abe at his car and took the streetcar back to the Quarter, riding silently. The day was warm, but she felt a sort of half-inch insulating coldness surrounding her, and wondered if she was catching cold, or merely giving off some sort of aura from having touched the palms soon to be blessed and got a glow on the skin like a saint. Then she knew what it was: a solstice in the "We"—a seasonal change in Jake and Julia.

Riding the streetcar, he took her hand and glanced down at her face. "Are you all right?" he asked.

"Sure I am. I'm all right."

He'd never asked her that before, not in a brotherly, solicitous way, on a streetcar, and it scared her.

"Why?" she asked him.

"You look pale."

"Pale," she echoed, knowing that was more of the same, and she was more scared than ever. "Get that tone out of it," she told him, but she hit off center with him.

"What tone?" he asked her.

"Christ," she said, pulling the bellcord. She got off the streetcar and left him, not returning to their rooms until night. When she did: "Are you all right?" he asked her, and she sat down on the edge of the bed. "I'm fine," she said, "just fine," and knew all she could do was pray for it to end.

What she called it to herself was the Charade. A Charade in human relationships is a mask over what is really going on. The mask is a false thing, but for some reason is temporarily preferred and clung to by the

person or persons playing the Charade. So then, Julia
recognized, you have the Charade conversations, which
go through the dead motion, covering over the real game
which is the illusion you have picked to live on, feed on,
which can't be exposed to light of day unless totally
believed in or it will crumble away to nothing. Jake's
real game was finally revealed to her. He revealed it
only after it lost the danger of vanishing, only after the
inner eye of his imagination had fixed and developed it
firmly and set it up on his private shelf as the one image
of the truth. It went like this: he wasn't getting anywhere because Julia was inadvertently destroying him.
It was their love, the great necessity of it that had sprung
up like a jungle between him and any career he was
meant for. He was boxed in by it. He had gone up to
Nashville, a real come-down even to decide to do it.
There, worst of all, nobody had wanted him. He'd been
insulted, talked down to. "New Orleans, where's that?"
some bastard in an office had said as he left. The one
audition he'd been able to swing ended before he got
through, cut off and no protest possible. He nagged at
Julia, drinking, all one afternoon. They went out to eat
and on returning he launched into her again, but this
time he had struck the real passion of it. Her fault! His
belief had been full sized before she'd known it even
existed. She was screaming back at him before she knew
it. It was one side of the room and then the other and
then, turning suddenly cold-hearted, even venomous,
she picked up her purse and walked to the door. I'll stay
in a hotel somewhere, she thought, but her hand was
hardly at the doorknob before he'd spun her around. He
forced her back and onto the bed, knotting his hand in
a fistful of hair, forcing her mouth open with his own.
She bit like a savage and got what turned out to be a
black eye. Half-stunned, she felt him prying her apart.
She clamped her knees tight and there was terror in her
now, but when he actually touched her it was like every

other time, she couldn't help it, oh, God she couldn't, how could she ever help it?

He could make her give up everything to him but the thing that mattered most—and that was the knowledge that he knew she had, no matter what illusion he decided to believe in, that he wasn't great, that he wasn't going to get where he wanted to go. He could arrive every other way but not the way that mattered to him most. And she finally gave up and took it, the full storm. This time she couldn't claim even to like it and when it was over she felt half-dead.

Daylight found her dressed and him sleeping. "You look nice," he said, open and fresh and innocent, waking without memory. His eye fell on the bag in her hand. "Where you going?"

"I'm keeping you from your life," she said. "I'm going to leave you."

He thought about it, pulling up naked on one elbow, the sheet slipping back. "Let's talk about it."

It was spring again. They had lived together a whole year. At some point, about a month before, he'd bought a second-hand car, to use on weekends, and getting it from where he had it parked, he now drove her out on the levee, outside the city, and held her tenderly. They both cried, and even in this they were together.

He was talking, his lips moving against her hair. Over his shoulder, she watched the barges go by in the sluggish current below, a ferry shrinking in size as it neared the river's great central thrust of current, a Negro tying up a skiff at a willow-lined inlet.

Julia felt smaller than she had a year before, and much less significant. In all the offbeat things she'd taken up with (people too) she'd imagined a purity of intention in herself which had been shared by whatever she'd been drawn to, else why would the attraction have existed at all? She knew now—it was written in her own aching flesh and bones—that any purity in herself was as tiny as the glint of a silver dime in a mountain of trash. And this went for Jake as well, and all the other things and people, people and things. So why did she think herself so special any more? Except for the *cum laude* degree at Tulane which only meant, she guessed, to ninety-nine point nine percent of the world's population that she should have known better. Would they be right or not? She did, at least, believe still in her own reality, that silver glint among the trash and rubble, the carnage and the gore. She recalled now that Aunt Isabel had written to her that Martin Parham had tried to find her; he had gone to the Devigny house and talked about her, but they hadn't told him where to look. Did she want to see him? She hadn't answered. Something about them had turned her numb. Maybe it was shame. . . .

She was staring at the river and all at once it seemed filled with people, with the numberless heads of all the multitudes of the earth, pouring out of the distance and sliding past on the mile-wide stream. At the beginning no single head was distinguishable from another, then separate heads began to appear, even features grew distinct and the color of hair, and age, young to very old, and men's distinguishable from women's faces, though some of both were clutching children, holding them up above the current. Some people were holding to one another, out of desperation or love, then all would vanish, some turning clockwise with the current while others came on and others, inexhaustibly.

"But I still think of it," Jake was saying, "and I guess I'm going to always believe in it a little bit. I think I see it, that all at once I've turned a corner and there's Canal Street with thousands packed into it, and all Mardi Gras is coming, me included, high on a big float, coming on and going past, and I'm playing with the rest, and they see me there, and then I think no, that's not all either, I'm really just in the band but playing along and I know it's good, it's got to be because the room is still and now they're with me, stamping and shouting, so it's bound to be good and it is and then it stops. But now that's going, going away. . . . They're shouting and clapping, the thrill comes up—and it's great. A wave of thrill. It's got to carry me on, on to somewhere, on to forever. But it fades, and I'm back where I was. All I could do was sit and watch it go, like sand sliding through an hourglass."

"Wouldn't it come back?"

"If only it had ever happened, then it might have a chance to come back." He shrugged.

"Life is where love is," said Julia, "that's what I thought you might have thought."

"I did think it till I saw. Love is a robber. It takes the true card out of the deck." He turned, righting her face toward his own. "I do love you. I don't want to go. It isn't a case of love or not love, of want or not want. It's a case of its being time. Time to go. I hope you get it, don't think it's been a put-on."

"You faked after Nashville," she said.

"I know that now."

"And took it out on me."

Their gaze stood pitiless with honesty each to the other. Faking was the worst, they always said it; faking was the real hell.

"Maybe. Except I always wondered—"

"Wondered what?"

"Wasn't it all a fake with you, all the time? Didn't you always know that a guitar player was beneath you? Weren't you always just along for the ride?"

"That first day was real, and the day that started in the Monteleone, that was real, the night of the murder, that was real, and the time after the trial, that was real . . . and on and on with times. Where's the fake in all that? Tell me!"

She was crying her truth out at him and he couldn't answer. One page in their book of total honesty she had left unturned. It said that he couldn't be, he couldn't become, what he had wanted to be, that good singer, that fine player, who didn't care about being great, but was anyway, out of natural excellence. None besides Julia knew that his silences all meant that he wanted to be seen that way.

Relentlessy, he turned the page. "If I'm just mediocre and you're due for first rate, it's time we admitted it."

She didn't agree with him because she came from Audubon Place, and that was what had made him say in the first place that she was just along for the ride. The impasse was complete.

In pain and outrage, she flung open the car door, jumped out and ran a way down the levee, only slowly to return and get back in.

The next day at the bus station, he kissed the black eye which was still crying. Would he be back? He didn't say. She didn't ask.

# 20. REMAINS

What had it all meant? Julia went around all afternoon after the train left, all through the French Quarter and elsewhere, trying to find somebody who knew and would tell her, and in the late afternoon she went to the hospital, to the out-patient clinic. Her shoulder had kept hurting, so much that she couldn't sleep and she thought something might have got broken. Sprained, they told her; that was all. The doctor who strapped her into place discovered in the course of his interview that she was talking in the detached and non-consecutive manner of the addict or the psychopath.

"You need somebody," he said. "Is there anybody I can call?"

"Call," Julia echoed, seeing again the sluggish stream of all humanity. You can call, she thought, but how can you get their attention?

"For instance," he said, "who was beating you? Don't tell me you ran into the door and then slipped in the bathtub? Is he sober now? Has he come out of it?"

"He's gone," she said. "A jazz musician."

"Then he can't be far."

"A Yankee. Gone back home, I guess. Can you beat it? A Yankee playing jazz?"

"Don't you have any family? Don't you have anybody else?"

She looked out the window. It was turning summer, full and fabulous. The great leaves of New Orleans were a rich green. Tommy Arnold, she thought, the first time in months. Nothing shocks him. At the idea of shock, which had not occurred to her before, and the thought of someone she had known a year ago, she looked at her face in the mirror, a white-painted frame mounting her face like a portrait. It was a picture she had just as soon not have seen. Something had been smashed. Not just the eye. What can anybody do to anybody? she had asked herself in passing, a year back. Especially in love? Well, there before her was the answer. Whatever can be done had been done, but still she did not know quite what it was (leaving out the black eye) or why it was even important. What's so important about me? she wondered, and saw again the slow progress of the river teeming with humanity thicker than a million schools of catfish. What was so important about any one of them? As this returned vision floated by once more between herself and the good square face of the doctor, she thought she saw a signal from out the throng—an arm lifted in its swift progress, a shouting face. A signal to her? Undoubtedly. Had it happened the first time she saw the vision? Had it?

"You're hallucinating now, aren't you?" the doctor asked, for the third time. Next he'd ask her what she was "on"; maybe he already had.

"I'm finished with it," she said, ambiguously, but suddenly turning into her old self—the Julia Garrett who had shown up in front of Tommy Arnold at the Squiremeister party. "It was all just like something for a change, you know. All my time with him. An adventure. Anyway, he's gone."

"Who's gone?"

"The man, of course. Not that I wasn't involved. I really was. It's the honest truth," she added, and that remark went back to Martin Parham's sister, up in Mississippi, who always used to be saying something was "the honest truth."

The doctor did not laugh. "What did he do?"

"He wanted to be a musician—a good one. In jazz, guitar. Not so much to be great, but be really good, be right, you know. Then all of a sudden, he couldn't. He thought our feelings did all the wrong things. Thought I drained him, I guess."

"Did you?"

"Who knows?"

"The red lamp at the parties," the young doctor said. "The sessions, the songs, the crazy sex——"

"The sex wasn't crazy," she said quickly, snapping back even more. At least she could say that. "Ours wasn't. It was straight—and good."

"It's going to be hard not to go back," the doctor suggested.

"To that sort of life, you mean?" she asked. "I don't mind finding a different life. I guess I have to now he's gone. Of course I can recover. I don't think I was even born a virgin."

He grinned without wanting to. "I'm going to put you on the out-patient list. Lay off everything, even sherry. Come back in a week."

Sherry, thought Julia. She remembered the Misses Mulligan. Probably they kept some.

"Write it down for me, the date and time," Julia said. "Write down your name for me, too. I'll forget."

"Call me before if you need to. For pain take Anacin. You ought to go to somebody, you know. Some friend, or family. You must have family, haven't you?"

"Family . . . now?"

"Friends?"

"Well, there's . . ."

"Somebody sympathetic. A couple . . . a girlfriend."

"Yes, that's right. . . ."

She walked straighter when she left, feeling the tug of pain in her injured shoulder, but also feeling the sureness of the bandages that held it in place, along with the memory of the strong impersonal hands that had bound it, the way she hadn't said it hurt or anything. A good job done well . . . it was something to count on, a little step in the responsible sort of life which was now, she thought, to lie before her, a plank over the Grand Canyon.

But who was she going to? She turned into St. Charles Avenue. The street car trundled by, under the thick shade All along she had thought of Tommy Arnold; he had un derstood her, liked her, they could have a good talk in a drugstore. He would laugh about the sherry . . . she liked to make him laugh. But she kept walking, away from downtown.

There was Edie, planning to marry Paul in June. She had fascinated Edie. Country mouse and city mouse. But now what did they have to say? And Paul would have his snide triumph, seeing her down on her luck.

She discovered her direction by noticing where she was going. Audubon Place. Uncle Maurice and Aunt Isabel. What am I? Oh, what am I? They had a ready answer. A female prodigal. (They'd be too nice to mention it.) What could we talk about? Well, something would get said . . . they're good at that. But they'd seen Martin Parham of the good lost days, oh yes. And so the slow dance toward matrimony would be ready to com mence again. She stopped dead. Her blood surged up, alive and quick, insisting on its right to remember. Wild-wet, strong and avid, a mouth pressed against her own. Her hands clenched up. An arm struck across her, rough-tender, tender-rough—all the good times before the last. He was gone now, gone for good. Because he was not a New Orleans name player—how could somebody from Ohio ever be one? He must have been crazy. What will he do? Vacuum cleaners, she thought, through raging blood. It's what his father did. She could have hurled every one ever made into the Mississippi River.

She turned away from Audubon Place where all her passion would have got smoothed over like a wrecked playhouse in the sand. What would they care about mine when all they really care about is their own?

She walked toward town.

Small and dark, hair trimmed in angular lines around her irregular features, her legs thin and straight, one shoulder hunched with bandages under her copper-colored tunic, gray skirt, pointed shoes, dark glasses over the livid eye, she looked like everybody in an age when everybody looked like nobody. She was one of that silent flood she had thought she was merely regarding, and there was no use signaling to her. Maybe she had signaled to herself.

Nearer downtown, past Lafayette Square, traffic thickened and brown skin mixed with white. She looked at the grimy shaft that supported the great patriot, the hero of America and France.

A fresh spirit had been hers the day of the Squiremeister party. It had dressed in pale green linen with a bright scarf, like a bloom on the new-grown stalk, and had drawn Tommy Arnold out of his drunkenness to delight in her. He had compared her to a deer wandering into a city by starlight. She walked twice around Lafayette Square.

She had to get a job. Jake Springland had left her a little over three hundred dollars. Better than leaving her bills, though it might later appear that he had done that too. He had at least turned the car back for what he owed on it.

She returned to the old apartment. There was the two-century-old battered remains of a courtyard, what would have been called a patio if they had been able to live in a more fashionable district. As she turned into the street she saw someone come out of their entrance, a woman who leaned for a moment against the doorframe, glanced two ways, then walked away. Julia could have sworn it was Wilma Wharton. Looking for what? She didn't know but felt afraid. She remembered the garishly tipped nails, groping in the greasy knapsack of a handbag. "No, I never had anything to do with her," Jake Springland had said. "Never laid her, even back when she looked good—and didn't smell. You think I wanted to? She wasn't my type. Anyway, she and Marnie were about as shacked up as you could get." Julia had listened, barefoot in a cotton shift, standing at the window, morning wind against her arms and throat. Clean and fresh, in and out. It had been a good time.

Now, as beat and broken under the hot day as a garden after a hailstorm, she crossed the courtyard and climbed the stair as usual, groping for her key. Sweat dampened the sockets of her eyes and she was damp between her legs with the iron-smelling damp of menstruation. That, too. Once she glanced back—if it was Wilma Wharton, if she'd seen her . . . if she was following now. Julia knew by now what could happen, the touch with the razor that didn't sting even after the blood rose.

"Did you do it?" she had asked Jake. "Did you and that woman kill him? Tell me . . . tell me . . . tell me." And when he said, "No," I had to believe him . . . I had to believe him. But did I really?

Her body ached from the blows of his hands, the wild pounding of his sex. She put her key in the lock.

It was a place of departure, empty, that opened before her, no longer a home. She went inside and looked around. The fight had torn everything upside down. The banana painting had fallen, a chair was turned over and broken. She straightened up a little bit, not too much, and heated up some left-over chicory coffee on the gas burner.

Below, on the stair she had just climbed, she heard a single footfall sound, then stop.

Looking through the window down into the courtyard, she only saw the green fronds of an ordinary plant growing in a corner separate themselves and take up a new position, having grown that much, silently.

She heard and could not explain a second footstep on the stair. It was then that she knew she was going, and she knew where. But as she left, the stair was empty.

Her steps fell behind her, retracing her earlier path, back to Lafayette Square again, and the building where the *Picayune* lived. At the door of the city room she saw him at a desk and she said, "Hi." It took him a while to know her. Once he did, she saw him recognize that everything, somewhere along the line, had gone wrong. She saw that he wasn't any too surprised.

He took her somewhere; where was it? She couldn't remember. All she knew, they were in an apartment, empty but for the two of them. Some friends of his were away, he said. Then he was giving her chocolate milk in a mug, on the sofa. Sitting by her, stroking her hair.

"You're nothing but a child."

"No, it isn't true." Correcting kindness—it always had to be corrected. "Wrong again, Tommy."

"Too much circus," he insisted, smiling. She gave in to the kind game and not for the moment having to worry whether somebody was going to kill her, she felt herself falling sound asleep, leaning on his shoulder, holding his hand.

Why didn't I find somebody good? she was asking herself, and had been, all this time. Now she heard the question, she could answer: she hadn't because she hadn't wanted to. . . .

# The
# In-Between
# Time

# 1. OLD RELATIONS

 People who knew Julia's story were always inviting her; among a certain set who wanted to be in touch with "real" life, she got to be a living specimen, somebody fabulous. The details of what had happened to her in her low-life adventure were not to be got out of her, nor was even the broad outline of it a subject anyone got anywhere with, in conversing with her. But odds and ends came to general attention from any number of sources—a fact here, a conjecture there, all were worked with embellishment into the general pattern of Julia Garrett.

Julia herself saw a number of different lives she might have at least made some effort toward creating rise up before her eyes and sink from sight. She did not follow, or so much as reach out her hand. The man from Texas came and went; the Frenchman—half-Creole, half-Parisian, with a plantation out from St. Martinsville and an apartment in the Vieux Carré—came and went; the New York businessman with an interest in art, boating, and old coins came and went; still she was there in New Orleans, Julia Garrett, ostensibly settled down alone, in a small modern apartment on Prytania Street, the kind of edifice that Aunt Isabel and Uncle Maurice lamented ever having been built, for certainly it had displaced something finer than anybody would know how to put up nowadays, even if they had the will and the means to try it. Jobs she could have taken which would have placed her among those prominent in the city were talked of as available to her. She might have taught in a private school, done research for Loyola and Tulane professors, allied herself with a promotional group for luring capital to southern Louisiana. Instead, she buried herself in a small job in a hospital. It had to do with medical terminology; she had had considerable Latin in her early years at a private school called Miss Powell's, had studied French later and taken two years of German. A three months' training course fitted her to take the place in the hospital of a woman who was retiring without fanfare after thirty-five years, just as, she realized, she would also retire, if she stuck for forty years. (And she saw herself, brow and mouth all time-smudged and blurred, eyes circled in tortoise shell, turning neatly arranged shelves and files over to whatever bright-faced young girl would stand there, ready for a first job. Would it really turn out that way? She didn't know.)

Almost daily, coming and going for four years in her simple linen and cotton dresses, her two good wool suits, her standard beige raincoat, she wondered what if anything was really going on now in her own life. Had she after a stormy time simply gained that calm shore that life was meant to be, having its own routine and sense of small usefulness to carry it along? Was that all? Maybe she had really belonged only to Jake and he had taken all that mattered most with him when he left. Similarly bereft by her—so they'd wound up equal this way—her old fiancé Martin Parham at least could see her whenever he felt he wanted to; he was apt perpetually to be in the environs of her life, Julia decided. Once in the heat of his first onrush of emotions about her, he had said that to him she was the whole city of New Orleans; its life was hers and hers its own. If that had any truth, Julia could think of him, she guessed, as a shady town suburban to herself; anyway, a fixed point.

Martin had married somebody his family approved of, but he still just needed to see Julia occasionally, so he would ring her up. It was a time-honored custom, something to do with Mississippi men in that old Louisiana town. What did being rich mean anyway, if you couldn't have what you needed most right when you wanted it? What Martin needed was in New Orleans, not so far away.

Julia had a drawerful of stuff Martin continued to buy her from Vieux Carré antique shops—a carved silver cigarette case, a collection of garnets, brooches, and rings, a drawing by a local young artist he thought to be really going places. He claimed for ages to be concerned about her relationship to marijuana and who knew what else. To look after her was his frowning motive. When she said she never touched much of anything nowadays he wasn't sure she was telling the truth. Who could ever be sure Julia wasn't lying? he wanted to know. Especially as she didn't know herself, he would add. Was that true? She would nod, seriously following him. He wanted a clear look into her life, he would explain to her, knotting his fist and striking the table between them, way over in the corner in the Pontchartrain Bar. Why couldn't he understand her? he pursued. Julia, who was also hard pressed to understand herself, tried to explain the difficulty.

"I came unstuck some way. The thing that happens is, you get more shocked than you can reason about, then you're all numb. I can't find my life thread any more."

"I didn't know there was such a thing," said Martin; "I thought there was just life, the same for me as you."

"Then why do you say you can't see mine?"

To those few persons to whom it could be a matter of gossip that Martin Parham and Julia Garrett still saw each other, it was also apparent that Martin had got Julia to move. For she suddenly changed from the modern apartment house to an old airy white house across the same street, in which a whole second floor was her own apartment, all chalky fresh, with high ceilings and some modern alterations, new wallpaper and lighting fixtures, warm with houseplants. "If only the rubber tree would quit growing," said Julia, when Uncle Maurice came to call.

Maurice felt freer in the atmosphere of her new place and noted with satisfaction that she had finally got herself into a frame, at least, that he could understand. He couldn't get out of her where she had got the money for it, if not from Martin Parham. He didn't exactly ask her that, but she got the point anyway and denied it. "It's cheap," she said. "They keep it that way because they don't want just anybody. I've known the owner for years."

"Known the owner for years," thought Maurice, in an echo. The innocent surface of the remark could be masking anything or nothing. Who, for instance, was the owner? He wanted to go make inquiries. He could have found out if he put his mind to it. But he hated being in that position, having to explain he didn't know, showing that he worried. Reassured about Julia's looks and health, he went away undecided about how much interest he should take in her concerns. Not unless asked, was his final decision, arrived at reluctantly, after talking to Isabel.

Then unexpectedly one Saturday afternoon, the Devignys got the fresh-sounding phone call. "Come to tea tomorrow." Maurice was downstairs and Isabel above, so they were both on the line when her voice came through. To them it was music where they might have expected the telegram-shock of bad news. They hastened toward each other, meeting on the stair landing. So she was coming about like a ship, she'd be all right now, they could pick up where they'd left off, a part of her belonged with them . . . all this they packed into her call, giving its meaning to them. They felt they had been rained on after drought. It had mattered more than they admitted.

Isabel wore her best afternoon clothes to tea, and Maurice turned himself out with care in blazer and flannels, brown shoes smartly shined. He had shaved and smelt faintly of lime. It was autumn in New Orleans, though warm still: the city made no definite response to that season. No fallen leaves whispered and crushed beneath their feet as they drove the familiar blocks by taxi, commented on places they had known always, reminisced over stories and scenes and people they had known first-hand or heard about. Agreeing that they walked too seldom, they alighted three blocks too soon. Then, a little nervous, they were mounting Julia's stair.

She was alone, and they were the only guests.

Isabel kept up an admirable line of compliments about the apartment without asking how its furnishings had all got there, and Maurice got comfortably off on some of the stories he had recalled along the way. Isabel asked Julia if she would like to have the old piano that had been in the upstairs hallway unused for years. It had been out of tune since the time lightning struck the drain pipe on the northwest corner.

Julia was silent. She could not think whether she wanted a piano or not. She finally said, smiling, "It's good of you to offer. What I'd really like is a picture of Dev. I lost the one I had."

"You want another one?" Maurice asked. "Why of course! Why certainly!"

His wife looked at him curiously.

On the way home he was talkative and wanted to go to an oyster bar he knew of on the river side of St. Charles. Nobody they knew would show up in a simple place like that.

Across the table from her in that plain little eating place, his wife saw him sitting with his eyes like flashlights.

"That old man," he kept saying. "That old man."

"Your father?" Isabel inquired.

"He's responsible for everything about her." Excited, he wanted to go on and on. "She isn't coming back to us—she never will."

Isabel, over his head, looked at herself critically in the

restaurant mirror. Did last year's clothes ever quite do? If
the answer was in doubt, then how could clothes three or
four years old do at all? The dresses she wore still showed
up well at home and in the houses of friends where her
name, Isabel Devigny, defined who she was and shed its
grace about her. But "out" even in a cheap restaurant—
no; especially in a cheap restaurant, where the surroundings did not make up for anything, she was far short of
looking the way she would like. She took off her glasses,
now that she had read the menu. Not only would she
look better without them, she would not be able to see
herself so well. These times came when money was short.

"It's your father you mean?" she repeated.

"Of course it's him I mean. If I had it to do again I'd
get a nurse straight out of the bayous. He made her life
for her, always in defiance of you and me. Always!"

"I offer her a piano, she asks for his picture."

"Exactly." Served by a drunk little old Negro, the
oysters arrived, a dozen for each in their gnarled brown
shells, glistening gray on the fleecy white inner shell.
"Though to tell the truth, I wouldn't much want a piano,
either," Maurice added.

"Oh, for parties and things, great fun," said Isabel.
"Why are the lights in these places always so bright?"

"To look for pearls," said Maurice, taking up his fork.

"You're still trying to track down Julia," said Isabel,
"even though you've found her in the flesh. I don't believe,
Maurice, that she's as complex as you think. I don't think
women are ever as complex as men think they are."

"Then please explain her to me, in a few well chosen
words."

Isabel was enjoying her oysters, which had been
chilled to the right degree and were exceedingly firm
fleshed. She thought of the coldness of pearl and of
chilled silver.

"I don't think she's happy," said Isabel. "Happier than
during the Springland period, but not happy. Maybe she's
crawling out of it slowly."

"Up to where we are, you mean? My dear, where we are says nothing to her. Never has. We wanted a child and she came; then we couldn't have her. Someone else stepped in."

"You always sound," said Isabel, "as if your father seduced her. You must think that, the way you say it."

"I don't know what happened. Who has her confidence? Is she really finished running around with a lot of crooks and guitar players?"

"Maybe Martin Parham knows. You can ask him."

"It's an idea," said Maurice.

Secretly he was more stimulated than he would admit. He and Isabel were happy, no happier couple had ever existed, but happiness is placid. The stir of life, its harsh brightness, its murky side as well, all this had thrashed up in his head since seeing Julia that day. The dead father—why had he rejected his son? Why had he chosen to steal the child's love away from them? And what were they saying, deciding, knowing, still—the little girl, the old man—she living and he dead? Why, nothing, everyone would tell him if he asked. No statement. None whatever. He had taken tea from gold and white cups and eaten some currant cakes Julia had bought at Holmes and looked at the things she had assembled, possibly ninety percent provided by Martin Parham. But sad to say they had not thought of even Martin Parham as being as alive to her as Henri Devigny—the fleshy dark brooding face with its shag of iron-gray hair like a frame, heavy hunched shoulders, old black coat in winter, rumpled linen coat in summer, intense eyes. Smoking. Stained fingers. Soul knowledge. Like a Negro in some respects. And he'd got to her, possessed the child. Here an expression Maurice knew well broke through—"got with her"—with its obvious sexual note. And that was it, a lower depth—that was what was causing him horror. For child and old man had circled him for years, gone off and off and off again from out the framework of his household, to play their games together, whatever they were. He al-

ways saw them walking away, out of Audubon Place, like
two escaping, gone into something instead of away from
it. *They* should have been outsiders, with their extremes
of age to cope with, putting them on opposite rims of the
circle, or to say it another way, at the windows looking in
on the warm life he shared with Isabel. Instead, they'd
turned the tables, made him and Isabel feel in a cage, ig-
norant and uninformed, while they roved free.

He finished his oysters.

Isabel came out with it, again: "If your father stepped
in, as you say, then you must mean sexually."

"Oh, I don't mean literally. Not necessarily. But the
life course—yes, he did it. Cruelly, maliciously."

"At one time you hated him."

"I did, yes."

"And still?"

"I could work it up. But mainly I—"

"You what?"

"I'm sorry for myself, Isabel. Except for you what life
could I have? No mother I remember. The rich stepmother I was never close to, the old man hated her, I do
believe. Then our life hedged in by him, and then no
children possible, until Julia. He knew all this, so what
did he do? I ask you. That massive ego, swinging into
motion like a huge machine. Remember the night she
came. Why couldn't he have stayed out of it? Inexorable.
Inevitable. He couldn't."

"Stop," said Isabel. "You're spoiling the oysters for
me."

He could indeed enrage and sicken himself, when he
thought of his father, whom he had loved so much, who
had refused him love out of his own soul knowledge, per-
versely and forever. But Isabel's lyric side came to the fore
when she remembered coming to that house as a bride,
charming the rough old man who wanted to live upstairs
alone and "stay out of the way," he had said, so touch-
ingly she had almost cried, tears shed into a lion's mane.
Still, she'd finally been allowed to sit beside him on a

garden bench, at last, miraculously, to lean against his shoulder, and hold his hand. He had frightened her in general, she would say, not directly. If he'd had anything against her she'd never felt it. But Maurice—oh, families were all a tangle with some black mystery at the heart.

She snuggled into her jacket; they were about to leave. "Anyway," she told him, "your father would be hopelessly dated in this day and age. Can you imagine him coping with the fifties? And we're nearly to the sixties. It gets a little ridiculous."

"I guess you're right."

"But *you* can cope—and handsomely. You know that, don't you?" She could come up with this, even when money was short.

He paid the bill smiling, opened the door for her on the cool night. Once again, she'd fished him up out of his well and set him down in a garden. "Let's get a cab home through the park," he suggested. "Sweet is the night air."

It was the day before they brought the new telephone book to Audubon Place and to the whole city, leaving it propped between the outer and inner doors.

And that was one more year.

# 2. THE MAN IN HER LIFE

To Martin Parham, who spent most of his days contemplating whether or not to get a divorce, what little he had been able to do to rehabilitate Julia Garrett after the Springland affair seemed decisive, and a good thing. He had been able to tip the scale toward getting her in a right sort of setting for herself, and he took an interest too in her job, which he had had nothing to do with but which he approved of. Now, though she went a bit mechanically, like a wound clock, at least she was what they called "a going concern."

Her soul wasn't in it. This was how he thought of her at present. Julia was more explicit. "I think I departed this earth," she would amiably say. "Somewhere along the line, that's what happened. Either that or I've changed into something, a cat maybe."

Martin's concerned eyes would follow her. He had a good youth-producing grin when he was happy and he was happy when everything was going right for everybody, including himself. People that things did not go right for he wanted out of sight, and ninety-nine times out of a hundred out of sight for him was out of mind. But anybody around, he wanted them happy and he would do his level best for them, if he liked them at all. There must be people he didn't like, but why think of them? If he looked at Julia with an anxious frown indented between his brows, then the anxiety had to do as much with himself as with her. She knew what it was: he was always facing it that even if he did get a divorce Julia would not marry him. She could torment with the knowledge without seeming to, cat and mouse. "We should have got married—but, oh, back there somewhere. It's too late now, aren't you glad? You're too polite to say so, but I know it's true." Then he would know that the whole business of doing the thing, which would mean so much to him, would mean practically nothing to her. She had lived on the underside of things, after all, and security had little or no meaning for her any longer.

"It's going to dawn on you someday how awful all that low-life business really was," he would tell her darkly. "Then you'll look at it as your wild stage, something like that." "Do you really think so?" Julia would ask. Why had she done it, Martin would pursue, ordering cognac after his long Creole meal. Well, she would say, she had fallen in love. Another time she said that when life knocked at the door you had to let it in, then that was your fate. Well, okay, said Martin Parham. Still, he didn't see. In that case, he said, suppose you just got the wrong address sometime and went to a junk yard; that don't mean, he went on, you've got to settle down in it. Well then, some kind of nightmare must be what she really wanted, deep down, she said. The way you invent your own death, she said, flipping this off in a light tone. He started to say, Well, deep down why don't you get to wanting something else. But he didn't. Then he did. By then they had moved from the restaurant to a courtyard, banana fronds leafy above their heads in the velvet air.

"If we got married," Julia would point out, "what you like would go away. Part of what you like is escape. You like to keep your route open. I'm your get-away."

So they argued, through balmy evenings, or through languid afternoons at her place where she might have cooked crabs for his lunch and shared some wine he'd brought.

So she would put her hair up, after making love; it had grown about a foot long. Sometimes if he overstayed his usual number of hours with her he would ask if she'd had somewhere else to go, anything else to do.

One thing they could agree on: they were engaged in
a long quarrel, perhaps a life-long quarrel. It had to do
with his family, their standing, their millions, their self-
righteous ways.

"They have to put up a kind of order for themselves,
make rules and all that," Martin would insist. Being a
good Parham was part of his life-game, though slyly he
wanted far more out of life than that. "They had to make
some sense out of all their good luck, didn't they?"

I don't know why, she would almost say, but didn't.
"It's not my business, is it? They're not for me."

"Then look what is for you, when you start picking and
choosing. Do you come up with anything better?"

"Certainly different."

"Better?"

She would set in a hairpin. "You never understand."

On any excuse he would linger—rain, or the Mercedes not ready yet. (He had bought one because he had
to bring it to New Orleans for servicing.) If it was rain,
their minds and thoughts might rove back together to pre-
Springland days, back to when she and he were first engaged. They had known each other so long and one of the
joys of that was to know what the other was remembering
and go along, tandemlike, a handsome pair pedaling the
same bicycle down memory lane. So they moved together,
back in years, to that Sunday afternoon up in the south
Mississippi country, pines and azaleas, a time after rain.

They had been to his fishing cottage, the one he had
built out over the small lake, four or five miles from his
parents' home or the homes of his two brothers and their
wives, his own idea and doing; relatives kept their distance when not invited. He used to take Julia there, a
nearly open secret. So they were there that Sunday, both
during and after the rain.

The rain had come on with thunder and lightning and
a dark torrent of wind. In the late afternoon a quiet clear
green light, pale spring green, had followed the storm.

Then she had got up and dressed quickly and easily—she was always a quick dresser—in order to run up to Martin's parents' house in the car, to get her things from up there. She always spent nights in the family home, sticking to proprieties, doing the right thing under his family's nose. For instance, every Sunday she solemnly placed wired strips of velvet, crossed and curved and ornamented with a velvet flower, on her head and accompanied Martin and his family to the town Baptist church where she sat appearing to listen to sermons that before she had stopped paying attention to them had sounded to her like the ravings of a lunatic. She had wondered after the first one or two if the preacher would not have to be taken quietly away and locked up, but noting that everyone took everything he said as a matter of course and nothing out of the ordinary, she decided that no one listened anyway, or that they heard this flushed, excited little man, hopping around in his lunacy, as one might hear an incantation through a mask.

On that weekend when it had stormed on Sunday afternoon, delaying slightly their departure for New Orleans, Martin's parents were away visiting relatives in Texas, and his sister and her husband were away too; the house was supposedly empty and Julia had taken Martin's key in order to let herself in. Martin, whom she'd left in the shower, wanted to get to New Orleans in time for a Sunday night supper at Antoine's in a special small dining room he kept for them for Sundays and occasions generally—Mardi Gras balls and football days. Julia stopped on the gravel of the front drive and ran up the steps of the nondescript brick house of wealth which could not even be called ugly, it was so uninteresting. She thrust the key in the front door lock and had already opened the door and entered the shuttered and curtained hallway before she realized that she had had to turn the key twice, back and forward again, the reason being that the door had already been open, and not through oversight. Somebody was there. She knew it, the sense of pres-

ence was strong, even before her vision freshly come in
from outer light could master the shaded interior and
make out the figure on the stairway. She did not retreat,
though the approach was not lacking in an ominous
quality. It was a faded woman, slow, and uncertain of any
motion she made being the right one; Julia thought at
once of sickness—she was probably sick. So how had she
got in if not with a key: maybe the key, like entering
the house at all, was something she had a right to but
wasn't really supposed to make use of. Now Julia understood why the telephone had rung so repeatedly in the
cottage and why Martin had jerked it angrily off the hook
and laid it down, unanswered, something he would never
have done if his parents had been at home.

On she came.

"Who are you?" Julia asked, up toward the figure on
the stairs, seeing that the dress she wore was neither light
blue nor dark blue, but just blue.

The figure stopped. The tiny laugh that came down
to Julia seemed like something from behind a closed door.
"I should ask *you* that, shouldn't I?"

"Oh." Julia opened a blind near the door, switched on
a light. "You mean you belong here."

"Maybe you do too."

"I'm Martin's friend," said Julia.

"You're going to marry Martin?"

"Something like that."

"He's my brother. I'm Lillian, didn't they tell you about
me—"

The voice stopped. Where it had been going was as
great a mystery, Julia felt, to the woman it belonged to as
to herself. But after it stopped, the whole house seemed
hushed, more steeped in a quality of silence than Julia
had observed in it before. It seemed less commonplace, for
though rich, with expensive objects of furniture and fine
carpets, it always had been to her supremely ordinary.
Now she saw the truth; its latent poetry was in this
woman's hands. She seemed to have come out of the

woodwork, the minute the elder Parhams got out of sight.

"I've been better recently," the woman said. Then, impatiently, "Where is Martin? I wired ahead and then came on the train. I haven't seen Martin, oh, in years, it's been—" Again the voice did its curious stopping trick.

"Martin's not far away," she said. "You stay right here. I'll go for him."

As she hastened back to the car she noticed the heavy wetness of the gravel in the drive and the wide sweep of light, a distant crystaline horizon, washed by rain, and light falling in raw, green cadence on grass, and the spring-charged trees. This country is raw and wild, she thought. And that too seemed more real, now she had seen the woman she didn't know existed. She drove back to find Martin.

He got into the car, behind the wheel, first placing his coat on the back seat. "Where are your things? In the trunk?" He had got his head set toward Antoine's now.

"Martin, I must tell you. Something has happened. A woman named Lillian is up at the house. She's waiting to see you."

"Lillian!" His hands dropped from the wheel. He had started the motor and was spinning backward to turn. Now the brake, slammed down, fixed the wheels in deep gravel.

"Oh my God. Oh my God." The strong capable hands, so recently put to pleasing and caressing her, were lifted and raised to his own face, covering his vision. He pressed them tight into his features and pulled them slowly downward, expelling breath. "The family spook. What'd she say? What'd she do?"

By the time they got to the house he seemed thoroughly in charge of things in his own mind. "I won't be a minute," he said to Julia.

Julia waited. Martin came out presently, carrying her bag and wrap. "Was this all?"

"Yes."

Lillian came out behind him, closing and locking the door. She got into the back seat of the car. Martin drove her into the small town nearby, to a large comfortable house belonging to his Uncle Noland, and let her out on the sidewalk. He said he would see her the next day. Then he was speeding recklessly fast through the little town with its multiple garages and filling stations, its one drugstore and four-way stop light, where everybody knew a Parham and a Parham car and no one would stop such a car or question its driver.

"She's not really all that crazy, you know," he told Julia, whipping curves. He slowed to a stop at the intersection, then swung onto the highway, going south. He was going to hit ninety if it took that to get there. "She's just touched, I guess, a natural. She took up this idea to be a missionary to the Indians, something like that. She went off to West Texas, then to New Mexico. She's come here now, I bet anything, to try to get some money out of us. Oh, not for herself. She never spends a penny on herself. It's all in trust, her share, controlled by the estate."

"That means she can't touch it," Julia remarked.

"She had a breakdown some time ago. Her being here at all means some doctor said she was okay for the trip. But who wants her to come? Mamma and Dad go out to see her every so often. Who wants her around? She thinks nobody does, and I guess that's right."

"Martin," said Julia. "Don't you think just being your sister, that that has a right to mean something?"

"I think it ought to," he said.

"Then don't you think running off to Antoine's after it's so long you haven't seen her must make her feel like hell?"

"What are you trying to say? She bugs me, always has." He drove silently, like a silent wind, eyes set on the road. "To most people I'm nice. Ain't that right? Ain't I?"

"You're nice to me," she said after a long time. The

swamps along the road dump turned to dark liquid in the twilight, sliding past.

"Means what?"

"Means you're nice to me." She rode with her legs crossed, one foot pressed hard against the floorboard, seeming completely relaxed until the two rigid tendons appeared above the ankle. Their senses still in some way linked through all this good physical period they enjoyed so, Martin was as conscious of this tense ankle as she was of his too-relaxed hands on the beautifully sensitive wheel.

They had got as far as Slidell before Martin said, "What right do you have to object to how I treat my sister?"

"I felt sorry for her . . . not sorry, no, that's not true. I thought you needed her. I thought you ought to know it."

"Need! You must be in a mood."

Julia knew Martin's ambivalence toward his family, and that it was a deep source of his whole personality. She knew his aversion to the church he had to appear at was of the same nature as his aversion to Lillian, and to his family's taste in architecture and furniture. He was always repressing his feelings, but they were there. So what did he do but seek out a New Orleans girl with French connections and (oh sure) dark cropped hair. He liked to lie in bed by the hour with this girl, stretching out his good trim legs and making jokes about the family in a not unfriendly drawl mimicking country talk —his father and his mother's timid courtship (his mother was taller than his father by about a foot), his sister-in-law's visits to Paris, London, and Rome (staying in all the right places but doing all the wrong things), his younger sister's finishing school sophistication, his grandfather's money-shrewdness always unbuttoned. Then he wanted to go down to the farm outlet store and be called the sweetest one in the whole connection—the only one who wasn't money crazy. Well, that was true; he wasn't money crazy except for spending it, a real democrat. His looseness with money made the family wary of him. They wouldn't care so much if he slighted his sister, but if he slighted money, the religion of money—was he quite sound? they would soon begin to ask, might already be asking. If he wasn't quite sound, the first thing you knew they would group him with Lillian, who cared nothing whatever for money. Julia reflected that that same Lillian who had been helping Indians out West might possibly have wanted at one time to help Negroes in Mississippi, in which case they would have found it easy to decide she was off, touched, a natural, and get her the hell out to somewhere healthy. Mentally regarding this total picture, Julia could draw her brows together with secret, inward concentration; she could go to work for Martin like a good hound, coming up with something for him intact in her mouth, dropping it at his feet.

"Lillian represents your danger too," she told him.

He glanced at her sharply, past the expensive chrome dials glowing multiform in the velvety dark which had seeped fully in upon the highway and the land.

He seemed to get a glimmering of her thought process, for he protested at once his full status as a Parham. "I'm good at business," he said. "Don't think I didn't do a trial run—came out better than anybody so far. It was a cross-breeding experiment on the cattle farm—did I tell you? With Indian cattle, Brahma. All one damn year I lived, breathed, and slept the sacred bull." He lapsed into a long funny description of their sexual natures.

"See?" said Julia, laughing. (She'd heard it before and both of them knew it.) "You make it a joke. That's dangerous."

"I'm not joking for one minute. I was the high priest of the Hindu cattle cult, the one they allow into the seraglio."

"That makes you a eunuch," Julia laughed. "More dangerous still."

"You can vouch for me there." He reached over to caress her thigh. "Don't you think we'd take prizes? Why, just this afternoon, who'd believe it if they'd heard it told?" His gum cracked in his contented jaws. "Listen, Julia, I'm thinking seriously. After we're married, do you want to keep a second place in New Orleans, or Florida? It's an important decision. Something like our real life will form wherever it is. I favor Florida, frankly. Palm Beach has got this winter season. Maybe that's too glittery to be interesting. But there're some other places. In New Orleans, it's more family; your aunt and uncle's social round—lots of purty houses, the best of the Mardi Gras balls."

She was silent. Marriage . . . this taking it for granted; she wondered if she wasn't beginning to pull back from him a little. And hadn't he taken her sexual compliance for granted, too, right from the start? Why else would he come to New Orleans to see her? An attractive boy two years out of the university, with a world of money. And no steady girl up there.

She had met him after a New Year's Sugar Bowl game, among a whole rich group of victorious Georgia Tech backers jammed in a railway car, the bourbon flowing, it would seem, from a central fountain. She had wound up standing, he seated on the edge of a table, so their eyes were on a level and not an inch apart. "Sorry," she said, "I can't move." "I'm not complaining, am I?" She saw for the first time the easy important whiteness of his good smile. "I tell you seriously," he said, almost nibbling her nose as he spoke, "I'm the only Mississippi boy here, but don't tell. If they knew they'd tear me up. I'm incognito, trying to make my Georgia accent sound right." "What are you doing here?" she whispered. "My father's a friend of the railroad," he told her. "Very big deal . . . what about you? Are you a friend of the railroad?" "My uncle's firm—it handles their account. Lanier and Weston Brokerage." "Is he Weston or Lanier?" "Neither. Maurice Devigny. He's right over there only you can't turn your head to see." "Don't tell me your uncle escorted you?" "It wasn't quite like that. Some people dropped in on us after the game and they said come on down here. It was more like that." "But you're not with anybody special." She did not answer. At that moment, a fat man joggled him aside; a tiny blonde girl came up between them like a daisy growing up and blooming, out of nowhere.

When Julia left the party, Martin had attached himself to her group and had moreover acquired a girl—yet another girl, tall and smooth. As information not precisely stated spread among them not so much to the effect of who Martin was but of how much money he had, it also became clear that they were all off for an evening and that the evening was on Martin. Julia had come with a young law professor from Tulane who had taken her to the game and had come to Audubon Place afterwards. Before the evening was over, Uncle Maurice had gone home to Aunt Isabel, who did not like football or the messy occasions that the big games brought them. Others had drifted away to hotels, or taken up with other crowds. The law professor got drunk and sang sentimental songs; the girl from the railroad car had turned out to be a public relations woman from a Georgia finance corporation. It was Martin and Julia who quietly discovered at 3 A.M. that they liked to dance together. By the time Martin took Julia home it was early morning. He had either bought or stolen a fresh pineapple for her and she stood in front of the house on Audubon Place, waving him good-bye in the early pale lemon-colored light, with the pineapple dangling from her fingers as though she casually carried a chopped-off head by the locks of its hair. She kept it till it began to reek and Aunt Isabel chilled, split, and served it one Sunday evening. They dipped the chunks in powdered sugar. "Now what's his name again?" asked Maurice Devigny. "Parham," Isabel supplied. "Martin," Julia said, as if he didn't know. . . .

"If you're trying to say," Martin said, "that the entire family is given its meaning by that woman you found wandering around, I think you're as nuts as she is, I really do. It's land that gives my family meaning, that and their religion—more likely land than religion, it's where they got all the money from. Then there's their feeling for each other, love for each other, that's a kind of meaning too."

"But she's where it all stops," Julia pointed out. "You say she can't get any money out of you, it's all in trust, so she's got no part in the land; and you certainly don't love her, you can't stand to be around her, so your religion doesn't reach to her nor your family feeling either."

"Even if I did love her, I don't have any authority to help out half the Indian tribes in the Southwest because she thinks I ought to."

"Oh, sure," said Julia, "but that's no excuse for not loving her."

Why can't I stop? she wondered. Do I have to analyze it all out loud? It only makes him drive faster, and I'm terrified as it is. The red diagonal of the speedometer line touched into the nineties, sure enough, but they were only minutes now from the first of the city speed zones which Martin, not being so widely in control of New Orleans, had more or less to obey. Yet he succeeded in making it to Antoine's by nine-thirty and the usual waiter, Joseph, was there. Martin got his huîtres Bienville and Julia her écrevisses, and the wine was a chilled white Burgundy. What did it matter, she wondered, all this luxury? It was fun for a little while, if you'd never had it, but who would keep on and on racing to have it, pushing the sister aside onto Uncle Noland, just to have it, again and again and again?

In Julia's sleep the plain face of Martin's sister began to appear above a blue dress—neither dark nor light blue, just blue—along a staircase, descending toward her, with supplication, asking, "Where are they? Where have they

all gone?" And Julia trying to make her voice work, trying to articulate: "They don't care. They don't care about
you. Understand it, face it; it's why you're mad."

A few dreams like that and, before she knew it, she
had broken off with Martin Parham, no amount of money
could hold her; and now at long last he had married
somebody else, but came to her anyway, had returned and
would keep returning, from time to time.

# 3. THE OLD MAN

 Reunited after the Springland period, now it was Julia who was worrying to Martin.

She was, for instance, in the habit of observing nearly a month of the year in remembrance of Maurice's father, the old man, Henri Devigny. Martin Parham had run into this habit many times, and each time his irritation with her for it increased. "This is too much," he used to think. She didn't want to see him or anybody else during this peculiar season. It irritated him more than any single thing she did. That he should come all the way down there only to be told she was observing the anniversary of the death of an old man not even her own kin. After all that he, Martin (living), had gone to the trouble of doing for her. It irritated him more than trying to get her to weed all the fairies out of her semi-Bohemian circles. "I can't," she said. "They grow in New Orleans same as Spanish moss. Anyway, if you get rid of them everybody just pairs off, so then pretty soon all you have is the country club and the church bazaar."

This time, on the phone from the Mercedes garage, he blew up. "What the hell does he matter so much now for? Not even kin to you."

And that made twice he'd turned the phrase (once in his mind, once out loud on the phone): "Not even kin." Thinking it again, hanging up the phone, refused admittance to her mourning presence, the words opened up their own latent contact to him for the first time. Why, that's just the point, he thought suddenly, and was aware of the whirring about his ears, as though a swarm of mosquitoes and other, perhaps uglier, things with wings had risen from a carelessly opened box.

Nervous and hot, he slammed up the phone and now having nowhere down there to go and amuse himself —how could he amuse himself when he was so mad at Julia?—he decided to get to the bottom of it. He took a cab to the *Picayune* office and asked for the file on Devigny. Which one? He didn't know. The first name escaped him. The one that died ten years ago. He got a handful of files instead of one. "If you go out in the other room you can smoke. Just sign for them here." He sat down at a comfortable blond wood table near a window with an ash tray beside him. He laid the files before him. He placed his cigarettes in a soft leather case close to his right hand, the silver cigarette lighter, an excellent German make, beside them. He wore a gold ring with a fraternity crest—ΣAE—on his right hand. The ash tray, aluminum dipped in bronze paint, did not please him. Arrogant he might be about his possessions —the minor tasteful swagger that money allowed a well-set brown-haired Mississippi boy to make was to his pleasure. Yet when he bent to the files, unwinding the strings that held the flaps in place, he felt like a college student again, about to learn a lesson. Only in one way he felt more than that. What was it, if not dread?

Martin spent an absorbed two hours in the newspaper offices. He did not smoke once. What did he discover? A sensual face—powerful, lowering, withdrawn, observant —and a handful of facts. Henri Devigny. Born in Iberville Parish; died Audubon Place, New Orleans. Two marriages, one son. Minor political offices. Prominent in Comus. Campaigned in two mayoralty primaries, known as friend and supporter of the city and region. Knights of Columbus, landowner, publisher of regional books (folklore, myth, legends), president of wildlife conservation, arraigned once on suspicion of murder in the case of Elvira Nicolson, but never charged. . . .

And who was Elvira Nicolson? He searched again and found reference to a law suit. The Tulane Law Library might have other information, of course, the girl in the newspaper clipping library pointed out. Still, enough was on hand to get an idea. Elvira Nicolson: a Negro woman who distributed voodoo instruction manuals, some lurid sex literature, arrested, tried, convicted, and paroled, found stabbed to death in the entrance of a mock river boat, kept for excursions only, docked for the night and no one aboard. Some of her "literature" collected by Devigny Regional Publishers, for publication, others said to have been printed in these same offices on Carondelet . . . purveyor of obscene . . .

The whole house on Audubon Place suddenly rose up before Martin Parham's bemused eyes. The side garden charming with camellias. But that had been bought— oh, Julia had told him—from a man in real estate who had made his money from Yankees during the twenties boom by selling lots in an undrained swamp down near Grand Ile on the Gulf. Henri Devigny had got it cheap after his second marriage to a Northern woman who didn't live with him all that long; they made each other unhappy. She was handsome, but not very pretty or gay or anything that was fun. So Uncle Maurice had told Julia, who had never seen her. Nobody had liked her, poor thing, though being from New England somewhere maybe she didn't even know it or didn't care. Who knew what people from up there thought? She was rich. She poured out money on the house, then left it. But there hadn't been any divorce. She spent "seasons" in New Orleans occasionally. "The thing was," he could hear Julia's clear voice repeating, "what was a season to her wasn't a season to anybody else, so nobody could figure out what she meant by it." The house was still in the Devigny name. It was something about Louisiana law and the old man wouldn't give in. He had had his love, Uncle Maurice's mother, his first wife. Having had his love, and seen death claim her, what wouldn't he be

allowed to do? Nothing. Everything was understandable
after that. Martin raised his head, to rest his eyes. Almost
visible before him, the figure of a dark-skinned heavy-
shouldered man, iron-gray hair, legs carelessly, almost
vulgarly, open, was to be seen seated across the room,
and there too came the weight of his breathing, the
lowering intensity of his regard. Martin shook his head,
clearing his vision. No mention of Julia Garrett, after
all, was to be encountered in any of these folded and
labeled, collapsed and condensed versions of what went
on in the life of Henri Devigny. Yet to Martin she was in
them all, like an elusive but definitely recurrent track
along a swamp path. He shook himself again. Gathered
up the clippings. Dropped them in their folders. Picked
up cigarettes and lighter. Returned the files. Obsessed!
How could he stop it?

He went out into the sun. How could he stop knowing that she had, aged six, but already visibly a potential
nymphet, come to that house which contained that man,
that marrier for money, that printer of obscene literature,
that murderer of a Negro woman who might tell what
she knew on him. He remembered dining with Maurice
and Isabel Devigny one fall twilight and the shrewd,
amused languor of Maurice's voice from the end of the
table: "Anything you suspect about New Orleans is apt
to be true, plus a lot you'd never think of." Sweat now
ran down the back of his neck, beneath the Egyptian
cotton shirt, the Brooks Brothers cotton glen-plaid jacket.
He reached, scratching savagely. Had he been supplanted
before he ever saw her? He could never know. He had to
see her. Lovers imagine horrors only when apart . . .
together the flesh distances the image; it goes up in smoke
like so much tissue paper, turns into a toy mask for a
party. A whole month for a dead old man! Crazy!

He came out on Lafayette Square in a nervous rage
and sat down on a bench. It was where the winos
gathered. He saw doddering old men, thin in the shanks,
grizzled, some smiling in a euphoria of recollection of

all life, not only theirs but everybody's all the way back to Adam, all, all collected like spit from an aging throat. Where does the terror start? When does it get in? It had got in for Martin Parham, so beautifully turned out, waiting for his Mercedes to have its generator minutely adjusted, like a Swiss watch running a minute slow a day, when he read ten percent of the facts and imagined the other ninety, when he saw the photograph and imagined that face on a lightning-flaming, thunder-racked New Orleans night bending above the sleeping body of a dark-haired child—had this ever happened? Who was to say it had or hadn't? What became of Martin's own joy, when his secret spring was so contaminated as that? One thing he knew: Julia would never tell him. The other thing he knew: there had to be some way to explain her, and this did. She had never been frightened of that old man; she loved him. She wasn't frightened enough of life. Did she deaden the fright on drugs? He didn't know. Why couldn't he see her?

He went to a phone and said into it: "Julia, *why* can't I see you?" "If it matters that much, come on over." Christ! He leaned against the phone booth in the lobby of the Lafayette Hotel, panting with relief and cooler, as with a welcome summer breeze.

Late in the afternoon he asked her: "Why is it I can't get close to you? As well as I've known you, as long? Why can't I have you completely?"

Here Julia got practical. "By that you mean get married and have kids, but then you're married already." "I know, but then you wouldn't anyway." "We had the quarrel over your sister." "Oh not that again." "I was born to be somebody's mistress. You said that yourself." "So . . .?" "So I'll keep on being yours." "But you *aren't* mine!" This was when he started coming apart. "Martin! You're nuts today. How can anybody be totally possessed?" "I'm not suggesting that anybody can be . . . it's just that you . . . Julia, what's all this about that

old man?" "Dev, you mean. Nothing. I loved him. Nothing. That's all."

"If anybody asked you, What about Martin Parham?
—would you say 'I love him'? That quick, that right, that
certain?"

"It's only when you're a child you know something
like that," she replied.

"But you thought you loved Jake Springland."

"Well, I did. Well, yes, I did."

"Then why don't you love me?"

"I do love you . . . we've been through all that."

"I'd like to strangle you."

"Go right ahead."

They would end up laughing, and he would be up,
dressed and in still another mood by midnight, ready to
be purred plushly back into his "real" life by the newly
tuned Mercedes motor. But now on the road home he
would be whistling and satisfied the way he needed to
be—none but she could turn a trick so well. Little old
Julia, she turned into a fancy woman. Then he'd laugh
aloud to the dark rows of swamp going past, and the
flat, quiet-colored country lying patient under the moon,
for nothing could be less fancy than Julia's simplicities.
Her style was all as simple and right as the plain chairs
and white napery of the great restaurants in her city—
and this he knew to be, in snob terms, the fanciest of all.

He had forgotten his hang-up, all about her fixation
on that old man. The old man's face, the idea of it, was
gone completely from Martin's thoughts, as though a
little black cloud which had crawled across the beaten
silver-gold complexion of the moon was now lost small
as a fly in the fair enormity of a night sky. Nevertheless,
just as he had had to go and search out old newspaper
clippings, so the mood would come again. He might even
go and find the old man's grave one day, and wonder
what secrets it was holding.

# 4. JULIA WRITING

 *Martin has no belief in the things or people I know, just in me personally. This is why he can't see me or know me completely—because he won't accept anybody in connection with me, starting with Dev. If I write it and show it to him to read, then he would have to understand it, or recognize it, just because he was reading it. So I'm going to do like this.*

"Dev came from down Iberville way, down in the French country. At least his family had had a place down there on Bayou Teche since the beginning. They shot slaves that ran away and put them up in trees, dead in their coffins, to rot, making an example to anyone else that wanted to try it, all they had to do was look up and see the buzzards.

"The whole Devigny family never was so devoted to country living, but wanted to be in New Orleans all they could. When Uncle Maurice showed their pictures around in the old leather album it was clear why the women wanted to move. It had to do with hats, which they liked big and new and fashionable, and the biggest, newest, and most fashionable were in New Orleans. What about the men? That was power, its exercise and growth, or so I guess. They could have more of it in the city by testing it and improving what little they had to start with; they could watch it grow. Dev was like that but he brought the country with him; he had swamp country friends who believed in soul transfer to animals, lots of things like that. When he went into law and bought a job in politics, he didn't know even though he had to buy it that he was getting in with a machine. When he found out, it was too late because it seemed everybody did it that way or they weren't mixed up at all in anything that mattered. In New Orleans, there were more Negroes and mulattoes, quadroons and all and they didn't have the old animal faiths, but held to the Haitian mysteries and passed them down and around, selling conjure packets, and grisgris. To whom? That could be vague like most things can be when people don't want you to know. They'd sell to you maybe, they'd say. What did you want done?

"When I followed Dev around after he retired from law practice, politics too, I used to sit in a back room in an antique straight-backed chair on a faded red carpet, all in a house out toward Bayou St. John. Sometimes they let me watch a hand of cards played, when there would be all men playing, with one or two nice quiet light-skinned Negro women around and a fan turning softly, or on a very hot day a colored boy standing to fan everybody with great big palmetto fans. Sometimes when there weren't any men in the room, somebody would bring me a glass of iced tea; one of the women used to talk to me. Once I walked in a rock garden enclosed by a high board fence. A rock castle had been built up taller than I was and water trickled out and around the rocks where flowers had been planted.

"Years later Uncle Maurice asked me where I went with Dev when he took me into town and I said, 'I don't remember,' because if they didn't really care then why start caring? What was I but a throwaway child from up in the hill country? They look down on everything from up there."

*Didn't care*, she thought, but did not write, *until a rich boy fell in love with me.*

"Then one day I was there with him in the house near Bayou St. John where he liked to go, and he was playing cards in the front parlor under the fan, but he let me walk back past the stairwell into the back gallery—I was

going out to walk in the rock garden. But there was a
commotion on the stairs and then in the kitchen, and
then in the gallery, where I saw somebody come in and
fall on a couch, and then a tall, nearly white Negro boy
coming after saying, 'What is it, Mamma?' and she saying 'Hot, oh God, I'm 'bout to burn up.' He went to the
water cooler and when I got out there he was spreading
a white handkerchief over her face so it clung and stuck
there like a mask and that was the first I saw of her up
close, as if her face had turned chalk white, and she gave
a long trembling breath, an 'Oooooo . . .' sound that
didn't seem to want to end but then it did end and I was
scared, rooted and planted in the door, and scared half to
death. The boy couldn't move either but he shouted out,
'Somebody get here quick! Somebody got to!' It was Dev
that came in behind me, brushing past. 'Get this child
out!' he said and hustled me out to the garden. I didn't
look back but heard them, Dev calling 'Fanny, Fanny!' to
her and saying 'What you trying to do, smother her?
Looks like you killed her, you fool.' And the boy saying,
'God no, sir, I didn't.' I had circled the rock garden by
then and was just seeing them dim through the latticework, Dev raising his cane to hit the boy and the boy
turning his shoulders side to side and warding off the
blows with his arm, until Dev fell back, landing in a
chair, I guess, and I thought, 'Oh, if he dies too, I'll just
have to stay here, I don't know the way home.' So I didn't
know whether to run off or not, but finally I went and
stood at the bottom of the back steps and heard him
speak (so he wasn't dead): 'Call the doctor, be sure the
bill gets paid in cash . . . I have to get this child away.'
And he called me."

*But I'm going to leave out the thing that had most to
do with me, for on the way home he started holding me
against him, struggling with my body and when we got
home he held me to him on the bed and cried and then I
don't know what happened. He was convulsed, panting
and heaving, and I was not thinking anything at all.*

*Later I thought, he didn't know what he was doing, he just didn't know. I still think that. He didn't know I was even there, I was just a body he was holding on to.*

"I know now she was his mistress and that he must have loved her, and the boy was probably his son, and maybe he thought the boy had been too careless of whether she lived or not because he stood to be provided for out of whatever Dev was settling on her. But I don't know this, not at all."

*He fell asleep in the afternoon's quiet and I stayed by him, awed and close, not moving, until finally he waked and said clearly: "God help me, the child is all that's left to me," then he said, "How can a child save anything from itself, can it know enough to save anything out for living with?" Then he said to me, "I wouldn't hurt you, I wouldn't hurt you, baby." They were all gone, Uncle Maurice and Aunt Isabel and some guests they had, over to Plaquemine Parish to a garden party— Aunt Isabel had been in blue and white lace with a wide blue lacy hat, and maybe they were cool. But back here it was hotter than hot, July in New Orleans in Dev's high-up apartment with all the heavy rich furniture. Oh God, what really did happen that day, what happened between us? It was a day with blood in it, as though the water around the make-believe castle in the Negroes' garden was all bloody, but I never saw any. I remember a white handkerchief stuck to a woman's face. Of course I'm not going to tell all this to Martin. He'd never . . .*

"After that, for some reason, he couldn't be good enough to me, I had all his attention, I was sun, moon, and stars to him, he chose my dresses himself and took me everywhere. I had a pink parasol and a matching dress with ruffles. One day at the races a man came up and chucked me under the chin. 'You get 'em lighter all the time, Dev,' he said, and Dev roared at him, raring back on his heels, 'You got it wrong, George,' and then he took him aside and whispered a while, holding him by the arm and looking back at me, and I didn't know why until years later I remembered the phrase, You get 'em lighter all the time, and I realized the man had mistaken me for being part colored and Dev's offspring, probably, besides. It was a kind of reputation, I would think. False word gets around same as true. The false word becomes part of the true word. It can't help but be.

"I could tell word for word about my whole childhood before New Orleans, but I think you know enough about that. When I look back on it, I'm glad I grew up in New Orleans instead of up there; up there it was just boring. You worry about Dev, but he needed company, that was all, and maybe he felt sorry for me and wanted to give me whatever I wanted to make me happy. That was all."

# 5. JULIA THINKING

Her pen stopped, hovering above the diary page she was meaning to give to Martin to silence him about her past—what did it matter if he knew the truth or not?

She was remembering the town—Towson, Tennessee, up near the Alabama-Mississippi border. It was the thirties and they had boarded, the three of them, her mother, her father, and herself, in a tall white Victorian house, one of those houses meant from the first, no doubt, to be boarding houses, else how explain all its divisions into unexpected cupboards, passageways, stairwells, and entrance rooms? She remembered the smell of medicine on the many stairs, also the dark closed doors of actual sicknesses. In the rooms windows were seldom raised in winter, as both coal and the cash that paid for it were scarce. On the street, going uptown to the drugstore, she took the hand which swung by her head's height, and it was her father's though she could not see him. She saw straight ahead and down, cracked sidewalks with prints of cows' and horses' hooves, or far ahead, up, treetops, telephone wires, and clouds. Her father had a side-to-side walk: she was always being shoved at by it. When this came back to her in later years, she wondered if he drank and she didn't know it, but decided it was a certain gait that went with run-down brown shoes, a single suit to wear, and discouragement. He couldn't get a job. That was the dead knowledge that lived with them, a fourth member of the family. It was like living with a corpse.

Then there were the days when letters came to them,

usually from New Orleans, sometimes from one of Papa's family down in Birmingham. Then a long discussion: "Why not go back there?" "We've been all over that." "It's a big town. Everybody has forgotten what happened. We can live in another part of it." "But who can I ask for help then?" "There's nobody to ask for it here." "But it's so much cheaper." "That's right." "Little goose." Mother would smile. Were they both stupid? Julia wondered, years later, with her detached citified curiosity, leaning back toward the sharp mouse-face of the dark little girl who had been herself but wasn't anybody any more.

The letters from New Orleans were always on white stationery. The texture of the paper was interesting to run a finger over; it made a terrain, something like hills and valleys on a map. But all was fleecy white except for the gold initial in the corner: D. This was for a French name, unlike her own plain one. People in town knew it soon enough, the way they knew everything. It accounted for the special way they looked at her mother and spoke to her, and for the way her mother could look slightly interesting and modish still in her old frail dresses, one flowered green and black, one blue dotted swiss, one dark blue with a peach-colored collar. She leaned back slightly when she met anyone, and when she walked her heels swayed a little bit. Julia was aware of these habits as what people called your ways, your airs. She knew that people said, What'd she see in him?—meaning her mother was above her father. Yet he must have had some distinction. Years later, Aunt Isabel said that they had met during a Mardi Gras dance, somebody having given her father the chance to come down there and go to one. Maybe for that very reason, to find a well-off girl who'd marry him? "He was a good dancer," said Aunt Isabel, and that was about all that Alice wanted to know. "Of course, she was very young," she added hastily, lest Julia think she was being critical.

Sometimes the letter with the golden D had money

in it, a check. Those were really the good days. There would be more food, maybe dinner uptown at the hotel with smiles to all who saw them out together, and surely a bath beforehand, good cigars for Papa, and Mother smelling of cologne. And talk, with reminiscence and optimism. Julia's memories of those lost days, so abruptly cut off, as if a pair of scissors the Fates held had snipped, came now, because of that neat action, in a package which she occasionally took out and opened. Or was it more like a deck of cards she could play carefully out, staring at card by card? When the card showed up about the white letter and check enclosed, the hotel dinner, she always lingered over it, letting fragrances come out of it, still fresh there, her father's leisurely cigar (the band handed over for her finger), her mother's cologne, the hot biscuits smoking on a plate to themselves. Then quickly to be run through in memory, there was the New Deal job Papa hadn't wanted to take but did, and the quarrels and the drinking and Mother sick and the doctor and the rain in winter and the winter death. And the numb funeral . . . What's to become of them? What's the little thing going to do? Going to New Orleans? Relatives? Well, that's what they say . . . she had a sister there, never came here, but they say she . . . Mumble, mumble, murmur, murmur . . . Pore child, pore little old thing . . .

And the train ride. She had laughed once, sitting opposite Papa, legs hanging down. She had been looking out the window at a field, watching two boys tugging at a mule who wouldn't budge. The wind was whipping at their clothes and they strained and jumped against the mule's bridle, but the mule would not move. It would not move and nothing could make it move, not twenty boys, nor fifty boys. And Julia laughed, thinking, Where's mother? Mother, look! And knew, finally knew, knew finally, that Mother was dead.

They got there, got to New Orleans on the train, and it was morning, and though winter still up there in the hills, up in Memphis where they'd changed, here it seemed a different sort of winter, almost warm, the station wide open, quiet, with lots of windows, and she was walking toward it, and carrying what she could. The breeze pressed through the station, lightly; the air was calm in texture and in the depths of the swept waiting room a woman was standing who looked enough like her mother for her heart to jump. She and Papa both stopped, having seen the woman at the same time, and two groups of people went past, one rich and one poor. Then Papa put his hand on Julia's shoulder, pushing his hand down to the center of her back and giving her a shove forward. "That's her. That's Aunt Isabel." The woman had not seen them, but was examining the incoming travelers. Julia did not move, but looked up into her father's face. They seldom conversed, but she felt close to him in an unspoken way, and she knew now what thinking he had gone through, what decision he had come to, how he meant to speak and act and be, but how at the same time he couldn't do it. It was the moment of his failure that pressed between her shoulder blades, a shove she was going to feel printed in her senses forever. She looked up at him in helpless fright, but he only smiled and nodded at her:

"Go on . . . it's her . . . go *on!* Say, Hello, Aunt Isabel, I'm Julia. . . ."

The woman, so like her mother that some part of Julia was rooted still before that insight, but her mother transformed, transfigured—died and gone to this heaven where winter was warm with sunlight and air smelled free and good—was wearing white wool with a loose blue-green coat and a touch of gold somehere (Julia remembered the gold D on the stationery), knelt suddenly, brought her face on a level with Julia's and put her arms around her. "Darling, child . . . darling."

Then, standing up and holding to her hand, "Where's your father?"

"Back there . . . he was . . ." Turning slowly. The bags were there, sitting side by side, but no father.

There was a sense of eyes from somewhere as they went back together toward the spot where her father had been standing. Of eyes hidden, regarding. Oh, Papa, Papa, where are you? Papa, how could you . . .? But both female creatures, standing together, knew all the reasons already, knew how he felt when he knew he couldn't put a voice to the hypocritical scene he had been about to enter. What they couldn't know was that he was gone for good, Frank Garrett, as though he'd given her up, this misbegotten child, for adoption, gone through the whole torturous process as the act of a moment, an impulse, then having found out just what he'd done had decided never to undo it, widening the distance between them forever. Every time he thought of her for the rest of his life he probably moved another hundred miles away. Had he left her out of cruelty or honesty or courage or cowardice? There must have been, Julia finally decided, some good in it, because at least he couldn't make an act of it, pretending that the poor light-headed girl he had married so impulsively had been anything less than killed by him, by poverty, by cold, by boredom, by absence of hope. So Julia believed. She thought that she believed it even before the letter which finally arrived, long, gallant, labored over: "You will understand someday. . . . I really loved your mother, just as she loved me. . . . I had to ask what could I give that was the greatest gift . . . it was to go away. Going away was my heart."

The scene in the station returned to her, in various forms, all her life. In a sense she was always walking on the air that is all you have to walk on when the ground plays out and you don't know it. Like the creature in the movie cartoon, she was always at the moment before you look down and see that there's nothing underfoot. So the point is not to look down until you get to Aunt Isabel and she is holding you. Mother had died. In the still room in Towson before Papa got back from going down to let the doctor in (for the third time that day) Julia had touched the white hand and the hand had not touched back. So she had learned there is a time when a hand does not touch back, and that is mother, but then she reached Aunt Isabel. The trouble was she had then to learn that there is a time when you turn to find Papa and Papa isn't there, and that is Papa. Aunt Isabel took her finally to Audubon Place and there were two men there but neither of them was like Papa. No resemblance, and no blood kin. Women are mothers or not, but all men are different. She got the lesson early, from the first evening onward. The first evening the heavy step had sounded on the stairs, as they went to the table, had crossed the hallway, had entered the dining room. A long pause and everything was suddenly rearranged. And there he was, massive, at the head of the table. "Was this your first train ride, young lady?" Opening the great white napkin. Great splotched hand reaching forward for the heavy silver spoon. Had a black wind rushed through an open transom in the as-yet-strange house on Audubon Place? Had a great bird ridden upon it? She felt a sense of thunder and of a broad banner traveling above them. She was a child and liable to enchantment.

She remembered him still as eating, just as on the first evening. His table at Arnaud's, she was to learn, was always one of two he favored. At Antoine's the maître greeted him in French. He would fasten a commanding glance upon her, his small companion, and the glance had anger in it. Then he would dip his spoon into steaming nectar.

What angered him? What anger fed his mind? She felt in deep communion with his thoughts without knowing what they were.

"Like sleeping with somebody and yet never touching them," she once said to Martin Parham. "But you did touch him," said Martin, touching her himself, "and he touched you . . . don't give me that." She shook a

tousled dark head on white linen, in the dark, thinking
of the great white napkin: "Not the way you think." "You
gave him life . . . it was a beginning." "For me. An
ending for him." "So you admit it, see. Your beginning.
His ending." "All right, all right. I began with an old
man!" She laughed, a low light sound she heard as if
from nearby, sliding into sleep, half-hearing Martin say:
"I've seen it all a hundred times, it runs like an old home
movie in my head, the home movie that turns into a
peep show. A little girl in a cotton night dress on a hot
night with sheets rumpled back and maybe a rain storm
at the windows and that old man entering nurselike to
close the blinds and the big head poked in above you
through the mosquito-net . . . Jesus!" She woke with
Martin's hands clutching her. "What the hell are you?"
he was crying. "Say you didn't . . . say you didn't. . . ."
"I've said I didn't, a hundred times!" "It's a lie!" "For
Christ's sake! You're obsessed with it!"

# 6. MISTRESS AND WIFE

Martin Parham, Julia coolly decided, about a hundred times a week, was a mixed blessing. He had loved buying the house she lived in, in somebody else's name (a firm in Baton Rouge was said to own it), getting the entire arrangement worked out so that it was nontraceable to him in any form, shape, or fashion, but then one day up in Mississippi (for all she knew it was down at that lake house where they used to go before they would drive back to New Orleans) he decided his children were too wonderful for anything and that furthermore Julia had to meet them. This was of grave importance to him.

He made careful arrangements. She was to come to the St. Charles Hotel lobby one Saturday afternoon, go to the mezzanine, walk along the balcony, look down on them while he kept them occupied on some excuse or other, then come down, look closer, mingle as closely as she could (but giving no sign of ever having seen Martin before), then quietly leave. She would never know what it would mean to him if she would just do that. Then his knowing that she had had this contact with them would fill his heart whenever he thought of it. And didn't she, really, want to see them too? Her heart would ache, said Julia, but she would do it for him.

She dressed as carefully that Saturday as if the whole world was going to parade by and see her. It was a sort of role, she guessed, a part in Martin's charade. But he had touched, unbeknownst, a great unspoken desire of

Julia's: children someday. She consented, for one reason, because once she saw them, they might come, in her own private game, close to being her own, those two.

Thus she came to the hotel and the heavy red carpets and the gilt and the great clocks in a lofty room. She climbed to the mezzanine and walked about casually, then stopped, leaned, and looked down. She saw Martin first, then the two small beings he had fathered. One at a time they wrote themselves on her permanent vision—boy and girl, one brownette, one tow-headed, and their daddy with them down there. She let the whole fill up her vision to the brim. . . . Then she saw the other one, the wife.

She was right down there beside them. She was appropriately part of the group, a blond girl who belonged there, stocky-legged and rich and confident in a new expensive red coat. Martin stole a forlorn glance at the balcony. If Julia had brought her opera glasses, as she had intended, she would have thrown them at him. The total Parham power was down there, the addition of the wife in person was all that was needed to parade it in full before her helpless gaze. And if Martin couldn't help it, it was because finally he didn't want to help it.

Mad as hell, she stormed out of there and decided, as she had often decided, to move. If he can't take a step without first consulting them why do I keep on letting him pay the rent? When she let herself into the apartment, the phone was ringing: it was Martin, imploring, but she hung up. He was there in fifteen minutes, ringing the bell. His wife had decided to come on her own hook. He'd had no intention of bringing her, but she had suddenly turned up with something she insisted she had to see the doctor about, so he couldn't stop her, could he? —and when she heard one of the children say something about the St. Charles, well, nothing would do her but to go there too, she'd been heading right up to the ladies' room when Julia left through the swinging doors of the entrance. It was just the barest coincidence, a kind of synchronizing of a fatal five minutes, that Julia had seen her with him and the children at all.

"It's all a mess, because you made a mess of it," Julia said, crying through the slit in the door, which was chain-bolted. "Oh, come on in, then." She lifted the bolt.

Martin entered, taking her in his arms, holding her, reassuring her.

"That's not the point, not the point," she kept saying whenever he ventured to say anything. "You can't do anything with them up there, you never could. Not for me, not for anybody. You couldn't even give me the moment of seeing them alone with you, you just robbed me. They're Parhams now—nothing to do with you and me. For good and all."

"But aren't they beautiful, aren't they wonderful-looking kids?"

She began crying harder than ever. Oh, damn him forever, she thought.

"You got to admit it, Julie."

"I never thought they wouldn't be," she said, having seen about a thousand photographs already. She stopped crying abruptly. "Yes . . . yes, Martin, just beautiful." She couldn't honestly deny it, but all the worse, she thought. Don't men see anything? They weren't hers, those bright-haired little things, and when he left (to pick up his wife from the clinic) she went and fixed it so that she ran into a man she used to date. They had a drink and she got around to it. "What are you letting him hold you for, if not for money?" the man asked, with the encyclopedic knowledge of a man one doesn't know very well. "You just don't want to say that's what it is."

"I know how much I mean to him."

"It won't be guaranteed to last if he's so self-centered. He might even fall in love with his wife, how can you tell?"

Oh my God, she thought, Martin in love with his wife. "He couldn't be in love with her because of me."

In a way she was right.

The girl Martin had married to spite Julia was un-
commonly sweet, pretty, and good-humored. She was
bewildered in life for the first time some months after
she married when she discovered that Martin's total
attention was not to be her own. She had thought she
had it, then she felt she might begin to claim it more and
more, finally she knew it wasn't happening that way
at all.

Her only trouble was being young, sheltered, and well
brought up. She believed in the encouragements of her
family and of other girls. When she first met Martin she
had thought he was just flirting, then she believed that
they were just having a good time together, then that he
would surely stop very soon sending her such nice pres-
ents, then that he couldn't be serious when he proposed.
Following this modest line with the state of Mississippi's
most eligible bachelor, she was in white before she knew
it. Her grandmother's veil—they'd got the yellow bleached
out of the lace mainly with the aid of sunlight on a slope
of grass—floated before her eyelashes down the aisle of
the Ridgeland, Mississippi, Presbyterian Church, as she
clamped to her father's trembling arm—trembling partly
(she knew but did not criticize) at the thought of the
Parham millions and that huge estate.

It wasn't long before she heard about the other one,
the one in New Orleans. How? Some overheard conversation, a letter found, a straight talk from somebody who
thought she ought to know. It was too terrible for her
to divulge the source, even to herself. By then she was
pregnant. She gladly let her soul run toward her children,
even while they were still unborn and making her sick
every day. The real reason she didn't let Martin and the
children get off without her that day he wanted to take
them to New Orleans was that, for one thing, the boy
had a little cold and the weather wasn't any too warm.
For another she was afraid he'd do something silly like
take those children to see Julia. It had been astonishing
what she could accept by way of disillusionment and

accommodation for herself—a young woman, brought up a strict Protestant, timid and warm. But an equal and opposite reaction had set in where her children were concerned. Here she would lie as coolly as a riverboat gambler, and she would fight—fiercely, coldly, cunningly —gone beyond hate, which had not even been a whistle-stop. She knew Martin by then, knew his ego which excused him everything and how he could corrupt them without understanding what he was doing. So she got it to stick that she had to see the doctor that day and went with him and stayed religiously beside him, stayed at the St. Charles while he was out on business, met him for an early dinner at Commander's, and then drove home with him, not a word exchanged about Julia, who might, as far as either of them seemed to be conscious of her, not even have been born.

Yet Julia had been born all right—or misborn, as she sometimes thought—and lying across her white-painted old-fashioned iron bed that she doted on, in the high white rooms Martin had got her so well fixed in, she wondered now what was to keep her from that complete derailment, that final goofing-off known as ending it all. With Martin gone—and he was gone, though he didn't know it yet—she had no inclination for love any more or for finding another lover. Sex was something else again. I'll start wanting it like a drink and a good dinner, she thought. Getting it that way. And getting nothing else to go with it. The prospect did not even alarm her.

She'd keep on staying in the house, she suddenly knew. He wouldn't, she guessed, give it up, sell it, and so turn her out of it. She hoped he didn't show up, though, and nobly tell her so. For she had no inclination to be noble in return and refuse. She was comfortable here. She liked it. She got up slowly, feeling sore in her spirit. She groped toward the mirror and looked in cautiously, like peering down a well. She had just given a whore's excuse; she was settling for a cast-off fancy woman's bed. Is it like me to do that? she asked herself. She guessed it must be, since she seemed to be doing it.

She picked up the silver mirror, the back embossed with a lady's face and long flowing hair that streamed out, undulant, in every direction. She put on lipstick. Still young; still attractive. She sighed. The pang of Martin—of the thousand blind spots that went to make up the lovable whole of a rich man's boy—struck her fresh and whole. Her face streamed wet again. "Fool!" she thought. "Oh, that fool!" Then she thought, Who knows the danger he's in better than me? When he gives me up, starts being good instead of bad, they'll turn on him. They'll start to hate him. They might even come back and root me out.

(She was used to studying "Them," way up there in Parham land, with her mental telescope adjusted and her mental note pad and her sense of accuracy about Them and their self-important ways. He was in danger from Them all right, and they would get at her all right. There was just enough difference between him and his own family for him to be turned on by Them; he was just that much of a gentleman among the mob. If I do nothing but sit here, she thought, I may turn into an instrument of revenge—getting my own back without doing a thing but living rent-free.)

She blew her nose, dried her eyes, and started refreshing her make-up. For his sake she ought, tidily now, to get out, bury the corpse of their love and good times decently, and cover all over with the neatest of white sand. Then the Parhams would find nothing at all to attest to Martin's wild days and general heartfelt disrespect toward the straight-and-narrow path they went every Sunday to hear preached about.

Now Martin will start loving his sister, Julia thought. He'll get around to it because I told him to. That sister. The bone that had stuck in Julia's throat. That lens of a person who had given her her focus on the whole lot. Through her Lillian Martin will get perfect. He'll be Jesus

Christ. Because what evil will there be left for him without me and Dev to think about? What kept him so tensed up was that it had the ring of evil about it, a good, hard, iron sound. And I——

She saw too much and could have screamed with the seeing. All too much seeing is a failure of love. Suppose, further, that she was right about it all? She recoiled as from an abyss. Words—"whore," "fancy woman"—had snaked up out of other times and tried to circle her ankle, to strike at her. Watch out for snakes, Tommy Arnold had advised. What else would get at her? She wondered just how narrow a ledge she now stood on and dared not look down. Instead she looked steadily into the almost-perfect circle of the little hand mirror, her level brown eyes looking back.

The great life snare, who's not in that? We're all in it together, in the great muddy stream flowing toward the sea.

# 7. REFLECTION AND DECISION

 Julia went on writing.

"In a certain manner of speaking, Dev used to say, We've none of us got anything outside our love. Some people never know it.

"He gave it full value, way too much, and he didn't really mean it all the time, but from time to time he did mean it. This is how love is. After all, he had known in the salt smell of Charleston and the static beauty of Jamaica what he had found out in the bayou country, having traveled far with the knowledge. He was with her, in all those places, a diminutive small-boned English girl. He was always picking her up as though to carry her over a perpetual threshold, marveling at her lightness. She had come to New Orleans, with her family, from Jamaica. Her father was English, they were all English. He was in a firm for imports and exports—words like rum and hemp and indigo lingered about the whole visit there, talk of cargoes with some space to spare for Mexican silvercrafts and New Orleans tinned seafoods. To find suitable accommodations for an extended visit, the family had made use of certain letters of introduction and credit. One was to the senior member of the law firm where Henri Devigny was a new associate, having come in to New Orleans two years before from St. Martinsville. He was invited, more or less, to call and see if they were faring well in the quarters that had been rented for them. The thought of Jamaica came to him along the way. A hot jungle grew up in his mind: it was rich and green. Along the way he traveled its edge; when he turned to enter it—their suite was at the St. Charles—a brown bird with a snow-white breast flew up; and that was his, flushed out. He knew it right away.

"The little bird. Tiny as a handkerchief. Ladies' lace pocket handkerchief. White. Always white. Her health no good. Probably she never knew his full passion, how could she have and still have him think of her the way she seemed? But hadn't she looked on those flaming red trees in Jamaica and seen the full-set Negro women come and go? Proud heads on necks straight and strong as mahogany trunks, hips swaying? Well, in a distant way maybe she knew, maybe she sensed it all, with a sigh. She was frail, one reason for leaving Jamaica. They told her the New Orleans coasts weren't exactly healthy, but she said at least sometimes the weather was fresh and there was some change of climate. They said it got drizzly gray with cold and rain. When she asked about sunny days, they said, That, too. She and her mother offered people tea.

"Dev had seen pictures of women like her all his life in magazines. The wise New Orleans girls were not like her (got stodgy later, after marrying). The pretty little Southern belles, from up in Mississippi, up in Louisiana, up in Georgia, Alabama, Tennessee, Carolina—always coming down on excursions or getting a bid to one of the balls they'd frame or keep forever in a cedar chest or paste in a scrapbook, pretty and prim or pretty and flirty or pretty and wild, all country girls (turned into good managers after marriage, Dev said)—they were not like her either. And the Yankee girls with what they were on the lookout for too firmly mixed in with their charm and their elegance and their money. He'd had a chance to see them all, all types, in the way of the New Orleans young, man or woman, without stirring out of place. So he waited and there she was. English. From Jamaica.

"I have often seen her picture. He kept it in the top drawer of a big mahogany chest of drawers he had upstairs at Aunt Isabel and Uncle Maurice's, and I think maybe he got it out when he was alone, too. I remember the finely worked gold frame, the miniature beautifully tinted, oval, and the face not abashed to be so prized as that, the eyes gray and even, and the soft pretty artless hair. The dress, too, was quite fine.

"Uncle Maurice's birth nearly killed her. It took him two days to be born. (He once told me that birth was the family curse.) He was a September child, but it was nearly December before she could get up. In February Dev wanted to take her down to the bayou country to a house he had there, with a formal garden. It was beside Bayou Teche and he wanted her to be there, beside the inky water fresh with its own nature and the willows slanting. 'Same as in England,' he said he told her. 'Willows are the world over. There must be willows in Alaska.' And the cypress. Big knees in the swamps and long fronds of Spanish moss. Birds, egret and heron, mockingbird, robin and owl. Camellias would bloom now, and poinsettia, azalea, bougainvillea, forsythia, wistaria, spirea. Althea, crepe myrtle, japonica, magnolia. He showered her with names, the stranger the better. So they took the baby and the nurse and set off by train, on a cold clear sunny morning, the kind she'd come there to find. A carriage and driver, ordered well ahead, met the train.

"Late in the evening and almost within the last of three forests along the road, with swampland among the oaks, a wheel came off the carriage. The nurse was scared of this part of the country (she thought it was full of voodoo spirits, especially among the Spanish moss), so she jumped out of the carriage and ran back through the dark, down the road toward the town of St. Martinsville. For all they ever knew she might have been trying to make New Orleans. Did the spirits get her? They never saw her again. The driver was scared too and whipped the horses forward to reach an open field he thought he saw ahead. It was Dev who jumped up and holding his wife under his arm seized the reins and brought the carriage to a stop.

"But the baby had fallen out—Uncle Maurice in swaddling clothes—and rolled off the road halfway to a ditch. He had to be looked for and then they were calling the nurse over and over, fruitlessly. When they reached the house that night and opened it there were snakes in it sheltering out of the cold. Nobody could sleep for fear of finding one in bed and the English girl sat all night holding Uncle Maurice in her arms.

"I had a dream once about that house. I was a young girl in white and gold, an afternoon dress, standing before a forward-slanting mirror over a mantelpiece, a heavy rectangular mirror with a golden frame, putting up my hair and hearing a call from below. A date come to get me. My heart was running down the stairs already, in golden sandals. . . . Life should be like that, always like that."

She broke off. She was sitting on the veranda of an old comfortable run-down hotel on the Gulf Coast, writing. She had got her vacation from the hospital and this was what she had decided to do with it. She looked out of the hot midday shadows into the even more intense heat, the almost searing glare, which lay across the wide green lawn and glossed dazzling up from the highway with its brightly passing cars and shimmered above the misty blue quiet flatness of the Sound water. Out in the water a wooden pier and gazebo had miraculously escaped every hurricane up to the present, though she had overheard two old people talking at dinner the evening before, saying that another one like '47 would wipe out everything. Nonetheless, the gazebo remained with its own jaunty attitude toward the world. It had a cunning peaked roof like a child's party cap, with a brass knob on the center pole. Hexagonal, it was surrounded with white latticework, and within had benches painted green, like the top railing around the bright red roof. It was like a ferry stop, Julia thought. Should I go to it and wait? Wait for what? She had sat in it and smelled hot paint in the sun.

She stopped writing. Presently she turned a page in

the journal which was slowly filling up, and wrote out a list of names.

> Dev, deceased
> Uncle Maurice and Aunt Isabel, in love
> Mother, deceased
> Father, gone . . . deceased?
> Jake, gone
> Wilma Wharton, gone
> Ted Marnie, murdered
> Tommy Arnold, out of touch
> Martin Parham, gone?
> Edie Williams, gone

She added the last name after reflection and after more reflection crossed it out. She tore the leaf off the wire spiral which held all the leaves in place, folded it and put it in her purse. Her whole life. What wasn't a graveyard was a junk pile of memories, assorted and some scarcely related, and she could go sort through it when she wanted to.

So far she was refusing to talk to people who seemed to want to get acquainted with her. At night she read instead of joining in games and dancing. All she had to do, really, was finish the memoir about Dev and give it to Martin Parham to fulfill her sense of what she owed him, then settle down to the nothing life like millions of the earth's inhabitants, or jump into the gulf, what's the difference?

The day before she had found a sandy piece of driftwood in the hotel corridor. A child had brought it and left it there. The colored cleaning man had been about to throw it out but Julia took it, getting a superior look from him. Then on the yacht club pier she had found a piece of heavy rope, frayed at the end and smelling of the oil which had stained it, dark with the oil and wear and frayed as well, the end like a hank of hag's hair, hanging down. And last she found a small handful of shells. They were all in her room and she would dislike leaving them (she would do it nonetheless) but they had so far kept her company. At night she had laid the driftwood on the bed. Once she lay face down looking at the rope: it looked like something female, drowned and dead. When she looked at it she thought of the Misses Mulligan: it was an antidote to them, they were its distant pole. Hag-drowned, wicked, and nameless, the opposite of precious little white non-touchable souls who whisper away a lifetime over fine china, and are loved by God.

She would pile the whole together on the dresser when she left, and whoever found it would be assured she was a nut. For this was Mississippi, not Louisiana. Mississippi was where you got disapproved of.

On a new page, she wrote:
"Father, of course, could reappear someday, never having deserted me, but only having had to go to the men's room in the station that day over twenty years ago. What if he did? The only person afraid that Father will show up is Uncle Maurice. Uncle Maurice may be a good uncle but to be a father to me is something he never wanted, so he let Dev take over, evil, vice, sex-mania notwithstanding. He let it happen, for all he wanted passionately was to be with Aunt Isabel. By reappearing now that Dev is dead, Father would reveal his failure to him. Perhaps he has discovered how to keep Father away. If so, there might be a way of getting that out of him.

"If Father reappears at all it will be to Uncle Maurice. Father saw Aunt Isabel, after all. You always take up where you leave off. This is the life-thread."

This page too she tore out a day later and put it, not in her purse with the name list, but in an inner pocket of her suitcase.

The next day about three o'clock she took the list of names out of her purse and, working with an automatic pencil, the sheet resting on the page of a book she was reading, she lightly shadowed over the inscribed names in slanted lines like falling rain. She had two days left and, except for occasional trips by bus up the shore drive to the beach near the Gulfport yacht club, she had yet to go out in the sun. She never played badminton in the dusk or early morning and when she swam in the hotel pool she swam alone.

Late that same afternoon there was a terrible thunderstorm which seemed to be happening not without but within the hotel. It was a wonder to everybody afterwards that nothing got broken and that the old walls were still standing and that no one had been killed. The dusk was clear but lined far out on the horizon with bold green and purple clouds, the first like that she'd ever seen, and green light was spread clearly and evenly over both water and land. After dinner, sitting deep in a wing chair in the lobby, she was bent over her book when she looked up and saw a young man come in. Once through the doorway of the wide-spread lobby, he began searching here and there with quick glances into alcoves and wing chairs, threading among the various groups. He was a good searcher, she saw. What makes a good searcher? her quick mind asked her. Somebody who knows what they want, she at once answered. She wondered what or whom he wanted and was about to read again when he saw her and everything snapped together, because she had run into him the day before at the beach. He had begun a conversation, bought her a beer, and must somehow have got out of her where she was staying. His face lighted up. He leaned toward her with the careful gaiety of a young man who wants to measure up to the top mark more than anything else. He had a face it would do no earthly harm to know better. It was good and clean and the taste of his blue linen coat and gray slacks was faultless. "I didn't know your name, but I remembered you mentioned this place. I called and described you, but no luck." She remembered now: somebody saying she was wanted on the phone, she saying there must be some mistake. "I just wanted to see you. I—I'm stationed down here, over at

Biloxi. I think I told you. Would you—can't we—talk? Have a drink?"

She lied to him. She told him she was waiting for her fiancé from New Orleans. He went away.

Julia was left after the young man departed in a sort of vacuum that seemed to be singing mildly and constantly in her ears. Tomorrow was her last day. And tomorrow came. The pier and gazebo stood bright in the sun as she taxied away round the wide arc of gravel drive. She had not even gone to wait for the ferry which looked as if it might appear and stop there. It was an instinctive motion, like refusing the young officer. She had chosen to crawl into her own worn leather handbag and nestle by the names she had written down, though they were as fleshless at present as the marks of pen on paper. Some in the graveyard, she thought, some in the junk pile, and some not much concerned with me.

The coastal scenery fled by first taxi, then bus, bright cut-outs in the sun, not joined to her own nature.

This was how it was.

# Part II

# 1. A RETURN

 Up at Parham Station, up where Martin Parham lived with his wife and children and all that family of relatives, one of the day's few major events was the arrival of the bus bearing in its underparts—along with suitcases, young unplanted balled trees, parts of farm machinery—the wire-tied package of New Orleans papers. The storekeeper cut the wire with a pair of wire cutters, then left the package on the counter. During the next half hour everyone in that community—mainly Parhams or their relatives—would stop before the door in their Cadillacs and Lincoln Continentals and Oldsmobiles and wander inside casually, asking before they picked up the paper for milk or cream or butter or soap or salt or maybe a package of frozen shrimp and some tonic water if company had unexpectedly arrived. If children ran up the steps and inside ahead of whatever adult was with them, they would want popsicles and Dixie cups.

There was a good smell about the store, Martin always thought. In fact, he knew his children best when they were running ahead of him into it, up the broad unpainted steps, each worn down like a saddle in the middle.

The hangers-on, the old men and loafers of every age, sat around and waited to speak until spoken to in that sly mock democratic way that said all were equal in God's eyes, but that it had a special meaning to own that much land and drive that type of car and that one of the things it meant was you'd better learn to speak first and to speak well, with just the right tone and manner. Martin had always had the knack of doing it. You would think he really meant it, every time.

On that day he noticed something for the first time: the children had quit running ahead of him. Today, they walked quietly. The girl, Mary Nell, sweet, brown-haired, and shy, was inclined to duck her head passing the men on the porch. As she bit her nails at times, she clenched her fists up. Martin guessed that awkwardness was torture. The boy, Davey, more extroverted, used to ripping up the steps two at a time, clambered evenly, head up and grinning generally. They had both been instructed that they must always speak and they did so, each after their own fashion. They went through the screen door ahead of him.

Martin stopped and looked round, exchanging a word here, a question there; then he entered the dim interior, removing his dark glasses, then letting his eyes adjust on their own.

"Well now," the storeman, Mr. Williford, was saying. "Agnes's been in and your mamma. Toots came early but the paper hadn't come. Said he'd be back. Noland's off fishing, I hear. How's your girl?"

It was Martin's wife he meant. She'd been sick off and on for years and kept having to go to specialists.

"She's been a little bit better the last two weeks. Let's hope she don't have to go back."

"I sure hope it. She's had a hard enough time." He put the milk and bread in a bag, along with the foil-wrapped chill package of cream cheese. "Be anything else?"

"Just the paper . . . unless y'all want something." He turned to the children. Mary Nell shook her head but Davey had a magazine already—*Mad.* His wife hated it, but Martin, as always, laughed and paid. So, picking up everything, he put his change in his pockets, set his dark glasses back in place.

"Warming up," said Mr. Williford.

" 'At's right."

Back to the car.

He did not open the newspaper until he reached home and then only when he was in the large modern kitchen on the ground floor of their split-level house with bedrooms above the short flight of horizontally elongated stairs, whose dark wood planking hung in space like a mobile, suggesting an airy passage, hung with vines and decked with plants and sculptures. (The plans for that stairway had existed for years in the architect's original sketches before the children were deemed out of danger of falling down it; then they installed it.)

Martin put the milk and cream cheese in the refrigerator, drew out a chilled glass with ice cubes already prefrosted in it, and set it in an orange-colored woven straw container from Italy. He dribbled gin over the ice, sliced off a thin moon of fresh lime and tossed it in, snapped the cap from a bottle of Schweppes tonic. "Ready for a drink?" he called, in general, not knowing just where his wife was. She wouldn't be. She had begun to question if drinking was really "right" or not; her parents had never thought so.

On his way for the stirrer he saw his face in a mirror and as always recently he got a jolt. His impulse, restrained, was to lean closer, peer longer. He had a name for that impulse: "Say-it-isn't-so." He had invented it himself. The years had not been so good to Martin Parham. His soft brown hair was thin and wispy across the top of his brow. His stockiness, appealing in a younger man, giving the air of a good tennis player after a fast game, had got lumpish of late. In a dinner jacket, at times in one of his very good suits, he could still look like the cleanly-got-up boy who had met Julia Garrett after the Sugar Bowl and been inspired to buy her a pineapple, but otherwise . . . Oh, Martin, he could hear her chiding, Martin, you once were so handsome . . . tu étais si beau . . . dommage! He laughed; his amiable streak had grown wider with the years, so that he didn't worry very hard for long at the time.

He stirred the drink, waited for the glass to sweat, withdrew the stirrer. Leaning against the cabinet, opening the paper, he took his first sip of the evening.

Then there it was—the front page, and the story.

He read it once, then as his shock faded, once again. He had forgotten about his drink.

What would it mean? he wondered. He combed through it a paragraph at a time, but no mention of Julia appeared. What would it mean to her? Anything at all? He was curious, nothing more.

Presently, he folded up the paper for taking it up to his wife, as though nothing had happened.

The thing was, Martin always had to pretend that everything was "all right." Not only "all right" with his family, his immediate family and his whole family, but "all right" with the Parham business, "all right" with the State of Mississippi, "all right" with the South, "all right" with the United States. Nobody brooked anything much different from this fixed line. If he went so far as to oppose American foreign policy, as he at times mildly did, they would all look at him in silence, as though he was expected to do and say odd things.

They would remember that he had bought a house in New Orleans into which he had installed a former girl-friend, and did his wife know about it and if she did how did she put up with it?

The only deviation the Parhams were permitted from the universal "all-rightness" of things was illness. Illness was something you couldn't help, so you could at least be in bad health. Come to think of it, nearly all of them were. Martin's father suffered from arthritis and varicose veins; his mother had had breast surgery; one sister (not the mad Lillian, who was physically sound) had some mysterious bone disease which could be arrested only by expensive treatments in a New Orleans clinic; his brother had a rare skin trouble and had been written up in a journal. He himself had had a scare the year before with a chronic sore throat, and time would not suffice to tell the complaints, both major and minor, with which his poor wife's days were marked.

As far as money went (and who was to say it didn't go nearly a hundred percent of the way in anything that really mattered?) the Parhams found that all was possible. Travel, beautifully built and landscaped houses, the finest clothes and furnishings, the best cars, servants, hotels, and restaurants . . . what else was there?

Martin found himself thinking more and more often of Lillian. Once, a year ago, telling no one, he took a quiet flight to Arizona to find her. She impressed him for the first time. She had a little hacienda out from Yuma and she had interests in Indian work; some oddball or other was always on the phone, but having met one or two of them, he found them not all that odd. She had found a life. "Do you still go to the clinic?" he wanted to know, staring at her: he had heard her openly despised and mocked at in every house on the estate as "the only ugly Parham," "nutty as a fruitcake." He guessed she was ugly, all right. "When I need to," she said calmly. "I've learned to know the signs." When he left, she said, also calmly, "When I write, I won't mention you came to see me." He had been about to ask her not to, and their joint perception of this state of affairs let him have it clear and straight, for the first time, what an awe-inspiring inferno was the family they both sprang from. In the plane back to New Orleans, he discovered a love for his sister firmly planted in his heart. Claiming his car at the airport, whisking on throughways and bypasses along the outskirts of the city, he remembered Julia and that strange weekend when Lillian had showed up at the main house and he had shunned her. It had been a crucial point with Julia, that one, he now realized, just as whether she had actually as a child been corrupted by a dirty old Frenchman had been a crucial point with him. How crazy people were! But if you weren't a little bit crazy maybe you got sick.

Signs of craziness had been observed in Martin himself two years ago when he proposed putting a large sur-

plus profit from the estate into a summer artists' and
writers' camp. They had the land, he argued, and the
whole scheme would be tax deductible. God knows the
state had talent to burn. Painters all over the place, writers
by the dozen. Things like this had been done in New England for centuries; why not here? His sane sister Agnes
sided with him, and it looked for a while like they would
carry the field along with them. Then his father got nervous, Uncle Noland retired from the discussions by saying
mildly that he didn't know anything about "all that type
of thing," his grandfather (consulted like an oracle in a
house up on a hillside where he shuffled from wheelchair
to bed with the help of an old Negro man and read all the
farm journals, occasionally telephoning down some entirely correct new idea for crop and soil improvement or
cattle breeding) sidetracked everything by suggesting that
the money be simply donated to the nearest university for
promotion of art and writing. Martin complained that this
defeated the whole spirit of his plan, that it would now be
"administered" in an academic way and would lack the
creative atmosphere he had envisioned. It would not, in
other words, be free. "No hippies," said Uncle Noland,
and brought a burst of laughter from everybody as no one
had thought he would know the word.

Now Martin and his sister Agnes grew closer and con-
soled each other over a great many too many martinis and
let their hair down on what they thought of everybody.
Agnes would be above using anything that Martin said
against him in family circles, but her husband Norris
might not. Cautiously one night, admiring some new
crystal she'd ordered made up in Paris, Martin asked
her, "Just getting one thing after another, anything we
want, that's kind of getting old sometimes, ain't it,
Agnes?"

"Oh, I think that too, but you've got to pass the time."
She was a dark smooth-looking young woman, not pretty,
not ugly, and encouraged by the distraction he often
noticed in her expression, he carefully asked if she ever

dreamed of anything, another sort of life, other kinds of people. "I don't mean to be sacrilegious," he grinned.

"Oh, sure I do, sure. Why do you think I go to all those places, Italy, France . . .?" She trailed off. No lover, Martin reflected, had ever actually showed up or even been rumored to exist. He dared go no further.

Agnes adjusted a piece of translucent tortoise shell in her hair and poured another martini. "Listen, Martin, you know how Uncle Noland is. When he wants his kicks he heads straight back up into Goose Hollow, up yonder where they still go to buryings and church suppers and hoe-downs—he can go up there and start carrying on like he never left off. But after Uncle Noland there was just money to get worked up over, and I can't manage either one. You can't imagine what trouble I went to about that crystal." She looked at it, the shimmering goblets for cocktails, claret, champagne and water, all ranged before her.

"It's terrific stuff," Martin encouraged her.

"When I go away," said Agnes, "I don't pick up with men. God knows I don't pay young boys for the pleasure of their company. Norris is more than enough that way—you know that. I guess what I like is just being nobody, being where Parham is just an odd American name."

"And watching the pretty sunset," said Martin, and saw in the strong character of her glance that he'd almost gone too far. He thought he'd come close to discovering another side to her, but that with any Parham was a dangerous exploration, especially dangerous for another Parham to undertake. And more especially for Martin. His younger brother Craig was gaining on him, just as Agnes's husband Norris might have done, only he had no Parham blood. Craig was not interesting but he was "sound." He was also thought to have matured wonderfully in the last few years, though Martin so far still retained his hold in two important quarters: Uncle Noland liked him best, no matter what he did, and he was still the favorite of the grandfather. New Ideas were what Martin was deemed

capable of. Important, and the life of things. So spake
the grandfather, alone up there on his hill except for Buzz,
the faithful Negro manservant, who earned enough to
change his car every year. Regularly on Sunday evenings,
Martin was expected up the hill for supper, a drink of
Scotch, and a long chat.

If no hidden life was to be smoked out among his clan,
Martin thought, there was only Uncle Noland whose
hidden life was not hidden but wide out in the open for
whoever wanted to go up to Goose Hollow with him and
whoop out loud about how much he loved them folks up
there, just couldn't get enough to satisfy. Of course, there
was always Lillian, whose other life had become the one
she led and so of course she was crazy. For the rest,
money and property, finer houses, bigger cars, better live-
stock, richer pastures. We've got all the way to French
crystal, thought Martin, and I guess that's a step beyond
swimming pools.

Such was the state of affairs when he went to the store
that June day for the New Orleans paper.

Standing in the kitchen he read it, and whereas the
moment before he had stood inland on the driest of dry
land, reasonable, routine, regular, sane, and sound as he
could ever be, the moment after he was up to his chin in
a surrounding element as strange and alive as if the sea
had risen to reclaim its own. And for what? All that was
said was that Ted Marnie, thought to have been murdered
eight years before, was not dead at all, but had appeared
—alive and well, walking down a street in San Diego—to
somebody who had known him in New Orleans, a member
of one of the groups Jake Springland had played with,
though no significance was at present attached to this
fact. The man who had seen him had had a drink with
him, then had gone straight out to telephone the New
Orleans police for whom he had done undercover work
off and on over the years.

Details . . . details. . . .

Martin Parham, standing and reading, soaked them all up and still had an appetite for more. He had reached and passed and now, like a distance runner, was reaching again for the name which twined with Marnie's, the name that had concerned Julia and through her himself: Jake Springland. It was Jake that New Orleans was intrigued by and it was he they wanted back, or what would such a long piece about a two-bit crook, part-time evangelist, possible dope-pusher, be doing on the front page at all? So he reasoned, wondering if it was also true that Julia herself wanted him back. From a distance it was possible for Martin to think that Jake and Ted and Julia Garrett simply were New Orleans, and that newspaper reporters scrambled all over each other to write them up because their true story was not quite known, nor could it be quite known as it was, simply, life, the way that city knew it. As he thought of it, that city, he felt it pull him, draw him, as it pulled the great river down a whole continent, going South to its very street-tips.

But Marnie died, Martin thought.

It was supposed to be true.

And Springland had left, just disappeared. But the name at least had stirred again. What would it say to Julia?

Martin had understood that she had got clear of any notoriety over the murder because a man she'd known (had more or less fascinated, he could only suppose, a sexy girl like that) had worked on the *Picayune* and had moreover been assigned to the case. But the name on the new piece, the by-line, was altogether new.

Martin sank in a chair, sighing. I can't get mixed up in all that, he thought, father of two young children, with an important role in the management of the Parham estates: oil, cattle, timber, tung oil, pecan orchards, peach orchards, nurseries, and a dozen other related industries. Julia had it made here and she hadn't wanted it. Why? Because I didn't love my sister. Funny, but if I have any clandestine relationship now, it's to Lillian. Is this Julia's power still? How different secret selves are from the outer face of things.

He broke out laughing. He had wandered into the living room which was closed and shuttered, air conditioning muted, curtains drawn against the glare. His wife had come downstairs into the kitchen without noticing him, and found the paper where he had refolded it and replaced it on the cabinet as though it had never been opened. Now she was standing over him, opening it for some election news. The national news was her daily meat. "What are you doing in here?" she asked.

"Cool," he said. "It's got hot outside. How you feel, honey?"

"Some better."

"You always feel better at night."

"I don' mind seein' that evenin' sun go down."

She'd said this before, about a million times, but Martin didn't hold such things as a little repetition against people. He sat thinking he ought to check into it about the house Julia lived in, to see if upkeep was needed—termites, plumbing, mold, and mildew, damage from lightning, fire department requirements, etc., etc. Also he could go back to the newspaper library, a quick trip, and look up clippings on the Marnie affair. It wouldn't hurt to have the straight of it. That reporter's reportings . . . what was his name? Hardy? Arnold? Arney? Julia had liked him. If she wasn't mourning the old man she was thinking of somebody else, maybe of that reporter, from time to time, maybe of Martin. So he imagined. She didn't seem to be mourning when she said she was. Just thinking of them, she said. What did she think?

He hadn't seen her in years.

He remembered the smell of the newspaper office, the day he went to look the old man up; it returned to him vividly enough for him to analyze what it was like. It was like a spring—dust, dirt, and black smears of ink like the loam or mud or slime in the spring's surroundings; and as in the eye, the core of it all, the clean water welled out, so the clean steel smell of the type was central to the grimy experience of visiting the newspaper. It would be better than the first time, certainly, when he went to look up Henri Devigny and had confronted the face of that heavy-mouthed, avid-eyed old sinner, and hadn't been able to bear thinking of— Of what? Did it matter now? What did the seduction of a child by an old man matter if you just said it that way and didn't think of who by whom?

Then he remembered a line from English literature in college that had impressed him at the time, a writer grieving for his girl's death, with a piece of her hair before him, writing: Only a lock of woman's hair . . . And Julia's hair, short, was dark encirclement of his fingers, or long, coiled lively about his wrist. . . .

His son Davey had crawled up on his knee, then up his lap and shoulder, and was trying to hang upside down over the chair back. His wife sat companionably, turning to inside pages. "You going to break your neck that way, Davey," she said without looking up. "How do you know what he's doing?" Martin asked. "I just know," she said.

How could people see without looking? Maybe that was the trouble with Parham Station. You didn't have to look to know exactly what people were doing all the time. He didn't know, really, what Julia had done with Henri Devigny or with anybody else. But knowing or not he had gone wild with jealousy anyway, and with revulsion— abnormality: that awful thing. And here he was, getting right back into it.

As he went up the stairs the houseplants and small bronze sculptures (Maillol, Degas, Picasso, and Matisse) were ornamental no longer but alive with their silent message, and when he came down again to switch on the lamps before dinner, the discreet paintings, drawings and graphics (Vuillard, Picasso, Matisse and Chagall) glowed with energy and fire. He had wondered from time to time, why spend so much on name artists when others did as well, though when his father pressed him on this point he defended the choice by speaking in an advanced way of "art." But in this moment, now, he knew better than that, too. At last, he saw again.

The next question awaited him as silent as a cat. What in this place battled against these things? What tried in every way to question, deny, or at least neutralize their statement, reducing them through that purposeful ignoring which is the lowest form of ignorance into nothing more than a clod by the roadside or anybody's plot of irises in a yard?

It was too much to answer.

Two days later he descended on New Orleans down the state highway like something being poured out of a pitcher.

At the St. Charles, where for a long period before his marriage he had kept rooms, he was still known and could get his car parked at once by the doorman, a room quickly apportioned to him at the desk.

A cab now took him deep into St. Charles Avenue and the Garden District, under the horizontal arms of great spreading oaks. A blurred sense of longing had invaded his whole being; he longed for the sight of Julia so much he could not even imagine accurately an image of her, since she was going to seem as she always seemed in memory or present with him, like a spirit filling to the corners, nooks, and brim every part of whatever room she was in with him, but he could imagine (and did) the white-painted iron bed which in his dream of two nights before he was simply sitting on, clothed, in the same room with her, talking to her, his talking and his looking and her presence all mingling together, both patterning and filling the room as patterns of sunlight through shutters and foliage both remain themselves yet give light everywhere. He should have called. But he hadn't.

Her stairway was a side one, a private entrance from a generous spread of lawn below, spaced out casually with camellia bushes and jasmine, crossed with a flagstone path. No one answered the bell. She was working, of course. He knew about the hospital job, but had forgotten it. Dashed, he circled the house—his, after all—and rang at the first-floor apartment. He did not recognize the woman who answered. She was speaking to him through the screen which he supposed she was keeping latched throughout. Her head was wound in an orange scarf which grated on his vision. Her voice sounded orange.

"Miss Garrett ain't lived here in some time . . . she moved just before we bought the house. . . ."

"Who sold the house to you?" He thought for one wild moment he might have the wrong house.

"Those people up in Mississippi . . . some big family, never lived here, but her relatives or something like that. . . . Somebody else took that apartment, now they've moved. It's empty now, but we hope——"

"But where's Miss Garrett?"

"She don't even get no mail here any more, so I couldn't tell you. Look in the phone book, why don't you?" She shut the door. Yes, why didn't he look in the phone book?

Numb to his fingertips, he began walking on St. Charles Avenue, blundered into the bar at the Hotel Pontchartrain for a drink (at 10 A.M.!) and back onto the sidewalk with the sun slamming at him and sweat around the rims of the dark glasses. He was shaking now. What was coming on was rage. They had gone behind his back.

In waves, the first a mere wash of feeling, a disappointment so easily alleviated (he could, as the woman said, look in the phone book), disturbance rose up about him, moving swiftly higher. Psychic in nature, it struck at his vitals as a physical force; it was a personal storm. His private barometer had fallen to zero while he'd taken the drink, trying to stave off full knowledge of what had happened; when he finished it, the sky in his head had turned black as ink. He had moved, love- and memory-drawn, in a deceptive path of sun, all the brighter because of the darker formations gathering around, but he had not noticed.

To go behind his back! He had slammed money on the bar and reentered the street with slashing heels. The full force was on him now and he was literally seeing red.

It was their damnable power of attorney, father acting for brothers when brothers were on a Mediterranean cruise, brother acting for brother when brother was on honeymoon or in New York for the theater season or up moose-hunting in Canada or on an art-buying spree in Paris. He had wanted to secrete, exclude that house from the estate, knowing the Parham nose for everything a Parham owned, and that it should have been discovered and then the discovery not disclosed to him. . . . He had thought himself the crown prince whose gentlemanly indulgences would be put aside without too much notice, and somebody had sniped him down. Silently—without even telling him! What right had they had? Added to everything else, it had been an innocent arrangement. Not since the ill-fated day he'd wanted her to see his children and his wife had been hell-bent on coming too had he even seen Julia, much less touched her. To him it was pure soul-luxury, a native generosity of spirit, to let her live where she could give herself a good style.

I'm going to stay drunk for two days, thought Martin. If I go back up there now I'll tear the place apart.

And he couldn't, no, he couldn't. Too much at stake for that. A split would follow, a real showdown. Unless, keeping it in his own four walls, he took apart the house he'd built, broke expensive things, squandering his wife's inexhaustible loyalty. (She'd have to go back to the specialist.) No, he couldn't. He kept walking.

He was already at Tulane University, about a mile further out St. Charles. A question occurred. Why hadn't

Julia herself told him, appealed to him, if she was being put out? Maybe they hadn't even communicated with her. That would be just like them. So then she might have taken the move as part of his desire as well. Out with the trash. Out with Martin's little piece of tail. And high time too.

Or maybe Julia herself had done it, got tired of the whole thought of anything to do with Martin, picked up with somebody else and, not wanting to wound him, had quietly informed his family that she'd just as soon they sold the house, it made her feel— He didn't know. Her uncle might have handled it with that smooth Devigny touch, vanishing before you saw it happen. But here too he didn't know.

He came full stop, plunged into a drug store, purple and white with banners and balloons and streamers— big sale—and scrambled through a phone book. She was still listed at the old address. So it was recent, this move. He called information but got no new number. The hospital! Why couldn't he remember that she went to work like ninety-five percent of the world? Five days a week, maybe six. He called the hospital. Now they were saying "Miss Garrett in Medical Information," plain as anything, and a phone was ringing.

"Hello . . .? Martin? Martin *Parham?*"

"Julia!" Half-exploding with relief, he sagged back against the wall of the phone booth. Sweat poured down his temples. She said she would meet him for lunch.

*Another one*, Julia thought, unbelieving, having herself read of Ted Marnie's reappearance in the land of the living two days before in the *Picayune. One and two, then three and four. Maybe . . . maybe.* Among her files and queries, between her telephone and her typewriter, she felt a coming life, as inexorable as that of a tree in spring. *First Ted; now Martin; then . . .*

They'd started coming back.

Not at Kolb's, as he suggested, but in a crummy-respectable, semi-nice cafeteria near the hospital (she said she didn't have time for a long lunch, but was really concerned lest they bump into Uncle Maurice, who liked to eat at Kolb's), there she was in the door in dark slate-blue cotton with a peach-colored scarf. He was coming toward her. Taking his hand, she turned for his kiss a cheek spotted with hasty rouge, neither as soft nor as fragrant as he remembered it.

Whatever this was, it wasn't like old times.

Martin Parham had probably never eaten in a cafeteria since he left school. They had never stood in a line together, holding brown trays and making sparse conversation. They had never, trays loaded, chosen a table, and had never stolen glances at each other over glasses of iced tea.

"Tell me from the first," said Martin finally. "What happened about that house?"

"Nothing spectacular," said Julia. "I heard through a letter from the new owner, somebody who heads a real estate firm, that the house was now in his hands and that rent on my apartment would be such-and-such a month until the property was sold. I paid it one month, then it seemed too high for me, so I gave notice and left. I guess they sold it after I left. I never met the new owners."

"And nobody talked to you?"

"Nobody."

"So what did you think?"

"I didn't think anything. I wanted to write you and thank you for all the years there, but I——"

"You what?"

"What if you didn't want to hear? What if your wife got the letter? What if nobody had ever known I was there? I felt like a nothing-person some of the time."

"A what?"

She was smiling. "A nothing-person is somebody who gets forgotten or misplaced in some way. Their files get lost. They were told to stay on in the fine summer house after the family left, but then nobody ever comes back. Finally people remember the property and return and open the door and out walks a little old woman."

"Some book you're reading."

"I didn't read it. I made it up. In other ways I was ashamed, a little, to mention it. I should have left long ago, on my own steam. I'm the party girl who didn't leave the party."

"I had to call you. I was afraid they'd been rude to you—hurt you some way."

She shook her head. "The hard part was not knowing. Now I see it really was impersonal. But maybe that's the worst hurt of all."

There was a silence. She finished up some cafeteria goulash. He forced down some dry roast beef covered with gravy. She had laid her dark glasses aside to eat. He hated it that she looked older.

"Do you mean to say," she asked, "that you didn't know about the house?" The question, certainly, was there to be asked.

"Not till I got here today." Of course, she was going to know that, no matter how he answered. He was letting her in on it. Was there harm in that? So far as his experience went with her, and that was pretty far, he had never known Julia to act with calculation. It was why he loved her. He guessed that was how you wound up being a nothing-person, if you didn't calculate anything. Yet he wondered if he would have seen her again if he himself had calculated how much he would have to let her in on. He had just been eager to see her, that was all.

"Why did they do it?" she asked. It was the "they" that stuck. Everything spilled out of it, including the con-spiratorial status the two of them used to enjoy, when they were going together, toward all the other Parhams. When she said it, she picked them up again, where they'd left off, so many years ago.

He shook his head. "It beats me. Probably something came up while I was abroad last fall. Nobody wanted to broach the subject with me. Maybe it was a way of finding out if I still saw you."

"But you really don't know why it was," she pointed out, going straight to the sore spot.

"I get angry when I think about it," he said, and began to shake again, the way he had that morning. No drink at lunch—that was one thing. He quit even trying to eat. "Julia, I— So much is wrapped up in this, can't you see it?"

She nodded. "Maybe a little, maybe a lot."

"I can't know! I can't know!"

"You think that *I* am going to feel sorry for *you*?"

"It's more than just finance," Martin said. "It's that they've got power over me. How far do they want it to go?"

If you hang around a family, Julia almost said, but stopped herself.

Martin glanced around him. "We should have got together somewhere better than this." He felt closer to her than he ever had, he had just decided. He was knowing something of what she had always known. The uncertain backing, the lost security, the sense of standing alone. A color T.V. set in the far corner was broadcasting some overexcited local news about a councilman's quarrel. They were advised to stay tuned for national and world news. The garish colors tore a distracted hole in the regular order of dull tables, chairs, cafeteria rail, hot tables, cashier's desk, and hat rack.

"Let's find some way to do better than this. What about dinner? Somewhere new and good, none of the old memory-lane places. I'll stay over."

She paused, liking the idea of "new and good," but not trusting it either to extend beyond the single evening and whatever else grew out of it. Still, she had always liked being with Martin. More, she felt how shaken he was now, and his genuine need. Her lashes had dropped. "If you insist," she said, making it funny.

And he grinned and she, eyes raised now, grinned too. What more is life than a moment's happiness? In that moment, Julia and Martin were happy.

Not till Martin was driving home the next morning did he remember it: the reason he had been moved to go and find her. Ted Marnie. He hadn't mentioned it once. The outrage over the house had filled his being; it had really struck him at the crux of things, had released for a time an anger that was blurring and intense. She had taken the mood off him during the good dinner and the wine and later through the night. Like a good girl should, he thought. She had whispered to him that part of her would always be his.

But if part of her belonged to him, he thought, by the morning's cool light, then of course a bigger part still must belong to Jake Springland and those old days, and she just wasn't saying so. And back of that was the old man she still thought about (it went without saying). And back of Martin, receding into swamps and mystery along the highway he was pursuing north through the dewy morning, the whole city lay teeming, not his property, not even aware that he had entered there and now was gone. And if she came back to him as easy as that and then let him go again, he couldn't have mattered much, couldn't have hurt her much, could never have touched her deepest love.

Had she ruined him? His fancy over her and that house, which had seemed only the right and decent thing, once known about in a property sense might work against him powerfully. Oh, those ever-loving Puritanical hearts, speaking the money language, every beat!

Whore!

He had stopped the car between an elbow of swamp and a rise of sunlit field. A new barbed-wire fence glowed tautly strung against the low horizon. His hands clutched the wheel. Whore or not, his ruin or not, she had been a meaning for him outside of Parham Station, and it was Parham Station she had rejected when she wouldn't marry him.

He did not realize until later that he had cried the word aloud.

# 2. THEY KEEP COMING

 She had been sitting in Jackson Square when it happened and though many things happened to her to which she could not attach any special meaning and did not try, she would always know about this and write it with a capital letter.

From the instant the anonymous outline appeared across the park, framed in a small area of light between the sloping roof of the French Market on the horizon and the straight upward thrust of a corner store which sold ships' salvage, she knew she had entered her own element. Her nerves woke up. It was as though she had been living the pictured life of an illustrated book and now the book had closed and let her wriggle out newborn.

The man was small, dark, she supposed, but she could not see his features, nor did she try. He sat down beside her on the bench, having approached interminably across the park while she looked elsewhere, at trees and sky which no longer really mattered.

"Thought it was you," the man said. (Now she knew the circumstances: Jake playing late and this was the one who usually came, hanging around, waiting, an exchange near the men's room door, and Jake saying: "I've got to burn bright till the sun rises—you know that.")

"Who else could it be?"

"That's right." The man leaned forward. "So it wasn't you he married?"

"You mean settled down and all?"

"I mean, you knew he wasn't all that good, so you wouldn't."

"That was his theory."

"You shouldn't have known it," the man said.

She said nothing.

"That's how you lost him."

"I didn't lose him. Maybe not. If I'd lost him completely you wouldn't be here."

"Umm," the man said, thinking it over.

He wasn't long about going. But when he left, just barely touching her, brushing her, along the shoulder and the bare back of her neck, she knew she would never get back into the book again.

This had probably been why she had taken recently to bringing a sandwich and an apple, some celery and carrots wrapped in wax paper, to the park. She was one of those who waited. The encounter would have happened somewhere. If not the park, somewhere else. The day was serene, not hot, not cool.

After work she went to the book store and the clerk was still there, the blond one with the long jaw. He had had, she now remembered, nice blue eyes and still had them—what personal life? She didn't care and, the way he seemed, neither did he. He said would after dinner be all right, so she met him over on the edge of the Quarter, over near Rampart Street just after dark. What was it she'd been missing all this time and why had she come? The what was the quick, furtive look of people in the backs of shops which sold used books or third-rate antiques, and the why was the conversation, the common language, sometimes unspoken, that went right to the point of what your life was, no regard to time sequence. She hated time sequence and filing systems. There was the uncoiling spiral you lived on, the escalator peaking away as you walked over the top of it all the time. The same steps under your moving feet bending to pass downward into voices which would entwine, pursue, and vanish. Oh, Uncle Maurice, where are you now? She had sat on the corner of a daybed in the black-trimmed white-walled two-room apartment all evening, and leaning back on the large cretonne-covered pillow, closing her eyes as she took her first deep drag, hearing the murmur of voices that would remain anonymous recede into velvet silence, she slowly projected about her the room from years ago where the Negro woman had died and then another time entirely when she had sat on a settee with a tasseled throw and read the *Illustrated London News* while Dev went off with the dark-skinned woman they were visiting for a little conversation alone. But that day no one had died.

When Julia got out on the street at last, the stars were shining at her in a formal manner, and she thought, I'll never do that again. Of course, it wasn't that old house. That house was over on Bayou St. John and anyway it's long since torn down. She refused the blond boy's offer of sex.

"There's this girl in our office," she told him, "who counts money all the time. She makes little lists of figures about the year's expense, the month's expense, the week's expense, the day's expense. . . ."

"The morning's expense," he continued, "the hour's expense, the minute's expense. . . ."

"That's right."

"So how much do you think she's spending every minute?"

"One point seventy three cents or just a fraction under."

"Exactly."

They parted.

The way it was, she could go back to that bookstore the next morning or anytime at all, and if a book or a record was really what she wanted, instead of what she'd been after this time, he wouldn't notice her, not personally, not for a second.

Then two weeks later, there in the paper, there was Marnie, back to life, but she held out and wouldn't think

about it, remembering the stars and their formality. And
after that Martin Parham reappeared, after all this silence
for so long and letting her get run out. Why did she see
him, then? She liked him.

Uncle Maurice and Aunt Isabel had rented out certain
quarters of their big house to selected "guests" they tried
to keep a secret, all because the brokerage firm, in spite
of all Uncle Maurice had tried to warn them about, had
kept running into problems with bad stock issues, some
weak, some actually fraudulent. Uncle Maurice finally
resigned on principle—he couldn't defend them any
more, in all conscience. He returned to private practice,
and money was short. Why did they stay on in Audubon
Place? Julia wondered. Surely the house alone couldn't
give them back their old-time prestige. Maybe they were
pretending that nobody knew. Who was the strange man
in the backyard? An antiques dealer, they explained, come
to do certain evaluations for the Committee on Preservation of Authentic . . . etc. Who were the couple on the
back stairs? Some distant cousins, they said, finishing at
Tulane. They did not dream of moving. When Uncle
Maurice sank into his green cut-velvet armchair and
lighted one of his brown Egyptian cigarettes drawn from
the flat tin, his hand heavy as usual with the onyx, family-
crest-incised oval gold-set ring, he was within himself in
exactly the same mood and position as when Julia was a
little girl in pink or blue or lavender cotton pinafore over
white blouse with puffed sleeves, going up the long back
stairs to call Dev down to lunch. In his heart he was
there in those days, in those hours, which was why he
kept the same brand of cigarettes, and had to have Julia
to dinner on Sundays. And didn't mention the roomers.
And didn't notice Isabel's getting round-shouldered and
thick in the ankles with broken veins in her feet. Something would happen. There would be money somehow.
He had kept his real life, Julia sat and realized, because he had reduced it to dream, had never put it to

the test of losing it and finding it again, pretending that taking risks didn't matter. So then his life became a dream.

Observant, Julia did not share her thoughts with them (catlike, she never had), but further she scarcely dared acknowledge them to herself.

If she so much as drew her breath, she grew heady with the thrill, the shock, the fear, the joy.

Was it coming back, her real life? Was it?

They could say they had found him in San Diego if they wanted to, or in Santa Fe or Denver or Nome, Alaska, or Lima, Peru, Madrid, Taormina, Cairo, Beirut, or Cuernavaca.

But to her he had risen from the dead.

# 3. THE COURSE

 She got the letter in the mail the following week and it said: "I know you'd be glad to stop by Ellis Candies on Coliseum & St. Mary & carry pkg. to the Wilsons over near Amelia because you used to live over that way." And there was nothing else in the envelope but a folded piece of paper and an address for the Wilsons. At Ellis Candies the gray-dressed little old Greek or Italian or anyway foreign-looking woman handed out a parcel to her and at the Wilsons' she was left standing for a short while on the porch of an ordinary house with a gray-painted front porch. It was one of those houses (she stood noticing) that were looked down on about fifty years before as being scarcely apartment sized and very middle class, but which were bought up later for careful refurbishing or were held on to by those who had inherited them or had always lived in them, as good solid property which was increasing enormously in value. Once thought small, they were large enough in present times to house a small family and be cut up into two or three efficiencies, and to have a number of separate entrances. Then the door opened. The man, like the house, was one of many.

Julia said: "Hello, Mr. Wilson," and held out the parcel, which was small enough to hide in her own hand.

"Name?" the man asked. He looked at the doormat she stood on.

"Wilson," she repeated.

"No, yours." The words came up from where she

stood, as though, like smoke, they had floated down, then risen uncertainly upward. "It's Garrett, isn't it?"

She nodded slowly as his hand received from hers, then turned away. Dropped it like a snake, she thought, and on the steps heard the door close softly, felt the chill finger of fear touch her spine. The sun fell hot on that very area of flesh and warmed it. Suddenly reassured, she moved away in a coil of slowly unspiraling joy.

So that was all, then.

Maybe they wouldn't ask her any more. Or at least not for a while.

It was Saturday.

Her day off.

She went and bought a paper and sat down.

Ted Marnie, now connected by the police to the murder of an unknown man whose body had been found in a swamp eight years before and identified (by a button, a thread sewing the button, and a broken and badly reset wrist on the corpse, among other evidence) as Ted Marnie, was being flown back to New Orleans for questioning. The police would also search for and bring to the city for questioning the one-time night-club performer Jake Springland, who had been Marnie's accomplice in several small filling station robberies at the time of the supposed murder. New Orleans readers would remember the many bizarre facts about the case, which had created widespread interest and speculation at the time. The woman Wilma Wharton, Marnie's common-law wife, was being searched for, though a friend of hers had anonymously called up the newspaper and said that she had died in Texas two years ago.

Julia put her coffee cup down empty. She looked around her. This was the same café, or one just like it, she had sat in so many years ago when the police suspected Jake of having murdered Ted Marnie. And it was hot again. If only Tommy Arnold would wake up and

come, she thought. It was his by-line she was missing. It
was him she wanted to see.

She imagined he was sitting across from her so
thoroughly she could hear what he was saying: "You're
getting your kicks from some crazy idea that you can
reevoke part of your life that's over and done with, kid.
And you can't do that . . . even you ought to know
better, you're smart enough." "But suppose it does start
up again, all by itself, starts over, only transformed. Not
less but more alive. More. Forevermore." "It can't be,
kid." "You mean, chuck it?" "I mean dump it. You're
going in for the nonworld." "Suppose that's where the
joy is?" "It isn't. Period." "If only my job were not so
routine, Tommy. If only I had got married and had kids,
if only I had shown a little sense, or used my opportunities better, if only I knew intelligent and fascinating
people." "If only." "That's right, if only." "I used to feel
a lot of if-onlies." "I know you did. On the other hand, if
I had it to do again, I think I would do the same." "The
joy of commonplaces——" "Isn't mine." A pause. "Is it
yours, Tommy, is it?" He vanished, dissolved.

I'll stop it now, she thought, gathering up her bag
and paper. Stay out of this small-time crook world which
has to have its little mysteries to satisfy the New Orleans
reader's taste for some real-life pulp fiction happening
at present. She'd go back to the parttime theater world
(there was a group she'd given up of late); they were
always doing plays about sex, lust, and blood and that
was one way of working it off. She'd charge a new dress
and hope to pay for it soon and if another letter like that
came in the mail, she'd mark it No Longer at This Address
and drop it in the nearest mail box.

Walking, she glanced at herself anxiously in a
diagonally set shop window, wondering if the gray strands
were now visible from a short distance away, but decided
not; wondering where her joy had fled.

Damn Tommy Arnold, talking sense into her head!

She stopped at a light and there beside her, waiting

also, was Wilma Wharton. Unnoticed, or so she believed, Julia turned at right angles and crossed Canal Street in another direction. Hallucination? She'd had them before. Or—had it really been true? The breath she drew came up from her deepest self.

At the hospital on Monday a plain envelope arrived for her, containing two fifty-dollar bills folded in a sheet of white paper.

# 4. A CALL TO ARMS

 Tommy Arnold, who had forsaken the newspaper five years before to edit a publication on Louisiana products which the Chamber of Commerce put out, did see the article on Ted Marnie's reappearance. He was at his house, in the evening. A grilled-gate, white-painted Spanish-type stucco bungalow on a corner, out near Carrollton Avenue. His wife was proud of it—a home of her own on St. Charles (what if it was nearly to Carrollton with the best areas ten blocks back?)— and he at least breathed, slept, and ate in it, though many years ago he had decided that he had inherited wandering blood and that the tie he had felt to Julia Garrett was that she was homeless same as he. He thought of her when he read the aftermath of the strange affair. It was getting stranger all the time. Like the victim, it wouldn't die.

He pored over the details, rereading to the point of eye strain, returning in twilight after the dinner his wife had had to call him to three times. Death and resurrection.

The man had been seen in San Diego, going down the street. An old friend had hailed him from behind before remembering that he was supposed to be dead. "Ted! Oh, Marnie!" With the unmistakable response of a man hearing his own name called, the spare frame spun round ("Like a stiff long-limbed figure knocked together out of the wreck of an old rowboat," Tommy Arnold thought). Ted Marnie too for the moment forgot that he was dead. Maybe he had got homesick for himself and was glad to be called right again, glad to reunite himself with that shadowy ghost of a past supposed to lie murdered in a swamp. And there stood the smiling friend. "So how do you get away with a thing like that, Marnie?" Even then the spell of being himself again did not break, or maybe he recognized in the face addressing him somebody he had known from past years as a fellow traveler in the shady world. Anyway, the lie he had been living these five years was still knocked out of him when he replied, straight out, "You have to be smart." By then he was sitting in a barber chair. The old friend had followed him within the emporium of shaves and haircuts. What Marnie couldn't know in his hour of release into his own name was that the old friend stranded before him as they tilted him back and forth in the barber chair had jumped the fence and worked for the police off and on for the last two years, and was in San Diego for a day or so en route from Tijuana back home. What he couldn't know either was that there was still a reward on the New Orleans books for information leading to the arrest of the murderer of Ted Marnie.

Tommy Arnold jotted down the following:

"What had he been smart about? If events in his unknown world had forced him into a position where he could only disappear, leaving the impression that he himself had died, no choice to do anything else, what events were they? And who was the corpse so like him, dressed in his coat with the button sewed on by Wilma Wharton, thread traced to his own possessions? How, if you wanted to disappear, could you find a corpse of the right measurements, hardly weighing 130 pounds? And with a broken wrist just like your own? (That could have been hastily examined.)"

Maybe Marnie had had a twin brother. At this point Tommy Arnold's imagination could carry him no farther. "What are you doing in that room in the dark?" his wife

called. What *am* I doing in here? he wondered. Maybe
Ted Marnie on the other hand did not have a twin
brother. Am I going back to work on this case? It looks
like I'm already doing it.

His present job, though lucrative and secure enough,
bored him. It was a good job and he was good at it. He
met a lot of fine people, the well off and the wealthy. The
articles he wrote or commissioned, the world he learned
about—of various industries which thrived especially well
in Louisiana and which the outside world should know
about in case it wanted to invest in them or had others
to add to the list—were grounded in that splendid profit
motive which had been handed down intact from the
fathers, be they French, English, Scottish, or German.
It was a world that wanted clean politics, honest government and as little crime as any society can possibly have
in order to get on with the great realities: business and
progress and the greatest economic good for all. In the
old days it had bought and sold slaves, rum, molasses,
and cotton; now it dealt in such diverse products as oil,
cotton (still), salt, fish, shrimp, tabasco, and nutria
pelts. Come on down; you'll like it here, we do. Year-
round climate. Southern charm. Gracious living. Hous-
ing plentiful. Always room for two more. You'll love it.
The people he met who knew this to be a game intrigued
him more than those who took it halfway seriously. But
these were the very ones who openly boasted of the tricks
they used to mesh the gears and keep the wheels in
motion. He never met one who wasn't above a trick or
two. He wondered sometimes at their men's club lunch-
eons how they could face each other across the shrimp
Arnaud and chicken Clemenceau. But to them a few
compromises did not cripple the idea of honest and fair
dealings without which nothing in this great society could
run at all. One swallow did not make a summer. What
was he thinking about? Rip the mask off everybody and
you've got your work cut out for you comparing blemishes

for size, depth, and age, for who can show a smooth face? Was he saying that everybody was a crook?

"What are you doing up so late in there?" Now his wife was in the bedroom.

"Coming," said Tommy Arnold.

What *am* I doing? Right now I am worrying about Julia Garrett.

If they bring Ted Marnie back and reopen the case, then they'll have to try and find Jake Springland. Then she may be caught in the net again, if not the net of the law the net of those feelings which do not, in Tommy Arnold's belief, grow old or change.

But of course she might get caught in the law too, thought Tommy Arnold, or plastered across the front page of some newspaper. I kept her out before. He did not go to bed without looking up her name in the telephone book, finding it still listed at the address on Prytania which Martin Parham had owned and then discovered sold out from under him.

He went there next day but got a door slammed in his face. "People better quit worrying me about that girl," the woman said. She was wearing a bright orange scarf. Now really worrying (his anxiety had turned orange), he went to the *Picayune* office and looked in the city registry, finding that she must be over thirty by now and that four years before when the registry was published she had been working at Tulane Hospital. There were always her aunt and uncle he could call. He went out into the hot street, newspaper smells enveloping him to the ears, printers' ink strong as dye on the soul, and smells of newsprint and copy paper, all beating on his parched nature like summer rain. And it was coming on to rain literally now, with a bold flash or two of lightning; the straight heavy tropical afternoon downpour, so typical of New Orleans in summer, commenced. Not wanting to wind up a drowned rat, he ran and sheltered in a doorway dedicated to shoe repair on

Carondelet Street—this shop too because of its use of
iron and blacking smelling not unlike the newspaper
office. A solid wall of white water poured straight down
inches from his nose and the St. Charles Avenue streetcar
thrust through a sudden sluicing river where two minutes
before a street had been. Do I want to find her? Isn't
what I'm really looking for with all this urgency really
just my old job?

The rain suddenly stopped. The sun came out with
a smack of heat like a slap or a clap of actual sound. He
went quietly back to his own office, entering the neat tall
new building which housed the modern offices of the
magazine. It came out each month between heavy covers
of enameled paper brightly adorned with some brisk
photograph that underlined the local world.

Sitting down at his typewriter, he spattered out a few
good lines: "My dear Julia, I remember the day you came
to me at your nadir, in other words, your point zero. We
went to the apartment of a friend and you fell asleep.
Your neck looked white, defenseless, twisted aside as
though awaiting a fatal blow. I also remember your dark
hair. Call me if you need me, don't if you don't. Tommy."

But all that was past, he thought, as the address (care
of the hospital) and his return initial materialized upon
the envelope. Long past and gone, he thought, and sent
the white stamped rectangle gliding down the slot in the
corridor.

By then the phone was ringing. It was Ed Clements,
former colleague at the *Picayune,* now city editor, who
had glimpsed him when he came into the office that noon
but hadn't had a chance to speak. "Hey, Tommy, you
know what's kicked up again, I guess. Remember the
Marnie case? I thought when I saw you maybe you had
it on your mind."

"No, I didn't," he lied.

"Why don't you get it on your mind, Tommy? Don't
tell me you're busy sixteen hours a day harping out hymns

of praise for the cat-food industry, the sugar refineries, the japonica nurseries?"

"Not that busy, but— Well, what's wrong with your staff? All gone to Maine?"

"The boy that's on it doesn't care for it. Nobody can get the mileage out of these yarns like you could. You had a real hang-up about this one, as I recall. You ate, breathed, slept it, as I recall."

"I know I did, I know I did."

Then he knew he was going to say yes. Like the willing girl who just wanted enough conversation to go by. Wasn't she beginning to look a lot older? Wasn't he a lot older? Never mind about that.

Anyway, he thought. Anyway, anyway, anyway. He called his wife to say he'd be late getting home, that Ed Clements needed to talk to him about something. When he said it, he heard in her replying voice something totally absent in recent years, the anxiety that the newspaper years had brought down on her, and he saw himself by the early dishwater-colored light that came filtering through smudged windows into the city room, hung over, stiff from curling up on the copy desk, covered with an old quilt he kept in the back of the car. A miserable life, wasn't it? But he'd missed it all, hadn't he? He wrote among the scribbles and doodles on the long blank sheet of copy paper on his modern Scandinavian desk top: "Man's needs are many, but perhaps one need is for his own particular sort of unhappiness." He wanted to add, but did not: Let my wife be worried for a while, I'm alive again.

Then, morose and thoughtful, he wrote the creamy story which said what it had to, about the wonderful wonderful Louisiana shellfish industry, and closed up on the dot of five.

# 5. EXCHANGE

 "Hey, funny thing, Tommy," Ed Clements remarked. "You remember that guy, that Marnie? He thought he was a Jesus type, or some such thing, now it turns out he was right. He's resurrected, don't you see it? Took him years instead of days, but he's finally got there."

It's dangerous, thought Tommy Arnold, to get back into all this again. Why would I do it, he wondered, except for her? Or am I making an excuse of her, and it's me that really wants back in? Do I really like swimming in filthy water? No answer to that. He was no longer sure that what he meant by Julia Garrett existed.

# 6. SURVIVING

Julia had found a fairly nice place for herself after the Parhams had eased her out. It was a little too far over toward the Negro district for her to care to reach it much after dark, at least not without catching a cab. But she had her livingroom-dinette, she had her kitchen, her bedroom, even her little balcony, which was great for sitting on bare-legged, in something cool. She never had enough money. A better job was indicated, marriage was practically a necessity, yet she did nothing at all about either.

She must, however, have said yes—more or less inadvertently—to a widower with one child who used to take her out to dinner, for she was announced as engaged and Aunt Isabel and Uncle Maurice gave a party for her. The man's name was Joe Delaney and he was in insurance like Bucky Squiremeister used to be, only it was a new company trying to edge in, and they'd sent him here from outside. The Squiremeisters were at the party and so, to her surprise, were Edie and Paul Fowler. Edie was pregnant for the third time and wanted Julia to know that her career was not defunct, she was progressing a course at a time toward her Ph.D. which she probably wouldn't reach till 1990, but at least she hadn't let go. She had to keep going to be able to converse with Paul, that was one motive.

"And then the children have to talk to him, too," said Julia, "all about physics, biochemistry, and space capsules."

"Why certainly," said Edie, over her great basket of a stomach, content to be teased.

Paul had scarcely dressed for the occasion. He had come in a dark brown suit and dark brown shirt, wearing loafers and red socks. On purpose, or in scorn? He scarcely spoke to anyone and seemed to be nosing about the house as though it were a museum which all the guests had paid to enter. Tulane had made him a full professor recently, so Julia could reassure Aunt Isabel that he acted that way out of brilliance of mind. Maurice observed Julia and Edie in deep conversation at the turn of the veranda. The pleasure of the sight struck and held him, for Julia had on a flounced-out dress in off-white net printed with great fronds or wings, while the little pregnant thing in flowered cotton looked like a comment on what marriage ought to bring. The insurance man had already brought Maurice some business—and there was the Parham business, too, which had been quietly handed over to him some little while back. (Who could sound as full of authority and mystery as Maurice Devigny when hinting at the perils of the Napoleonic Code to those whose tradition for generations had been nurtured in the English common law?)

The young women were smiling at one another while they talked, and, moving past with empty glasses, he heard Edie say she had never expected a regular marriage to interest Julia, but it just went to show you never could tell, the most way-out people turned around and plunged into housekeeping and the baby business, it happened all the time. "Oh, it hasn't happened *yet*," said Julia, and Maurice had a freezing moment before he decided she was just in a mood and walked on.

It was a mild party as those things went. One of Julia's former professors climbed to the landing above the big entrance hall—the stairs broadened and the banister went into a curl at the bottom where a bronze goddess with flimsy garments fluttering about her charms held up a candelabra—and began reciting verse which started with Shakespeare but grew off-color as more was requested from the crowd below. It was not wise to do this only from the point of view of scaring off Joe Delaney, who perhaps was fearful of New Orleans ways, being from somewhere up in Alabama—Birmingham, wasn't it? Julia moved around enough to hear people talking. She heard it murmured once, as a question, how much the young man knew about her, and she wondered what was meant: the Springland affair, lost and done with? Or the old rumor she found more interesting than otherwise, that Negro blood had touched her, she who had come from way off mysteriously like that. She didn't know which. At a turning there was Paul Fowler, drink in hand, saying, "You've kidded too often not to be kidding now; come off it, why don't you?" He'd always had hard eyes, but before she could answer someone said, "Who was that other young man, Julia, from up in Mississippi, wasn't it?" And she said, "Oh, you mean Martin Parham, well, he died, you know." Then somebody came by to whisper, "I really was sorry to hear about Martin, Julia, don't you just feel awful sometimes?" She said she certainly did.

It was late and after all was said and done, drunk and eaten, Aunt Isabel was the woman who had silently prevailed and now seemed everywhere, admirable in her new blue-green chiffon, myopic without her glasses, but drawing gazes she had no need to return. Joe Delaney missed Julia and could not find her, Maurice also was looking around for her. . . .

It had happened some weeks before that a car had edged into Audubon Place, a Cadillac, so large it had all but filled the wide-flung gates. Maurice had been sought for out in the garden, and news brought him that Martin Parham had been killed in the crash of his private plane, while flying over Texas.

It was through the Parham account that Maurice had been able to get rid of the roomers that had embarrassed him, except for a German bachelor who lived in the backyard house where Dev's old servants had once lived. But, indirectly, the Parham business had been due to Julia, as she could now bitterly remind herself, smarting from all those remarks, both chance and deliberate (Paul Fowler's had been deliberate). So she'd climbed up to her old room and sat alone, looking down into the garden, while the engagement party wound to a close.

Grief for Martin was what she felt coming on more strongly every minute. He had been going out to see his sister Lillian (nobody had to tell her that) when he'd flown into a great silver thunderhead, probably innocent-looking without, even beautiful, but alive with turmoil and treachery within. She thought of him as she first had known him, still feeling in memory the sharp spikes of the pineapple pressed into her fingers, and a gentle winter dawn lifting about her. She had promised to marry Martin, too, and there had been a lot of parties.

The door opened. Uncle Maurice had found her. "The guests are leaving," he said.

"I was sitting here thinking of poor old Martin," she said.

"I thought of him too," said Maurice, sitting down beside her. He put his arm around her. "I've also been thinking that you look great." He shook her gently. "Don't let the past pile up, darling. It's bad, but it's gone and we can't help it. Think of the wake of the boat."

"Oh, no, that won't work . . . it's all around . . . around. . . ." She shook her head.

"Come down with me," Maurice firmly advised, "come on, now, Julia, come on down." She rose and followed him.

Joe Delaney, her fiancé, talked to her constantly about what a fine man her uncle was, how lovely her aunt was, how splendidly they entertained. "Creoles," he came right out and said, going on to add, "You can tell they know everybody." New horizons, he told her, were opening up for him; he owed it all to her. But the party itself was something he would never forget, not if he lived to be a thousand and one.

"Or maybe two," said Julia after a time.

"Two what?" he asked.

"A thousand and two," said Julia.

"Oh," he said.

# 7. SURVIVING (Continued)

 She had stolen the dress she wore to her announcement party, the one of off-white net printed in black fronds. It had been like a game and a much more tricky one than the first time she had stolen something, which had been a white bag. That first time, she had really surprised herself. All she had been doing was shopping, spending some money Uncle Maurice had sent her until it went in some other way, God knew how. She had gone first to Holmes, then to Godchaux's, then back to Holmes, and she couldn't get the clerk to pay attention. It was getting later and this was the bag she wanted for her new outfit and her day-long date on Saturday, a trip outside the city with the insurance man. They would take a drive to St. Martinsville, to the bayou country, an all-day jaunt, this time without his little girl, who had gone back to stay with her grandparents up in Birmingham.

In the store the clerk saw her twice but each time waited on customers who had come there after her. Suddenly impatient, she wondered what would happen if, instead of complaining, she simply walked out with the bag, and she did and nothing happened. She got nearly to the door and thought, Now I'll turn around and come back, but something made her want to know if they'd stop her at the door and what it felt like, so she kept walking, and they didn't and then she was on the street.

It was like something that never happened; the store was forgotten like a station passed through on a train, but she had the bag and must go back and pay for it, the next day. How? She looked at it, after supper alone, in her small apartment, getting ready to bathe and put up her hair and do her nails for the next day. It was handsome and right, fresh white calf with a gold clasp, made in France. Just never do it again, she thought; but whatever it was she had felt in the park near the cathedral that day when the man had touched her and spoken of Jake Springland, she felt again. Well, Jake stole, it suddenly dawned on her. He was in those stick-ups. Why, that's pretty awful, isn't it? Wasn't it? They had talked about it, she and Jake, had discussed it openly between them. They both thought of themselves as having the intellectual approach—it is intellectual to discuss your own lawlessness. Jake's talking face came back.

He'd had a way of looking at it. He had wanted to soak his very soul, he had said, in something that wasn't the straight-side-up U.S.A. If you went in for the straight life, he said, you wound up killing the ones who weren't straight. Just to teach them a lesson, you threw them into outer darkness, that was the absurd goal of the 100 percent red-blooded American. Why? Well, nine times out of ten because they didn't believe in the sacredness of money. This was Jake's philosophy. When he talked like this, she remembered Martin's sister. "A man in business," Jake had said, "knows and secretly accepts it that his actions will sooner or later have to include murder or he is not a good businessman. People in politics know this—the ones who aren't bureaucrats. But every businessman knows it."

Remembering how Jake used to go on this way, she thought of the insurance man's even profile. She thought of his kindly humorous eyes when he looked at her, his firm touch whether driving the car, paying bills or kissing her goodnight. All that Jake thought was wrong. Jake was sophomoric. He belonged to her immature years. To hell with Jake.

The next morning saw her on another errand near Amelia Street, and just for old times' sake she walked past the Mulligan house under the trees. As she did so, change as sudden as a chemical transformation came over her. She could have been a maiden bound to a stake while flames started up around her ankles and climbed her legs, and a drum sent its first thudding throb out to the scarcely stirring village, waking first the dogs. She leaned against the old tree. She saw why people did well to leave a town when life went wrong in it; she saw too that sooner or later they would find that same life again. She pressed her face against the dark rough bark and wished for her own life—that mysterious good-bad thing —to whisper to her out of the trunk's heart. Instead she had only her own living body and the sigh that rose to her lips.

On her way to her apartment she bought a paper, as she had vowed she wouldn't, and, while getting herself well turned out for the day with Joe Delaney, filling the smooth white purse with lipstick, compact, comb, and cigarettes, read that they were flying Ted Marnie back to New Orleans, that Jake Springland was being sought for questioning. Tommy Arnold was writing it.

What was she calling life? The old one or the new?

# 8. MARNIE'S RETURN

There was a crowd at the airport when Ted Marnie was flown in. Tommy Arnold, whether he would once more fail to get that story out of New Orleans or not, had his chance to recapture it for the city. His daily stories, recalling elements of the old crime, replaying them, theme by theme, once again took up the New Orleans imagination; its softly wicked consciousness only occasionally could be lured to seek its own self-image, for mostly it would rather live it than look at it. Sex, dope, jazz, voodoo, et cetera—the dear old mysteries of the low-life. Why was the heiress to the something fortune found in the upper story of the absinthe house with her throat cut? Was it really Louis Armstrong's ex-mistress who sold junk on Burgundy Street until the police moved her out for what she had hidden under the crockery? Who killed Ted Marnie's double if not Ted Marnie? Tommy Arnold was shameless, and he loved it.

All the time, in the back of his mind, he kept the thought of Julia, how he didn't want to involve her in all this again. He should have gone that day to check up on her but had let himself get rained out in front of a shoe repair shop.

One story was entitled "The Resurrected Man" and ran in boldface under the heavy headline, MARNIE FLYING BACK TO NEW ORLEANS: FACES POLICE INQUIRY IN GRETNA SWAMP MYSTERY.

When the plane arrived, Marnie, in custody of the city detective, looked down at the crowd and wondered aloud what they were doing there. (His ego, supreme

in private matters, had little public reference.) When the
door opened and the steps were rolled up, people watching (among them Tommy Arnold) said that his slow
emergence from the plane (he was stooped far forward
to get through the low door, hesitant, squinting in the
sunglare, stumbling at the threshold) was really remi-
niscent of some bizarre kind of birth. One half expected
the plane either to heave like a parturient animal or to
explode like dynamited earth to let him out more freely.
It was the second step down before he straightened up.
Holding on to the hand rail of the steps he swayed
slightly, like a mast in the wind. Only then did he notice
that the crowd was there because of him. He half-raised
his hand, debated (perhaps) what to do with it, then put
it to his head, thrusting back his hair. The hair was
mouse-gray, somewhat oily, cut straight from the thinned-
out area of the brow, so that when it fell forward it
seemed long. Christ, is he corny, Tommy Arnold thought.
He's Jonah from the whale's belly, he's coming singly
out of the Ark. He dates back through everything. Okay.
The cornier the better. More grist for the mill.

The photographer who had come out with Tommy
whirled in, snapped the camera twice like a cagey jackal
springing in to a gathering at a carcass, then whirled off.
The thin man moved through the crowd. The trousers
were seedy, creaseless; the cotton tweed jacket was
frayed and hung unevenly, high on the hips. Tommy
Arnold thought, there are people so poor they have to
eat out of garbage pails to keep alive, or is it their cats
they can't afford to feed and are scavenging for? They
drink up everything welfare or the government gives
them. I'd rather think it was cats, so I always do. Mainly
lack of intelligence is at the bottom of it—that and dope,
alcohol or something, some little thing, funny in the
head. But after all some Ph.D.s turn into bums, and
assistant secretaries of state, if I've got the plural right,
have been known to wind up in house arrests.

A few minutes later the police car, prisoner folded

within, was tilting out the ramp of the airport, and Tommy Arnold was scribbling away on folded pieces of copy paper from the office.

Driving back to town a thought struck him and, being hung up in traffic for a moment, he wrote it down:

*One reason for going crooked: some people are just not comfortable in the straight world.*

Later, before a stop light, he leaned once more toward the paper on the seat beside him and wrote:

*Why?*

He had got all the way to the office and was at his typewriter in the far corner of the city room where Ed Clements had arranged for him to work on special assignment before he wrote down the answer:

*They don't trust it.*

Tommy's answer to the question of where Julia was turned up on the society page. She was engaged to be married, the brief notice said. The man's name went through Tommy's brain and stuck somewhere, filed away for reference. What stayed in the foreground was "insurance man." He read on. Very high up in a national firm. How straight could you get? She's overdoing it, he thought. Delaney: a Baptist from Tuscaloosa, Ala., more recently resident in Birmingham; Kiwanis Club, ex-Army captain, etc. It didn't figure. He turned the page, then later came back and read it through again.

September wedding. The dangerous thirties. She was in them, barely. Maybe she had children on the brain.

At this juncture, Tommy Arnold's youngest child came down with pneumonia. His wife was mad at him all the time for missing meals and not being concerned enough that any of them lived or died. He gave in to family love, to its ordinary glories, and spent hours with his flesh and blood, until, danger past, his boredom flowed back. He said that he had to do extra work on the newspaper to get extra money for the doctors. This made his wife mad all over again, thinking that at his stage in life extra work for extra money should not be necessary.

Harried, badgered, and depressed, he left the quarreling behind with the closing of the door. And back at the typewriter, sleazy, disreputable, and ripe with decay, the Marnie case came alive beneath his fingertips; it glowed in his heart, reviving like a signaling mirror the shine of that long distant afternoon at the Squiremeisters' party when the clear voice had sounded: "What are you sitting there thinking?" And there she was.

They had found Jake Springland now. Was Julia reading?

# 9. THE NET

She was.

She was reading sleepily, having tired of going out every night with her fiancé, Joe Delaney the insurance man, then having to get up and work every morning. In the humid New Orleans weather, as warm from nine A.M. onward as the inside of an overripe watermelon in the sun, she was now having to expose herself to still more heat by sitting under a hair drier in the beauty parlor nearest her house. Opening the evening paper, she saw it there: the story of how they'd now found Jake. As she read the drier roared like the amplified inside of a gigantic seashell.

They had found him in, of all places, Baton Rouge. So he never left, she thought, with wonder. Catching that train north and then getting off still in the South, what did he mean? Or maybe he left and wandered back again. So where exactly did they find him? In a grocery store, shopping for the week's groceries, after payday, with his wife and children.

He was reaching for a can of tomato soup. Tommy Arnold, she thought, he's gone wild. He'll have to know everything, every detail, down to what kind of soup. Tomato, but what brand? She read on and there it was: Campbell's.

During her comb-out, she placed the folded paper on the beautician's dresser under the big round mirror, beside the white bag she had stolen. As she sat there, watching the small rollers being disengaged from her crisp, thick, cropped head, she reached into the bag for a compact and the paper fell on the floor. The operator returned it to her.

"They've caught up to them people again," the operator said.

"What people?" Julia asked.

"You remember all that. That singer and that preacher and that woman. You know what she was: a addict. Heroin, they said. You don't get free of that—not ever. Say they can't find her. Wherever she's at, if she's still alive, she's worse off than ever. I had a brother on marijuana for a while, and I don't want to hear nothing more about it." She whispered. "There was speed in it, too, honey."

"Don't blame you," Julia murmured.

The three of them were lined up together in equal panels on the front page: Jake and Wilma and Ted Marnie.

"He looks a whole lot nicer than them other two," the woman remarked. "I remember thinkin' that when all that come up the first time." One finger struck the page. It landed close to Jake Springland's temple, on a spot where Julia's kiss had lingered, over and over, endlessly. She paid and left, paper beneath her arm, out of air conditioning, entering the soup-thick late afternoon air, passing the smell of shrimp creole coming from a third-rate restaurant.

She turned two corners and entered her dull little building: mirror in the hall with table beneath, convenient for putting down mail, bag, and parcels while groping for key. Inside the door she found her cleaning, her figured dress, brown leaves and black branches on a white pique background, and went to find her white sandals, turn on the bath, dig out fresh underwear. The insurance man was due at seven-thirty. It didn't give her long.

The phone rang. She picked it up. "Hello?" There was not a word, only breathing. Man or woman? And what connection, if any, to—? She didn't know. "Hello?" she said again. There was a sudden click. If it hadn't been for the Marnie case waking up again, she would never have been so convinced that a woman was out there, wherever the wired connection ended, and that her name was Wilma Wharton. Trying to scare her, or just keep in touch, as an old acquaintance should? Jake would never . . . Ted Marnie? He was locked up, and, anyway, his visions had ignored her.

Jake had laughed once, telling about Ted and his visions. "You know Marnie? . . . Well, he's had these visions. He sees souls, the nucleus in the soul, that's what he looks for. You weren't in his visions. He knew I knew you, but he couldn't make you live. He saw you only once, he said, that one day he actually saw you, up in the doctor's office. After that you vanished, face, body, nuclear soul, and all. You were not even a faceless face. He used to see faceless faces sometimes."

"What's a faceless face?" That day when they were talking in bed had been a slow-passing Sunday morning, window open, church bells, murmur of distant voices.

"A face that's just an outline, I guess. Wouldn't it drive you crazy? Think about it."

"I'd rather not."

"Don't blame you."

"In my opinion he blocked me out because he——"

"He what? Because he what?"

"He was after you—a good-looking boy, I bet he liked that."

"Oh, hell, Julia."

"What's that mean?"

"Means you're off the track."

"I might be like this with you, but not with him."

"You mean you thought he had a bitch side too."

"I mean there wasn't any part of me enough like him for him to find it. So I don't guess he could find any soul I've got, nuclear or otherwise."

"You imagine things. Ted was always struggling with the Lord. That was his hang-up. I said, 'Christ, Ted, if you want to fight the flesh off, pick something more attractive for an excuse. That was after Wilma got fat all of a sudden. But he was too preoccupied. He thought it was some soul flaw made her gain weight. So he kept trying to cure it. He had to be adored and Wilma worshiped him."

"No reason to kill him," Julia remarked. "No more than ten dollars was a reason."

"What are you saying? I never killed anybody, not even accidentally. For a while I thought maybe Marnie died of wounds received, but then I took heart when the police started knocking hell out of me. I knew they didn't know either. I think maybe he wanted to get away from her, for some reason she had got too much for him, so he'd started making life impossible and then maybe she'd killed him more or less accidentally, trying to hold on to him. Does that make sense?"

"Wanting to lose her, that makes sense," said Julia.

She went into the bathroom, trying to rid herself of the idea of Wilma Wharton, but the amplified breath from the receiver still coursed in her ear passages, she could almost smell it as well. Odor of shrimp creole, masticated and swallowed, tomatoes, cooked green peppers, rice, and shrimp. She threw up, quietly, sincerely, into the toilet.

But by the time Joe Delaney appeared, she was fresh, clean, cologned, pressed, powdered, and gleaming, her hair rich and dark, clustering thick as grapes or hyacinths, and she knew she looked good. The dark floor of the living room, run over hastily with an oil mop, shone softly and added a comfortable, clean breath to the twilight air. She gave him a drink—gin and tonic crisp with ice—and he sat smiling in his dark summer cotton suit with the maroon bow tie. ("A bow tie!" she remarked as though she'd never seen anything so nice. "For a change," he smiled, grateful for her notice.) The chair was covered in gold cotton with a satin finish and looked considerably more expensive than it was.

Through evening after evening as she talked, walked, dined, drove, and attended movies with this nice man who wanted to marry her, she watched him, sometimes forgetting his name, like losing something in the bottom of a purse, and sometimes finding it again. Finally she identified him in her private geography: he was that one she had met in the hotel near the sea—not literally, but in a manner of speaking—the one she couldn't go anywhere with, not if she lived to be a thousand and still looked the same. She remembered telling Martin Parham: You can't choose your life, you can only discover it. She remembered a nurse she had had as a child, a young mulatto woman who still wore, even as late in time as the 1930s, the red bandanna of outside servants, knotted at the top. A tignon, they called it, in the old French dialect. She remembered the girl's quarrel with Aunt Isabel and Uncle Maurice, a quarrel even Dev had got in on, though how she didn't remember, and how the nurse was fired and then the doll had appeared in her room; she'd found it the day after. Who had got in to leave it? It was lying face up on the floor of the bedroom, arms flung wide, as though run down, a rag doll out of nowhere. "She left it for a present," Aunt Isabel quickly assured Julia, who had been frightened of it. "She liked you, so she left it." But how did she get in? Julia wondered. "She didn't," said Aunt Isabel, kindly inventing. "She put it up on something and you didn't see it and then there was a breeze blew it off on the floor." But Julia didn't believe that and knew she was being lied to. Was it a threat, a warning, a punishment, a spell? She'd never quarreled with the girl herself, but Dev said, "She's getting back at them through you." Herself represented by the doll then? "Don't tell her that," Uncle Maurice warned, too late. She had already felt the chill, a thrill out of a world she vaguely sensed to be there, but able to reach out and touch her . . . and the sense of her own particular life roused for the first time, spreading silent and powerful. The single yucca plant bloomed white that summer in the corner of the Devigny garden, and its mystery was always its own. Whatever had brought the doll there, however it had happened, she had seized it to her, like a personal fate, and kept it yet; it was both mystery (like a sign of hate) and joy.

"Julia," said the insurance man, "something is the matter, you've hardly said a word."

When he took her home, Joe Delaney let her know that he understood what the trouble was, whether she would tell him or not. He'd tried continence—"being good," he called it—since his wife's death and had mostly succeeded. But now . . . he was tender and persistent, and half-distracted she let her feelings coast as he held her, noting the catch and rise of his desire as though he were one of a foreign race just landed on these shores. He broke away. They ought to think things over, was his murmured conclusion; he didn't like to take her as being all that easy.

"It's your ideals," Julia came up with, wondering if nice girls talked like that, "that make you so good to me." She pressed his hand, slipping out, and went inside.

She could wish a few minutes later that she'd brought him up with her, no matter what risk she ran of losing him—this man she had determined she must settle down with—for her apartment in her absence had been entered and turned upside down. There was no one in it now, though she had fearfully to substantiate this by switching on lights and walking cautiously through each room, checking closets, finally daring to search her balcony with a flashlight. In the bathroom, the wash basin had drops of blood in it, though the reason she understood no better than the reason for the doll she'd found in childhood. It was during that anxious search that the cold truth went steadily with her as it had come to stand beside her at equal measure with herself from the first moment. There was nobody she could talk to, for she had nothing that she could tell without revealing a self within herself which took every means that came its way, however dangerous or shady, for maintaining its secret life.

Ted Marnie was in jail. Jake Springland was being brought to New Orleans, had perhaps already arrived. And Wilma Wharton? Was she imagining the odor in her rooms . . . no, she wasn't. It was a dense syrupy perfume of the sort that Wilma had preferred. Jungle Gardenia: the name returned. There now returned too a name that proved her wrong in thinking nobody lived she could talk to.

In the corner of the restaurant booth, across from Tommy Arnold, she writhed like a tortured cat.

"I think she came there and got in somehow. Don't think she wouldn't know how." She saw in waking nightmare, crossing her threshold, the bare, messy, big, ugly foot with crooked toes, a corn or two disfiguring them, the garishly painted nails, the thin straps of a cheap, varicolored sandal with high pointed heel.

"What would she be after?"

"To get me on some sort of terms before the trial. I'm still Jake's alibi."

"Nobody knows where that woman is. I doubt if God knows. And you think——"

"I've got no proof. Oh, if I had I'd tell you."

"You haven't even let me say I'm glad to see you," Tommy Arnold said.

"Oh, Tommy. You're the only person I could call."

"I've thought of you. On and on, you might say. Ever since the scarecrow decided to rise from the tomb." He put his straw hat aside on the wooden seat and taking out a wad of handkerchief, swabbed the bald top of his head. "What would settle you, a drink?"

She shook her head.

"I don't go in for the other stuff," he pursued, "An

old-fashioned type." And when she said nothing, he went on, "We ought to go somewhere we can be alone; like that other time, remember? over in Hattie Tremblay's apartment."

"I never knew whose place it was."

"She works on the paper, lives near."

"Was she your girl? Not my business."

"Hattie Tremblay? Her age is unknown. Some think she has an artificial leg. Others think she has two artificial legs. A few think she has an artificial body, down from the collar bone."

"Let's walk somewhere and sit by a tree." She said the word tree as if uncertain that such things still existed.

"Jackson Square?"

"Not there. Please. Not there."

They took a cab to Audubon Park, coming in from the river side so as to miss the sight of Audubon Place. The whole city had emotional landmines in it; cracks on the sidewalk concealed razor blades; this, thought Tommy Arnold, was the nature of terror.

Arranged beneath a tree, beside a lagoon where swans drifted, Julia resumed her pseudo-French poise, the kind she had a special talent for. Tommy Arnold had always liked her smile: she knew it and gave it to him. It was slightly comical, slightly clownish, like a mime might wear.

"Did you know I'm getting married?" she incongruously brought out.

"I noticed it in the paper," he nodded. "Small world, I have to say. Hattie Tremblay probably wrote the article."

"I want children, a house, I want to bury myself in all that. Come to think of it I always wanted children. This guy has a child already, a little girl. She sleeps in my lap in the car sometimes." She lays her head on the shoulder of my stolen dress, thought Julia. She gets a Kleenex from my stolen white handbag. We walk through gardens owned by the Mafia. "It's the first time I've felt I could

really work it, that it would work out. It's not just sex, you
see."

He wished she hadn't said that. Of course, he knew
that she and Jake Springland . . . that she and Parham
. . . that she and God knew who else . . . Still, he
wished she hadn't said it. How many of them, and when
and where and how? But did she have to come out with
it?

"Tommy," said Julia, her voice trembling, "I've been
getting payola for something, I don't know what."

"You *what?*"

"You know: money. If that's what they call it, it's
what's been happening."

"Happening how?"

"It's always just a letter, anonymous. To take some
small package to an address. There's nothing but just
directions: where to pick it up, where to take it. Then I
get it and take it and it's nothing, just nothing, not even
requiring me to go into a bad neighborhood, except that
once I had to go upstairs over a place on Royal Street that
wasn't all that healthy-looking. But then I've lived in
worse places when I knew Jake than anywhere they've
asked me to go. Then a few days after, the money comes,
cash in an envelope, so I can buy a nice outfit or two, to
go out in, you know."

"A girl has to look nice," said Tommy Arnold.

"It isn't just that. I feel if I didn't take it something
bad would happen, really bad."

"Ummm."

"Then I think maybe they'll forget me. It won't happen
again. They can't use the same people over and over,
that's the whole trick of it, isn't it?"

Tommy Arnold said nothing.

"It's only been a few times," she said.

"But what's in those little packages, Julia?"

"I don't know. I never look."

"You've got a pretty good idea it isn't paregoric."

"Why do you think it's something to take? Maybe somebody is smuggling something through in code."

"In that case they could use the telephone."

"Okay, the lost crown jewels of the Holy Roman Empire are being slowly reassembled."

"Not by those methods they aren't. Do they always pay the same amount?"

"Yes. The last hasn't arrived."

"Suppose it *doesn't* stop?"

"When I get married, we're going to live in Mobile." She said this with the triumphant air of a desert-crazed wanderer describing a mirage, cool and green, with sheltering palms and cool fronds ever dripping from a plashing spring.

"Your fiancé," Tommy Arnold inquired, noticing with what skilful disinterest, by the use of one foot, a swan could change direction upon the water. "He's in insurance, isn't he?"

"That's right."

"Did you ever know any artists, writers, etc.?"

"Mainly queers."

"Professors?"

"All married."

"Antique dealers, historians, archeologists, doctors, lawyers, researchers of every variety, both scientific and classical, book dealers, musicans, theater directors . . .?"

"What are you saying?"

"I'm saying I've got to get back to work."

He rose from the grass under the tree beside the lake and put out a hand to her. "At one time I thought anybody, any life in these parts could have been yours for the asking. You tossed away young heirs to great estates, dashing cavaliers shed their blood in your lap. . . ."

They had strolled across the park, this time toward St. Charles. A young woman passed them on horseback, riding a spirited bay with dark mane and arched dark tail. Julia and the girl nodded to one another as she went past. In the near distance, summer hazy, the cool shadowy recess of Audubon Place looked faintly violet. Its huge houses, rich vines, tended lawns, and spreading trees brought to Julia a memory of Mozart. They did not mention being near there, but turned right on St. Charles and walked a few blocks under spreading oak shade before crossing to take the streetcar.

At this unlikely place, a streetcar stop with no car in sight or hearing, she turned to confront him, having been silently aware the whole way across the park that his criticism of her had been meant to cut deeply.

"If you're saying I can never act to my own advantage, why that's true. If you're saying I can't connive and scheme, why that's true, too."

"So it really is the insurance man's idea?"

"Oh, altogether so. I don't deny that what he likes is my—what is it—my New Orleans something."

"Your continental air."

"Something like that."

"Well, I like it too."

The heat was still at noon time and the empty track, both directions, looked long and deserted. Julia laughed. "I've never even gotten to New York, let alone Paris."

"You're just trying to get to Mobile, I take it," Tommy Arnold said. He was thinking how if you looked deep into the heart of continental mysteries you found that they said bordello instead of cat-house, but he did not say it. He guessed you found other things as well. From either direction now, the trolleys were approaching. They'd both be late to work by thirty minutes, and there was the emptiness inside of doing without lunch which went with the great spaces of sky on the gigantic clear noon of summer down there.

Tommy Arnold said quickly, "I went back on this case for the paper partly to see it through again with you out of it. One of the other papers may hook onto you. I hope not. You haven't asked me about Springland. That's good. Don't even wonder about him. Don't go to the police, call me if you need me." His voice drowned in the old-timey lumber and screech of the two cars that approached from opposite ways as evenly matched as though timed on purpose, both stopping before them. He gathered her to him with apparent carelessness, one arm pressing her to his shoulder, uttering into her ear: "I'm scared for you. Remember that."

They clambered on, dropped money in the box and rode together side by side. On her way back to the hospital, having waved him good-bye, her mood shifted and she decided he was exaggerating, going too deeply into things he couldn't know, conjecturing darkly. He was a worrier, she thought, all his thoughts now like hounds nipping at her heels, panting in her wake, while she kept on and moved ahead of them, light and free. One way or another she would go a good distance beyond anything he could imagine for her, she decided.

Blood in the washbasin. Doll on the floor, sprawling, face up. She hadn't asked about Jake because he had a wife; that was it. Not fear.

When she got to the hospital there was the letter on her desk and the bills inside, twenty dollars more than usual. Her price was going up and who knew why? Beside the letter a scribbled note said she was to call a number and extension she'd never heard of.

I won't do it, she thought. I will not do it.

At three o'clock she was alone in the office when a busy intern burst in without knocking to find the correct definition of articulitis.

She had her head down on the desk and was crying.

# 10. HOTEL CROYDON

"Hotel Croydon" was what a voice said when Julia called the number. She did not ask for the extension. She said "Wrong number" and hung up, to evaluate things. It was one of the cheapest hotels in town. Who could be calling her? From that sort of place? Nobody connected with anybody she would do well to know, including Tommy Arnold. Maybe it was something that had to do with her message-bearing and the money she got for it. It might, even worse, be connected with Marnie and the Wharton woman. But then, too, it might be something to do with Jake.

The next afternoon, after work, she went down to that part of town on the bus and saw it from a distance. Earlier there had been a thunderstorm so severe several people at the hospital said it looked like a tornado was striking and patients who had to have intravenous got scared they'd be blown away with needles plugged into their veins. Those with stomach pumps felt worse yet. There was some joking after it was over, but not much while it was going on, black and turbulent. Julia had gone out into the cleared air.

Even down as far toward the river as the Croydon Hotel, the sad little streets looked freshened from the storm. Blown twigs and broken branches still had the look of victims. From a drugstore across the street from the hotel Julia watched and at last saw a girl—a girlish young woman really—walk from a grocery store and turn into the hotel.

Who would that be if not Jake's wife, the one on whose

account she'd been abstaining from even looking at the
paper in order not to see her picture? He would do that,
she thought. Just pick out somebody nice with a good
figure, somebody who'd adore him. Young. But am I even
right? She felt she was right and turned away. She went
to the back of the drugstore and called the number and
this time asked for the extension, too, because I'm going
to do it sooner or later, she thought. And a girl-voice answered. Why, I was right, she thought. She could have
laughed.

Yet her heart had started hammering and her fingertips throbbed against the black smooth texture of the telephone. "Hello, hello. Who is it, who is it?" So far she
hadn't said a word. Because she couldn't. The voice was
tense. If there was such a thing as a T.V. phone they'd be
staring at each other's eyes, like one woman into a mirror,
both knowing the eyes belonged to Jake.

"Hello." She got it out, even disguised it, with a stagey
sort of accent she could do. "Somebody sent this number
to a friend of mine."

"A friend! Who? What friend?"

"Her name is Julia. Does that mean anything?"

"Oh yes. Yes, it does. I want to . . . can she . . .
Can I see her, talk to her . . .?"

"She's out of town, but she——"

"She what? You see, she knew my husband once and
now they think . . . well, you must have read about it
in the papers. Marnie and Springland . . . all that?"

"What's Julia got to do with it?"

"Well, you see, she knows . . ."

"Knows what?"

"Listen, it's her I want to talk to. Just for a few minutes. Not to anybody else." The tone's tension mounted;
in a moment the girl-woman would scream or cry. God,
thought Julia, she's strung up like a piano wire. She hung
up, knowing well what the silent click would do to ears
like that. And gentle to him, isn't she? And soft at night,
and oh! She leaned her head against the toll box, the

plastic covering above the directions. Does she know his songs?

The songs were rocking through her head, all the old ones. The boxlike booth echoed, filled to the brim with the resonant strings. She fairly burst open the door and gulped down the sweetened air, which had even got all the way into the drugstore.

On the way home she bought the paper she'd been denying herself. There were pictures, front and inside both. The girl she'd seen and just talked to. Jake, looking older, but much the same. Marnie. Where was Wilma Wharton? And the biggest question of all, according to Tommy Arnold, who was pounding out stories, she saw, like a race horse in the stretch, was this:

*Who was the corpse?* "The location of the grave is being checked through the city cemeteries office, but no answer has been given as yet, partly because the cemetery where the grave is located was previously privately owned but has more recently passed into the hands of the city. Hence some confusion in records and personnel is to be expected."

It dawned on her as she walked home from where the bus left her, a hope green as the grass that glimmered with light after storm. If I can help Jake then I can see him, and if I can see and help him, then he might get them off me, call them off me, these letters, these errands. I'll be free of it all and why shouldn't I be?

# 11. AUDUBON PLACE

It may be that human life without its dream qualities would not be human at all, as we know it, but something different. Not totally in on Julia's life in the sense of having directly to do with it, Maurice and Isabel Devigny were nonetheless deeply affected by it. It became like a play they were watching in a mirror; they could not see things happening directly, but could see them reflected. At times they bent closer toward the depths. All was there. One gift was granted: they could turn it back and play it over. They were always doing this.

Martin Parham dead? It seemed like something they had both dreamed, like that whole afternoon of Julia's announcement party, people spilling out over the veranda and into the garden at the side, around the old cistern with its peaked roof, people on walks, living, yet decorative as paintings of themselves, clustered in the large rooms. Then, before that, had come the dreamlike twilight when the black Cadillac had nosed through the gates, bearing news of Martin. Dying alone in that spectacular way. "Somebody on the ground way out in Texas," Maurice related to Isabel, "said they saw the plane go into a thunderhead, great big thing. It just didn't come out the other side." "Some sort of disturbance," Isabel wondered. "Maybe hail," said Maurice, for no reason. He knew little of thunderheads, was not a country man. The great commanding silver cloud became a dream. In the dream they saw the little plane go silver into it, grow molten, wings falling off like feathers from a struck bird. The plane seemed a toy, Texas and the cloud momentous giants, only Martin of human substance, of human solidity, but so a victim. So they thought.

"That makes two," Isabel observed.

"Two what?"

"You remember that one she knew who shot himself by accident with a dueling pistol? Don't tell me you forgot that? There I go: making too much of it, aren't I?"

Maurice laughed. "Too much of her, you mean?" The eternal feminine, he thought. Isabel doesn't want us to make too much of Julia.

"I'll tell you one thing," said Isabel. "She'll never marry the present one. I gave the party but it was a waste of time."

Isabel was wearing a white blouse softly frilled and ruffled down the front, and among the raffles lay a strand of pearls which she enjoyed twisting lightly in her fingers, occasionally watching herself tap a pink tinted nail against one of the larger pearls as one might also for no reason tap a countertop or an eggshell. She had a habit too of barely touching her teeth together when considering something, and with these gestures, never overdone or repeated nervously, she enjoyed arresting and commanding her husband's attention, noticing in slight ways that she had it, that his very breath ran in one current with her own.

"Does it strike you as odd, that whole Marnie case coming up again?"

"*Outrageously* odd!" Maurice was explosive. His gaze broke away from his wife's charming blouse and manner. "Isabel," he said, "everything about Julia, everything that affects her, strikes me as—well, what? strange, wild some way, even a little mad."

"You used to say that about your father," Isabel reminded him. "And yet she—"

"She what?"

"We are personally better off because of Julia, Maurice. I want to be fair. The Parhams came to you. Who is better able to protect their property here than you?"

"I know, but that wasn't so much Julia as Julia in reverse. They just met me through her, that's all. I think they feel sorry, maybe, that I'm stuck with her. But then, as you say, they take advantages."

"And *you* take advantages," Isabel murmured, her clear little humor at work. "Merrily we roll along."

Maurice laughed. The grand delight of having his house back free of roomers was almost a counterbalance to childlessness. "Luck," he said.

"What?"

"Luck. Occasionally, I have luck."

"Then you know what to do with it."

"I can only try."

They were conversing in the small sitting room, a sunny southern exposure with bay-window recess, off the main dining room. It had been newly upholstered with cream-colored draperies, beige cotton brocade, and a splash of crimson cushions.

"Let's not gloat too soon," said Maurice, himself a grand one for gloating. "We may have to go up and visit the Parhams again."

"They gave up asking us," said Isabel. "They even left us out of the funeral."

"Oh, that's strictly family."

Her hands straightened a thread in her blue skirt. "If something goes wrong in Julia's engagement, will this Delaney man stick to you, too? All that insurance company's business—he's already consulting you, isn't he?"

"How can I pronounce on it, love?"

"But you've thought of it."

"Certainly I have. Insurance companies need a great deal of legal help."

"I keep wondering if he's ever heard of Jake Springland."

"It won't come from us," said Maurice.

"I never thought it would," said Isabel, "but someone——"

"Ought to tell him? Now the case is reopened? Then let it be her. That is, if she——"

"If she what?"

"To be grown up is to be responsible, or so I've always understood. We take it for granted Julia is grown up. Rather by reflex, I think; that is, she's old enough to be, so she must be. But is she?"

"Julia——" said Isabel and broke off. "Only what Julia loves matters. I know it's true. You know what I think she loves? Evil."

"Evil!" His wife's church-going was still a mystery to Maurice, who could be got through the door for special occasions and nothing else. He said she kept the pew warm for him. But occasionally Isabel's religion came full force to the fore and he had to think it meant large things to her. Yet she had tossed the statement off. In a few moments, using almost the same tone in which she had summed up her view of Julia's immortal soul, she inquired whether he, Maurice, on a Saturday evening, would prefer to dine on chicken or veal?

# 12. AND JAKE

And Jake.

But it was not Jake but Dev whose head leaned to her out of a bougainvillea vine dark as wine or emperor's blood, who said once more as in days gone by: In a certain manner of speaking, we've none of us got anything outside our love. And she remembered the strong clean Negro scent of the house near Bayou St. John, the splash of water from the rocks in the enclosure behind. But it wasn't what was there he meant; she never thought so anyway. Now, she wondered, was it or not? Had he really loved the octoroon woman who had died that day they had both been there, a wet white handkerchief set chalk-like over her dark face, like taking a death mask in plaster? She wondered at the old legend which put down roots wherever it could (and it could particularly among romantic Southerners), that you only "really" love once and no more. That was why she had assumed he did not "really" love anyone but the English girl from Jamaica, Uncle Maurice's mother. Yet decor is important and memories do not turn to dust. They live wild as young colts, powerful as floods, in the minds they have taken up with. Maybe love was what he really felt for that colored woman, which was why he'd gone into madness, seducing a child, immediately afterwards. Which was why he'd never gone to much trouble to correct it—nothing like quarreling or fighting—if somebody brought up the idea, seeing him in Julia's company, that she had a touch of the tar brush. In reality, neither Negro, nor French, she had got all her life's mileage from illusions. Jake was closer to the truth: he equated her with the city she had come to and grown into, its nerves at last like her own.

And Jake.

She dreamed her dream again, the white and gold one, white dress and gold sandals, down in Dev's house in the bayou country. Upstairs before a mirror with a gilt frame. Yellow Bavarian wine glasses on the table below, her elbows leaning on the plum-colored marble mantle piece, and a young man's step crisp on the flagstones, his knock at the door. And her heart running, flying down the steps, in golden sandals.

Jake was in jail; what was she doing here? Her life had doubled back on itself: like a symphony it was repeating its great theme. She bent to her work daily with such ease and accuracy, she wondered if she might not be a genius.

How to fill up the great sensual image that life was to her, the life Dev had given her? It was like a great marble basin waiting to be filled to the swelling brim. Jake had filled it once, that much was certain. Would he again?

"Oh Jake!"

It was a whisper. He was there before her, in the visiting room at parish prison. They had brought him in and left him. All her hungry nights came back, all her missing time. Was he on the way back to her when he stopped off in Baton Rouge? Got a job for a while, got a girl pregnant? Had to marry her? Would there be time to ask him, now or ever? From the moment he entered, her senses woke and fled to him, nestling and close; he could walk in that splendor same as his skin. If he wanted to.

With the wire mesh between them, he sat before her and then her knees' force disappeared to land her in the chair, level with his vision. She leaned her head down low and his hand reached to her cheek. Through the screen she could feel the pressure of his touch.

After a long while she said, "You should have left me a pet dog."

"I know. I should have."

"Or a cat. I often thought about a cat even."

He said nothing. She looked at his large hand which was the same as she remembered it. His eyes had been a clearer blue and could be again. What made them flash blue? Music and love. His blond hair was ruffled softly at the part.

"This man's jail don't want to let me go," he said, with half a grin.

"Oh Jake, are you all right? They didn't—didn't do it again?"

"What, the rough stuff? Naw. I told them. Hell, I had it once. I'm just here till *you* learn something. That's what I said."

"Don't rile them up, Jake."

"Something's going for me. I don't know what. They're all making circles around me. Maybe it's the press, waiting to catch them. Maybe it's magic—Marnie coming up again like that. That damn Marnie. I'd just as soon he stayed dead. He's in a different cellblock from me."

"With him around, something else would shape up."

"Something like that."

They were silent. First, she was looking into her own lap, then raising her eyes, meeting his; they drank up each other's hands and mouths and brows, shoulders, ears, and hair, all there was to see.

"I wish we could be together, Julia," Jake Springland said.

"I wish so too."

"I'll be out soon. You knew it, didn't you?"

"I knew about them not finding the body. I saw the paper and it said that legally. . . ." Her voice dropped away. It ended, as though speaking power was not something she had been born with or ever known.

"Yeah, I know, legally. . . ." His own voice stopped, like words written off the edge of a page.

Julia gave him her number to write down. "I'll wait," she said. And then: "Tomorrow."

"Maybe. Maybe afternoon. Maybe not. I'm not sure. . . . Julia?"

"Jake?"

"I just wanted to ask you things. Wondering if you'd forgotten."

"I don't think I forgot anything. Not feeling this way."

"Lost your black eye." He was grinning, reflecting within himself, apparently, what had gone before. She might have been a toy he had damaged once which had somehow got mended, and that was what she'd hated, she remembered. She hated it that she could sweep him in but that then he could get out again and go his way, even get married. Martin Parham had never really got out the way Jake had. Her knowledge mounting distant and high as the Texas thunderhead that had killed Martin, she knew she had been in on it, part and parcel with his death.

"Did you see it in the paper?" Jake Springland asked. "All about me?"

Yes, thought Julia, and all about that girl you went and married. She nodded.

"Save all the clippings till I get out. You know that guy that writes it—Arnold? You used to. He keeps coming here. The police have got image-conscious. They're showing me off all in one piece, no scars and bruises. . . . Julia?"

"Umm?"

"We've got to be together again, haven't we? Isn't that what you mean, coming here?"

"Jake, I came because I'm scared. Somebody is getting me to do things for them."

"What things?"

"Things like taking messages. It must be connected with Marnie, so you've got to——"

"Why do you think it is?"

She remembered the man in Jackson Square for one, then the boy in the book shop for two, and then she didn't know any more. It didn't have to be Marnie.

"I'm just on the outskirts, Jake. And still they—— Will they use just anybody? And can't you . . .?"

"You're trying to level off, aren't you? Maybe getting married or something straight. I know how it feels, you know. I——"

"I know you got married," she stopped him. "And kids too. So maybe you'd rather I didn't come."

There was a long silence from him now, but finally he said, "Nobody is you but you, I guess."

"That's how I feel."

"Christ, it's printed on us both like headlines."

She laughed. He suddenly began to laugh as well. The stinging salt wave of desire that had crashed over them had withdrawn and they were now like children standing ankle-deep in swirl, laughing.

"There's a lot to tell you. The good ones are looking for me, the music ones. I've got word."

The police attendant was moving in. "It's time."

"I may take a new address, with another telephone," said Julia. "If I do, I'll let you know."

It was the day that Jake got out of jail that Julia moved. She took sick leave from the hospital on the grounds of being really sick, and put out from her apartment where she had gotten afraid to stay, having been twice broken in on and no one to appeal to except Tommy Arnold, who advised her to get out until the Springland case was over and done with, then to go to the police or get married, anything straight. Nobody could protect her from every small-time operator in New Orleans, that was for sure.

"What makes you think they're small time?" said Julia, over the phone.

"Are you out for the big shots?" he asked. "Nothing but the best?"

She hung up. He was right, always right, but she didn't like her terror being made light of.

The place Julia found was in an old white three-story house over near Prytania. She had the corner of a sleeping porch which had been sealed in. A dresser and bed had been installed and a hanging cupboard made of pressed wood and reinforced on the inside with unpainted, roughly cut widths of pine. A cheap ugly object altogether, which depressed her, standing like an upended coffin. Only for a little while, she thought. That's all I'll be here. A week or two and then. . . .

Then what?

Jake would get the word through Marnie or somebody that they had to let her alone now and by that time she and Jake would have had their second time around and then. . . .

And then what?

Her fiancé, Joe Delaney, the insurance man, was not to know where she'd gone. She knew that Uncle Maurice would know just about where he was, but getting in touch with Uncle Maurice was out of the question. Joe Delaney was another one that Uncle Maurice was going to keep for his very own. He knew how to do that without seeming to, Uncle Maurice did. Julia sat on the cheap but clean chenille bedspread in her rented sleeping porch and thought about Uncle Maurice. She had admired him when she was a child, she wanted to touch, to be touched by him, but he kept her at bay more often than not, was placid before her wonder, and aware, too, but not too responsive. Even that was know-how. A sensualist about everything, he didn't bother; he had simply let her bring the young men to him. If she had known what they were good for in her way, so had he in his. It wasn't fair, but which of them wanted it differently? He gave value for value received, would never think of letting them down in business dealings. Or socially. The Parhams owed their New Orleans standing to him, as well as their legal protection in these parts; they were bound to expand in the

direction of this city. Now she could be certain he wasn't
going to let go of Joe Delaney. There would be amiability
in it and genuine enjoyment of a sort, perhaps, except a
distinction would be implicit in the relationship, namely
that as far as "real" New Orleans society went, the insurance man, like the Parhams, would not be entirely
"in." He would know it and accept it. It would be why,
having met Uncle Maurice and Aunt Isabel, he could
never find his life quite the same without them. Everybody is a snob somewhere along the line. Julia was such
a snob that she went so far as to reject what other people
sought. She had read in the international news a story
of a young Spanish countess with the oldest possible
name who had turned into a protestor for working men's
causes, and she knew why the girl had done it, just from
a snapshot of her petulant face and lank hair.

Yes, Julia admired Maurice Devigny. He was not only
a man who knew what to do with life but how to do it.
Furthermore, he cared enough *to* do it, even though he
sometimes gave the appearance of not caring at all, or
conforming simply because he was too lazy to break out.
Yet things did work around him; he lived in a house
where, even when he had to rent out rooms, the clocks
always ran and the lawn looked good. (He had lied about
his roomers; having to take them in even temporarily
had killed his soul.) Julia had grieved him because she
had cast off advantages that might have been hers and—
not only that—she had acted disgracefully, she guessed
he would have said, but said it only to himself and Aunt
Isabel, never being disgraceful enough to say so to Julia.
(He disliked getting worked up.)

Why did I act the way I did? she wondered. Why do I
still?

If she could see far enough into her uncle to admire
him, she could see only a short way into herself. His
outside life had no interest for her. The intricacies of the
Devigny social connections, the glory of New Orleans
ornaments and furnishings and houses, local disputes

and marriages, protocol of the business world—none of this was hers. Why not? she wondered, since so much of her life had been spent around and within it. It just never took, she realized. It couldn't make her feel alive.

So this was how you wound up on a crummy sleeping porch with your clothes hung in a cranky wardrobe, longing for a breeze, a breath of air in the smothering humidity, and looking down on convent grounds where nuns walked, sometimes together, sometimes alone, rhythmic and thoughtful.

Rhythmic and thoughtful. She watched through her window, lying on her stomach, sighting down through a rift in a high brick wall at the nuns, walking on the convent lawn past the heavy summer shrubbery. They had a regular schedule for appearing and disappearing. What did they do inside? Back when the Church had power and frightened people a little, there used to be stories about sexual orgies or weird relationships, but Julia never thought them to be true. She guessed the nuns were good —tranquil, praying, writing letters for their order, eating, conversing, reading. She'd gone to a convent school for a while and still thought of herself as Catholic—for some reason she had never been confirmed, though Aunt Isabel had insisted for a time, then had dropped the subject. Julia had had a professor at Tulane who edited a literary magazine and said that nuns were fairly good poets; he used to publish poems by Sister Mary Joseph Something. Gave up everything, their own names even. But could you give up your sexual nature? It would have to be repressed, or sublimated. How? Suppose it woke up, live and kicking, a great green vine writhing with life, sprung up one fine morning, wanting to burst into bloom under sunlight like a hundred morning glories, and there you were, you'd already done it, taken the veil, the cool veil that kept you in shadows—and suddenly you wanted sun. Well, you could get out whenever you wanted to, so she'd been told. What if you weren't sure you wanted to? Then you stuck like somebody in a half-baked marriage, not happy, not unhappy, just in limbo. I'm tricking myself into thinking about Joe Delaney, she thought, and I just won't do it. If he doesn't know now that we aren't getting anywhere, he never will. He'll get somewhere with Uncle Maurice. He'll never have a notion that all that New Orleans society that Uncle Maurice is making sure he admires from a distance without ever exactly getting admitted to is a bore. Martin knew that, in a way, though he too liked the idea of its being there, the way you like the idea of having all seven volumes of Proust on the shelf. Maybe I'll get married and mark time for the rest of my life: penance. Right now it's only a chance to live a little while in the old way that I want so much. The old sleazy way. Some rickety little room with maybe a little sun coming in, a breeze maybe, and not too much of a smell. What's holding up Jake? What's stopping him? Maybe he's not coming at all and I won't have it after all. Tied down with the little wife. The nuns passed out of her vision. She rolled on her back, tasting solid heat that glazed even the indoor air. From below the phone rang and presently the woman called her: "Miss Garrett?" The ringing and the call had split the desert silence of her heart.

She ran downstairs in a cotton housecoat and straw slides. Would she meet him at such and such a place near the Cathedral and she laughed, remembering Dr. Pollard and the March wind of so long back. Knowing he'd remembered too.

She floated back upstairs, breathing happiness.

Then she was bathing, she was dressing, she was working with mascara and powder and lipstick, with a hot iron on fresh colored cotton, blue and white, and white shoes and the bag. She was zipping and hastening, the old straight easy open step coming back to her on the stairs, in the hall, out the door, dark glasses on against the sun glare, lipstick moist, fresh and carefully drawn, under trees to the bus and wind in the bus door against her bare legs, her thighs, feeling the slim straight brown line of her legs—this was it, now and always, it was forever. Why did it run away? Sand through an hourglass . . . if we were married it would ruin everything, Jake had said. She had agreed because she agreed to anything to everything to nothing. All she knew was they weren't married, hadn't stayed together, but now he was back so it hadn't gone. In her at this moment was all of life, what she meant by life, twined softly vivid and real as wind rain sun and green were real. She was off the bus and walking, clipclip of heels and stop and eyes turning for traffic signals, aware of the turning of men who had eyes for seeing with and knew by their eyes she was a good sight to see with her dark head close-cropped and high, gleaming, as she crossed and entered Chartres Street, weaving through the Quarter until the old square opened up before her and he was there, up ahead and watching, grinning.

It was Jake watching while Julia walked to meet him in the white shoes and blue dress.

They sat in a poor old rundown bar in the French Quarter, no tourists in it, and didn't talk or drink anything though Jake finally ordered a beer to get rid of the waiter.

"They couldn't find the body?" she finally asked him.

"Never did. No." He smiled.

"Why was that?"

"I didn't inquire."

"It said in the paper they got you off because of double jeopardy."

"I know it. Double jeopardy. The lawyer dug that up. He was pretty nice, that lawyer. A pretty nice guy."

"It meant you couldn't be tried twice for the same crime."

"He had to argue quite a bit because the prosecution claimed it wasn't the same crime at all. Claimed it was Marnie first supposed to be dead, pronounced dead and identified, now somebody else was dead but that somebody was still connected to me, Jake."

"How?"

"They found my flashlight out there, and there was Wilma Wharton's button she sewed on."

"But why couldn't they find the body that was really murdered?"

"Because the Negro couldn't remember where he buried it."

They spoke at long intervals, forgetting there had ever been a murder or a trial, then remembering again.

Jake said "They opened a couple of places where the Negro said he had buried it, but they finally said they couldn't open up the whole cemetery. That was when he admitted he couldn't remember, though he'd been the one who filled in the book four years ago."

"Did somebody bribe him to forget?"

"Maybe. Maybe he just plain forgot. Who'd have thought to look for him to pay him to forget?"

"Whoever thought that Marnie ought to disappear in the first place."

"You think Marnie's with the big time?"

"I don't know, do you?"

"I never knew. I don't think so. I think he personally may have wanted to disappear."

"Then did he find his own twin or somebody exactly like a twin and kill him and put his clothes on him and bury him? Is that what he did?"

"You have to ask him."

"You don't know."

"I've wondered about it. Maybe he just knew a way to find a skinny corpse. The question was, you see, how many times you can murder the same body."

She fell silent longer than before.

He leaned toward her and she to him. If they tried to stand it much longer (she had a feeling) the hands of vines and plants would spring out and snare them right then and there, thrusting them close and wrapping them round when what she wanted was his doing it.

He was touching, just the back of her hand, her wrist, and she said, "Where? Where can we. . . ."

"Near here," he said. "Why did you think I asked you here?"

"I didn't know."

She scarcely remembered leaving, going out into the street.

He'd found the room already and it was good, better than she'd dreamed of, old-fashioned in ivory, green, and gold.

He locked the door and pulled the blind and for the first time in forever kissed her. She kicked her shoes free as they landed on the good strong bed in a tangle. It was a fumble over clothes until she took over, quick and skilful, and at last she was really giving to him again, getting and giving, giving and getting. Sunlight sparkled thinly through a slit in the blinds. Even the pillows were right. How could anything be this right? she wondered, deeper than any right that was right before, she wondered, until even wonder left her, gone. Along with everything that wasn't him.

# 13. AND MUSIC AGAIN

 Jake had come down from Baton Rouge with his car full of instruments: guitar, banjo, steel guitar, and zimbalon. Up in Baton Rouge, he played evenings from time to time in some of the lounges, imitation New Orleans places. It was how he'd got away from his wife so easily to come back to Julia and her city: the fact that he'd brought the instruments along. He said he'd had an offer to play.

But a little something more was in it and this little something made Julia proud of the place she called home. A Negro group had sought him out: they wanted him to play with their band, first for a night in Preservation Hall, then for a week in Dixieland.

There was glory in this, Julia thought: something genuine. They were telling him, by asking him to play with them in those places, which were showcases in New Orleans for one of the things the city did best, that understanding was not withheld from him just because he might have burglarized a little, or got tangled up in some kind of weird-smelling murder case. He had come there wanting what mattered, their kind of music, and they were saying that his good intention had not gone unnoticed in the world they liked. It made a kind of blessing, and a forgiveness.

When the musicians actually started appearing (and Jake for a while had seen none of them, had only received a note of invitation from the band, which had been mailed to him in jail), Julia felt that they bore out what she had thought in advance about them.

Her flesh satisfied, set as deeply in place in her own life choice as a garnet in a gold ring, she lay in long afternoon silence on the green and gold bed, musing about this new turn of things, about how the city had come through. She dwelt on the instruments of music, each fitting into velvet compartments made to receive them, brown, white, and rose-colored within their scuffed black cases. For a while, back when she first knew him, Jake had tried to teach her to play. She would hold, cradle, examine the guitars, tilt up into its correct slant and position the bass which he rented for a time to fill in with a group who needed it; sometimes she would pluck the strings, hearing the vibrations as much through her fingertips as in her ears, and the thrill in it was part of what she thought of him. So too she used to hear his heart in his rib-cage, or his voice speaking beneath her hand, down in the length of his chest.

"I bet you got them first through Sears, Roebuck," she would say. "How'd you know? Of course I did." "I can see you, a little tow-headed boy, bending over the catalogue." "Way up there, where you've never been." "Oh, probably it's just like anywhere else," she would answer. "I guess," he would absently agree.

Once in the years Jake was absent she had heard someone say at a party, "Nobody can love a guitar player . . . they're all stamped out like figures on a tin. It's a modern symbol . . . no individuality." She was shaken just to hear the mention of loving one.

Jake laughed about it himself: "I wanted to do something original, I took up with a guitar."

They went out together to meet the Negro man, a clarinetist, who would wait for them up on Rampart, in the lobby of a cheap hotel that catered to Negro meetings and banquets. He was there, tiny, shriveled up, wearing a carefully brushed black suit like a preacher, and, also like a preacher, apparently not thinking about such earthly things as heat. He was a lot like an old cat. He had a retracted, shrunken-back look, not so much from physical age as expressive of an attitude toward life; and a mottled eye-surface, dark gray, dark brown and black, opaque of feeling. One thought of the narrow little hands with long fingers and yellow nails moving sure, strong, and tremulous up and down his clarinet. Julia, retired behind her dark glasses, saying nothing, was entranced. She caught everything about him without trying to render or interpret him in some other terms: the sunken cheek, the crossed knees, the folded hands, the dignity.

"We are not the most famous of the groups," the little black man said. "More famous groups could invite you perhaps, Jake."

"No, Bunny. Don't look at it that way." He spoke honestly. "Bunny, yours is the only one."

"We can just try it on for size, I would propose," said Bunny. Julia could see a little way now into the opaque surface. Bunny had liked Jake's admitting that nobody else was after him.

"I don't think I'm great," Jake said, and she felt it inside that Bunny liked that, too. "If we hit the right feelings, all pull together, maybe I'll get going with something you can like."

"It's all we ever do," said Bunny, after a silence. He slowly extended his fingers along the red plush sofa where he sat and drew out from the corner a small black bowler hat, which he now set on his forehead. "I must return to work," he said. "Come tonight." He looked at Julia for the first time. "We find it better to work alone." He gave a suggestion of a smile, a momentary gleam of a gold tooth back of the flat dark lips. "However, another time."

She nodded her understanding and withdrew with Jake beside her.

They must have been several blocks away from the hotel, following streets from one patch of shadow to another, when Jake said that it was the old dream back, like before only better. To work with the music, the real stuff. To have Julia at home for him. That was all he ever wanted life to be.

"Now it can't be," said Julia.

"Why not?"

"Just a little matter of what you've got up in Baton Rouge."

"Yeah, I guess not. You mind if I go up there, this weekend?"

She walked on in silence. A long weekend of walking alone anonymous in the Quarter or along the river or the lake, hoping not to meet anybody she knew.

"I guess not. Better than her coming here."

"I thought that too."

"It can't last, can it?" Julia finally asked. She had called the hospital to say she was still sick and would be out another week or so.

"It's lasted so far," Jake said, after another transit through midsummer sun to ninety-degree shade.

"Bunny Terrence doesn't ask just anybody," Julia said.

"I know that."

They entered air conditioning in a ten-cent store for a time just to get cool enough to continue their return to the green-and-gold room.

"I want you to live your dream," she said as they strolled through refrigerated air. They passed cheap makeup, notebooks and office supplies, then blouses, bras, house slippers and aprons. Back among kitchen utensils, she remarked that the bubble would burst soon enough.

"But not yet," his voice followed her shoulders going steadily before him. "Not yet."

It was the city that had reached out to him. Did he know that? Did he know it? He knew it, yes, he said. Too great to mention even. Music was his real thing and now that his ambition was gone maybe he could live it. What had thrown him before was wanting the name side of it, the fame, all that. Now he felt purer, purified.

They had gained the room. She was turning up the air conditioner, stepping out of hot shoes.

"We're counting a lot on Bunny Terrence," she said.

Turning from the door, Jake Springland smiled. "But maybe not too much," he said.

That went for hope, which they had to have.

# 14. MARKING TIME

 Julia sat in a cool square waiting room which was really the living room of a Negro house she knew about. She was the only one there. There was a false cool in the room simply because it wasn't in the sun and she waited until the false cool, the idea of it, evaporated off her mind and left her as hot as the inside of an oven in an old blackened cook stove.

At last the cretonne curtain in the back of the room stirred and the voice said "Miss Julia?" And she went in.

The light in there was dim. She had known about the place for years, had gone from time to time since childhood, but had never known it to change. There was a tomblike changelessness about the box of a living room, surrounded by enlarged photographs of serious-faced Negroes, with a jar full of prince feathers or cattails on a table in one corner, a radio, a victrola. The victrola might have changed. It was a record player now, and the stack of records themselves, though silent, dusted, seemed to indicate that a teenager might have been choosing them and even playing them sometimes.

But the dark room with the dim lamp had always been the same.

Businesslike, the Negro woman, whose name was Mildred, sat down.

"Yo' birthday in February . . . you got the fish sign, you got to let the other folks decide. You can't be the big ole miss, ordering this and how you wants that. You got yore man now, how you goin' to hold on? It's yore problem, maybe you do it one way, maybe you choose

another. Lemme see yore han'. . . . You livin' out yore
curse line, almost done with it. Worse to come. Pore
young woman! Maybe it won't strike so hard as what I
sees, maybe it will. Remember who is who. One man
gives you yore needs, but one man never goes the en-tire
way with you. What one wish to call all, you always sees
as not all that much, not all that fine. You live out yore
curse and then come back, you know when it's done,
ain't nothing nobody can tell you before then. . . ."

After she paid she saw the purse was nearly empty,
money nearly gone again.

When she got home in the twilight, Jake was there.

"I went to see Marnie," he said, "just for you."

"About the breaking in, about the messages?"

"He doesn't know who's doing it, or why. He got mad
because he didn't know about it, and he says he'll find
out. So if anybody can he will, but once he's found
out . . ."

"Maybe you shouldn't have asked him."

"You wanted me to. Marnie's something like a blood-
hound, you know. He can track things down, here or
anywhere, but what he does with what he finds, that's
a different thing. Nobody can know what he'll do. He
explores these mysteries, you see, and when he finds a
course of action, then he actually does it: he acts it out.
He might have disappeared because he found some sort
of impasse in his labyrinth. I had a role with him but
he wouldn't tell me what. Son or brother, how could I
tell? He said I was a truth-bearer. He thought some people
picked up truth sort of like a microbe, a germ. Then you
were stuck with it, it was a disease that limited and
defined your life. He felt he couldn't see you, he said
today, because you were a person without limits. You
had no definition, you could be anywhere, be anybody.
That makes you dangerous."

Julia thought privately that she and Jake had gone
to their own private fortune tellers, but she said nothing.

"Did he tell you whether or not he dug himself up?"

"You mean he *was* the corpse? I don't think even Marnie thinks he could make that happen. I didn't ask for the secret. You know what? I think nobody's ever going to know, Julia."

He was picking up soap, moving to the wash basin, scrubbing his hands. His teeth flashed at her as he turned his head; she loved the line of his neck, the smell around his neck and shoulders, her teeth bit at his neck. She was tiptoeing. She could not remember, with him, from moment to moment. . . . In love, memory is an afterwards invention, and with it you try, she thought, to fill up what experience has left behind. Memory is a handful of gravel thrown into the Grand Canyon, a gallon bucket of minnows emptied into the Mississippi River. I've remembered him for years and here he is and going from me every minute. This was what Dev couldn't stand about love, he said; it was eternal and passing both, and at that suddenly she sat straight up from the bed where she'd lain back to think and said:

"If you aren't going back to work we've got to go to the cemetery, the St. John's one."

"But that's where they thought the grave was, but couldn't find it."

"I know," she said. "This is something else entirely."

"I don't want to have anything more to do with all that gravedigging. I'm willing for it to be a total mystery."

"I know," she said, "I agree. This is not related to that, not in any way." And she dragged him by the hand, laughing and urging him, till he said all right then, all right, okay then.

She said there were reasons she had to go there.

They took the bus.

The old cemetery they went to had been private for many years, with a neighboring acre or so owned by the city where paupers and unclaimed corpses were interred. Now, of recent date, the whole was the city's property. Burying had always been a problem in New Orleans.

The first settlers had found it so. If you dug even two feet below the surface, water flowed in. The dead therefore were put in little houses, which were more or less ornate marble houses above the surface of the soil. Lesser souls rested sealed in drawerlike tombs, only name and dates chiseled without. Sometimes whole families shared silently a single tiny house. Pediments as small as triangles drawn for geometry mocked the classical style. The miniature columns—Doric, Ionian, Corinthian, sometimes Egyptian or some Gothic innovation, twined with ivy or made with fluted and creased designs—framed the closing slab which stood where doorways were to be thought of. Here inscriptions might be written in flowing script, poems, Bible verses, or private thoughts about the dead, or mere facts set forth.

Julia bought flowers near the gate and took them in, dividing the bunch in two. Above her head at times, at times only measuring to her quickly passing shoulders, the white tombs rose. She hastened, knowledgeable, and Jake Springland followed, down intersecting pathways, under moss-hung trees. Late sun, blinding doubtless at noon, now streaked over the marble in patterns that, hourglasslike, moved with the eternal changes. Their passage, for an instant, interrupted the usual rhythm of these changes. One aisle, one corridor after another went past them, giants moving in a silenced village. Then she stopped, in magnolia shade. She bent down, not kneeling exactly, but not without reverence either, and put down the flowers in their two separated bunches, side by side. One large façade showed two names, entablatured.

Jake Springland read

> Henri Devigny
> 1869–1949
> Valerie Laughton Devigny
>   b. Kingston, Jamaica 1885
>   d. St. Martinsville, Louisiana, 1916
> Beloved wife in all eternity

Then he noticed the smaller tomb beside the first, in pink marble, the only one that was.

Diana McAlister Dwyer Devigny
b. Newport, R.I., 1888
d. New Orleans, 1931

"Two wives, I guess," he said. "But the second one, she was like a parenthesis. When he died he went back to the first one."

"Something like that," said Julia. "The second one was rich, what did she expect? That was her house," she added, "the one they sent me to. Audubon Place. Where you wouldn't go."

"Oh, your swanky relatives." He was laughing, and she thought, to him relatives are just natural landscape, something like mountains and rivers.

"I'm one of the wives," she said. "And he—he's the only one I can't bring back."

"I think he's with you anyway," said Jake. "The way you talk about him."

"I think so too. I think he's why I never married, always looking for somebody here like that, or thinking what he'd say of the ones I went with."

Jake Springland did not ask what Henri Devigny would have said of him.

"They're going to close the place," he remarked.

She turned then and walked away, straight, not looking back.

"He'd understand how you make me feel," she told him, for her desire was coming back again; with every step she took, it would grow.

"I like the way you talk about him, feel about him. It goes all the way through you," Jake said. "It's why I have this thing about you, things go all the way through with you."

"I know that," she said. "I know that."

It was like an hourglass running out. When she got to the gold and ivory room, the last grain would go through the narrow funnel.

The last aisle of tombs released them and they turned left to go toward the high arching wrought-iron gates of the cemetery. Here she came up short for a moment, stopped stockstill. Why? The small house near the gate, done in concrete in vaguely classical outline, had a glass-paned door which stood open, showing in the dim interior ranked powermowers and grass clippers hung from a board, rakes and hoes and other tools stacked in the dimness within. But out of it all, now emerging, came a little dried-up-looking colored man, bent permanently from the work he did there, studious over the dead in their white houses, their little lawns before them. Julia was sure she'd seen him somewhere before, a feeling not unusual around New Orleans, but the thing that brought her up short was Jake. The fact that Jake spoke to the Negro as they went by.

But it wasn't until late that evening, after dark, when they were eating in a cheap place with booths and a service counter that she asked him, "Who was it, Jake? The little colored man you spoke to at the cemetery?"

"It's funny. He's the same one that buried the corpse supposed to be Marnie. They had him in for questioning. They asked me if I'd ever seen him before and I said I didn't think so."

"Well, had you?"

"No. I'd never seen him before. I can't think why they asked me, unless they think he was in cahoots with Marnie and so with me too. Maybe he knows how to get a dead body, thin as a rail, with a broken wrist, on very short notice."

"But you don't think that either."

"How should I know, one way or the other? The corpse came from somewhere and if Marnie had a twin who showed up and got murdered, I never heard about it and neither has anybody else. The city couldn't issue permits to have every pauper tomb in that cemetery broken in to."

"Only Ted and Wilma Wharton really know the truth about all that. And they won't tell. But they tried to frame you."

"We think that because they dropped my flashlight out there. But they may just have dropped it in the dark and then couldn't find it."

"The reason I knew that colored man, he was the one the Misses Mulligan used to get to garden for them. I just remembered it. He used to come along with a wheelbarrow and garden tools. Now I know where he borrowed them from. I've got a feeling he knows everything about you, me, Marnie, and the whole story. But he won't tell it either."

The only way to find out if he really was the colored man who used to garden for the Misses Mulligan (and for all she knew still did) was to go and ask the Misses Mulligan. She could of course go to the cemetery and ask the Negro, but she doubted getting a straight answer. She had come and gone past him for years without noticing him, but probably he had noticed her. Doubtless he noticed everything. If she went to the Misses Mulligan she had a feeling they would tell her exactly. They probably knew everything legal there was to know about him: how many times he'd been married, whether his wife was alive or dead, how many children he had, how old he was (about), what sort of health he was in at present and last year also. They must have got him as gardener through their cousin on the police force who would have said, "Go round and see about their garden once every week or so." What gardeners do the police know except these keepers of silent gardens, the buriers of derelicts, suicides, beats who drop down on Royal or Dauphine, Conti or Rampart or Tchoupitoulas or out on Carrollton between two-thirty and five A.M. with nothing in their pockets but a few coins, some cigarette butts, an address of some cheap rooming house, a photo which when traced leads only to a long-ago address of a photographer's shop in Memphis, Nashville, Cincinnati, or

Birmingham, long since demolished, so most of the time there's no way to trace anything.

The more she thought of that little colored man, the more she could imagine him anywhere, as an article lost can be imagined almost anywhere with great accuracy. She could think of him waiting on tables, cleaning public stairways, shucking oysters, trundling service-tray wagons in hospitals, drawing weeds from the Mulligan ladies' flower beds as carefully, slowly, as a seamstress drawing basting from fine lace. Obsequious, furnishing a corpse decorously procured from God alone knew who—he must be in touch with people who for a price would get anything done. A broken wrist—there must be ways of getting that. In fact, some of the money Jake hadn't been able to extract from Marnie that night of the fight might have gone to him. How could you get information like that? You could go and ask till your face turned blue, you wouldn't get it. She got an inkling of what the police were up against. At bottom, humanity is intractable, its true motives are kept desperately secret, too dark to bring to light. Or just too shamefully trivial. Through some contrivance, it would seem, that black man looked like a hundred others. Bent back and grizzled hood of native hair, face drawn together from squinting to see. One just like him that night at Jake's session (for, for the first time, she was allowed by Bunny Terrence to come in and listen) was banging the piano, bending down close to the keys and sending out his long arms with an expertise of fingering, hands flung out like birds in flight. Every once in a while he hollered, cried out, and the bass echoed him. Jake and his banjo were going pretty well, she thought. Occasionally they threw it all his way, letting him see what he could do with it. They seemed to be saying they were wanting to give him as much as he could take without giving it all. There was a lot in the way the music shaped up, a lot they didn't say that came beating through the music. They said it in general, then they said it about each other, then about

Jake, then they said it again, but now it was enriched and fluent and wanting to say itself what it was and how it was and everything.

Julia sat on a folding chair back against the wall in the dim, bare barnlike room up above the restaurant down near lower Canal and listened quietly, the way she had to. It was a practice place, nothing more. Sometimes one or two people might wander in, somebody who knew one of the musicians, like herself. It was off the tourist track. It was not like a public place at all.

A chill line was running on a sort of invisible double track with her thoughts and with the music too, and that was: suppose that colored man is in thicker with Marnie than we know, and suppose he tells Marnie we were out there today; but surely he knows we didn't go for any *reason* and if he's noticed at all he's seen me there before. He knows why I come if he's noticed me at all. So is he reporting anything to Marnie? Does he even know Marnie?

She knew nothing of how the crime world worked, only, having brushed against it, that it had snaked out to catch her. Or had seemed to. How deeply was she in, how much did they have on her? And why? Uncle Maurice, getting rich on what the Parhams had thrown his way and now with an in on the insurance front as well—was he too all but down on some long list of possibilities they were drawing up somewhere? And who was "they"? Who starts syncopating where? When do they throw it to you?

Jake's blond head bent studiously over his rattling banjo looked innocent with concentration. Within that head was a knowledge of what everybody involved in the Marnie case could or might have done, what they'd tried to do to him. Yet he didn't hate. That was what his music was saying. If he did hate he wouldn't be there; he'd be up in Baton Rouge with his wife and child looking life grimly in the face and putting his shoulder to the wheel and seeing order restored and dull things unfold. A raise, a missed sale, a quarrel with the boss. He wasn't a hater and so he couldn't really be a victim, either; all this had to do with why his love pleased Julia through and through. But by the same token he would leave when leaving time came, the way he had before. She'd be like any mourning colored girl singing *The Empty Bed Blues*. But right now the true, the ever-living happiness was hers, the right and final kind, hers now and because once then forever.

She heard herself thinking (the thinking almost made a noise like footsteps in leaves or a fire in dry grass) that if he'd do great, do big, hit the big target, then he'd never leave her. He'd always be coming back to have more of it. But she couldn't push on that point, it was her ambition before that had landed them in that impasse, had driven them to disastrous collision. It was where the black eye and the hurt shoulder had come from. And the broken heart. Should she go to the fortune teller? To church maybe? Jesus, she thought, who can I pray to?

So she thought, sitting back against the wall.

Jake Springland.

## 15. OPEN DOOR

Bunny Terrence's band was booked at Dixieland Hall for one week only. But following the one-night engagement at Preservation, there was a write-up in the *Picayune* and a longer one followed the same afternoon in the small weekly paper the French Quarter published, not only for tourists but for the whole city. The second night the hall was packed, and the next and the next. They were turning them away at the door.

Julia noticed how the decor of New Orleans persisted through these evenings, allowing the players to be quiet and faithful only to the music they played, to pack up instruments and pay no more attention to the audience than if they had been part of some great ritual, like priest and acolyte, to give out the air of its making no difference whether the church was packed or empty save for two or three souls.

She overheard scraps of talk: "Can't tell me that boy ever killed anybody." "Just a killer for music." " 'Killer' Springland, huh? Let's name him." It was one of the hall managers talking this way. He had caught the dark upward cat slant of her glance, overhearing him, and grinned at her. "Okay by you?" She smiled back. So they would try to make that stick. Somebody had done the same, she guessed, with Jelly Roll Morton and Pee Wee Russell and Satchmo, though here he was mainly known as Pops. The story would fill in around Jake too, she guessed. Tried for murder but they couldn't find the corpse . . . either that or the corpse got up and left for California. Other lore would pile up as it did in the

casual wash of life there, barnacles sticking to the new
surface, once it got firmly fixed in that dirty sea. Could
he rise to the high level that demands a nickname? He
would have said he didn't know, added that he didn't
care, not any longer. She didn't know either and saw that
she too had to say she didn't care, had to learn to master
it, mean it, no faking, not ever.

After a break, they were filing in again, picking up
music sheets, tightening strings, getting settled, while
the audience shifted, settling too.

There it went again—slow and easy for a starter.
. . . "I like you baby but I don't like your low-down
ways. . . ." Then picking up through *Tiger Street Rag*
and *Lazy River*. Music hammered around her ears. She
could mark the point of improvisation beginning, of flinging the theme back and forth, then of breaking through
entirely, as they now had the luck to do. She knew the
moment too when for the players in the whirl and
spin of sound the audience itself had dropped away and
there was nothing for them but the take-off from the
improvisation, the off-spun statement, far from the
original beat itself abandoned for flight after flight, the
return to question and answer, to repeat and wondering
and hesitation, until renewed inspiration sprang from a
single player who was hailed and joined by one and all,
so that all went traveling down the road together into
gladness pure and simple, and discovered flight and soared
to rapture until now, altogether . . . Halt! There was
the wild applause that came at them, waking them out of
their trance.

Julia knew they were cutting a disk that night, for
the second time. Whether the players knew, had thought
of it, she didn't know.

She edged toward the door with the crowd, leaving.
Hearing "Where's that mulatto girl?" "You mean that
girl he——? Part French, I thought." "There she is, here
every night." So she knew she was in the legend too,
getting to be, because the press had praised him by name,
both for banjo and straight jazz guitar, a difficult feat,

and now the jazz buffs had come crawling out to approve or not.

But what it mainly was, she thought, was glory.

He hardly mentioned it; which was how she knew best that he felt it because like the name of a beloved he didn't want to say it. Getting up, shaving, not talking about it even when he said good-night to the other five, standing at the wash basin in the green-and-ivory room splashing water in his eyes where the smoke had stung them, he moved in the ebb and flow of glory, and she got it, caught it (she also wordless about it) every which way.

Jake played with three Negroes, one on drums, another on bass, and that monkeylike one at the piano. Then there was the trombone, so white as to pass for white, and the trumpet, a mulatto with French and Italian blood and God knew what else. And Bunny on the clarinet made up the band. Julia remembered Martin Parham's family with their pure Anglo-Saxon talk, pure bloodstream talk, how they'd wondered (she'd heard them) if that dark tight-curling hair of hers didn't mean something foreign at the very least. She'd told them, when right-out asked, that her mother's family had some French blood, she thought, though Aunt Isabel claimed that if this was so she didn't know it. How did you go about proving such things? The French in the early days had intermarried cheerfully with Indians, only Indians had had hair straighter than a board. They were given to melody only when whooping it up around a flaming corpse lashed to a pole, if she'd heard correctly. No, it took the black strain for the real jazz beat, which had come out of the voodoo drums, Lake Pontchartrain torch-light dances, and fancy doings on summer nights in Congo Square. Others could learn it, but the true beat was African.

Jake and Julia went to Morning Call near the wharves for coffee and doughnuts after the show, or they found a hole-in-the-wall for gobbling down eggs and toast.

So he would finally have to open up, talk about it,

and he did. "Hey, did you hear that double beat tonight . . .? Lakey kept it up at me till I thought it had
gone behind a cloud and would never come out again.
Sometimes I think I'm still hammering, just waiting for
him to come through."

"Then he came zooming out," said Julia. "You both
did."

"We did, all right. We sure did."

"It was grand after that, it got just great . . . really
going. It was just about your best."

"They're coming fast now, don't think that's all. And
they're cutting records, too. You knew that?"

"Knew it! I was helping them set it up."

He took a long exhausted sigh, burst into laughter,
caught her hand up, kissed and dropped it. "It's too
much. But great . . . just great. You'll bring me luck
forever."

Forever. Something kept repeating it without her will,
way back in her mind. There must be such a thing as
forever. But what did anybody ever have forever? If he
said that, it only meant he was feeling the glory again,
more and more, increasingly. He was rising to it and
wanting to ride with it, with self-knowledge, self-
awareness. That was his forever. She was a part only.
She didn't, couldn't, want to take it away from him.

But his rising sense of the big moment and the break-
through was not shared or even felt, in his particular
way, by the others in the band. Julia saw that—she had
expected to see it—when she went along with him to a
gathering of the whole group, near the end of the week-
long engagement.

For Julia, nothing could have been more gratifying,
more mystically fulfilling than this meeting. It had been
prearranged among them in the briefest and most under-
stated of terms and it was the dumpy bald little mulatto
trumpet player who had mentioned it to her just as she
was waiting for Jake near the door.

"We will be over to the club room later on, Miss Garrett."

"Where is that?"

He told her, the address being in the far lake side of the Quarter, up near Rampart.

"Will you come?" he asked.

She nodded. "I think so."

And so they did, entering, around twelve-thirty, an old-fashioned house with dark red wallpaper, one small dim crystal chandelier burning just below a steep curving stairway. And mounted to a large room with deep easy chairs and several posed sepia photographs—framed and hung around the walls—of other bands posing with instruments held as tenderly and consciously as mothers hold young children. There was a piano, dark, in one corner, and a fireplace which in winter was actually used, she could guess, for the brasses were polished. A Negro waiter passed around a big plate of hamburgers, warm and covered with a napkin, and there was beer in steins set out on what looked like a card table, and peanuts in a large bowl. No one spoke.

Jake Springland seated himself quietly, not trying, she was glad to see, to talk with anyone, these men he had practiced with for days and had now played out his last ounce of inspiration with nightly six nights in a row and one to go. She herself sat near him with her hands folded, heart tremulous and high, for the time of testing was there for both of them and she knew it. She knew it, she felt, better than he. Its importance, its ultimate nature, were everywhere unspoken in the room.

Of the two other Negro musicians besides Bunny Terrence and the piano player, one was big, formidable, black, and habitually sullen-looking. The trombone player, the one who was either white or could have passed for white, had a thin supple mouth and was limber and ugly. He often looked at Julia in a way that was not at all unpleasant, more meditative than otherwise. He seemed to want no conversation with her. His wife had appeared with him that evening; that is, a woman had entered with him and climbed the stairs beside him, and now Julia knew she had been there in the audience once or twice before, a sophisticated-looking woman who tonight was wearing black with a sheer sleeveless tunic in gold embroidery on chiffon. It took considerable taste, Julia knew, to find and wear that sort of thing, which might not have been so expensive. Other wives or women or girls, ranging from chocolate to nearly white, had appeared almost silently, to sit carefully in the background, speaking to one another in low voices, saying what Julia could not imagine. Everyone was eating hamburgers and drinking beer. One of the darker women got up and passed the peanuts around.

Bunny Terrence at last stood up and said:

"We have to some extent to thank Miss Garrett for the interest of Royal Recordings in our performance."

Everyone looked at her, but no one said anything further, and Bunny Terrence sat down.

"I didn't know about it," Julia whispered to Jake, who said aloud, "Miss Garrett wants to say she didn't know anything about it."

There was a pause. It seemed that no one would speak again. Then Bunny Terrence said: "Her name was mentioned."

Julia whispered again to Jake: "By whom?" "Does it matter?" he whispered back. She didn't know.

"One night is left," said Bunny Terrence.

After another silence, the big sullen Negro spoke. "Jake here," he said, "he live in Baton Rouge."

The mulatto stood up, said "We know that," and sat down.

The silence resumed and another plate of hamburgers came in, borne by the same Negro waiter. He passed them with that kind of pace and decorum about which nothing could be said because it was perfect.

Finally Jake Springland leaned forward. "What's it supposed to mean—I live in Baton Rouge?"

"Placing you ain't easy," said Bunny Terrence.

"Is placing what he want?" the big sullen Negro asked.

"I doesn't know," Bunny Terrence said. He turned to Jake: "Is it?"

"Placing how? With you? A steady member?"

The small Negro nodded.

"Sure I want it," Jake said. "I'd thank you for it."

He'd not been offered it, that was the point, the reason for the silences, the source of the solemn concentration.

And then Julia stumbled on it, on what was there, and her own luck. It was communion. It was why people did things, why they went so far as murder and uprooting, loss of all they seemed to have. It was the world within the world, and she remembered something: Dev.

A month from his own death he had spoken to her from the big mahogany bedstead, upstairs at Uncle Maurice's, saying: "I was so glad to be a member of the Uptowners' Club, young as I was and chosen. A year or two later and I was in with the inmost few—'the little Napoleons' we called ourselves, in a jovial way. Then came the night I drove the surrey out there beyond Chalmette, a cold night. I waited out with the horses while they went and knocked on the door and though I heard the cries it was only later on I faced it, what they'd done to the man who'd discovered he had a conscience toward the federal government rather than the city, only he hadn't reported to his friends and comrades just when he had discovered it and how, nor what he had gained from the discovery and how he meant to use it. That was why we were there in the surrey. I drove silent on the way home. Did they kill him, threaten him, ruin him? Either my memory's getting bad or they never told me. I know he wasn't around any more. By the time I found out why—though now I forget—I'd already made my peace, that peace being of this nature: that whichever one it was I still wanted to belong with them, with the Uptowners. I had to belong with some crowd or other and they were mine. If you belong to anything, you belong to something that is wrong some of the time. If you don't belong to anything at all, then you are alone."

She had sat listening to him, days on end, long hot afternoons, silent near him, her young womanhood held waiting in the wings; she had this particular time to spare him. She was now a good part of all he had any feeling for, so she let his words come straight to her, straight into her, and watched the big head turn restless on the high pillows in their heavily embroidered cases.

Smiling. "You're thinking I'm alone anyway, aren't you? You're thinking, well, where are they now? I'll tell you where. Dead. Mason and Belliveau, LeGendre and Barnett. Oh, I meant to move with the times, make new friends, but put it off or something like that. Then it was what they did at the capitol, what the governor did . . . oh, it was financed there, that college man's study. He published it! They wouldn't stop it!" He was shaking now, coughing now, a red face turning as purple as aging grapes or old blood in the heavy hand-veins. "Wouldn't listen!"

"Dev." She got up. "Now, Dev. Don't think about it." She sat closer, touching the hand that was enlarged, grown monstrous with age. Touching it without revulsion.

"Think about it!" But he had quietened. "I have to live with it, why should I think about it. A cold study, a cold college study, making us out to be cheap crooks. It was the governor's policy. They hated us down here. An exposé. Brought out in the press. It was meant to be a college boy's paper. You know what it was? A plot. Calling us by name, making us out to be some Cajun outfit, drinking cheap wine, some bunch of shrimpers, instead of——"

"You were all grandees," said Julia, soothing.

"I tried to stop it." The old eyes turned to her, sad and eloquent.

So it was the day he knew he couldn't stop it, the day they brought him that note, that was when he'd rampaged, tearing at the very house itself. Who had had the right to "expose" gentlemen of Dev's class, who provided for the children of their mistresses and chose their wine carefully and gathered for their café brûlot in plushly carpeted rooms? Keeping the city well in hand, keeping their business matters in smooth order, keeping what was theirs in the appropriate fashion, all the while living a concept of themselves, knowing that nothing is simple and nothing is pure. How well she understood. She felt as though it were her own property—the large unhealthy head turning restless on the hot pillow, its knowledge all packed up within it, but coming to life at times like a volcano, seething, bursting out occasionally in jets of molten rock and spurts of flame. Don't mention too much, be careful. What if a cold-blooded little girl at the day school had told her once that Dev had printed filthy literature for sale and then had the black woman that sold it for him knifed to death near the wharves when she ratted on him, or tried to get money out of him not to rat on him—one way or the other? What of it now? What if that was his mistress who had died that day in the house near Bayou St. John and he had loved her? Do we have to talk about it? Once knowing is enough knowing. There was Julia's own secrecy as well. Back in those days, if she skipped on the sidewalk it was not from childish high spirits but because some thought of what she'd allowed to happen only the week before might cross her memory, but she wouldn't do that any more, wouldn't find herself allowing it, to Buddy or Billy or Paul. We have to have communion, call ourselves the little Napoleons of the Uptowners or something else, an infinite list of choices—why? Because we can't stand ourselves, it is unbearable.

"Read to me, Julia," he'd say. "Read, child. I'll correct

your French." He had said once that the poems had
become a fascination after the women went. The poems
were like the women had been.

And she would read:

> Quand, les deux yeux fermés, en un
>     soir chaud d'automne,
> Je respire l'odeur de ton sein chaleureux,
> Je vois se dérouler des rivages heureux
> Qu'éblouissent les feux d'un soleil monotone;
> Une île paresseuse. . . .

So it was no confessional they held, those final days.
She knew, not everything, but enough. She knew he'd
kept his communion, had found and kept it, until they
died, and then he died, with memories, with the picture
of his bride, with the living hand of his son in his, with
Baudelaire—and with Julia, "that child."

It was enough.

And now she'd lived to find a company of her own.
It happened when Jake said he wanted to belong to
them, and there in the room she'd felt herself immersed
in their common knowledge, their sacrament.

Yet she was helpless, she recognized: she couldn't
play two notes herself. It all depended on Jake. Now
more than ever in her life she wanted him to measure
up, for the testing hour had arrived. A steady member?
He'd be happy to belong, he'd said, waiting, not hastening ahead of them. When she saw the action of the group
open intricately toward him, toward the moment of including him, Julia drew the kind of breath a tightrope-
walker's wife might have drawn in midcourse.

She glanced around at the circle and noticed that the
wives, the women of the men there, were sitting a little
back from the circle of men, that only she had, by chance
that was not exactly chance, assumed a forward position in a large chair near the fireplace, as though placing

herself among the musicians. She now rose, on the pretext of putting aside a greasy napkin, and reseated herself back in the shadow-line. The atmosphere of the room shifted. The move had been correct.

"I got nobody working for me," Jake said, into the silence. "It was the Armstrong story, the one I liked."

"Satchmo." The voice, male, Negroid, and rich, came out in the room, but who had spoken it was not clear. "Pops."

"That's right: Louis. He didn't want to leave that river boat so they couldn't pay him to get off it for the longest time. It was just his playing broke him out of it. When the playing swelled too big to be held within it."

"The melon on the vine," a voice noted.

"Big old peach, man. Bound to fall," and this time it was the big black Negro; it was him for sure.

From the shadows Julia felt that supreme joy in a woman's life, pride in the man she loves. He had got it, she thought, caught on. And he wasn't even from there. It had been the mystique of the group playing, the music thing. Now they were in it together.

It was a cool night, having clouded over, blown, thundered, lightninged, and rained while they were inside, and when they reached the room, Jake Springland raised the windows and let the night air in. Julia put her cool arms around his neck. For moments in the mellowness of desire they swayed together, like dancers.

"That went off all right, didn't it?" she asked.

"I think so. I hope so."

"You were right. You played right, too. Everything you did went right."

"You were thinking that, there in the room. When you got up and moved back, that did it."

"Can we stay with them forever?"

"Will they let us?"

"Maybe." She drew in the possibility, like breath. "Maybe."

The wind swayed through the room, stirring the curtains. It was a shabby old house, not pretending to either respectability or nonrespectability. Happiness is one room, Julia had sometimes thought before tonight. She would never think so again. From that time on she knew the truth: happiness is communion. Why had it taken her so long to find it? She remembered once some weeks back seeing Edie and Paul Fowler in their station wagon, baby carriage and picnic hamper, the whole bit, stopped at a drive-in grocery before the outing, and how she'd curbed her impulse to go and greet them, how something had appalled her about it all, the sight of American coziness, all the accoutrements, every sandwich wrapped in cellophane and extra diapers packed in the plastic carrying case. Well, how would *I* do it? she wondered, turning away depressed. Not that way, she thought. She turned up a side street so as not to have to speak to them. He always hated me anyway.

Yet she thought freely of children now. Unborn, unnamed, they crawled up her shoulder, breathed against her neck, wakened her when she napped alone. One of the musicians was a barber, another a shoe repairman, a third sold insurance, and a fourth was either unemployed or did something illegal. Did what they did outside the group have to exist even? She thought not, and having run low on money, went out and stole supper. On Canal Street she glimpsed Joe Delaney striding purposefully by. In thick with Uncle Maurice, who was getting a fat fee, she could guess, he was brisk and forward-looking in his stride, eyes set before him. (Did she detect an inner puzzlement?) She turned and glided into the Quarter, but not before the whole structure of her present dream had shivered.

At length she reached their doorway, and was mounting the shabby stair. Jake was there. Offers had come in, he said, but he didn't know what would be accepted. It would depend on the others, what they wanted, what could be worked out. He went off to practice for an hour.

In the room shc gravely savored happiness. To her it was the city that had reached out and taken Jake in. It had reached all the way into jail, where he had first got Bunny Terrence's message, like a soul reprieve. Now the city was trying to give him his forever. The garbage heap of all that Marnie trouble had grown a lily, pure white and flawless. She recalled a hundred other stories, images of all that had gone before—Marie Laveau, the voodoo queen, bringing food and magic potions to condemned men, calling down thunderstorms to reprieve them in torrents of livid rain; and others condemned, shuffling out with a smile and bow on their way to the gallows, written up with tenderness in the old-time press, as if their humanness could and did exist side by side with the awful things they'd done and were now paying for. And Dev, reproached by his cronies for keeping up, more or less, an aging quadroon he had long since lost all sexual interest in, seeing that her children got to good schools and into steady jobs: "What harm she ever done to anybody, what harm? Anyway, I might be one of 'em's daddy for all anybody knows." "Including her?" "That's right . . . including her." After forgiveness, Julia discovered, you could never fully return to guilt. That was its beauty. And that, too, the city understood.

Then he was back, a step on the stair, an opening door. She was sharing a slug of cheap bourbon with him out of a thick glass, she was bending to cook the stolen meat and red beans and rice. It was the last evening. They did not mention it.

That night the hall was packed tighter than ever before, and the performance was as solid as ever—strong as a stevedore's arm, muscle riding smooth and fluid to the surface, when required. Some of the band shouted when they played, a muted call. She sat against the wall as usual, eyes closed. Then it was late, and the show over. She knew, gathering herself to rise and go out, that it was time it was over. Something new would grow up now, out of that great week. What was to be forever known would happen. Now.

It was late, and the clapping toned down at last, then stopped. She took Jake's arm as they went out and it was just at the door that a flash, a glare, burst unexpectedly, once and then again across her face. For a moment she was frightened. But it was Jake they were after, she decided, and as a musician now, the stories about the trial, Marnie, and all that having faded. They were after a story on the last evening's performance of the group, so he'd have another clipping, that was all. Still, she should have waited down the street for him as she'd always done before, met him in the dark corner of some bar or other. Why hadn't she? She didn't know. Her long dream was opening into fulfillment, so she had moved like a dreamer to catch his arm. She thought of Tommy Arnold, who had kept her out of the press God alone knew how many times, and that maybe he would do it again, if she could find him in time. Once again, under the gracious spell of memory and a gone day, she walked with Tommy away from Audubon Park, a silent pair beneath a sweep of trees.

But she did not call him, did not ask for anything. When she thought of the flash of light it seemed to blaze into her brain cells, to turn her inside out with fear.

"What's on your mind?" asked Jake Springland.

"Nothing," she said, reverting forcibly to the week's splendor. "You were good tonight. So was everybody."

"A great week," was what he said, tender, exalted, tired.

There was a cheap paper, a magazine-size tabloid published in New Orleans, and the weekend discovered her on the front of it, looking dark and smart under a tousle of hair, stepping through the door of Dixieland Hall on Bourbon Street, clinging to Jake Springland's arm.

In a morning-fresh café down in the Quarter, Julia,

wearing dark glasses the size of harness blinders, sat looking at the paper. It was bound to happen sometime, she thought, not daring yet to turn inside. Uptown they would soon be selling the record. She knew that because the record company had called up to say so. She thought that things had a way of meshing in the dark basement machinery that ran America, of working together down there where nobody could see. Were the record people in touch with *The New Orleans News*? Many was the time Tommy Arnold had sweated away down in that symbolic furnace room for her, but he couldn't control the whole machine, no matter how many contacts he made use of for her.

SOCIALITE MYSTERY GIRL IN MARNIE CASE
*Springland's Secret Companion a New Link*
*In Swamp Murder*
*(See Inside Story, Page 3)*

It was a long hour before she could turn to page 3. At last she did, quickly, and read. She felt the words catch fire under her eyes and squirm upward as though caught by fire, wriggle, and wither into ash. When she finished she touched her eyes and the area under them seemed burning with hot sweat. In this interval she closed the paper up like a surgeon closing an incision above an inoperable truth.

Children! Nameless future children, who had climbed, hurting her, across her, pulled her hair, laughed into her ears. The life she had projected trailed now through her spirit like an old-fashioned lighted Pullman of the sort Dev must have liked once to ride, passing, curtains drawn and lights mellow, through the heart of some honky-tonk over-the-river strip of dark human wilderness garish with neon. All she knew of that train now was that she wasn't on it, that it carried her dream swiftly, but not herself.

How can a woman have two lives? The question landed before her clinkerlike, an empty oyster shell. She had played around in the forest too long not to have been noticed by the Indians. She sat chin on palm, thinking of hers and Jake's love which this story would not, could not, touch, the jewel in the junk shop, and thinking too of the music which, swelling and torrential and truthful, would go on anyway. And the door behind her darkened and a form stood at her shoulder. She looked up: Tommy Arnold.

She did not move or smile. Her eyes moved perhaps, following him as he came to her, hat in hand. As he sat down, she could see no more, tears poured out. He caught her wet hand in his.

"The day the bubble burst, the day the money ran out, the day the telegram arrived. Everybody has them, kid. They're all the same. What I keep asking myself is: did you honestly think you were kidding anybody, that your good square Kiwanis Club insurance executive was back there waiting patiently?"

"Oh, I think he is waiting! Why not? I thought, if Dev could swing it, so could I."

"Who?"

"Oh, somebody—somebody from childhood. Long dead."

"Devigny, you mean? The old man that raised you, wasn't it? Brought up to lead a double life, is that it?"

(Tommy Arnold, like Martin Parham, had looked him up, too, had seen the sly fox within the heavy-eyed regard, the principle of concealment, layer on layer, deeper-skinned than any onion, insoluble as a Chinese mystery box. What was at the center? A something? A nothing? Julia would know better than anyone else, and, if she thought it was a something, then it was.)

He led her by the tear-wet hand to the back of the bar, to the empty but neat, cleanly swept room where people sat at night listening to a half-French, quarter-Negro, quarter Anglo-Saxon play a muted slow-beat as an emperor passing through town might have done if he had noted a piano and remembered that he liked to play.

She put her head forward on the clean red-checked cotton cloth.

"Marrying Jake," she said. "It's the last thing I can do."

"One thing," Tommy Arnold said with patient good humor, "he's got a wife already."

She was sobbing now. "I had to live it. When he came back like that, I had to live it, didn't I? What else could I do? You're nothing if you can't live it."

"I know. I know that. No matter how outrageous, how ridiculous, how violent, how outlandish. You have to live it. I know that."

"And the children."

"Children! You mean Springland's?"

"No, I mean children—someday."

"I'll give you some of mine. Nothing surprises them."

She managed a wan smile. Dear Tommy. The perpetual wisecrack artist, hat laid sincerely across his heart.

"What are you on now?" he politely inquired. Her arm rested near him on the table, and he turned it deftly, looking for needle stings. There was a mark or two, but that could have been mosquitoes, anything. "Just joints? You haven't graduated to something else, going on to more and better things?"

"Nothing. Nothing."

But anything could be a lie.

"It's not fer me to say," said Tommy Arnold.

She pushed the tabloid toward him. "All this. That's what I'm on. Have you read it? Read it all?"

"Every word. I would have stopped it if I could. It's a new bunch that turns that thing out. They don't listen any more. Either that or I've lost my touch. The world's got tougher."

She wiped her eyes. "You're back full time, aren't you?"

"The *Picayune*. Yeah, it seemed realer than the other job. You've changed my life, see?"

She laughed. "My life's changed thirty times already."

"Now let's not go in for melodrama. It's just what you get for going to work for an eye doctor."

"It's what you get for dropping by the Squire-meisters'."

"You can always marry a Texan," said Tommy Arnold. "Texans don't care if you're the lead story in a tabloid."

"Uncle Maurice and Aunt Isabel. They're probably deciding right now that they've had all they can take from me."

"What had you planned on? Going back and marrying that guy, that one in insurance? I can't think of his name."

"I don't know why not," said Julia. "I've lived my wild life, literally. Most women do it some way or other . . . some just live it in their heads."

"There's something else here," said Tommy Arnold.

From the chair beside him, he lifted a brown paper envelope, obviously containing a phonograph record. He drew it out and placed it before her, sitting quietly while she took it in.

It was not a Dixieland Hall recording primarily, but a Springland recording. Jake's picture, a singing face, guitar in arms, was large on the front cover. He looked like himself, but like a million others, too; he was a reminder that America was one. JAKE 'KILLER' SPRING-LAND, the lettering read. One side was of his own songs, the ones he and she had composed together out of all the old poetry texts and other things, scavenging up collages of life, bits of words and intonations, like pieces of tin foil, old string, and rusty mousetraps: scavenging to hang songs together. That was from eight years before. She remembered now: back when she had wanted his success more than anything, she had got one of the young men at the artist's studio where she had worked as a model to cut a disk of Jake and his songs. The words would be there, cut in the black plastic now silent before her, but the technique would be his older style . . . but never mind the fine points; he had a name now because of the Marnie case, and they were milking it for profit. On the reverse side was the Dixieland Hall recording, with the Bunny Terrence band. God, she thought, nobody intended this; Jake and I, we never heard of it. But who's going to believe us? And what does believing matter? The thing had been done. Terrence and his gang were background for what the record guys had done. And they weren't going to like it. That much was inescapable. No good Jake saying he would have stopped it if he'd known.

"What's happened to that guy, the one you say you're still engaged to?" Tommy Arnold asked her.

"He went to Chicago to a convention. He got run over by a taxi and had to stay a day or so in the hospital." She added this rather automatically, wondering why she made up things. Lies or not? A put-on. "I hear from him," she added, another one.

"A convenient absence," Tommy Arnold remarked. He returned the record to its envelope and gave it to her but she refused it. "Keep it," she said. "I'm going to say I never heard of it."

"It will be a flop," said Tommy Arnold. He replaced his hat, put the package under his arm, and prepared to leave. "The story of how it came to be will interest no one. It won't get around to anybody. When your what's-his-name fiancé gets out of traction in Chicago and returns, everything will be back like always. You're Cinderella in reverse, that witch that set you down in a rumble seat with a rat at the wheel will order you home at stroke of noon. They don't get tabloids out on Audubon Place, I trust. You'll be back buying your trousseau in a week. Can I come to the wedding?"

"You're on the list," said Julia brightly, putting her dark glasses on.

She kissed Tommy Arnold good-bye at the door, thinking Jesus, how can I know, how can I know anything, how can I know it?

# 16. POINT OF CONTACT

In New Orleans the Springland record made a better than average sale, and for a week or so it went pretty big. But the town, which had started taking Jake for granted (he was a character in it now), was not really going to go to the point of doting on him, or of giving him more than a certain quality of fame. If he insisted on more they would let him starve first; he would starve, it is true, in the New Orleans manner, but would do it, nonetheless. Even if he went away now and made a big success in New York, Chicago, or the West Coast, and then returned, they still would give him no more than they had before.

"And we were almost inside the charmed circle," Julia said, as she had before. "We almost got there."

"The record did it," said Jake, as he had said before also. "The record was a betrayal."

"Not even my fault," said Julia, regret rising steadily up around her like a tide full of trash. "If it had been I could just find some way to dramatize getting out of your life and pure intentions."

"Like how?"

"Like jumping out of a window." She began to laugh. "The bad part is, we can't explain."

"They aren't the kind of people you can explain things to," Jake said slowly. It was the Bunny Terrence bunch he meant.

"Explain or not," she said, "you think they need us?"
"No."

They were walking in bright sunlight, along Jackson

Square near the docks, and pigeons fluttered up before them, landed a short distance away, circling with quizzical glittering eyes.

"Together, together," he said. "Thrown out together."

"That's something, yes, I know. But it's not enough, Jake. No it isn't!"

She had burst out so that he stopped still and swung her by the arm around to face him. "It's all we can give each other. You've got that guy, that insurance guy. We've talked about it . . . agreed. . . ."

"But then it happened. Oh, it happened to me. You remember."

"The night at the club." He began to laugh. "A society girl like you. You've had champagne by the gallon, but you finally make it on hamburgers and beer."

"For Christ's sake, it wasn't what they ate. Just that they were eating, I guess that was it. We were part of it, Jake. Oh, you're always just passing through, aren't you? To me it was belonging. At last. Then it's snatched away. The record snatches it away. Your coming on as a star. Using them to make yourself something else that's not them. That did it. I think you could try to talk to them, Jake. Try. At least, try."

"Not after Bunny's call this morning I can't try. Maybe we can cool it and start over. I doubt it. Time passes . . . passes." He walked on, meditatively, past the high iron fence before Jackson Square. "I thought you were into everything here—everything from newspaper reporters to the financial world to Audubon Place. Now it seems you're begging for an in with a jazz band."

"I am into everything. But nothing's turned out to be absolute . . . nothing before the other night. First there was you, but you alone. Then: them."

"I understood it, knew it. . . ." He stopped and spread his arms wide, as if to the docks, the river, the pigeons, and the sky. "I can't drop my life, Julia. Not again."

"The wife and two kids. But you've walked out before

and you would have if the record hadn't. . . . Oh, we're
back again!"

"I *wouldn't* have walked out. I'd have had an excuse
for being here if I could have become important enough
here. Now—"

Julia's mind's eye could not blot out a black disk
whirling inexorably beneath a needle. She was mewing
about already in abandonment, a deserted pet unable to
leave the house that everyone had moved from.

Jake was standing silently, looking out. He did not
turn. The moments between them were stretching out
longer and longer like so many rubber bands. Presently
one was going to snap and then there'd be no going back.

She sat down on a bench. "Jake? Jake? You've got to
know sometime. I've got to let you know . . ."

Her voice was smaller than either one of them could
ever remember its being, and the note in it spun him
round. He looked at her, then sat beside her, circling her
shoulders almost companionably. "What?" he asked, and
"What's the trouble?" but in a way she guessed he knew
already, having been an attractive young man long
enough to know what a woman he'd been living with was
apt to say when she sounded like that.

"I thought so several times, but didn't mention it," she
said, feeling a little proud of this, thinking she might get
a prize for it.

"If you're sure, it's probably so." The way he looked at
her, gently kissed her cheek, pressed her shoulder, spoke
tenderly, they might have been longing for this very
moment, all safety and love of the lasting kind. The
next minute he was asking her what she wanted to do
about it. It was not an unnatural question; it was, in fact,
the most natural question in the world. It was just that
even the thought of what he might be getting to drove her
wild. She didn't want to think about it yet, even to know
as regards her own and Jake's child that the possibility of
such a "solution" had ever been mentioned or even
dreamed of. "No! Jake, please, please. For now, just no!"

She had pulled away and was standing, back to the bench, as he had just been, and the visible world had turned to dream. Within this dream a long black car she had already seen, she half-realized, several times that day passed in a slow, silent, pneumatic glide before her. Had it circled the square several times already? Or passed them once or twice earlier in the narrow streets of the Quarter? It was chauffeur-driven, curtained, custom-made, a Cadillac. Once she had known all about Cadillacs. Now it was turning right, with slow funereal decorum, at the corner of the square. Then she forgot it. Floundering in her own dilemma, but trying, too, to grasp, to hold personally to herself—and perhaps to herself alone—the joy of her conception, she began to walk deliberately away toward where the splendid car (already forgotten) had turned. Alone—alone then!—she was trying to start thinking, both heart-broken and exultant at once. I will continue . . . we will continue . . . I will have it that way. . . . She turned the corner.

Jackson Square. And the old general same as ever, snared in the middle. He'd gone away and they'd turned him to stone. And then the car, circling yet another time, went past her by inches, long as a freight train, and at the second corner, turning right, it stopped and waited.

Directions, was all she thought. She was always being asked directions in the maze of the Old Quarter, and she came on and a window let down an inch or two. One of the back doors cracked open. She saw no one, had through her personal turmoil only the impression of a chauffeur's cap. So it was more than half her own momentum, helped on by the sudden half-alighting of someone within the car, the swinging of an arm half round her and the quick tug forward, that carried her straight within the dim interior. Maybe she had been going faster than she thought, fleeing from the suggestion that had been about to come from Jake and was going, she well knew, to scar their common history forever. So her velocity was perhaps her passionate expression of how completely she did not

want him saying anything about "getting rid of it." So it
had been even easier than it should have been to snatch
her into the dark upholstered cavern where she heard the
slight expensive *chunk* of the closing door, felt the noise-
less smoothly powerful impulse of the motor, drawing
them purposefully on, and turned straight into a full-view
close-up of Wilma Wharton.

Wilma, despite all her work with mascara, eye-
shadow, lipstick, and various other products, must have
known deep down that the response she might get from
beautifying herself was not a gasp of admiration but a
shriek of terror, for she clapped her scented hand over
Julia's mouth. They were alone, small as tussling children, on the big back seat. Julia gazed off to the immediate horizon where like a figure at the far end of a drawing
room a man in a chauffeur's cap turned his head from the
wheel and looked back upon them. It was Marnie, as
natty as he'd ever been, and they were circling the square
once more, turning the third corner and now the fourth,
and so coming to that point, like an X on a map, where in
ancient times, all of five minutes ago, she had revealed
to her true lover that she had conceived his child, and
then had run off before he could even make a start at mentioning that she didn't have to have it.

Jake was still there. He had sat a good while thinking—this came out of what she knew of him—and now he
was rising to follow slowly after her, knowing she would
have gone back to the room because there was no place
else to go, planning how he'd handle her, calm her, how
they'd talk. And there he was, walking; and as the motor
slowed, a tiny mechanism could be heard or felt to mesh,
minute as a baby insect, and at the sound she knew finally
and completely that this was the capture, the take of both
of them, that the net was spread and she had walked into
it. Now he, moving downwind, as it were, innocent in
the singularity of his world, was about to be . . .

*No!*

Her mind shouted it, and she leaped, wild, at the turn

of the second corner, almost clear, her hand shearing against the door handle. She might have made it, she showed such strength, but long before she had ever had a bone in her to fight with Wilma Wharton had known the human jungle and trained for it. Julia had no force to make up for the natural size of her own species (she was like a female panther, young and black, in the fetid hold of a lioness, flea-bitten, but a lioness still.) Ted Marnie drove, as he knew he could, without a moment's strain, watching ahead toward the prey. Jake went sauntering on. If only she could scream once, to warn him, then they could knock her out, she guessed, but something had already resigned itself to their getting what they wanted— whatever that was. What was it, oh, what was it? It was Jake who knew, who would know. If she could warn him in time she could free him, and he could get her out of it, some way.

Julia relaxed, seeming to give up, but only to fool the powerful arms enough to get a final surge against them, but when she felt herself released by one arm the other tightened expertly across her shoulder and throat, its hand still smothering her mouth. Out of a sense-haze of gardenia perfume she heard the click at her earlobe and saw the blade before her, delicately lifted; the handle was made of white bone, gone slightly yellow. The edge was so fine as to be invisible as a silk thread, as softly glistening as a web in dew. All was possible and plain, with the plainness of things that cannot happen until they do. Then the car drew even with and slightly ahead of Jake Springland as he walked on. It stopped, motor still running, and Ted Marnie got out.

Julia noted that they were scarcely twenty feet from the entrance to Dr. S. M. Pollard's office. He must be up there, getting a bit grayer at the temples, a good deal more bald across the dome, efficiently applying all his serious training to helping out whoever made appointments and could afford to pay their bills. "Why aren't you in one of the big medical buildings?" she had asked him. "Oh, I always just liked it down here. My father's office was not too far away." "Was he a doctor?" "No, a lawyer. I told myself that if I didn't get enough patients because of the inconvenience of the location, I would move. But so far so good." And so it would always be good because Dr. Pollard had been, she now supposed, good himself. How could she get him from right upstairs to here, to help her? So near, and yet he might have been on the moon.

Marnie closed the distance between himself and Jake. He spoke a word and Jake turned, at close range, and saw the black gun rise up between them. Also between them now, between those two who in the past had been acquainted deeply enough to burglarize, compose music, get religion, and eat the same woman's cooking together —and all before she knew them—there seemed to Julia as she watched helplessly to be more than surprise on one side and triumph on the other, more even than recognition from both, but two confronting visions, twinlike. How deeply had Jake been committed to Marnie's world? She couldn't know that, nor whether he was still committed in any part.

Terror walks the margins of our lives. If the Russians aren't to blow us up, the neighbor's sweet child will one day cry bang-bang you're dead, and so you will be, for he thought from watching T.V. that guns weren't real and that shooting was just a game. From the coldness of her mother's hand which had not answered her touch that day in Tennessee to the coldness of the razor Wilma Wharton held, this thread had run through Julia's life, was part and parcel of it. Jake was getting into the car. One cry when he saw Julia, and whiteness and his hands knotting together, knuckles white—she knew that gesture.

When he spoke it was straight in front of him, without turning, but the words came to her alone, she could guess, in the school French again, the way they always played with it: "Le rôle est sa passion. . . ." And then: "Tiens froid."

"Shut that off," said Marnie.

So his role was all that mattered, that was his game, and she had to keep cool, remembering how a game gets to be everything, you can't break rules and get by. The car was moving faster, sure of direction, around and out onto the broad street, past the French Market, the fish market, ship salvage, sailor's dives, smell of ships, fish, and river. They were part of the present theater, she and Jake. There would be more to it than that, much more.

They gained, after a twist of narrow streets, a sleazy corner of the Quarter, off the beaten track, and stopped before a Chinese laundry. Marnie turned to address them, ceremoniously removing his chauffeur's cap:

"You've thought you'd hog everything for yourselves, now we're both out and free. But who had the message and gave you the spirit to play the way you do? It came from the message and you know it. And you know the message was mine—the spirit-power, that was mine. Without me you wouldn't have it. If this girl don't know it, then she has to learn it. Get in the back of that laundry and say your name is Edgar Q. Snow and come out with what they give you. You try anything and she here—she'll learn a fucking lot more than even I want to teach her. Get going. This part is unimportant. It's just a matter of doing it right, like playing the little tune, Jake-boy. Get going."

It must have taken all of three minutes to go inside and come out again. Why, Julia wondered, if they're doing tricks like these do they hire a car as conspicuous as this? She almost asked, Alice in a special sort of wonderland, always asking. But she saw the answer, or thought she did. The Cadillac too was part of Marnie's role; the trappings had to be right. Jake Springland returned.

"God, Marnie, it's heavier than lead. If all that's——"

"We're not discussing it," Marnie said. "Put it in there. Why you think I rented a car with a glove compartment this big?"

"Nothing if not practical," said Jake.

Marnie now, turning sideways, snaked out a long arm

and skeletal hand, deftly transferring the gun to Wilma
Wharton. She put down her straight razor to take it, balancing the former on her knee like some domestic object
relinquished for a moment. "Over there," she said to
Julia, releasing her grip on the girl's mouth and shoulder.
The gun waved, commanding. It was held just below the
level of sight. The razor teetered, sliding to one side
against the thick thigh, skirt drawn carelessly up, expos-
ing a length of black stocking. Now was the time, if this
was a movie or a suspense show on T.V., to grab the
heavy arm with its hammock of flesh and let the gun go
off in the air, while Jake lunged into Marnie. But you
didn't do that, the police being something nobody was in a
position actually to want to appear, for one thing, and
you didn't do it from fear, either, and Julia moved, half-
choking with the cheap-woman smell enveloping her now
like a supernatural cloud, breathing through her mouth.
She felt dizzy and weak, half-nauseated.

"Let her out, Marnie," Jake was pleading. "I grant you
the message, anything. It's too hot a package for her . . .
she'll get too large a label."

"She's got it already," said Marnie. "She's had it from
the minute you walked through the Chinaman's door and
said the name. It's time she graduated."

"Was it you in my apartment?" Julia wanted to ask
Wilma, and almost did, the way when stirred by fear or
hate or love words formed without her willing them,
formed and fell, formed and fell. It must have been her,
the world couldn't hold two women like this. . . .

*"Open the window, I'm going to pass out, I . . ."*

# 17. WEEKEND

 The blur was clearing. They were all in the country, the four of them, on a beautiful day. She woke in the room she had been in for what had been left of the night, and got up slowly. The windows were broken and fallen in. One had a curtain nailed across it. There were flies in the room, in sunlight, and these had waked her. She had a feeling they were near the Mississippi River and that she had been in the house for a long time. But maybe it's just the next morning, she thought. Jake, she thought, just the way she always did. They've done something with . . .

But she looked across the room and there in a second bed, painted white in almost hospital style, like her own, Jake Springland was lying, heavy and gravid, face down.

"Jake!"

Did she say it aloud? She ran to him, pulling at him, turning.

"God." He stirred at last, flinging himself over heavily, tasting his mouth. "Oh, my God."

Overgrown bushes, shrubbery once, she guessed, pressed to the windows. The windows were low to the ground, almost as low as doors would have been; one had a stick to prop it up. Everything needed paint except the beds. The one chair in the room (her dress lay across it) was dull, worn, unpainted wicker with flowered cretonne cushioning now ripped and faded. Somebody had picked it out once, she guessed, just as somebody had once put a curtain in a window. These presumed human actions seemed about as much encouragement as she

could wring out of a situation that had had nothing in it,
she was beginning painfully to recall, but debauchery
without resistance. She saw then she was standing on the
edge of where he had been sick in the night.

If there was pain for her in the act of leaning toward
him, of touching back with her hand and fingers the hair
along his brow, she knew it was because the motion
realized the truth of her body again and made it know
where it had discovered itself the night before.

Springland caught her hand and pressed it, genuine
in the gesture. The pain flared up worse than ever and
she turned her head away.

"Don't," he said. "Don't worry. Please don't think about
it. I'm forgetting about it myself. It was pretty bad all
right. But don't remember. Call it another hangover. It
was just what they gave us, made us take."

"We're nothing like that. Not like that." She was half-
sobbing, and spinning around, grasping herself across the
belly with both hands crossed. "The baby."

Jake caught her arm. "If it's there at all, it's okay still.
Listen to me."

She listened and believed. The stench of vomit came
on more strongly. "Let's clean it up at least." Her mouth
came wanly up at the corners. "Let's find an old wasp
nest to pull down and nibble on, and forget."

"You weren't any worse than the rest of us."

"If there was any worse to get," she murmured, weary
and half-faint in the increasing morning heat. "What self
have I got but a body? Oh!" It was gasp and sigh at once.
And knowledge. That none can break loose from words
spoken or from action done.

"Does he hypnotize?" she asked, a faint hope.

"I never knew, but after what we let him give us,
there's nothing impossible to——"

"Why did we let him do it? No guns, no razors. By
then he'd calmed down."

"We just did it, that's all." Looking across the room,
across the pool of drying vomit, he saw her back to him,

her body writhing against the white-painted iron bedstead.
"Look, Julia. Let's clean up."

His voice, she knew, was trying to erase it all, like a
blackboard, and I wish to God he could, I wish there was
a way to let it happen but I can't believe there is. She
moved, stiff, seeking a bathroom door and finding one
the other side of Jake. Inside she found a bath towel,
faded and frayed like everything else here, and wet it;
found an old bucket too and filled it with water from the
claw-footed bathtub.

"Give it to me," he said, and slid to the floor, bending.
"Go wash your face. Go on while I do this. Think of coffee.
You like coffee."

"Coffee." I'll think of coffee. She closed the bathroom
door. There were rust stains in the basin. The water
ran tepid, then freshened. She splashed some on her
face. There was something in me that wanted to, that
wanted it, wanted the worst that could happen. And
Marnie knew it. Jake's right, he can see through you, into
you, deep inside. It's his claim to all of us, and I had to
be a part, it's why he had to nab us, one reason.

As though the small room was on a ship and the ship
was reeling in a storm, she staggered in it, side to side,
and wound up, her face still dripping clear water, holding
to the wall. For a time the wall had folded down flat and
she had lain on it as on a raft on the waves; now it was
back upright. As long as it didn't fall on her.

"What am I? What couldn't I do?" A voice said plainly:
"There is nothing you couldn't do, Julia." It was the
demon's triumph. Demons tell the truth.

Slowly she gained at least physical control, and lowering the lid of the toilet seat, came to perch herself on it.
Leaning forward she gripped her arms once again, with
tenderness, around the deepest area that enclosed her
womb, gaining a fragment of sanity out of the pledge she
felt capable of making. I will protect you. I will bring you
home.

Home! Where was that? (She thought the terrible

voice was going to speak again, but it didn't: one message was enough.) She closed her eyes. On a distant green lawn which was sometimes right side up and sometimes upside down, Aunt Isabel, young and smiling and wearing an old-fashioned white dress with a high lace neckline, came forward to greet a guest, while Uncle Maurice stood correct and knowing; their smiles cut right through life with rightness, with love, too, while from a high window above—oh, don't look there!—it's a dark old face looking down. She looked anyway and strength was in it, for he had seen, done, things not even she could guess at, and so was with her.

Emile, she thought, suddenly naming a child not only unborn, but for all she could be certain of not even conceived. Emile, I'll make you safe. I'll bring you home.

When she came out of the bathroom Jake had made a good start on cleaning the floor. She helped him. The floor was wood with wide boards and being wet like that it shone with a pallid receptive look, as though it enjoyed a cleanliness that had happened to it time and again in older and better days, betokening care. Outside the sun was beautiful on a shaggy overgrown slope of lawn, and a fresh full rush of breeze burst through the window. The tattered, pinned-up curtain swelled. Something blue, lovely as a bluebird, which it might have been, flashed by.

"Jake," Julia said, putting aside rags and mop. After many changes the water in the bucket was a dirty soap-smelling gray, and the boards had a soap reek to replace the sour stench. The floor-cleaning had been a saving, ritual-like action for them both, a motion toward decency. They sat on the edge of the bed and held each other.

"Out of the pigsty into the palace," she said with wan humor, but still she felt beaten. He stroked her head. "What can we do? How can we live? How can we even get out of here?"

"How can we get breakfast?" He straightened and began to move toward his trousers and shirt.

"Jake?"

"Yeah?"

"I'm afraid for you to leave me."

"Then dress. We'll sneak out together. There must be a kitchen."

"What is this place?"

"It was an old river house, a home. Then an overseer's house. Then a hunting-fishing lodge. Now trappers put up in it, in the winter season. In summer it stands here with brush grown up all around it."

"Spanish moss," she said, looking out the window toward the slope of yard down to where the trees commenced, trailing their generous widths of gray, breeze-stirred. It must be about eleven. The day was edging toward somnolence.

Memory was fresh as raw meat. Herself stripped down to nothing in the soft red glow of light the color of a road-worker's lantern, and the cold direction-giving voice she had obeyed, not once but over and over, in front of . . . She clenched her hands to fists, beat her knuckles to either side of her head, as though to knock the knowledge out.

"If we have to go in that room again, I'll scream. I can't take it, can't . . ."

"You won't have to. I think the kitchen——"

"You were here before, then."

"Marnie uses this place. You got no idea how much he had out there in that cistern at one time. A gold mine. He found a place in the cistern wall. He used to let himself down in it with a pulley, me holding the rope. That's when I decided to check out on him. You and me, we took to smoking joints because it made the music better, us better too some of the time, but the hard stuff, you wouldn't have had any if they hadn't put a gun on us. Neither would I. You see what it can do." He was tucking himself together, dressing. "He's got his wish now. Something about putting his feeling for you so you'd remember him, too."

"Remember him!"

"Yeah, because you didn't know Marnie, see? You knew him on sight, but not the literal God-and-demon Marnie. Yet everything had centered around you. Even the nigger he got the body from, you, somehow or other, had known that particular nigger. You remember that day at the cemetery? I told him that, just as a curiosity. I shouldn't have. It was the last straw. You were in on everything but outside his power. You were drawing power. You didn't know how much, neither did he. He got worried. I know Marnie. If his role's not complete he can't go on breathing. He's the soul engineer. Whenever you touch him, he rounds on you. And he had to touch you, literally. You can't glide through his life without a body, above it all; you've got to have the scar."

"It was something in me, too," she said. "Something that wanted to go down forever, to hit the absolute muddy bottom where there's nothing but old beer cans, fishhooks, and garbage. And I—I must have wanted to get that gone, or I wouldn't——"

"Everybody was that gone. How do you think I feel? I let it happen. Christ . . .!" He ran out of breath, out of thought as well.

"So now he's the overlord?"

"You don't bug him any more. He can't lose ground because of you."

A quiver swept her. She shook herself like a dog coming out of water. She wanted to jump out of her own skin.

"I'm just going to call it an awful headache. That's what it mostly is, right now."

"Except my being sorry, always." They stood before each other, clothed and sane, with level, grave regard. "Something that started long ago, I thought it was in the war, out there in Korea, but now I know it was probably in me all along, some sort of not caring, not being able to see what difference anything made in the long run because I didn't think there was any long run . . . well, I think that's gone for me. Drained out. . . . Hell, when the sky's the limit, the well's got no bottom to it either."

It must be so, she thought. She said, "It must be so." Then she added, "You mean maybe he's saved us, defined us."

"Something like that."

In the kitchen they found hot coffee in an enameled pot which seemed to have been left there for them, as though by magic hands in one of those fairy-story castles. Wandering down the slope of lawn in back they came on Wilma Wharton in an old canvas chair with one rung rotted, which listed her broad behind nearly into the grass.

"Sit down, you two," she said. She was reading something, a paperback book she had probably found in the house, and Julia saw the title, something by somebody she'd never heard of; a forest fire was blazing on the cover. Trees were catching at their tops and smoke billowed up into the title. Just before Wilma Wharton the slope dropped steeply. A bayou lay sluggish below, a dark metallic stretch of green water under the morning shade.

"He said he was going fishing," she said. "It's a lie, like everything else." She put down the book. "I'd like to kill the bastard," she said, to no one of them in particular, looking out in the direction of the bayou. "I was a fairly good woman before I met him. That, last night, it's just a sample of what he's able to get people into. A sample of what I've gone through time and again. Why do we put up with it? Do you know, Jake?"

Jake sat down on the grass and looked out at the bayou. "We're all searchers," he said. "It's the promise of something beyond it all, beyond just common life, I mean—that's his promise. We go on following step at a time and pretty soon all hell's cut loose."

"If we could get together on him, we could do it, Jake.

If we do it and put him in a grave, suppose somebody does dig him up? Then it's just a joke. Because by now with what the papers made out of it, everybody's tired of it anyway. They acquitted you, the time it didn't happen, so you can't be tried again. It was legally done. Nobody on God's earth could keep a straight face if they dug him up again."

Jake broke off grass and twisted it. Julia sat beside him, gazing at Wilma. Wilma at last met her eye.

"I'm getting my sense back, you can see," she explained. "It's been coming off and on, for some time. I had just about kicked it, all the old ways, that's why I can sit here the morning after, cool in the head. Nothing the matter with my mind except Ted persuaded me to trust him about coming out here and all; there was money in it for him, and he said he had some soul business with Jake's girl. He's worse than ever, either that or he don't even know how bad he's going to get. Which is it, Jake?

"I was only a waitress," she went on, "and from time to time I worked in the ten-cent store and once shampooing at a beauty parlor but my skin wouldn't take it. I have very sensitive skin, and all those different soaps and things. But there's nothing wrong with being a waitress. Waitresses read books, they can be churchgoers, everything like that. You think when I started fooling round with Ted I went over to being a tramp? Not a bit of it. Ted looked good when he got fixed up. He's almost a Ph.D. If he went slouchy it was in an intellectual way."

She stopped, to let it soak in.

"I even loved him," she continued, "till his hair turned that color and he got on dope. About that time, I got fat, all of a sudden. My shape changed overnight. Jake remembers. What with those handicaps, our New Orleans resolutions got dampened. It took the edge off them. We were going to start out new, see, in a place where no one knew I'd been a waitress or he'd been out of work. When we made your friendship, Jake, we really meant it. Some-

body we really liked. Remember all the reading . . . tell
her Marnie was smart."

"Sure he was smart," said Jake. "We had a lot of good
evenings."

"And that time down at Grand Ile, how nice the sea
came in, the wind and all the gulls."

"It was nice," said Jake.

"Then there wasn't any more money, it started going
for dope again because he was trying to catch his vision,
he said. He'd started seeing too much but not quite enough
to hold it, to hold on to it. Prophecies, soul-knowledge,
the grace-state. You know how right he could be. The Salvation Army thing, that was just a stop-gap. He was after
a teaching job in a religious institution. They were publishing these tracts he wrote. He sat up nights. You never
saw any," she said to Julia. "We were back in New Orleans
by then, and needing money. Jake used to practice . . .
you worked by the hour, Jake, all that winter, and we
went down, sinking lower. Had to move, new place dirty,
and then—"

Julia got up and walked away. She'll be offering to let
me read his tracts next, she thought. Maybe I would even
find some truth in them, since Jake did once, enough to
be interested. She wondered how crazy the world could
get. At Tulane she had known an historian who got into a
fight with a critic who was visiting him and they had
quarreled slambang about an intellectual topic too obtuse
and controversial to interest even people in their own field
who might have known what it was, finally tearing at
each other and smashing with fists and breaking things.
The historian's wife had to come out and stop them. When
the critic went out to his car, he had found the battery
burnt out and had to ask the historian for a ride to town,
so it was as if the quarrel had never happened from the
moment he came back and knocked on the door. She'd
put it down (smart college girl) to their possibly being
suppressed homosexuals, but now she wondered if the

world in general wasn't crazy. Why could Wilma Wharton
think she wanted to read anything written by a dope-
ravaged guru who the night before had seen how deep a
debasement she could be dragged through, how much she
could be egged into actually desiring?

Yes, desiring!

Because she'd never had heroin before. The other
things, yes, from time to time. Joints and goofballs, hash-
ish once or twice, and things you sniffed without knowing exactly what they were, but being a good refuser she
could refuse too when she wanted to, and that was most
of the time. Now she'd known the depth charge and now
she would always know why people went for it. It had
reached to the inner kernel folded in the deep spirit, first
with shock, then with slow music. It had taken herself
from herself, and if that self did something, the other self
could sit and watch and laugh and know that it didn't
matter, did it, how could it matter, when the self wasn't
the self, the real was here instead of there; so the knowledge ran.

Julia went down to the side of the bayou and sat on
a pier. She took her shoes off and put her feet in the ink-
black water. Moss trimmed the gray supports of the pier
and water reeds grew up out of the mud. But where she
was the blackness of the water still looked pure and felt
pure, and she wondered if the black was a matter of reflection and how the water would look in a glass. Small
perch came and nibbled at her toes.

Jake came down to join her, squatting on the bank.
His white shirt and khaki trousers had gathered to him in
their own way and his hair, just dried from the damp
combing, sat as it ought to. He looked real again, and permanent. She wondered how long, really, they had been
there.

"How long?" he repeated, after the question. "I guess
we could get a calendar and figure it out. If we knew
what today was," he added.

"It feels like Sunday," she said. "Can you get back," she asked, "to Bunny Terrence and the group?"

He turned to look at her then, and as so many times before she felt herself dissolving, disappearing in the intensity of his direct gaze, but one thing was different now: there was the impersonal thought embedded in it, the sense of something beyond them both.

"I can't go back to anything here, Julia. Not after what's happened."

She felt such panic that she was afraid to show the smallest part of it. She looked quickly away. As if to grope for reassurance she touched his arm. Out of the very set of it beneath her touch, she knew there had been a displacement, that the earth, in regard to Jake, had moved. And still she could not look, nor even think about it. Not yet.

She took her feet out of the water and sat on the pier with her back to him, looking outward into the lake. "God help the fish, if he's really fishing."

"He's not fishing, why do you think that?"

"She said so."

"Wilma? She says anything. He's out in that little house."

"What, the john?"

"No, it's a house around on the other side of the big one. Modeled on the main one, only just one room, an old bunk or two inside and a bathroom. Neat."

"A garçonnière," she said.

"Come again?"

"What they had back when."

"When what?"

"When people had a life out this way, when there were houses for them to be born in, grow up in, live in. Then they had young men, sons, who went to parties and came in——"

"Drunk."

"Maybe."

"And way too late."

"Maybe."

"Or not at all."

"Maybe." She continued, "They could always go to the garçonnière so they didn't have to explain anything or wake the household."

"Neat. Like I said."

"So Marnie's out there."

"Sleeping it off or not sleeping. Christ, you think we had it bad. He's tied up in knots like a pretzel, I went and looked. When he comes out of there you know how he'll look? Holy. Sanctified."

"I don't want to see. Jake, let's leave."

"How can we unless we steal the car?"

"There are people. There are cars. There's bound to be a road."

"As long as you're here and breathing," said Jake, "that's like forgiveness. You've agreed to live even though it happened, and more than that to talk to me. But if you go, then it's just your spirit I'll have and that's no company. Now that she wants to kill him too. She really does want to, Julia. It's worse with her. She's a lifer. She can't throw him over."

"Why can't she?"

"He can always get her back. Didn't you get it with them? It's a gen-you-wine marriage, that's the power. He's trying to extend it to me and you. He's never got hold of me, no hold at all. You were his last-ditch try. If he can keep that, make me accept it, he'll have his claim staked. Where can we go and forget him? Either together or apart?"

"You want to kill him for us? Or for yourself? Or for me? Which is it, Jake?"

She glanced at him and saw the stubborn line form at the edge of his mouth and remembered the day when he'd stood up in the courtroom, lonely in a strange country, and showed what the police had done to him, knowing that no power was in his hands except the power to do what it seemed had to be done.

"He's got no power over either one of us," Jake Springland said.

"Jake," she said, "maybe I wanted what he did." She ventured this because she had to. All that sinks must rise. "Had you thought of that, Jake?"

"Not you the way I know you. Not that you." He was looking straight out, grim, absorbed in inner passion that seemed to be growing swiftly.

"*That* me!" she said and felt herself alive, created, the way he saw her. "But if you kill him, you'll go and won't come back! So there won't be any me like that."

His lips moved but she did not hear what he said.

A small water snake which must have been near the bank a few yards from where she sat, asleep or sheltering in the loamy mud, put out into the water. It swam with its head high, all wavelike motion for the rest, though barely visible except for the head; it might have been a chance ripple in water as dark as itself, barely stirring the morning-silent surface. From beyond the house, somewhere beyond vision, there rose a bellow of anguish and despair. There was something personal about it, though not directed at any visible being; Julia thought she must be right about its being Sunday. Marnie bellowed again, wrestling his angels.

"Yippee-yi-yo," said Wilma Wharton, not looking up from her book.

"What did you say?" Julia asked Jake.

"I said, 'Don't forget.'" In this peaceful, sunlit hell, where the cries did not resume, his words seemed almost to take shape and glide about her, like birds of blessing.

Across the bayou in an empty field that looked like the corner of an old lawn from which the house had long ago been burnt down, a tall yucca plant bloomed white, straight and silent, in Indian-like majesty. The one on Audubon Place when she was a child had come to her shoulder.

"I said, 'There will be a you if you don't forget,'" said Jake.

"Oh God," said Julia, and saw herself among the silent ranks of women who kept some pledge within themselves, through blank eternity. I won't be that, she thought, but at the same moment she knew he was going to do it. That something she had felt within him had caught and held. She rose silently and stood straight. *Couldn't we do something ridiculous, like just forgive him?* She wanted to say it, but didn't. The fights and justices of men kept their life secrets set in place.

"Then you're going to?" The question was almost a murmur, but Wilma Wharton picked it up, glanced up from behind them; her look was out to catch their seriousness.

"I certainly am," he said.

"Then the two of you—" Julia said and stopped.

"You see the difficulties," Springland said.

"My name's on that car receipt," said Wilma Wharton, and turned a page in her book. "I'm taking it in to where we rented it, paying, and getting to hell out of here. I don't lose no love. Nobody's going to see me again."

Julia saw then that whatever was or wasn't going to impel them on with it hadn't set in yet. "Let me stay," she begged.

"No," said Springland. "No, you can't."

"Why can't I? Why?"

"It's a final thing," said Jake, "and one I couldn't take. Not for you." He leaned and kissed her check, which was wet. "Killing wasn't much more than a habit to me, several months in a row. That was with the army in Korea. Julia, listen: saving is what you don't know about. Hear what she said—she wasn't going to lose love? You would lose love, if you stayed. You would lose it, Julia."

He was giving her limits, necessary ones, she could see that. She turned to nudge at his hand.

"What can I think about you?"

"Think we're doing what's necessary. Beyond that, I can't give you your new road. You have to find it. But take here as a start."

Then he was walking her down a rough drive to a broken, weed-grown cattle gap, a sagging fence.

"The end's to do with me," she kept telling him. "You're keeping me from it."

The arm was right around her, crushing, and it was all like the first time almost, the sense of being a cat he'd found, petted, kept, and fed, and now was turning out again.

"Some day you'll wake up and not be sure you didn't dream it."

"It's that I don't want!" She twisted free and leaped at him, fierce and wild. They were half-kissing and half-fighting, and desperate at each, until he got his hold and, tamer-style, held her off, arm twisted back behind her, firm, loose, comfortable, and helpless. They were standing dusty and panting face to face, on an open road, a well-kept-up gravel swamp road leading out of a curve and onward to the south, which was to Julia's right.

"If I don't see you, just remember you gave me all the life I had while I was there. You let me live my dream. Maybe it's the only life I'm ever going to have, all that's any good. Go that way. Tie your head in your scarf. Put your dark glasses on. A mile down the road more or less is a crossroads town called LaFourche. Get something to eat. There's a bus through in about an hour, heading for New Orleans. Take it. I'll love you always."

He let her arm fall free, then gathered her tenderly to him and she let herself be kissed like that, kissed and kissed, forever. Then she turned like a wound-up doll and started walking. She didn't look back. At first her sandals slipped on the gravel, but she learned to walk looking down, to find where it was easiest. She remembered the bloody streak on his fair face, temple to chin through light freckles, where she'd clawed him. He says I have to go because he's going to go in with

Wilma and kill Ted Marnie and to me someday it's all going to seem like I dreamed it.

Twice she thought the sun would be too much for her and once she got scared when a car passed full of Negroes who leaned out the window to look her over curiously, but she kept on, resting once or twice by the roadside in some shade, and pretty soon she came to the outskirts of a crossroads town. The sign said La-Fourche, just like Jake Springland had said.

*Maybe it's the only life I'm ever going to have.*

She remembered those words, riding the bus into the city, which seemed strangely cleansed. There had been a storm and a clearing; the sky bled scarlet.

In a state of sacrament, as one can feel at a sentence served to the last full minute before release, she set about knowing her own knowledge. Which was that she would never have left down there, they would have had to kill her too, except that she literally held within her life Jake had given her. Otherwise, killer or killing would have been her fate, equal as anything with their own.

# Battle

# 1. ARREST

 "The trouble with you, you're sentimental."

It was Julia's judgment of Tommy Arnold. She had often felt it and it was true.

As for Tommy, he couldn't see her as other than an attractive girl who kept making mistakes, and worse, involving other people in them. Maybe she thought she was looking for "life's true meaning," or at the least an interesting time. He thought all this in the face of her strenuous underscoring by her actions of what she believed in, in the face of her refusals to follow any other course but her own, her personally worked out systems of life- and death-keeping.

She had had the child, she argued with him. Actually had it. Wasn't that proof enough that she'd never been playing except for keeps? She had a job, and somebody looked after the baby all day. Who? She gave him a puzzled look for two reasons: one, that she hadn't seen him in ages and ages and here he showed up in her place on a Saturday after work; and two, that she wondered what business it was of his. But she answered. The child was seen to daily by an old fortune teller she had gone to once, a black woman down on her luck at present.

He sat silent, aging in his mind, divorced for a year now. Lonely? She didn't ask and he didn't say. Gray hairs speckled around his temples were about all he had left to call hair, but Julia reflected that he had always looked a little bit crumpled and woebegone, like a sketch of himself.

"I tried to give the baby to Uncle Maurice," Julia astonishingly confided.

"To give him the baby! You mean, give it away? For good?"

He had jumped when he got that message. Something snapped clear in his brain, for the first time in years, it seemed. Surprise would do it, only that.

The baby in question woke and fretted.

"What's its name?" asked Tommy Arnold.

"Emile."

She went into the next room to change it and brought it out, held to her shoulder quietly, in a sober passionate way, no affection or cooing, it seemed.

"When I was still in the hospital," she told him, "Uncle Maurice got the word somehow and came up there to see about me. When they brought the baby out, they gave it to him to hold; they mistook him for the father or grandfather or something. It took him straight back to when his own child had died, so long ago, and some idiot of an intern had put it dead in his arms. He never got over it, so there it all was for him again. When he saw me he was crying and he told me that. When I was up and around, I went down to Audubon Place and tried to give it to them. They always said they wanted one. But they said no." She paused, got up and got a bottle from the kitchen, and returned. Tommy Arnold had had his ups and downs in the baby world. He still saw his children but alone, without the bickering. It was worth every penny it was costing. Nothing quite like children, but his had all been noisy. He looked at the quiet savagelike supping of the child on Julia's arm. Did things always go along this well?

"They didn't want him," she resumed, "but just the act of saying so must have set them up some way."

"Set them up?" Tommy Arnold asked.

"Let them know where they are in life," Julia said.

"And where is that?" asked Tommy Arnold.

"Uncle and aunt, great-uncle and great-aunt to half

of uptown New Orleans. Oh, all those girls who got by with it all and still wound up marrying in church and all those boys who knew it but pretended not to. Pretty dresses, Sunday church, football, carnival, and a real good time. Now they're all learning bridge and joining charities. Okay, that's it. They've chosen now. Because if they had taken the baby, I would have seen him, no way to keep me out. Not that they say I can't come back, but how is it to work? It isn't, not for the next twenty years."

"It's the Devignys I came about," said Tommy Arnold.

She stopped rocking. She was wearing a brown cotton wrap-around skirt, a printed blouse laced at the neck, and sandals, the sort of sensual, casual thing you could buy for little or nothing around the Quarter or the docks. A towel on her lap held the child comfortably. Tommy Arnold had climbed quite a way to reach her. A tall old building was what she'd found to live in; it was kept in more or less decent order, though God alone would know who the occupants were, and what they were. She had a fair view from the top, and one enormous room, plants and all that, but to him hardly worth the four-flight walk up. Then he saw she had a basket she let down for groceries, and noted the spring lock and chain on the door, and the telephone. This was about all, except for a table, bucket chairs and a bed, that she did seem to have. A walk-in closet seemed to be a whole nursery. Squaw woman, thought Tommy Arnold. It was the way of the age, to make a style out of no style at all, life stripped to the bone.

"Your uncle came and found me, down at the office," he told her. "He would have come to you, but he's afraid to."

"Afraid?"

"The house was bombed again. You didn't see the papers, I take it?"

"Dear Lord. It's the cistern," she said.

"Care to explain?"

She was white now, drained out, and not wanting to

go through it again. She kept her mind away by force each day, like keeping a child out of a dark corner that scared it. Yet she made herself tell him, at least in summary. He had to know.

"There was a package of the real thing, the hard stuff, you know, terribly valuable. They picked me up about it—not the police, but the ones who knew about it —and they tried all one night to get out of me where it was, thinking I knew. I didn't know, but finally I made a guess. I said, In the cistern. A member of Bunny Terrence's bunch was there in the gang. I don't think Jake ever knew there'd been a tie-in from Bunny's band to Marnie . . . he thought it was talent, pure and simple, that made them interested. But the night they nabbed me, right when I was coming off the bus and five months pregnant, I began to wonder if it all wasn't what they call an inside job, with music on the side. Who knows? They'd all known Marnie, the ones that I was with. Marnie was a drop point. I hadn't known it before, but it all fit in. When things got hot and the pushers couldn't operate, they'd let him hold it but they didn't know where he hid it. Nobody knew. It was dangerous for anybody to know. That was part of the game. It was Jake told me something about a cistern and I passed it on, thinking well at least they haven't found Jake and it's taken them this long to close in on me, so maybe somebody's been protecting me and I didn't know it. The reason I gave them any lead at all was that I was scared for the baby. When I finally said 'cistern,' they let me go. A few days later somebody must have come up with it that Uncle Maurice's house had an old cistern out at the side, left over from former days. First they sent somebody out there who pretended to be from the city sanitation department, to look into it. Then when they couldn't find anything they went out one night and put an explosive between the cistern and the house, to loosen up the structure—all this with a guard right on the gate. I don't know how they manage things. . . ."

"I saw the story," said Tommy Arnold.

"Maybe you even wrote it. It wasn't till the newspapers got hold of it that anybody knew the first investigation was a fake—the sanitation department never heard of that cistern. After that, Uncle Maurice took to sleeping with a gun in the house and Aunt Isabel almost had a breakdown. I got all this through the Negro grapevine, since my babysitter knows their maid. So what's made it break out again?" she said frowning. "After all these months, it must mean they never found it. And that's odd, Tommy."

"I certainly hope that, in addition to odd, it's the last try," said Tommy Arnold with a sigh. He got up, walked to the window and looked down on the irregular rooftops, higgledy-piggledy, squares and triangles, all like a modern design in a painting, he supposed he might have interestingly remarked. Who's watching who? Who's after what? A package of heroin big as a brick, a flower pot, a hot plate, weighing five pounds or eight or ten, worth twelve thousand, twenty-five, forty-eight? Down a cistern that Julia Garrett knew about, but where? If they'd wanted to know couldn't they have got it out of her? No, he guessed, if that one word was all she knew. But if she did know more and wouldn't tell . . . oh, now that was either an extreme of courage or else somebody was protecting her. Protecting her, or themselves? Who had called it off the Devigny house the first time, so that only after these many months had they returned for a second round? He brought out a good part of this to Julia.

"I really can't answer, Tommy," she told him. "Some people from outside come here, every so often, I think. If it's not an inside job, it's an outside one. That chunk of heroin could be one of those little items that keep the books from balancing, can't you see that?"

"You didn't get it yourself, out of whatever cistern you happen to know about?"

"Me!" Her eyes sprang wider than mousetraps.

"Stop that innocence, damn it!"

"Tommy, Tommy, you haven't told me. They weren't hurt, were they? Uncle Maurice, Aunt Isabel? They're all right, I guess, or you'd have said."

"They're okay." He continued sitting, a still posture, eyes fixed on her. She could send her boy to college, he reasoned, on the proceeds of that heroin. And she had to have money to live. She'd done it before, in other forms. He let his breath whistle slowly out.

Julia observed his silent struggle, and recognized right along in step with him (in that room so high and undisturbed) that he couldn't help but watch with perfect awareness while her beautiful brown legs and structure-perfect sandaled feet moved to rise and she carried the baby back to its bed, her heavy dark head bending and rising. She could seem as wicked-innocent as a nymph out of nature, but how to make do with her on the human side? She knew his problem was a nice one, and once her back was to him she all but smiled.

Did any one ever look more quiet-featured and atten-tive, Tommy Arnold thought, at times like a studious girl, even conscientious, at times even demure? He puzzled. Her world-view was a little bit different from the common one—this was all he could come to.

"I haven't always been safe," she reminded him. "Throwing away your life, if that's what you're sitting there thinking I've done, is no easy way out. It's uphill all the way: why, you can make a career of it."

"I wasn't thinking of lecturing you. I think you're right in step with things, if you want to know. The world's working hard at the same game. I'm just watching and writing the story."

For the story was all too often like this, he considered. A nigger church . . . well, let's blow it up. A Jewish synagogue; well, fetch the dynamite. A store turned a nigger out . . . smash the windows, loot the merchan-dise, what you waiting for? If dope's there, let's get it, blast the earth to find it. If you want to die, buy a corpse that looks like you, bury it and disappear. Layer on layer, the crummy enfoldment spoke of a corrupt central core; something like a spiteful syphilitic midget was secretly in charge, running the whole show. Tommy reported it; that was all. But Julia had roved around to find it, had felt driven to discover firsthand its very terms and nature . . . once again, out of his own stream of thought, admiration for her flickered up. He quickly let it sink from sight.

"You're on the Devigny story, then?" she asked him.

"About the bombing last night, you mean? I got hold of it, yes, as soon as I noticed whom it concerned. I just happened to be on the night desk."

"So that's why you came, following up your lead." She smiled ruefully. "I hadn't seen you in so long, I thought it might just be that you wanted to see me."

"Well, maybe it was you. After all, why else would I want the story?"

"Curiosity, maybe."

"Maybe a little more than that."

"Good."

In the silence she had time to finish her cigarette, he to sink toward sky-gazing, out the twilight window. The child was sleeping, somewhere out of sight. The feeling of its sleep was present.

"Tommy," said Julia at last, "do you know how it is with you? You got all the way to the dead center when you finally got divorced, but you're still sitting there, Tommy. Stone dead."

"Thanks," he grumbled. She passed him, looking for matches or another cigarette, and passed him once again. The second time his hand reached up, connecting to her wrist and holding in a clasp of surpassing accuracy, simple and pure, as was the tug like a dancer's movement that pulled her down beside him.

"Oh, Tommy . . ."

"Tommy what?"

"We've come a long way."

"And wound up just the same, side by side. Front seat of the car, out on the lake. Remember?"

She nodded, then drew the sort of involuntary breath that told them both how she felt now. The room brimmed up slowly with desire, but not the young and racing sort that hastened on a strange stair, wrenched free of everything in any anonymous room. There was languor in it and some regret and a touch of hesitancy, a genuine inclination to leave it all alone. Just the same he bent his head and kissed her, a kiss she slowly returned. Back in its little closet bed, the baby slept as peacefully as any baby could; presently she went and looked in, closed the door and returned.

She sat down beside him again. "Now's the time to break it up, Tommy," she told him softly.

"I thought that too." He touched her hair, almost stood up to go, then turned to look at her, close-range. His large brown eyes were wide, glistening slightly, his mouth had unconsciously softened. Younger. He was pulling together, she realized, transforming right in front of her, whereas before he'd just looked beat. This touched her; it gave her the satisfaction she needed to feel she'd given in this way. She drew his head firmly to her for longer kissing and pulling back again saw it happen even more, the tired lines going, his face like a clearing sky. "Maybe I've always loved you, Tommy."

He could still manage to smile at her, even while loosening her blouse. "I want to look at you . . . look and look again."

"Nothing more, Tommy?"

As she never wore a bra, he came suddenly on what he was looking for. His gaze moved palpably over her, drawing up her full desire. Her teasing and affection stopped dead still. Like twin deer confronted at a path's turning, her breasts stood returning his gaze; she knew them to be more open than her eyes which she shadowed and guarded, out of habit private to herself.

"I'm no good any more," he murmured, kissing, touching, drawing back, tentative, older than in other days, but savoring still, and full of the value of moments prolonged. "No good since that divorce hassle. Just . . . feel out of it . . . something . . ."

"You will be," Julia promised. "You'll be good enough." She knew how to make it come true.

It happened late on a Saturday afternoon, as good a time as any. Afterward, everywhere he went, Tommy Arnold confessed to her, all the old sights were saturated in wonder. Everything was new. To have known her this long, let her grow on him, and then. . . . Words wouldn't do. He felt like an old plowshare, good for nothing but weighting a gate with, but rained on, washed clean, discovered shiny and new. Unintentional was what his visit had been (here he would raise a finger, though no one was arguing with him, let alone Julia)— without ulterior motive, he would go on, and Julia would nod, agreeing that if he said so, it was true.

Julia! Even the name fell on him at odd hours, like something soft and furry, leaping out of a tree. The world was more than the world, once it quit spinning. Strange foliage grew in it; it was dusky with awe, the unknown came up to lick his hand. Arrows, presumably, might come whistling out of it at unspecified times. She had said it hadn't been easy, starting where she had started, arriving where she had arrived. There's room at the top, but is there any at the bottom? Did Tommy Arnold imagine an atmosphere thick with threat and dread? It was hard to know, and Julia would never exactly tell him anything. He came often to her high big room and the four flights of stairs became a precious chore.

"Where'd you get it?" he wanted to know. He'd asked her this about so many things. Small habits she had,

skills and crafts; where'd you learn that or find that out?
was what he'd try to get at, try to have the story of, to
make her say. Sometimes she'd tell him. Most of what
she'd learned sexually, she said, she'd picked up listening to cooks and maids talk in the kitchen on Audubon
Place. But she wouldn't know what they meant, really;
only later it came to her that what they meant was this
or something more like that. One in particular was a
girl who knew about grisgris and such things.

But one time he said "Where'd you get it?" to ask
about a piece of sculpture she had in a corner; rough-cut
and nondescript at first, it grew a shape and the more it
was looked at the more exciting it became. She kept it
on a table near the window.

But when she said the name of the sculptor he didn't
believe it. Everybody in the world knew that name if they
knew anything.

"Parham gave it to you?"

"Oh, no, I got it just recently."

But where and how? He was worried, actually.
Things like that cost money, a lot of it, and where would
the money come from? Did she have a rich man, another
one, for God's sake, on the side? Was she pushing?
Did she find the money in a trash can, the way somebody in a Faulkner novel had done? Where did it come
from?

"Goodness, Tommy, you can't know everything."

"What's it of?" Reporters, thought Julia, would drive
you crazy, nothing but questions.

"I wrote and asked him."

"Asked who?"

"The sculptor, of course. I wrote and asked him."

"Don't tell me he answered?"

"He did. He did answer. He said it was of a saint very
little known, one who thought himself for a time to be
an animal altogether—in his soul, I guess, being ugly
and secretly wicked in some way. But then he couldn't

know this. The sculpture is him believing he is only an animal, not a human soul. He's sitting by a stream thinking this."

"That's great," said Tommy Arnold, imagining she'd invented it, but not asking to see the letter. Even if there had been such a letter, it would not tell him where or how she'd gotten the work.

He had called back, as he had promised, to Maurice Devigny, to tell him that Julia knew nothing about why the Devigny house should have been invaded, not once but this second time.

"Except that's not true," he said to Julia. "You do know, and I don't imagine he's convinced for a minute. He sleeps there with a loaded gun. There's a police patrol always on the street. What he can't tell is: will there be another time? And when?"

"I can't tell him," Julia said.

"You know more than you're saying to anybody. That's the point."

She did not reply.

"He's sent his wife out of town. She's convinced they're marked, because of you."

"Aunt Isabel out of town! But where?" The departure of her aunt from New Orleans, and alone at that, had a quality of enormity about it. But with this fact provided her, the whole grew clear: Uncle Maurice with a gun, high in the rooms where Dev had lived and died; the house torn; Aunt Isabel out in the world like a wanderer. "Where?"

"It's going to strike you odd, from your standpoint. Just remember they've got in thick with the Parhams for business reasons. Your uncle's been representing them in this area for some time, hasn't he? What I mean is, she'd go up there just to be safe. It's got nothing to do with you."

"I never thought it did," said Julia. But her atmosphere had shifted a little, nonetheless.

After this piece of news she was restless. A bad sleeper at times, smoking too much, irritable at work. Her lover's child was safely in the world, her old admirer had returned, but it was not yet enough . . . it was not all. She held the question of Tommy Arnold's actually moving in with her at arm's length. Talk about it was all they ever did. He could come when he felt like it; what more did he want?

She was like a woman in a lonely place watching a still bright skyline. The road which always passed across it was empty. Waiting for it to fill with some arrival, wondering if it should not be receiving her own footsteps and form, departing down it. She still knew, in the form of a great white undetailed space within her memory, the night she had gone through when they'd tried to get out of her where the heroin was. It went Marnie's horror treatment one better in that strangers had done it; there was no one, later on, to understand. She did not think of it in any detail, but remarked the result: if there had been any last corner of her soul where something of innocence might by chance remain unshaken and untried, they had reached it. Live cigarettes had threatened her, and words not even she had ever heard, but had just as soon never hear again. The child within her was not to be spared either, she was given to believe. One of the members of Bunny's combo, that group she'd yearned for as for her own human company, as a family whose sister now was coming home, had held her head back by a fistful of hair, until her neck strained to bursting and her breathing closed. After that she felt free to make up stories about anything, anytime she chose. She would gladly live like an animal, simply, instinctively, for the day only. The sculpture had come to her from the Parhams. After Martin's death, one of the younger ones had sneaked it down to her. Martin had collected those things in Paris, thinking of which ones would please her most. Heroin the size of a brickbat—Jesus! Thousands on thousands, mined out of one purseful. She bent her dark head and thought about it.

At times she thought that Tommy Arnold was merely sitting around in some part of his mind, waiting for what she would have to decide to do.

# 2. THEIR SEASON

 "It was you all the time, you all the time," Tommy Arnold repeated, into her hair, kissing her neck, in a tumble of bedclothes, a tangle of limbs. Sleep and waking, caught in the driving storms of midnight and darkness, breathing quietness by the morning sunshine, quiet and knowing as grass and leaves. She didn't give enough, he threatened. Didn't *give* enough? she repeated. Didn't give enough, he said.

"You're a soul-hunter," Julia observed, half-teasing. "Little by little, Tommy."

"You're the dark of the moon. It's where you live. I want there too."

"You've got your own dark, haven't you?"

"That's not the point. You're keeping yours, hoarding it. You're determined to."

"Not determined . . . no. I know what you mean. I can't help it, Tommy."

"Is it limits I can't reach to? Still dreaming of that damn banjo player?"

"Yes. No. Oh, if I don't know, why should it matter?"

"Of something before that, then?"

"And before that, then, and before that, then?" she half-mimicked.

Stirred and angered at once, he almost struck her. Tenderly, she caught his hand. Her soft insistence melted him once more: "When you know everything, Tommy, why then it vanishes . . . you lose it. Besides, how am I to tell you what I can't say, even to you."

Turning her hand, wistful with hope and fear:
"There's future yet," he said.

"Of course there is."

"Of course there is."

At the same time, something in him waited, she
felt, not for revelation but for the action that would bring
her over, trap, domesticate, and destroy.

Wanting to want was not much good, Julia reflected.
She longed to long for what was now again within her
grasp, marriage—but this time more of a necessity than
ever, bringing with it a father for the child (who but
Tommy would be that good?), some certainty in life.
The idea of goodness beckons forever to those who can't
have it, but once they catch up to it by luck or accident,
they immediately feel uneasy, restless, miserable.

Playing solitaire with a worn deck, lying on her side
on the daybed by the window, Sunday afternoons: "I'll
disappoint you, Tommy. I won't do you right."

"Oh, you're going to. I've stopped bothering about it.
Someday we'll both just find ourselves around the corner
and into the church."

"I want it that way."

"The hell you do. You see how you won't open up
enough. The trouble's there."

"Open up enough!" Her laugh had a hundred good
times in it.

"Mind, thoughts, head. You won't trust me."

"You can't have everything, not about anybody."

"It's not anybody I want."

"Just me." She turned to solitaire again. "Okay, someday I'll let you know it all, bore you to death."

"When? Now?"

"Oh . . . in the fall." She was yawning.

They were, of course, happy, these old acquaintances,
happy and lazy. What they argued about, what they
decided—it didn't matter much. Tommy Arnold's first

fine wave of passion had passed on, diminishing. It returned, from time to time. He had never yet got raving enough, apparently, to hit her over the head and drag her by the hair to the registry office. But that didn't matter anyway, he argued. Name on a paper, ring on a finger, what did it mean? If she eluded him without it, she would do so with it, even more. The idea of him reforming anybody—not really! All the while he knew his own life had turned a page. He did not go back to his old surly ways. The air was fine and the sky above the cathedral spire was soft and blue.

"I can't think why marriage is important," Julia said. "You'll notice as soon as people get into it, they want out of it." (Except Uncle Maurice and Aunt Isabel—they never wanted out. Apart they died: was she still away with the Parhams? If so, it seemed the very air was torn in the direction of thinking of them.)

Lotus-eating, Julia just out of her shower on a hot afternoon, Tommy Arnold agreed with her. Marriage was not important. He sat in the one comfortable chair, a bony rocker with a cushion or two in it, holding Jake Springland's child in his lap. He loved the child anyway. In his heart, he was its father. This was his family. It was just that he got his mail elsewhere.

Question: Where did Julia get her mail? (He had to ask twice—she was cooking ham and grits.)

Answer: At the shop. Downstairs, people steal it.

Julia worked at a shop in the Quarter that sold the work of local artists and some antiques, mainly interesting junk. She answered the telephone, met customers, sold but did not buy, and opened the mail. Her employer was a small crippled man who made flowers out of leather and metal, copies of swamp flowers and other wild plants. He had got the idea after learning what a fixed life he himself had to live, after the way the VA hospital had patched him up the last time. He was funny, direct, and quick-minded, a noble soul, Julia guessed. Tommy Arnold did not want to think of what mail she might be getting at the shop. From Springland still? She said she didn't but who knew if it was true? It was like his not knowing—not being able for all his reporter's snooping skills—to find out whether she was pushing or not. He didn't want to know. He saw that married, even completely in her confidence, he could have put a stop to it all, taken everything in charge, tidied up his paradise. By refusing marriage she was stopping his authority. He saw it, clear and plain.

One day she disappeared.

He found the apartment empty except for the baby and the old fortune teller who baby-sat for her, and who informed him that Miss Julia would be gone for a day or so. The Negress was clean, in navy blue cotton and white stockings, and the narrow ankles, big feet, and bulging calves that neat Negro women often have were appropriately hers. He sent her away—he would stay the evening and the night, he said, and wait all tomorrow too as it was his day off at the paper. And Julia, of course, had known this. Funny she hadn't told him she was going. Why? He lived in torment until her return, yet (he discovered) the happiness she gave was really given —it belonged to him alone. It's all right, she seemed to be saying, it's all right about me. Speaking, but from where? He would leap to his feet and run to the window and look down, and a hundred times imagine her footsteps on the stair, following to the logical second what he had thought to be the closing of the street door. He really didn't know how to look after a baby. Where was she? Where had she, really, gone?

It was nearly two on the second night that he fell asleep in the chair with the baby, exhausted by its own wailing, asleep too, held clumsily in his lap. But this was not before he had had time to get enraged, to see at last the helpless position she was keeping him in and how little, apparently, she cared.

# 3. NIGHT VISITOR

 "Uncle Maurice! Uncle Maurice!"

Maurice Devigny crawled out from behind the newel post. He had come as near as anything to shooting her. He lived locked in, up in the old rooms where his father had passed his last year and had died; he walked daily a certain path in those rooms and now knew why Isabel, back in days gone by, had often ordered the carpets turned. She was trying to keep them from wearing out where his father had walked also, thinking what? All those shady dealings . . . all that darkening world. Funny how the old man's activities, whatever they had been, had gone dead even within his lifetime; they had frozen and existed in outline only, or in the rheumy-eyed look of some old crony encountered downtown in a restaurant or at a funeral, especially the latter when the handshake made more of a difference to both of them and the knowingness in the eyes was worse, almost unbearable. His father had been mixed up in—in what? "All that" was the way Maurice used to put it to himself. All that. He had never exactly known, never wanted to know. He didn't want to know now.

He had committed himself to making this house a place of joy and music, that particular joy which denies everything that has gone before and anticipates no ill. Isabel. She had been its gracious avenue.

But now they had—oh, miserable inadvertence—the old man's progeny: *he* had adopted her, not they. And they were moved closer than ever before to that land which to them contained nothing but danger and death.

Maurice did not, however, when the property was first invaded, the cistern surrounded and searched, bring Julia's name into it. He would not, no matter what. The police had questioned him closely. His niece? He seldom saw her, but the terms they were on were friendly, oh, yes, indeed, the friendliest possible terms. No, he had no address for her; as he said, they seldom saw her.

All that was before the months had gone by and the second blow fell—an invasion.

He had been coming in from the study, holding his glass during a long quiet warm evening when he liked a meditative nightcap or two, and had found a stranger standing in the parlor looking at him. "Who the hell are you?" The words, spoken in his own house by his own voice, picked up no energy, for they seemed to go unheard and certainly were unanswered, stones thrown in an empty lot. The stranger was younger than he was old, he had black hair and the foreign olive skin of port people who are not Negro. His eyes passed over Maurice, looked beyond and around him. It seemed that like a life-sized (and incidentally living) ornament, he had been moved in to stay.

"Watch out, Dad."

Maurice stepped back; his glance, following the side gaze of the stranger, saw two more invaders descending the stairway. They were Negroes, but the fact was without consequence or meaning. The world Maurice sensed as theirs had gone, he instinctively knew, far beyond race. It had gone beyond property as well, beyond familiarity, beyond rights. They belonged together, and though for some reason he got the distinct feeling they were not necessarily from New Orleans even, they belonged because of their present endeavor on his stairway; they were more at home there than Maurice. He had merely inherited all this! How could he fight them? he helplessly wondered. They were as used to fighting as a pack of mongrel dogs.

Isabel! Subconsciously, he had been holding at bay

the very thought of her name, because she had been about to retire an hour before and, by now voiceless, must still be somewhere in the house. But where, dear Lord? The cold exploding terror within screamed silently, as others, shoulder to shoulder, came out of the dining room.

"Show us the basement, Dad."

"I'm going upstairs first," said Maurice firmly. "Then I'll show you anything you want." And walked past.

The two Negroes closed ranks.

"Excuse me," Maurice said. "I don't mean to argue with you. There is nothing here you could possibly want. We've nothing. A little cash . . . it's yours gladly, only . . . For the moment, I must——"

The forward Negro simply shrugged, and the other made a swift motion, swinging his fist past his thigh like a pendulum. Maurice spun round twice on his way downward, landing in a sprawl in the middle of the carpet beneath the chandelier, which, unlighted, looked asleep up there. He cast about him at last, hearing now the muffled sound of a voice talking inarticulately through cloth, and there in a chair in the butler's pantry not too far from him was Isabel, in her nightdress and robe, hair let down and streaming. She was tied, bound to a small chair, but had been trying to call to him.

"The basement, we keep asking you." The first of the men he had seen said that, approached and tugged at his shoulder, lifting him. He was trying to get a handkerchief from his pocket, as blood was coming from somewhere onto his shirt. His tie! Was that what Isabel was saying? It sounded like it. He pulled off his tie. The dark man tugged at him. He landed in an easy chair, facing in Isabel's direction, and felt a rope pass twice around his shoulders. "Are you hurt, Isabel? Shake your head or not . . . thank God. Keep still then. We'll understand in a minute. The basement's down a secret door. If you'll let me up, I'll . . ."

Before he could finish, Isabel, by working her mouth

frantically up and down, had managed to loosen the towel they had tied across her face: "Your hand, Maurice! A tourniquet . . . use your tie!" He looked down once more. Blood was jetting upward. He'd felt no cut, no touch of anything, but there it was. He began to lace and bind the tie at his wrist with the supernatural speed at which a man might snatch a poisonous viper's tooth from his flesh.

"Shut up from yelling, quiet it down!"

The kitchen door flapped and yet another was upon them; a stumpy, dirty, blond man in a black suit with a striped tee-shirt beneath gave Isabel's chair a shove. She fell to one side, bringing the chair down with her in a soft fall of nightdress and peignoir and her hair falling, too, infinitely. Then Maurice saw her little gold-rimmed glasses scatter off as though thrown by a spoiled child. They landed on the bare hardwood before the living-room rug began and lay splintered. He would never lose the sight. He drew the knotted tie tighter and saw the blood dwindle to a thin trickle. She had saved his life, he supposed. What could the two of them do further? The dark man he had first seen, in a gesture that seemed at that strange hour the height of courteous and just dealing, set the chair, with Isabel in it, upright. He pushed back her hair and said to her quiet denuded eyes: "We just don't want nobody to start screaming."

"I'll show you the basement," said Maurice, "if you'll let her out first. She'll mention nothing, not if I ask her not to."

There was a silence among the men, who now having emerged from every possible door seemed to Maurice to be numberless. At last the dark man spoke. His lips scarcely moved. "You'll do it anyway, Mister."

One wall of a closet in the kitchen unhooked and he showed it to them, turning on the light and watching emerge the dark little stairway where he'd often played as a child thinking of magic tunnels, enchanted corridors, treasures of gold and silver. They were down it instantly, all but one left to guard, who dutifully bound him back into his chair. He sat and held his arm.

"Are you all right, love? God knows what they're after."

"Same as before, I imagine. We didn't know then."

She was white and in distinct danger of fainting, he supposed, though gamely she insisted she wasn't. From the distance a police siren sounded, came nearer, turned —oh, blessed relief—into the gate of Audubon Place.

There was suddenly a thud; two more together; and Isabel would have screamed if the guard had not clapped his hand over her mouth. The whole house reverberated. There were sounds of crashing objects from upstairs and things falling in the kitchen, and before their eyes the chandelier awakened, not to light but dislocation, half-tearing from its attachment to the ceiling, and listing before them like a struck flag. What was it about? Would it never end? There was a noise of hasty digging, plundering and dragging from the direction of the basement. A hole, Maurice learned later in the night, had been blown out there, again near the cistern, probing its point of connection with the old reservoir in the basement. Some notion about clear water, uncontaminated, in this swampy place, had led his stepmother to put that cistern in. He sat wondering on its importance to whoever kept invading them—rats fleeing the house now as the sirens and the police lights swirled about on the street outside. It was then that, to his astonishment, Isabel wriggled free. Anything is possible. Before he knew it, she was heading upstairs, white blond hair streaming about her shoulders.

"Isabel! There might be somebody up there!"

She knew what she was making for, apparently: a little pearl-handled pistol she had got out after the first scare and kept in the bedroom. It would have to be fired. Oh, the weariness of agitations! thought Maurice, their ultimate uselessness. He sat still tied in the armchair and heard the gun go off out the upstairs window, proving himself right.

He sat there helpless, knowing that when they learned the truth it would all be to do with Julia. Julia, Julia! Cursed day they'd ever thought of her. She was exorbitant. Down to the last thing she could think of to do, everything about her was bigger than life, prodigious. More outrageous than evil, at times better even than goodness.

What had she meant, for instance, offering them a child? To him and Isabel up in their fifties, wanting only to pass quietly, beautifully, together through archways of imperceptibly merging seasons, attending the celebrations of old friendships, days linked each to each. She had visited on them the sharp hurt of gratitude, the explanation of refusal, and to him at least the ultimate pang of love that exists but is helpless to reach or reorder anything. He supposed she felt this love, knew about it. What else, from them to her, could there be? Nothing.

Luckily, Isabel hit no one. The wail of the police siren faded as footsteps struck the porch. Released, Maurice rushed first to a window overlooking the side garden, where he saw the mystery of who had called the police answered before his eyes. The German professor, left over from the lean days when they had had to rent out rooms and still living in the old servants' house, had not only observed dark figures moving against a window in the downstairs rooms but had rushed to his telephone. Then, intrepid (he had survived air raids and other horrors and so had good instincts in disaster), he had been charging toward the house when the explosions occurred, scattering fragments of basement wall into the garden, sending aloft soft earth, some of which had pelted him. Up and at them once again, armed with an iron skillet and a broom, he had merely got in the way, and figures fleeing the scene, masked now (Maurice was reminded of Mardi Gras), took turns striking at him, shoving him from the path as they made toward the back fence, each vaulting away. The last blow had really felled him, courageous and irate. He fell before Maurice could direct the police to him or indicate those in flight. He lay stretched out ominously upon the grass, a bachelor, passionately concerned that German culture should not be neglected in this country where prejudice understandably existed; and so he taught and read and worked his heart out. And there he lay.

Julia! Protecting her from the image she was determined to create, from whatever she was actually at any given point up to—even now Maurice immediately reverted to this lifetime habit; even with blood precariously stanched and apt to run out of him to the last drop, he made for her sake the quick decision to put the law on the defensive. Couldn't the police do anything better than they were doing? A guard on the gate must have been by-passed some way, and how did it happen, especially as he had been subjected to this sort of attack for the second time now for no good reason. Of course, he did not know any good reason. Would any man in his right mind, knowing a good reason, not reveal it and stop putting his very life in danger?

Hastening upstairs, whence no further shots had come, he found Isabel charging down the upper hallway like a mad myopic princess with streaming hair. "We've got to tell them, got to tell them. It's Julia doing this—"

"Isabel! You can't! You don't even know that! Hush, hush! They're actually inside . . . they've come. Isabel!"

She was writhing in the grasp of his one good arm. Where he'd caught her wrist was red and even her cheeks looked scorched. The side of her face where she had struck the floor falling (or been struck?) was already discoloring.

Maurice remembered the little fallen glasses.

"Demons! Demons! You brought me to a house of demons!"

"You're not yourself! Oh, Isabel, never say it!"

"I've wanted to! I've got to! Oh, Maurice, save me! I'm hating you!"

"Hating me! You're not! You can't be!"

It was late at night before he could even talk with her, for arrangements took them over—a shot for her nerves which made her sleep, a trip to the nearest infirmary for him to get sewed up. Not since his brief term in the service (World War II), which his fastidious soul had depised, had he known such downright discomfort. He swallowed down the pills. Returned, saying a courteous good-night to the police guard, he mounted to their rooms and sat on the bed beside her as she roused. He held her hand, and thought her soothed at last. But the next day she could not control her direction in the house, lost her way, kept wanting to climb the old stair up to his father's closed apartments. She thought that Julia was up there.

There was the police questioning, of course. Maurice's smooth skill . . . well, it was sometimes legitimate to be proud of oneself. He had never felt it more. And Isabel, too, under control again, after that one flash of wrath and flailing out, was vague and ladylike and distracted, unable quite to remember what had happened. He would trust her anywhere, except she was not well.

"They know all about it," she confided to Maurice. "They know that Julia's here."

A doctor was indicated, and the family one, a man more wise than not, having put her in close care for a week, told Maurice there was nothing really wrong but upset nerves and suggested she take a trip out of the city. He took her to a rest home, more like a hotel actually, north of the city, in different country, and there the Parhams got grapevine news of her and nothing would do them but to go and get her out for weekends, for a rest, for an extended visit. Maurice had misgivings. Yet she seemed totally herself again. Fair and clear-eyed and nearly radiant once more, she welcomed him when he drove up for an evening, but would not just yet return.

He got the feeling she was having a good time. Of course, she said in private, she wouldn't mention Julia to the Parhams—the idea. "What made you think I would?" "Not thinking what you were saying, maybe." "Now Maurice, what do you take me for?" "I take you for my darling, Isabel."

He stayed alone in the house on Audubon Place, going daily to work, and not liking to remain in his old apartments without Isabel, as he felt her presence from one moment to the next and at times almost found himself conversing with her (next they'd be putting him in a hospital). He moved upstairs to his father's old rooms, saw everything empty and in place with a qualm, but with a feeling too of human oneness, of reconciliation, and, above all, of rest; it was a kind of sheltering.

No pearl-handled popgun for him: he slept with a loaded shotgun in the corner. The police guard remained. Julia, the night she appeared, had stopped to exchange greetings, she told him later, with the cop at the gates, whom, it turned out, she recognized. He'd got her past the second, and there she was out of nowhere, ringing and calling in the deep-bayed recess of the front porch near the door.

"Uncle Maurice!"

He knew the voice immediately. Just the same, his nerves had frayed more than he realized, and he almost shot her. Instead he switched the light on after saying "Julia?" and being answered; then he put down the gun and unbolted the door. It was a little past nine.

The door swung open and she entered, alone.

"My God!" said Maurice Devigny. "Where on earth have you been?"

# 4. THE STRAY

It was true that she was scratched, scarred, and half-starved, but she was not as down-and-out as he'd seen her in what he would have called much better days. A frazzled-out, askew look in some haphazard way actually made Julia appear to have come to terms with life better than others who didn't look that way. In a torn skirt, with blistered feet in sandals with a broken thong, hair like a magpie's nest, and one bleary-looking eye, her good humor yet came flashing out when he opened the door for her. For days Maurice had felt numb; wondering what would happen next was what he'd been reduced to. Now that he saw, actually saw, the being he and Isabel had been regretting they'd ever thought of, both voicelessly and vocally for twenty-four hours a day, he was overcome with the heady delight she could always give him, and he loved her, loved that scarey girl (as he was given a year or two back to calling her) from the bottom of his heart. Still it was a shame. The flank of the house torn out, Isabel panicky, finally sent away, up to Mississippi . . . and he, stubbornly trying to stick it out here against who knew what perils or numbers or even against what reasons anyone would have for invading his property. And, as he suspected, and now had almost confirmed for him, she was at the bottom of it—Julia.

"Welcome home," he said.

It was a moment and a thing to say so excellently turned they both broke into laughter. He knew how to render it dramatically, standing in the dimly lighted hallway, looking a bit blear himself, from worry, age, lack of sleep.

"Aunt Isabel's away, isn't she?"

"You got that from that reporter." They met and kissed.

She had never, she realized, been here before when her aunt was more than temporarily out of the house. She went to the large downstairs bathroom to wash up, comb her hair, scrub her feet, put on powder and lipstick. When she came out, Uncle Maurice had gone into the dining room and poured them both a drink. He would turn on only dim side lamps, but these were of such crystalline quality that light played delicately on the polished wood of the table. He risked opening a window onto the street, but drew the jalousies half-shut. Night air came through to them. The amber liquor in the glasses looked beautiful. He had not neglected ice. They sat down together.

"Was the house hurt much?"

"Nothing I can't have put together again. It was the fact of its happening, that was the hard part."

"Not once but twice."

"Isabel just couldn't take it. It was like part of herself being torn at. Now she's gone."

"To the Parhams," Julia said, just out flat, not knowing herself how she meant it.

"You sure get all the news, don't you?"

"I guess so."

"I think we'll sell after all this, Julia; that is, if I'm not blown up in bed. We'll buy into the Garden District, near the park maybe. I can put up a high fence, install a burglary alarm, get a dog maybe. A lot of people live that way now. I don't feel that Isabel and I can keep on here. The house was always too big for two, and we've begun to be looked on askance, you know—a couple of Jonahs in this lovely neighborhood."

"All because of me." She had scarcely touched the drink. Uncle Maurice's was half-down already. The middle of a civilized city can feel like the heart of deepest jungle, he thought. We sit in luxury within the stockade, sipping Scotch or bourbon or fine cognac from handcut crystal, waiting for the next attack.

"And yet you let me in," Julia murmured.

"Oh, let you in! Of course. *I* never turned you out. You turned yourself out. You must know that."

"An alley cat by nature."

"I didn't say that; you did."

"I've fixed it now, Uncle Maurice. They won't worry you any more."

A huge night-flying bug whirred and thumped against the screen. She saw him blanch, tighten his jaw, and felt a sort of worthlessness that she did not get frightened any more.

"Do you want to let me in on it?"

"All I can. Listen. I happened by accident to know about where something valuable was or might be. At least, certain people believed that I knew where it might be, and I thought maybe I did, too, once they got to asking me about it."

"It sounds like an inquisition," he observed.

"It wasn't all that polite and gentlemanly," she said. I won't look back, she thought, if I do I'll scream. She did not dare then even to look up at her uncle, not wanting him to see terror in her eyes, the pit of fear opening. All would flash blackly out, and he would have to live with it. I can't give him that, can't and won't, she thought, and looked no further than at his smooth hands familiar on his carved ivory holder, inserting a cigarette, snapping the small always-efficient lighter to the brown Egyptian tip. She was walking a knife-edge of hysteria, thin as honed silver.

"I can't imagine atomic secrets or forty-carat diamonds being down my cistern, Julia. It's got to have been dope—heroin, something like that."

She did not answer for a long while. Then she said, "It's settled now. I think it's settled now."

"You might have gone through a lot of danger to——"

"To protect you, get it settled. Yes, and for myself too. But then it seemed more my fault than not. Getting you into things you ought not to have been bothered with." She lost her struggle at that point (thank God, thought Maurice) and broke into sobs. He crossed round the table and stroked her hair, kissed her cheek, tried to take her hands from her face, but failed, then went and got her a clean handkerchief. But she would not confide. She had a larger commitment than to him and Isabel. Life is a tree with twin trunks, one is love and the other corruption—if she had settled for anything weaker than that, Life would never forgive her.

Wasn't Uncle Maurice proving it with what he was coming out with next? "I've been looking around for real estate," he said. "Haven't told Isabel. Guess what I know is for sale? The old Mulligan house. One of the sisters died, the other's in a home. Want me to take it? I can even keep your old rooms, ready for you, up the back steps."

Her eyes, dried and swollen, flashed round the room. Those lofty ceilings, wide-banistered stairs, multiple rooms became as frightening as a white-washed cell. He saw that, in the white scared flash of her gaze.

"Julia, forget I mentioned it . . . you'd never come!"

"Have you forgotten that I offered you——"

"Yours and that boy's child. Yes, I know. We never thanked you enough, I guess. How could we?" The truth was neither he nor Isabel had ever known what to make of the offer.

They are like French crystal ornaments, Julia thought. Lalique. No life at all without what surrounds and admires and contributes. Yet they're beautiful; oh, yes they are. Isabel and Maurice. Maurice and Isabel.

"Now I have to thank you," said Julia, "for offering me some place to go." She cat-smiled at him, wiping up tears.

"You remember Joe Delaney?" Uncle Maurice gossiped, saying the insurance man's name, but she became vague about it the instant it was spoken, as though it had been merely mumbled.

"Sure I do. Why?"

"His little girl's in the hospital, something serious, I understand."

Back in those days of her so-appropriate engagement she had dreamed of nothing but a dozen children, a house somewhere quiet, maybe over in Mobile. Children clambering over her like vines. And during the days before the wedding that never happened, she and Joe Delaney used to walk around the gardens of old plantation houses turned into charming restaurants, best French cuisine available, good wine cellars, Mafia-owned, she knew, but did not say. The child had worn pink with a big sash, once; once white pique, embroidered, with rosettes, green, lavender, and rose, and shoes with cross bands that buttoned. Julia had dressed her, chosen things; oh, it was nice. Now he was married to somebody, she'd heard, but couldn't think who. Couples.

Julia rose. "I've got to get back to my own place."

"You'll come back soon, won't you? Bring the baby?" He was speaking in perfect faith, hopeful of heart, and easy to enchant; just being with her had cast its spell— he saw at that moment nothing to prevent a continuing relationship.

"I'll see."

He had been sitting nearly at her feet on a footstool dragged out of a corner, looking up into her face. Now he watched her rise with a frown of misgiving, for she looked as if she were about to reenter her own element, as if she would not have even breathed very much longer in his, and then he knew that there had been a real split, definitive. Maybe when they refused the child? Hers could be his no longer, nor his hers. He rose slowly. Now he could look down on her again from the accustomed distance, but it was only in a physical way that this was true—she had, in the deepest sense, become her own being.

Something about it was deeply stirring to him, having not so much to do with his own misfortunes—wounded house, wife fled, himself barricaded, anxious nights. After all, nothing had been literally destroyed; even the German professor had gotten no more than a bump on the head; on Audubon Place they had only caught the tail of the hurricane. What moved Maurice, what hurt him, was to think what things she had exposed herself to, never to discuss them with him, perhaps never to discuss them with herself, but simply driven into them, why he could not say. Some people give their lives to dangerous sports, for instance, but he knew now that this was the fear-challenge they were meeting, and that what Julia was meeting was different. Isabel, insisting on Julia's evil, did not see it, but he did. It was the evil-challenge, the response to that deceiving fire as a life-source. Maurice was chilled inside to think of it. Had she been trying now to get her misbegotten child out of it? Or was the offer in good faith, genuine, warm and real? Well, he guessed it was both; no Puritan, he—he could live with that, unfrightened but aware. But how could a child brought up by Julia not turn out to be a monster? Well, he thought, it could, certainly it could.

He frowned, turning to urge cold food on Julia; hungry himself, he thought of one of those quickly prepared egg dishes that she and Isabel both knew how to whip up. The minute he mentioned it, she got up to move toward the kitchen, accepting the idea so naturally it would seem nothing out of the ordinary had happened and whoever said it had had just had a nightmare. Presently they sat across the kitchen table from one another, bright mats laid down, munching toast and eggs with chopped mushrooms, crisp strips of bacon.

Yes, he thought, knowing with his wisdom why he had refused Isabel when she insisted that they "ought" to take Julia's child—Isabel, the Irish Catholic, coming all armed to the fore with Worry, Duty, all that fretful crew. Yes, he thought again, complimenting the food, a child can not only live but really live, be more saint than monster, be more human than either. The chances were against it, Isabel would complain, to no avail. Maurice's conviction, in a final sweet way, persisted even while he kissed Julia good night at the door. After her departure, alone in the house in the quietened night, he counted on her word that nothing would threaten them there, and so mounted, not to the high safety of his father's old quarters, embattled above the street, which, fortresslike, oppressed his nature, but to his own room and comforts, his and Isabel's, and with his niece's kiss still lingering on his lips and cheek, the pressure of her arms still remembered around his neck, knew that tenderness, compassion, and release all were in harmony in his feelings toward her. His depths had been touched. Soundly as a child himself, mysteriously blessed, well-fed, he slept the clock straight round.

The next morning, still trusting to Julia, he called for Isabel to come home.

# 5. ISABEL

 When she left to go away she was frightened, frightened at why she was going, what she was leaving, what might happen to Maurice in her absence, and frightend too because it was the first time she had ever been away without him. She remembered Julia, a little girl on the train coming South to them, and thought that she knew now how the child felt, the sense of stepping off into the void.

But once the Parhams got hold of her, everyone made over her, and she was praised and fed and housed like visiting royalty. They esteemed the connection so much. For one thing Maurice had represented them well over the years. For another his acquaintance had got them into things—Mardi Gras balls, old houses, names and legends, and the sense that the very best thing to do was by the Parhams actually being done. Now he in turn needed them. They would allow the impression to surround Isabel that she was Creole, of course, and explain that this didn't mean Negro blood, oh my goodness no, it meant Spanish and French, the aristocratic blend. Isabel, no more Creole than they, sat quietly, studying them through her glasses, now repaired. Her blond hair had passed quietly into gray, but in certain lights it looked simply fair; her dresses in their clear shades could have been worn at any season. Little girls in the family trailed her upstairs to see what her cosmetics looked like, and the little boys in sitting rooms watched her silently, from the edge of their chairs. She spoke to Maurice on the telephone nightly and by the third day was looking better, dark shadows gone; she even laughed a time or two. Her appetite picked up. She was passed out among the family members in their beautifully furnished secluded houses; they took turns with her; from luncheon, tea, cocktail, and dinner invitations she had no hour's freedom, and there were morning drives as well. So all passed until Maurice called her to return, and she returned as she had gone, chauffeur-driven in the family Cadillac, feeling small and demure inside.

What she had to tell Maurice was what had happened the very evening of his final call, when she had been at the house of one of the younger Parhams for drinks. He was a nephew of Martin's who had taken over the house which Martin had left, and which, soon after his death in the airplane accident, his widow had left too. For a while it seemed to Isabel that she had been forgotten. She had been brought in, and then a phone call had taken some of the Parhams back to pick up another member of the family. The host, a dark silent young man whose wife was not there, sat reading for a time even though Isabel was with him, then suddenly got up and left the room. Alone, she wandered about, admired on the stairway the French sculptures that Martin had collected, the plants that grew and trailed about their shapes, shadowing and softening, rendering them mysterious, she thought, for the plants were really like a miniature jungle; and at length the darkening room at twilight gave her the impression that she was visiting a ruin. She examined pictures and ornaments, and passing near the stairwell heard voices coming up from below:

"You don't mean Julia's aunt . . . I didn't know Julia had an aunt, or anybody . . . you know what she said that last time we . . ." There was a trailing off, and then: "You going next weekend? It's time we told her that . . ." Isabel could hear no more except, presently, a burst of male laughter, and then the car drew up, the door was assailed by arriving guests. And the footsteps of the host were heard ascending the basement stairs.

There was even a hostess, it appeared; a long-haired girl in a chiffon mini-skirt with long balloon-type sleeves floated among them. And this was all.

Back home, Isabel, sitting in the living room alcove relating this episode to Maurice, had been, he thought, unduly shaken by it. "They see her, Maurice. I know it now. Don't you see she's still there, in a sense. Just as she's still here." She sighed.

"Why does it matter?" he finally asked.

"It matters because— oh, Maurice, because of what I realize. I collect antique figurines, I join societies to preserve the old houses, the cemeteries, I belong to the best clubs, I go to church. But all of this is not life any more."

"The past is part of life, Isabel."

"No. No, it isn't. I have no life, Maurice. I go through the motions, that's all."

"Oh, Isabel, what nonsense. Shall I find a modern word for it? You're disoriented. Have a drink, for God's sake."

"I have life through you," she said, "that's all. For myself I'm like a piece of china, and I've existed where I was placed to exist. I've no reality, Maurice. And it's too late."

"Did the Parham visit bring this on?"

"Oh, no. The Parhams are worse than I. The motions they are going through have less taste, that's all. It was only in that one house that I knew all this, and when I heard them say what they did about Julia, and I knew—"

"Knew what?"

"That life was with her. That I can't have life. I can know it when I am near it, but I cannot have it."

Maurice got up impatiently to get her a drink. A double, he thought, for both of us. Menopausal fantasies, he muttered to himself. He would have to consult the doctor again if this kept up.

Later in the evening Isabel looked out on the garden at the side and saw a small Negro man wandering near the ruins of the cistern. When she ran to get Maurice she was half-screaming. It turned out that the Negro wanted work as a gardener, having noticed in passing that their yard had recently been torn up.

"Come here," said Maurice, closing the front door. He led her back into the kitchen by the arm. She was always more herself there than anywhere, yet on their passage through room after room, he was conscious for the first time in his life of the giant bulk of the house, ponderous around and above them, ramified, empty. He sat her down at the kitchen table and sat across from her. "I've come to a decision, Isabel. We will sell the house, buy something smaller."

"Safer," she said finally. And then her lips moved once more, but he could not understand. She said it again, and he finally heard: "It will be away from Julia, won't it?"

He looked into his wife's eyes, into their diminished eloquence, and knew that he had failed. An inner quest had driven him for years, a quest for reconciling, for bringing all together under the shelter of love. For this reason he had offered Julia a place, had said he would never refuse, never reject her. But Isabel said strange things now, from time to time:

"When a side of the house is torn away, what's there for it but bleeding out of it? What's to contain us?"

"It's all repaired," he reminded her.

"But still I see it torn."

Again, she once cried out wildly: "No stopping place! We've searched for years. We'll search forever!" It was all like a waking dream. He tried to dismiss it from his mind, but when next she came up with some such, he would once again know the mind-ʳhill, the thing he couldn't stop. It was enough to know.

"Julia will not come there," he now said firmly.

*But if I say that, how can I keep from dying a little if I turn her out, and turn her out I must if I say that. Dying a little, dying little by little, diminishing life. But I've said it already . . . we can't be stabbed in our beds, Isabel can't go entirely mad. I've said it already. It is already said.*

He saw himself as he might be years later, grayer perhaps but much the same, standing in a well-known house of an old friend, regarding a mahogany table on which roses stood in a silver vase. The lawn outside was perfection. On the table top one velvet petal had fallen. Ten years later, on a golden afternoon, this actually happened. He was standing as he'd foreseen himself, the roses stood just so, the lawn lay in late sunlight, the petal had fallen. And he remembered, all and everything.

# 6. TREASURE

 Julia Garrett and Tommy Arnold walked along the river. It was autumn, or rather fall, or something like it—anyway, a golden time, still with expectancy, laced with the sound of crickets, treefrogs, and—as these stopped for a time or cicadas wound to a slow, toylike conclusion—the insects that hopped or clambered in the day grass could be heard, living their minute, important lives.

The child could walk. Emile could walk. A funny child, blond and exuding wisdom, he provoked Tommy Arnold to laughter, at times on sight. Today he wore a straw hat and Julia had him on a sort of lead, a long canvas strap around his waist, allowing him to toddle ahead or behind, and when they found a good spot in willow shade and threw down the quilt, he rambled to the end of his tether to open up a field of exploration, and went into research immediately, gathering gravel.

Julia regarded Tommy Arnold, who was full-lipped and content, with gold-flecked eyes half-closing drowsily and neatly tanned dome of skull at rest on his arm.

"I guess you were a good-looking little boy," said Julia, studying his face. He was watching gulls above the river.

"A great beauty," Tommy Arnold said. "Photographers came from miles around. My mother had to make appointments."

"Where are they?"

"My parents? Dead."

"So are mine. I guess they are. My father—I always think my father's going to show up some day or other

and I'll have to look in his face. Just that frightens me.
Not anything he can say, not anything he can do or cause
to happen. Just to have to have his face printed on me.
I've got enough faces."

"Maybe he's already come back, looked through the
windows at fashionable Aububon Place . . ."

". . . seen me, in my pretty clothes . . ."

". . . got run off like a bum . . ."

". . . and left, renouncing . . . Oh, Christ, Tommy.
It's *my* father after all. We're drawing up second-rate
Tennyson."

"I couldn't think that one more bum around Audubon
Place would matter."

"Lay off it," she complained.

"Your uncle's well-off now. You know his latest client
is one of the Mulligan sisters. The other one died. She's
turned the estate over to him. Seems they had a lot of
money and property, those two. Didn't want to bother with
spending it, or something."

"Life scared 'em at an early age. They tucked back
into the womb."

In the silence, the insects wound, died, grew busy in
the grass, and, from the trees, wound again. There was the
flop of a jumping fish, like a hand thrown into the
water.

"You remember the little colored man the old Misses
Mulligan got to work in the garden? He was also the care-
taker at the cemetery where they buried whatever corpse
passed for Marnie, the first time. I think he was the one
who got that corpse. For all we know he may be a powerful man. I thought for a while he might really be Bunny
Terrence in disguise. Or else Bunny is him in disguise. In
a bowler hat and a black suit with a white waistcoat.
Looking—oh—like a funeral director." She sat up straight.
"I think he *is* a funeral director. It fits!"

"I wouldn't look into it," Tommy Arnold advised.

She lay back down. "Maybe they're twins," she said.
"I went to Bunny after I got the heroin out of the cistern.
He said he might know what to do. He made me take a

rake-off. Partly out of kindness, I guess, for I think he admired me, in a way, but partly because they have to have you on the books, you know, however they keep them. That's when the police got my name."

"Oh God, all that——"

"If it wasn't for you——"

"I turned loose everything I had for you. You can't be a police reporter slouching around in this ripe field for as long as I have without having the low-down on quite a goodly number of the higher-ups. To hear me talk I was about to pull the whole city down around my ears and everybody else's. Hercules and Samson weren't in it. Could I have come through? The paper wouldn't have printed it. Corruption in New Orleans isn't news."

"You bluffed."

"Let's just say I managed somehow. I exhausted my capital, my carefully kept store of information. Knowledge is power. You've stripped me, Julia. It's not good to go through the byways here defenseless as a child."

"I didn't strip you. You did it yourself. And you shouldn't have. Oh, Tommy, you know you shouldn't have!"

"I know I shouldn't have."

"Then why did you? Why did you do it for me?"

"Sometimes I wonder," Tommy Arnold said.

Julia still worked for the artist in the Quarter. Almost daily she had some hours of extra time, especially during the rainy season when the weekdays were spare with tourists, so she had taken to scavenging for pieces of colored glass, learning to do enough with plaster to fit abstract designs together. And she picked up other things as well: scraps of wood and iron, carved stone. Her finger-ends stayed scratched and her nails wore down, filling up with grime; a frown of concentration cut between her brows. Her work had a strangeness to it, the flower-artist said. But it had authority, he added. "A silent jazz," he said, giving her an oblique glance as he answered the phone. Later he said she could set a few pieces up for

sale. "The world's full of stuff like that," she overheard a
customer say, deciding not to buy, and she guessed it was
true. Maybe she was following Jake, trying to make it
without really trying. The flower artist was shrewd in
business, got private teas arranged for him by the state
wildlife and nature groups, got invited to cocktails with
group show openings, spoke to civic clubs, appeared on
T.V. It was a headache keeping him from knowing it
when the police rounded her up, along with dozens
more—he wouldn't have liked involving the shop.
But Tommy Arnold had called him (oh, indefatigable
Tommy) that weekend to say she had the flu; and somehow she'd scraped by.

    All this time Jake Springland was as silently absent as
Julia's father. She never mentioned Jake to Tommy
Arnold. No more for one than for the other did they know
the answer to would he reappear? Or what difference
would it make if he did? Fatherless and husbandless, she
went about the world.
    There was still a third about whom Tommy Arnold
did not know the answer, either, though Julia at last,
when she came out of the hospital where she'd gone when
her nerves collapsed from stress and terror, claimed to.
    "It's what I can't face, Tommie. What I have to live
with. His face down at the bottom of that well. I'd made
a rope out of scarves tied together, silk scarves so as
not to cut myself all up with it, and tied it to a tree
and then under my arms and then went down into the
cistern. I'd gone out there alone, remember? The property
smelled bad enough, but once I got through the mouth of
the cistern it smelled to choke a horse and then I knew
what the big bird tracks were around the edge—buzzards.
And I went down. I found the loose bricks and dropped
one and that was when I looked down and saw it, the
corpse after all those weeks and the buzzard carcass near
the face, all tangled in the gray hair, the buzzard that had

gone all the way down in the well, too greedy not to. Then couldn't get out again, maybe too fat, maybe couldn't get a wingspread. Tommy! Whenever I close my eyes to sleep, to nap, to rest them, even to blink, I see that face. Sometimes I see Dev's face too, in clouds, dark and thundery or looking out of high windows—the windows over in the house on Audubon Place—or dark on white pillows in that same house, fine old pillow cases trimmed in embroidery, saying, *Je suis comme le roi d'un pays pluvieux* . . . always looking down at me, about to say my name. He up high and Ted Marnie down low . . . Christ, Tommy, can you think how it is? I mean, for everybody there's a place where the thinking runs out and the world's held in place by something that's not known about really, a mystery, some people say God. For me, there's what I'm telling you. There are those two."

"Well, in between," said Tommy, "there's all of life."

"Life," she repeated, flat, then rose up on one elbow on the pallet where she'd been lying. "Life!" She leaned over and looked into his face and collapsed back again, laughing. She suddenly stopped laughing. "All of it's life. But my life's nothing without those two, that's the thing." She felt a sudden release, relief, and closing her eyes without knowing it, as if after love, she slept a while, this time without seeing anything, any face at all.

When she woke up she continued calmly. "I could never tell exactly what had happened. Did Jake and Wilma Wharton kill him and throw him in there? Did they think they killed him—this is more likely—and, just left there, did he come to life like a stunned snake, crawl to the cistern to get the heroin out, and then fall in? In that case, did he die at once or slowly, inch at a time, leg broken maybe, staring up at the blue blue sky and the stars at night and for a little while the moon? Hollering at times, but nobody heard. But if they thought they killed him, why didn't they go ahead and bury him? Did they just leave him alive, just walk away, and he fell in the well by accident? I don't know. Jake sent me away in order to do a job on Marnie for what Marnie had done to me, to all of us——"

"Kill him, you mean?"

"Yes, yes! He said so. He said——"

"Stop it! Stop it now! Wipe it out, Julia."

"That's the worst thing of all," she said calmly, after a long pause. "To say that is worse than anything. No, I'll have it, Tommy. All of it. I'll not refuse any part of it." She sat up, eyes fixed ahead and widening with the discovery she felt banging against her. "The joy's in that, Tommy. In not refusing."

The day before she'd found a whole rich cache of colored marbles—yellow, rose, black, and red—near the site of an old mansion that was being torn down; it must have had colored mantelpieces or bathtubs. She ached to start shaping them, smoothing, polishing, fitting the patterns in which her artist boss said she was finding a growing elegance. Fragments of a city. She thought of them as being allowed to find a new voice, though broken, fractured, torn from their original purpose. The night before she'd had an encounter with a rat. The beast had materialized, or seemed to, right before her eyes on the floor of her high room as she ate alone, and she'd sat shivering before its gaze, facing out some sort of long struggle within its field of recognition. They had known each other then, she and that rat, and in that moment she had felt love for it and a oneness with its relentless existence. That was before she thought of the baby and disease and getting rid of it, which she managed by hurling a shopping net over it, then dropping it out the window in a paper bag.

"Tommy, can you love a rat, I wonder? I thought I did, last night."

"Rat! Human rat, you mean?"

"No. Real rat."

"Once I thought of you as a deer—something soft and wild and a little wondering, a little scared."

"A real come-down," she said. "All the way to a rat."

It was the time of afternoon for moving on but they sat for a while, looking out toward the river, the child asleep on the quilt between them.

Hadn't they been past the house the Devignys had finally settled in, elegant, high, old, smaller than the Audubon Place house, but finer, stately and silent behind its high mesh fence, deep grown in fine camellia trees, gardenia, and box, where the metal tab on the gate announced the burglary protection it enjoyed? There was a tomblike silence about it, that was all.

Hadn't they both driven up-country to Mississippi on a newspaper assignment Tommy Arnold had? When, finding themselves within five miles of the Parham estates, he, wanting to go there, had talked her into it; though she said, in warning, they'll spot me, sure as anything. But he'd got his way—had to get it; anything about her fascinated him—and they'd driven through those formidable green acres, herds of Santa Gertrudis behind impeccable fences, sweeping slopes of pecan orchards, deepset barns and silos, oil wells neatly tamped into the soil, pine nurseries and forest and thick oak groves where white houses nested. The whole property was never barred or marked, the highway ran through a wing of it, yet it bore its own atmosphere, spoke of its own deep entity, made its own assertion upon the air, was more than itself, by power multiplied. And all might have lain beneath her feet. Tommy Arnold stopped at the old store for a Coca Cola. Julia put on her dark glasses and waited in the car—until the man came out quietly and leaned in the window. And she knew she'd been sitting there knowing he would come. Even then she did not turn her head, but, staying in profile, heard him through a scarfed ear. "Miss Julia? Miss Julia Garrett?" the voice said. "It's you, ain't it? If I'se you, I'd git on along, Miss Julia." She told Tommy Arnold, when he returned. And as the highway swung the long curve, once so familiar, left the self-righteous, potent, God-blessed acreage behind for the little humble farms and fields along the New Orleans road where poor sinners had a hard time to make a living, she remarked, "They think it was my fault about Martin."

"How could you engineer a plane crash?"

"I couldn't," she said. "But they think I'm something that weakened him—a sort of corruption maybe."

"What do you think?"

"I? Oh, I think I saved him. I sent him on a happy journey. . . ."

They did not speak of it again.

"You went out to that place," Tommy Arnold said, looking at the river, "and you went alone. Why was that, Julia? Wasn't it on Springland's account? You didn't know what you'd find and you didn't know what you wouldn't find. If anybody knew where the stuff was meant to be but wasn't, they'd get on Jake Springland's trail maybe. Maybe they already were. Then, a corpse is always awkward, too. You did it for him, didn't you?"

"Uncle Maurice, too," she said. "Aunt Isabel. They should be able to—"

"To what?"

"To walk in the park and look at swans. In peace. The way I saw them once, passing by, not long ago."

"Did you say hello?"

"No."

They rose then, by common accord, and began gathering up quilt, child, and picnic scraps, and placed the rubbish in a large paper sack. She carried the child ahead of him on the path through dense willows to the road. Walking single-file and Indian-straight, she thought how life longed to be done with its nightmare, to return to its natural state. "I think we're heading toward a grand reunion, Tommy. With the Indians!" Caught in briars, he did not hear her, and, as mosquitoes had braceleted her ankles and begun to sting viciously, she did not repeat what she'd said.

They found the car, a little better than Tommy Arnold's old beat convertible she had first known, but not much.

"I know what you did for me, Tommy, and I ought to thank you, but I can't. Why, I don't know. Lots of people go to jail, why shouldn't I?"

"Keeping you out mattered to me," he said drily.

"The giving mattered, the cutting back to nothing mattered."

"And love?" said Tommy Arnold, finally, after long silence, after considerable driving. "Doesn't that matter, Julia?"

He was emerging onto the cement road leading out from Chalmette, and in the distance the gray bulk of the city rose, a scarlet sunset drenching the sky to their right beyond the sweeping curve of the Mississippi, also beyond an open field, rubbishy, swampy, untended land, and a rim of billboards. A heavy diesel truck passed them and for a moment, like a plane passing through a black heavy thunderhead, they were totally enveloped in its thick sound. Her mouth had moved in answer: she had said something. But when the truck was a fading thunder, disappearing before them, he did not ask her to repeat it.

Just as well, Julia thought. Tommy Arnold went to meetings in company with people who earnestly desired to save the old city from the encroachments of new real estate, and she hoped they would succeed. But trying to get her to go with him made her as restless as talking about love. It was all a disguise, she felt, a way of asking her to repent of something. She wouldn't do that, as wild as she'd been. For in a sense she was always hanging at the end of a silken, multi-colored rope, knotted under her armpits (she had learned knots from sailing with Martin Parham on the gulf: "Never know when they'll

come in handy," he had said—you certainly didn't). She
was always hanging in the stench and the sight of
Marnie and the buzzard and thinking her fate was there
too, to fall in and never be heard from, if not to fall in
to let go deliberately; such reasoning as the old mad
logician once commanded seemed now to be tearing
into her again. She had scratched at the wall seeking
for loose stones, and stones fell. Once she felt the whole
side of roughbuilt cistern ease forward and again home-
made cement sanded down into her mouth and eyes, and
then suddenly she found the parcel, neatly wrapped. She
threw it out and over, into the grass, and scrambled out.
And fell in the grass herself panting and retching, and
crawled and reached the very slope where Wilma
Wharton had sat reading, and could see the rickety pier
beyond where she and Jake had talked. She went down
and washed the best she could, and in the woods on the
way back to the rented car was when she first knew
that joy, special and profound, which sang with the
mouths of all the wounds in the world. She had seen the
white egret then, regarding her before it rose with a
grace both ancient and new, and had looked in the fox's
eye. Joy born out of a dead buzzard, she thought, and
the dead face of an old madman.

The city knew about it—it was what they shared
together, she and the city: it was the joy that all came
to find there, whether or not they knew it. It was the
kept illusion, according to Tommy Arnold. Who made it
and kept it? Julia did, for one; he would have granted
that.

At a turn the old car entered the real town and the
half-shabby streets were there as of old. All to Julia was
like a jewel—real or fake, what did it matter? It
spangled around them in eternal light, silently rejoicing.

Tommy Arnold had to go off to his meeting for the
city. He let her off at her door. As he drove he thought
that he had no way of knowing what he would find on
his return—the apartment ripped apart, a clutch of

strangers within, demands on the end of a semi-anonymous call, and worst of all the way that none of it disturbed her. On his return he might also find a woman and child—love, serenity, and more peace than he could ever have imagined even the possibility of. It was better not to chance it. Sooner or later . . . sooner or later. It was better never to return there, never to go back at all, he thought. He had thought it before, several thousand times.

Julia went inside. The neighborhood cat slipped past her when she opened the door. It circled about her ankles, mounting with her. On one floor a pipe was gurgling. The sound faded as she climbed, and then, except for the sleeping child in her arms, she had only the cat, which moved about her footsteps, weaving endlessly.